The Iron Seal

Book Nine of the Iron Soul Series

J.M. Briggs

Contents

This book is for every friend who is buying the books to support me even though fantasy isn't their genre. Thank you, even if it is unlikely that you'll ever read this page.

1

Bracing for the Worst

Magic had some advantages. As much as it had cost her and complicated her life, there were still moments of wonder that Alex Adams was able to enjoy. Watching a Brownie bounce around their new living room with small items floating around him as he tried to organize the shelves was definitely one of them. Unfortunately for Timothy, piles of boxes of Alex's belongings filled the center of the living room. The number of boxes was far more than she'd ever taken to college.

There were items from her family home. Morgana had packed them: probably packed up her entire room and combed through the house for anything that was hers. Alex had dared to peek into one of the boxes and found a pile of family photos. She didn't know how Morgana had managed that. She didn't know the details of how Morgana had altered her brothers' memories and didn't want to know. That said, Alex hoped that Morgana hadn't just taken all of the family photos. Maybe she'd used magic to duplicate the photos without her in them so that Matt and Eddy would have something. Maybe someday she'd be brave enough to ask. Maybe someday she'd go through all of those boxes. For now, she was focusing mostly on the things she'd brought to college. The rest could be stored in the laundry room for later.

Nicki laughed from where she was putting some movies on a shelf. Timothy was sliding across the wood surfaces of the furniture that Morgana had bought for the house. Alex wasn't sure if he was having fun or cleaning dust that she couldn't see. The small creature was only a few inches tall with a pudgy face, tiny pointed ears, and little black eyes. In some ways he resembled the Sídhe a little, but he was something completely distinct from them. Alex still wasn't sure what the similarities between beings from the same branch of the Tree of Reality were. The Sídhe, Brownies, and other creatures from that branch of the Tree of Reality all shared a weakness to iron. Except for Red Caps, who had trained or bred that weakness out of themselves through contact with human blood.

Aiden huffed as he walked into the house with another large plastic bin. Setting it down on the floor, he groaned and rolled his shoulders. His brown hair was a mess from the wind and his cheeks were red from work.

"I thought I was in better shape than this," he said.

"Take a break," Nicki said. "You've got most of it in."

"Yeah." Aiden looked at the boxes and around the room. "You girls need to speed up. The others will be here soon, and we'll need room for their stuff."

"They won't be here that soon!" Nicki gave Aiden a stern look. A strand of her red hair fell over her eyes, giving her expression a little boost of danger. "So stop whining."

"Why do I put up with you?"

"Blackmail material," Nicki replied. She turned back to the shelves and shoved another stack of books and disk cases into place. "We'll never fill this place."

"Don't say that," Alex said. "You'll be amazed at all the junk we'll end up collecting."

"Besides," Aiden added. "It's cool to have our own place. I mean, yeah, it's weird that a teacher arranged it for us, but it does make sense."

"Morgana is hardly our teacher in the traditional sense," Nicki protested. "I don't think any of us have classes with her this year."

"I do," Alex said. When they looked at her, she shrugged. "I can use some of the history classes as related credits."

"For English Literature?" Raising an eyebrow, Nicki asked. "Is that a new rule that Morgana pushed through?"

"No." Alex laughed but knew that it was the sort of thing that Morgana would be willing to do. "It's long standing. It makes sense when you think about it: history provides context. Anyway, I've got a class with her this year about the Renaissance."

"Oh... that sounds interesting actually," Nicki said. "I wonder if I could take that? I didn't spend as much time working on scheduling as I should have."

"To be fair, there's a lot of other things on our plates," Aiden said. Slumping down on the new blue sofa, he stretched out his legs. "Between Arthur, the Fae, the Sídhe, Demons, and Old Ones, we're very busy mages."

"God, I hope we have a quiet semester," Nicki said. "My GPA is horrible."

"You're failing?" Alex asked.

"Failing as in not passing at all, no; failing as in not meeting my own standards, yes," Nicki said.

Aiden rolled his eyes but wisely said nothing. Shaking her head, Alex looked down at the boxes with her name. She needed to start moving them. There would be a lot more stuff when the others arrived, and frankly since Morgana had already furnished the house there wasn't a ton of room. As large as the living room was, it was crowded thanks to the super long sofa, loveseat, and armchairs.

The new house that Morgana had arranged for them was nice. It wasn't brand new by any means, but it was solid, and judging from the new windows and doors, Merlin had probably made some modifications. Alex was certain that if they pulled out the frames they would find lines of iron to help protect the portals of the house. Thankfully it didn't seem to affect Timothy too badly. Whatever protection she'd granted him from iron during her... unusual blood protection spell was still holding.

The house was fairly large, and thanks to the finished basement they had five bedrooms. With an open layout, movement through the house was easy, but if they were ever invaded it might complicate things. All told it was three floors and thankfully had two and a half bathrooms, which would help the college students deal with each other in the mornings. The kitchen was decently sized, with an island and lots of counter space that would hopefully make meals easier. Alex expected a chore wheel to end up on the wall there within a week or two, regarding at least cooking since they didn't have easy access to the university cafeterias anymore.

Officially Lance and Jenny still had separate rooms, though Alex wasn't sure if that was going to remain the case for long. Aiden and Bran had decided to share the massive basement room that had extra outlets. Alex knew that as soon as Bran got back with his stuff gaming systems were going to be set up. If Jenny and Lance did decide to share a room, then they would end up with one more bedroom for something. Alex was sure that something would come up soon enough. It always did.

She hoped the others were safe. There were blood protection spells in Portland, Eugene, and San Francisco, but that hadn't stopped Arthur from killing her parents. Whatever magic he'd used was still a mystery, or maybe he'd simply paid off some desperate man. Neither option was good. Looking around the room Alex was sharply aware of the people who were missing. Bran should be here; Lance and Jenny should be here. Bran would be helping unpack while Lance carried boxes and Jenny ran around organizing the books, movies, and trinkets.

"Are you hungry?" Timothy asked. His voice, while higher pitched than a normal human's, was surprisingly soothing. Still, it was enough to make Alex jump a little after being lost in her thoughts. "I could make something if you like?"

"No, Timothy," Alex said. Smiling, she shook her head. "I'm still full from breakfast. And you don't have to worry about cooking all the time. We are adults." Looking towards Aiden, she gave him a stern look. "And we do appreciate your help. Both with the house and contacting the Fae."

"I'm glad to help," Timothy said. He adjusted the hem of his shirt which had been tailored from old doll clothing. "And it's nice to be around humans that I don't have to hide from."

"Speaking of the Fae," Nicki said. "Anything new on that front?"

"No," Alex said. "Some are siding with Arthur and the Queen, and some are neutral. I'm not sure any of them except Timothy can be said to be on our side." Alex shrugged. "Not that I blame them for that."

"Still," Aiden said. "It could get ugly if we end up against a huge horde."

"We killed a lot of them," Nicki said. "I can't blame them for still being angry. Yes, they were controlled, but..." Nicki shook her head and trailed off. "Well, we'll just have to see what happens. Thankfully, the blood protection spell in Ravenslake does seem to be keeping out anything with violent intentions."

"Let's just hope it has some effect on those damn Red Caps," Aiden said. It was his turn to shudder. "I hate those things."

"We all hate those things," Nicki said. "Maybe next time we see them Alex will let you borrow Mjǫllnir to smash some of them."

"Uh, no thanks." Aiden shuddered. "Who wants to get that close to one? Fireballs work just fine."

It spurred on some kind of argument, one in good fun, between Nicki and Aiden as they debated fire or water against Red Caps. Alex didn't hang around to listen after Timothy bounced into the kitchen. He'd start working on food soon enough, no matter what she said about not being hungry. Someday she'd get used to the small creature bouncing around and moving things with his surprisingly strong magic. But not today. Instead, she knelt and picked up one of the boxes.

Carrying the box up the stairs, Alex went to the second door on the left which led into her room. It wasn't the largest, but it was the corner room with a nice view of the forest. Her new full bed was already made up and her stuffed dog Galahad was sitting on a pillow. It was a comforting sight, but it was mostly devoid of personal touches. Her computer was set up on the desk in the corner by the window, and a lot of her clothes had already been packed away in the dresser. Setting the box down on the bed, Alex sat down next to it and looked around.

There were only two things on the walls. A pair of vertical weapon displays hung just to the left of her bed near the door. The first had two small wooden hooks that were holding up Cathanáil. Her eyes traced over the sword that was better known to the world as Excalibur. Its golden hilt gleamed softly in the sunlight still coming through the window. It was just over two feet long, and Alex wasn't sure if it was technically a longsword or a short sword. Standing up, she gently took the Sword out of the stand with her right hand.

Despite being made of iron, it wasn't very heavy. There was only a slight strain in her muscles from holding it with one hand. Beneath her fingers, soft warmth radiated up into her skin. Stepping back from the wall, Alex gave the Sword an experimental swing. Swishing through the air, it produced a soft musical hum that sank into Alex's bones. Sparks of magic glowed just under the metal's surface, giving the Sword a soft aura. Someone who didn't know what it was would dismiss it as a trick of the light, but Alex knew that it was the magic her first incarnation Arto had put into the sword three thousand years ago.

Alex shifted into the starting stance that she'd learned at fencing club almost two years ago and adjusted the Sword. It wasn't like the rapier she'd practiced with at the club, but the principles were similar enough. Keeping the Sword steady, Alex swished it through the air, ensuring that she kept a firm grip on the hilt and trying to familiarize herself with the weight. Her room was no place for this, but maybe they could set up a practice dummy in the backyard. Now that they had Cathanáil back she needed to learn how to use it.

The second display held Mjǫllnir, the Iron Hammer, which was known to mythology as Thor's Hammer. Unlike the usual depictions it's two sides were different sizes. One was larger while the other end tapered into a smaller hammer surface. It was a reminder that before it was a weapon the artifact had been a tool. Her left hand pulled the Hammer free, and she adjusted her grip. Like the Sword, it hummed in her grasp. Magic reached up for her, caressing her skin while also gently pulling magic from her. An equal exchange for now, but Alex knew that if she ordered it to the Iron Hammer would release lightning bolts.

In her left hand, the Hammer was heavy. She'd almost exclusively used it in her right hand until the final fight in India. When she'd recovered Cathanáil, it had seemed most natural to put the Sword in her right hand.

At least it lessened the likelihood of her stabbing herself. Alex lowered Cathanáil and carefully swung Mjǫllnir. The heft of the Hammer wanted to keep going, but her firm grip kept it in check. A thrill-filled her chest and an unbidden smile appeared on her face.

Part of her knew these weapons. As far as she knew she'd only really wielded each in one of her lives, but something about them transcended her deaths and rebirths. That was an odd thought and she shook her head. Being the Iron Soul meant that she kept coming back again and again to protect Earth, but she knew very little about herself. What had caused the creation of her soul? What was a soul? What impacted the when and where of a reincarnation? Those were questions that Merlin and Morgana didn't seem to worry about anymore, and questions Alex was sure she'd never have answers for.

A knock on her door made Alex tense. The sound was too sudden, and her magic flared through the Sword and Hammer. Then the knock came again, and Alex relaxed. Shaking her head, she called for them to come in. The door opened, and Aiden poked his head in. He blinked at the sight of her and pushed the door the rest of the way open.

"Are you planning to dual wield?" Aiden asked. Grinning, he leaned against the doorframe and nodded towards the artifacts. "You did okay in India, I'll give you that."

"My arms hurt a lot afterward," Alex said. "I need to work on building up more muscle and endurance with these." She checked the heft of them. "They do seem bit lighter than they should though. I wonder if I'm doing that without knowing, or they were made that way."

"You might just be imagining it," Aiden said. "Don't forget that iron or not, Swords and Hammers were always meant to be picked up and wielded."

"Maybe; things like that just remind me of how little I know."

"We'll work on it," Aiden promised. "And we have a yard now, so we can work on fighting and practicing without going to Merlin or Morgana's place. That should make things a little easier."

"I thought that myself earlier," Alex said. "I just need to set up a training schedule. I miss running, but maybe Sword practice in the mornings will be a nice replacement."

"It might, and Nicki and Merlin are still exploring ways to hide Cathanáil with magic."

"That would be ideal," Alex agreed. She looked at the gleaming blade. "I'd feel better having it with me."

"Yeah." Aiden looked at the weapon displays. "I know that Arthur can't come here, but leaving them out in the open kind of freaks me out."

"Maybe a safe-"

"That has other problems." Aiden shook his head. "If you need them, you need to be able to get to them."

"True," Alex said. Looking at the plain wooden displays, she smiled. "Maybe Nicki could carve something into the wood."

"Well, she is determined to figure out how to make more interesting items. And Merlin's staff does prove that some magic can work with wood, at least for a little while."

Nodding in agreement, Alex's mind coursed with questions. A few strange memories tried to push forward, and the soft voices of her other lives whispered. It was odd. Two years ago, she'd been freaked out over visions when meeting her fellow mages, and now she was living with voices in her head.

"Alex?"

"I'm fine," Alex said. "Just thinking."

"Okay." Aiden nodded and smiled reassuringly. "I'll give you some space. Uh... oh yeah, I just came up to tell you that Nicki is going to run to the store; do you need anything?"

"No," Alex said. "Thanks."

Giving her one more smile, Aiden closed the door, and Alex exhaled slowly. It was nice having friends who understood her need to be alone. While she'd always loved reading, she'd never been a real introvert. Now she just needed to be alone sometimes. Moving across the room, Alex looked out the window into the trees. The forest wasn't too close, and there was a tall wooden privacy fence between them and even the closet trees. A hillside rolled up to the foot of the nearby mountains. It was a nice view, but one Alex didn't appreciate. Turning on her heel, she swung Mjǫllnir around a little and bit her lower lip.

Restless. She was restless. Alex shifted the Hammer and Sword in her hands again. There was a dull itch creeping up her spine. Everything was quiet; had been for weeks. She'd returned from India ready for a fight, but there hadn't been one. Bran, Jenny, and Lance had finally decided to visit their families while Aiden and Nicki helped out at their local family businesses. Even staying with Morgana hadn't produced anything of interest. She hadn't learned anything new, and the two had largely just passed by each other.

Something was coming, Alex knew that. It was just beyond the horizon, but what it was she wasn't sure. This waiting was horrible. This knowledge and confusion at once were clawing at her. Rolling her shoulders, Alex shuddered and returned to the weapons displays. She carefully set Cathanáil and Mjǫllnir back in their places. Then her hand went to the iron dagger secured in a sheath at the small of her back.

What else could they do? The others would be back in Ravenslake soon. It wasn't safe, but it was better than being on their own. Even now, she wanted to have Nicki open a water tunnel and take her to collect them. They'd made it this far and survived Arthur's plotting, but the Demons' fear of the Darkness nagged at her. She didn't know what it all meant, Merlin and Morgana didn't know, and her gut told her it was important. Yet, here she was, just bracing herself and trying to figure out the next move.

2

Waiting for the Right Time

The ring of the metal hammer against the iron bar wasn't as satisfying as Alex thought it would be. For a moment she wondered if she should have brought Mjǫllnir with her instead. It seemed over the top to use the Iron Artifact in Merlin's modern workshop, but that was what it had started life as.

She wasn't really making anything. Alex stopped hammering and used the tongs to turn over the narrowing iron ingot. Her fingers itched to push magic into the iron, but Alex kept the instinct at bay. This wasn't the time to accidentally make something; her thoughts were too scattered. The last thing she wanted was to forge another horrible item that would be used against them. Hitting the iron harder with the hammer than before, she felt a spark of tension ease and welcomed the ache spreading up her arm.

As the metal cooled she used the tongs to slide it back into the hot coals of Merlin's furnace. Well, one of them. The large detached workshop had two stations, originally set up for Merlin and Morgana, though Morgana wasn't much for smithing. As the metal heated in the fire, Alex panted softly and tugged a strand of blonde hair that had fallen loose from her bun back behind her ear. Heat rolled out of the furnace and filled the space, overheating Alex's already warm body. Between the heavy leather apron and leather gloves, she already felt dehydrated. Shifting back from the furnace, Alex took a long drink from the water bottle that she'd thought to bring. It helped, and she quickly returned to the anvil.

Time slipped away. She kept working on the bar of iron, trying to figure out what it was. Keeping a tight hold on her magic, Alex focused on just smithing the old-fashioned way. It was harder, and Alex wondered how often she used her magic to help shape the iron in small ways. This time it was rougher, and she still had no idea of what to make. Even looking around at Merlin's old projects didn't help. Fancy candelabras, railings, and artwork didn't hold any interest for her.

"Alex?" It was Merlin. Alex's muscles tensed at the sound of his voice. Holding back a sigh, she almost didn't turn around.

"Hey, Merlin," Alex said. Turning to look over her shoulder, she smiled at Merlin. "Sorry if I woke you up?"

"I was already awake." Merlin was dressed simply in a blue button shirt and jeans. He was holding a steaming mug of coffee, but his brown eyes were already alert and sharp as he took her in. "Couldn't sleep?"

"I slept fine," Alex said. "I'm just trying to build a routine again." She turned back to the forge, debating if she should keep working or give Merlin her full attention. "Got up early and stretched out. Didn't run; I still miss that."

"Running on your own would be dangerous."

"Hence the not running. But I wanted to do something, so I left a note and came over. You did say that I was welcome."

"I did." Merlin moved around her left side and leaned against one of the long tables that lined the walls. "But in my experience, you come here and work iron when something is wrong."

"I'm just a little restless," Alex said. She gave up and pulled out the iron bar. It had been narrowed and flattened out, but it didn't seem like a sword to Alex. "Feels a bit like I'm in limbo at the moment."

"Are you that eager for classes?"

"I'm eager for something to do." Alex watched the red glow fade from the metal. "I'm not a fan of this waiting game."

"I understand," Merlin said gently. "But we can't risk playing into Arthur's hands. Sif is still traveling and seeking information. The contacts Timothy helped us get are occasionally emailing in reports. Morgana has even tried scrying for Arthur. I know how hard it is waiting when you know your enemy is out there, but right now staying in the protections of Ravenslake is a good decision."

"You don't believe the Darkness is real, do you?" Alex asked. Merlin's expression answered the question. He hesitated, clearly searching for a diplomatic way to say it. Alex shook her head almost fondly. "Okay, so you don't."

"Alex, I'm three thousand years old, I'm sure if something like this Darkness was real, I'd know about it at this point."

"But you've never left the Iron Realm," Alex said. "Only Morgana ever has, and that was in a controlled environment." Shaking her head, she turned away from Merlin and organized the small hammers on the rolling tool bench. "There's a lot of things you don't know about the other worlds and what is happening there, Merlin."

He huffed at her but said nothing. He didn't lose his temper or snap at her. Alex was pretty sure that he never did. Merlin had never-ending patience.

"Let's go inside," Merlin suggested. Smiling at her, he gestured towards the door.

"Alright," Alex said. "Wasn't working on anything specific."

"No?"

"Nope, but that's the great thing about blacksmithing isn't it?" Alex said. She carefully put away her tools and secured the furnace. More heat washed over her face, but it was less comforting now. "You can rework it."

"True," Merlin agreed. "Bronze was much more difficult. I do not miss casting items in molds."

"Never?"

"Well... maybe from time to time."

Chuckling, Alex pulled off the leather gloves and shrugged off the heavy apron. Without it on, she felt a little cold. It only got worse when Merlin opened the door and let the summer breeze in. Alex shivered but quickly adjusted as she walked outside and towards the main house. The back door was still open. Clearly, Merlin had figured he could get her to stop quickly. A flash of stubborn irritation flared in her chest, but he wasn't going to change at this point. At least a few of the voices agreed on that, giving Alex a sense of solidarity.

"Clean up, and I'll get you something to drink." Merlin shut the door behind her and gave Alex a smile. "I'll be in the sitting room."

He was treating her a bit like a child, but Alex supposed that she had shown up pretty early. But it wasn't like she didn't have a standing invitation. She'd even texted the others and left a note on her door. Still, she went to the bathroom and washed off her hands.

Splashing water on her face helped. Exhaling slowly, Alex looked at her reflection. There were bags under her gray eyes. They weren't too bad, but they gave her face a slightly more sunken appearance. Frowning, she wondered if she'd lost weight. It was possible, but she'd never had much extra weight to lose. The others hadn't said anything, so hopefully, she didn't look too bad.

Merlin was waiting for her, seated in one of the armchairs. He had brought out another cup of coffee that was waiting for her on the coffee table. He looked up at her, his expression completely calm and patient. Her earlier irritation faded as Alex considered that he was worried. After all, waking up during the summer to the sound of clanging in your workshop couldn't be pleasant. Smiling at her, Merlin nodded to the chair opposite him, and Alex sank down on the edge of the cushion.

"You're frustrated with me," Merlin said.

"Not you, or not just you, at least." Alex picked up the cup of coffee and took a sip. Merlin just watched her silently. "Frustrated with the situation. It feels like I should be doing something more. Waiting around in Ravenslake feels like a waste of time. Morgana wants me to continue school-"

"It was important to your parents, was it not?" Merlin cut in. "Getting a college education? They saved for years and had high insurance policies to ensure that you and your brothers would receive a college education."

"Yes," Alex said. Swallowing, Alex pushed away memories of such conversations with her parents. "But that isn't what matters now. School isn't what I should be doing."

"What do you want to do?"

"Stop them," Alex said. She sighed and slumped back into the armchair. "But I know, I haven't a clue of what that means." Putting her left hand over her face, Alex groaned. "I'm a horrible Iron Soul."

"You are not."

"Yes! I am! I almost failed at getting my powers in the first place, and then I gave the Sword to Arthur, and now I don't know what to do!" Alex slapped her free hand down on the arms of the chair. "I'm a horrible Iron Soul!"

"You are not," Merlin repeated. He crossed the room and before Alex could twist away, placed his hand on her head. The large warm palm was a comforting weight, and Alex exhaled. "You are not, Alex. You were the incarnation born in a time of confusion and crisis. Not only have you been faced with the threat of the Sídhe, but also a traitor. You've had to face Old Ones and Demons, a war on many fronts." His thumb brushed her hair softly. "Not to mention your personal losses. Please, do not believe that Morgana or I are anything but proud of you."

"It feels like I'm not doing enough," Alex said. "I should be fighting Arthur."

"We don't know where he is. We need to concern ourselves with protecting the Sword. The new Iron Gates are holding the defenses of the Iron Realm strong against the Sídhe, but Cathanáil's power can circumvent that. The Demon's proved that." Merlin removed his hand but didn't put any distance between them. "Sooner or later Arthur will slip. There is a limit to what he can do."

"He has some Fae following him," Alex said. "That's dangerous. We have to stop them before they cause havoc."

"And I am watching for signs of them," Merlin promised. "As are the Fae I am in contact with." Shaking his head, Merlin took a step back and sat in the other chair. "I wish Frea was still alive: I did not appreciate her loyalty and desire for peace enough. Then again, dying of old age is a luxury." He shook his head and offered her a small smile. "I know waiting is difficult. But Arthur is...arrogant and cruel. I believe that he will slip up. That he will make a foolish choice due to his impatience."

"Maybe," Alex said. "I'm not sure of that. He's played long games before. And I'm not sure that we're the best judges when it comes to him."

Lifting her cup of coffee, Alex noted that her hand was trembling. She gripped the handle tightly and steadied the cup with her left hand, hoping that Merlin wouldn't notice. In the back of her mind the voices were whispering soft reassurances to her. Arto and Lokpal's voices seemed the clearest. It was a sharp reminder of her problems, but also calming in a strange way. Someday she'd have to examine why, but not today. She heard Merlin sigh and looked up at him worriedly. For some reason, he looked older. His hair seemed whiter, his wrinkles deeper, and his posture more defeated. Something in her chest twisted.

"I'll be happier when the others return," Merlin said. "I dislike them leaving the safety of the group." That almost seemed like agreement with her concern, but Alex wasn't sure.

"I know what you mean," Alex said. Rolling her head towards the window, she looked outside. "They'll be back soon." She was telling herself that more than Merlin. "And they know to be careful."

"Yes, but Jenny and Lance have no magic." He waved his hand and shook his head. "I know that Avani Desai started to teach them some of the basics that magicians use to borrow magic from the Iron Realm, but it isn't the same. And from what I understand they hadn't made much progress."

"We weren't in India very long," Alex pointed out, feeling the need to defend her friends.

"True, true. But that just makes them leaving all the more... mystifying."

"They wanted to see their families," Alex said. Not looking at Merlin, she was aware of a sharp pain in her chest. Her eyes teared up, and it was hard to breathe as guilt took over for a long, agonizing moment. "Anything could happen. We already know that."

"Yes…" Merlin suddenly sounded nervous. "Alex, how are you doing?" She didn't answer, and he was silent. "Morgana told me what you asked her to do."

"I figured she would." Alex waited for him to launch into a lecture.

"I know it must have been hard," Merlin said. "But I think you made the right choice."

That surprised Alex. Turning towards Merlin, she was surprised to find him smiling gently at her. His eyes were soft and sad. The ache both eased and spread at once. Tears gathered in her eyes, and she didn't know what to say or do.

"You do?" The words slipped out before she could stop them.

"Yes. Being a mage… it is a difficult life. You never know what is coming and your life isn't truly your own anymore. For you, as the Iron Soul, I imagine it is even harder. We've never spoken of it; maybe we should have, the knowledge that when you die, you'll return in another life to fight once more. As you know, that has had negative effects on your family in the past. It can be difficult for those that love you as kin to accept the burden you bear."

"Yeah." Alex's mouth was dry, but she pressed on. "I didn't want Matt and Eddy turning into Galath. His anger… I wanted them to be able to have peace. Arthur already killed Mom and Dad. I couldn't- I didn't want him able to find and hurt them."

"Commendable." Merlin nodded to her. Then he stood and came closer, once again putting his hand on her head. "I believe you made the right decision, Alex. And I promise that Morgana and I are with you. We've been here throughout your lives, by your side through many of your battles, and here we will stay."

"Thanks."

The word fell flat, and Alex knew it. Merlin chuckled warmly. Strangely, she did feel a little better. Sometimes she forgot what Merlin and Morgana's lives meant. They were three thousand years old thanks to their half-Sídhe nature and magic. For centuries they'd fought the enemies of the Iron Realm and helped her various lives. She at least had the kindnesses of death and gaining a new family, of being able to marry and have children, and age. They didn't.

"Thank you, Merlin," Alex said, trying again. "I know that you and Morgana didn't choose this life, but I'm grateful you've been here for me. No matter what form I take."

"We have not met you in every life, Alex," Merlin said. He looked down into his coffee. "And while I can honestly say that I have always tried to be a guide for you, I will not claim that I was always successful." Without meeting her eyes, Merlin shook his head. "You live long enough, and you learn that you can make many mistakes. Morgana and I both have things we regret, but Arthur is and will be one of our greatest." Then he looked at her, his brown eyes cold and distant as a new harshness crept into his voice. "I want him dead and burned. I want to find a way to destroy whatever soul he has so he can never return, Alex. Believe me, I do. I want them stopped, but sometimes you must wait. You must wait for the right time."

"When will that be?"

"I don't know," Merlin said. "But you have achieved a great deal. You have Cathanáil once more, the Iron Hammer, and the Iron Chalice. Shiva remains your friend and ally, and Sif is loyal. The right time will come, and you will be ready for it." Smiling, Merlin relaxed and leaned back in his chair. "Of that, I have no doubt."

3

Woes of a Farmer

Podlasie Province, Poland 983 C.E.

The soil was wearing out. He knew it, but there was little to be done. He'd tried putting manure into the soil and planted beans, but it wasn't enough. The crops were weak and poor no matter what he did. Sweat was rolling down his back, and his muscles ached from exertion. The warm summer sun was shining down, but there were only tiny and weak stalks of green in the earth for all of his efforts. Holding back a cry of despair, he stumbled away from the rows of his field to a nearby tree for shade.

Leaning against the tree, he stared up into the branches. Even the trees were in rough shape. Last summer the tree had been strong with large branches and leaves. This year he'd already cut off several diseased limbs. There was no end in sight. A heavy sigh escaped him, and he looked up into the sky. It hadn't been too hot, there had been plenty of rain, and yet the crops were struggling. Despair welled up in his chest followed by the grasping ache of helplessness.

He made himself move on. Everything had been watered and weeded. Lingering in the sun wouldn't do him any good or help the crops. He moved away from the long field that held his crops and walked down a worn dirt path to a small wooden and stone house. The foundation and the lowest part of the walls had been constructed with stone, a rarity for the area, but it kept the home warmer. Long logs had been fitted together to form the walls, and the sloped thatch-covered roof went nearly to the ground, providing cover for the woodpile.

A small fenced yard had been built around the house, and a few chickens were scratching at the ground. They at least seemed to be finding enough to stay healthy. Good; they would need the eggs at the rate the crops were growing. In the middle of the yard, carefully using a whetstone to sharpen a knife, was a young boy about six years old.

Looking up at him, the small boy smiled. His brown hair was a tangled mess and dirt was caked on his hands and nose. But he looked happy, with bright eyes and a warm smile. For a moment, the farmer was almost able to forget. Then the boy coughed. His whole body shuddered, and he fell to the ground, coughing into his hands. There was a glimpse of blood across the child's palm.

Dashing forward, he hoped that the boy had cut himself before realizing that a cut would be just as bad. He jumped over the fence and chickens scattered out of his way. The boy was still coughing, and the splatter of blood in his hand was bright and mocking. Kneeling, the farmer fought to control his breathing and pulled the child close. The boy curled against him as the coughing finally eased. The blood remained, and the farmer swallowed.

"Father?"

"Let's go inside." Scooping up the boy, he climbed to his feet and rushed through the entryway of the house.

Inside it was dark and cool, with only a little light entering through the small window cut opposite the door. In the corner was a large stone oven and shelves had been built into the wooden walls around it. They were covered with pots, pans, rolled up furs, and all other manner of supplies. Jars and baskets along the walls held food and clean water. Two raised beds covered with blankets filled much of the inner space, and he strode to the closest one.

Setting the boy down, he turned and grabbed a small bowl with old washing water. Without a word, he used it to gently wash his son's hand. His stomach tightened as the water took on a red tint, and he rushed outside to dump the water away from the house. When he returned, the boy had curled up under a blanket and was looking up at him sadly.

"I wanted to help," the boy said.

"I know, Slavko," he said. Reaching out, he rested his large hand on the boy's head. "But, please rest. You need to get stronger." The boy frowned, his brown eyes darkening. He knew what the boy was thinking of. "It will be alright."

"I miss Mother."

"I miss her too." The words were hard to say. It was the way of things; natural, but it still ached. "But things will get easier." Sitting down on the edge of the bed, he leaned forward and kissed the boy's head. "But right now, I need you to rest and stay out of trouble." His eyes jumped back to the whetstone. "Please."

"Yes, Father."

The words were soft but reassuring. He knew that the boy didn't fully understand. As weak and ill as he was, even the slightest cut and infection could finish the job. The thought made it hard to move, and his grip on his son tightened. Slowly, he pried his fingers open. There was more work to do. He couldn't just stay in the house. Standing up, he smiled at the boy. The child returned it, though his eyes darted across the small house to the spindle.

Of course, the boy would try to find something else to help with the moment his back was turned. Exasperation gave way to resignation. It was just the two of them now. He couldn't do everything. At least some spinning wasn't likely to worsen his health. Grabbing his axe, he went outside, and looked back to check on Slavko only once. The urge to stay clawed at him, but there was work to do. Always work to do. The crops were poor, so he needed to be ready for anything. Avoiding the chickens, he left the yard and went around the house to where several long trunks were waiting for him.

Grabbing the first log, he hoisted it half way up on an old stump. With several sharp swings of the axe he managed to cut it into two more manageable pieces. The sun beat down on his back, but he quickly found a rhythm in the work that was almost soothing.

"Dobiemir!" The voice jarred him out of the haze of motion. Stopping after the swing of the axe split the latest log, he rolled his shoulders and looked towards the dirt road. "Dobiemir!"

The man was short with broad shoulders and dark hair and eyes. Dressed in a woven tunic similar to his own, he had a satchel tied to his back and was using a walking stick. Dobiemir lowered the axe and set it on the stump he'd been using as a support. Walking over to the fence, he met the man alongside the road.

"Hello, Emond."

"Hello, Dobiemir," Emond returned. He was panting a little and leaned against his walking stick.

"Why are you out this way?"

"Doing some foraging," Emond said. Flushing a little, he shrugged and adjusted the bag on his back. "Crops aren't doing so well, but thus far the roots are still plentiful."

"I know what you mean," Dobiemir said. Nodding towards his fields, he felt the pit in his stomach opening once more. "My crops aren't as healthy as I'd like."

"No one's crops are doing well," Emond said. Looking towards the fields, he swallowed. "There's talk of famine."

"I know," he said. "I know, but what can we do?"

"I don't know." Emond shook his head and nodded towards the house. "How is the little one?"

"Not good. Rest isn't helping, not much." Shaking his head, he looked at the house and hoped that his son was at least sleeping. "He coughed up more blood not long ago."

"I'm sorry, but at least-"

"Don't!" Dobiemir scowled, hoping that his expression would silence whatever useless statement Emond was about to say. "Just don't."

"I'm sorry. I'm sorry," Emond said. "The worries... they're bad. I'm not thinking right." Shaking his head, Emond swallowed. "We have four mouths to feed. I don't think the little one will make it through winter."

"I understand." Dobiemir's anger faded. Emond understood just fine even if he wasn't tactful.

"Have you any plans?"

"The chickens are healthy, as are the sheep, for now at least," he said. "If we can get enough out of the harvest to keep them fed... or at least some of them, then we should make it to spring." Adjusting his axe, he tightened his grip on the long handle. "And... if necessary, I can trade some of Lyubov's trinkets."

"She'd care more for your survival," Emond said. "She was a good woman, a good mother."

"With only one surviving child." The anger flared back to life. His hands trembled, and Emond reached over to grip his shoulder. "And to die in childbed-"

"It happens, all the time," Emond said. "There was nothing more you could have done. And you're looking after Slavko like she would have wanted."

He nodded. There was nothing else to do or say. Ranting at the unfairness of it would do no good. His guilt wouldn't help either, even as it pushed up inside him and made an effort to choke him. Two children already gone and Lyubov lost along with the new baby. Life was hard and unfair. He knew it, but that knowledge didn't make it any easier. Emond squeezed his shoulder and continued on his way home. Dobiemir managed to not throw a log at him.

Frustration wasn't so easily dismissed. Even chopping the logs into small chunks did little to calm him down. His muscles were becoming fatigued, but the sight of blood on his son's hand kept flashing in his mind's eye. Images of Lyubov's still and sweat covered face and the silent infant followed, making his heart ache. He knew that it was the way that life went sometimes, but that didn't make it fair. It didn't stop his grief.

Gathering up the wood, he stacked some of it carefully against the wall of the house under the protective slope of the roof. It had the added benefit of helping to further insulate the house, but also the downside of providing a home for vermin. Keeping his grumbling to himself, he quickly lined one whole side of the house before looking up at the sun. There was still a lot of daylight left. Running through his list of chores, Dobiemir decided that he'd done what he could on the farm.

Quietly, he poked his head into the house to check on his son. The boy was asleep, his small face peaceful against the pillow that he was holding onto. He looked even smaller than usual. A small smile took over

Dobiemir's face, and the knot of worry loosened just a tiny bit. Then his son coughed weakly in his sleep, and the knot tightened worse than before. He was completely still, waiting for it to worsen, but the boy just rubbed his cheek against the pillow and slept on.

He stood there for a time, waiting and bracing himself before his muscles finally unclenched. It was one little cough. He tasted the old dust of the house and told himself that was the cause. Still, he carefully left the house while glancing back at the boy just in case he stirred again. He grabbed a large leather bag and swung it over his shoulder as he went.

Once outside, he took to the path Emond had been using and headed up into the hills. Gathering some extra food sounded like a good plan. If they could build up a supply now then anything from the harvest would last a little longer. Carrying his axe, over his shoulder, he kept his eye out for any newly downed trees. If food couldn't be found then at least wood was good for trading in the winter.

Stepping into the shade was a relief, and he eyed the towering pines thoughtfully. The bark of their lower trunks was thin and gray, turning more and more red closer to the top. They swayed in the light wind and his feet crunched on the ground against years of fallen pine needles. No matter how much they gathered them up for use in mattresses and fire, there were always more. While they weren't a great source of food, they were always useful in tea during the winter. Scattered amongst the pines were a few large oaks and one or two ash trees.

The forest was oddly still. Dobiemir stopped in place, tightening his grip on the handle of the axe as he listened. He heard birds, but they sounded muffled and far away. His eyes checked the underbrush around the trees, but the only movement was from the wind. Frowning, he waited for something to move. A bird would fly through at any moment, or some small creature that he'd spooked would finally run for its burrow. Nothing happened.

Suddenly the world began to darken. Looking up, he gasped in surprise. The sun was still shining down on him and there were no cloud obstructing it, but somehow it was darker. He blinked, both hoping and fearing that his eyes were betraying him. It didn't go away. Everything was just a little too dark, the colors were a little off, and he couldn't understand it. A shiver raced up his spine. The hairs on his arms stood up straight as he found himself fighting back a chill. He started to take a step back, no longer caring about gathering roots and berries.

Then there was a sound to his left. Freezing in place, Dobiemir looked around carefully. Something was moving through the trees — something long, black, and on all fours, shifting slowly in the shadows. Another rush of cold made his teeth chatter. Air was pushed from his lungs by the sharp chill. Lightheaded, Dobiemir reached out and caught himself against a tree, but did not take his eyes off of the creature.

No, not black, he realized. It was like it was... not. Something about it wasn't natural. He couldn't truly see a shape, just the outline where everything else wasn't. The cold increased but he stayed still, praying to both the pagan gods and the new Christian one that he wouldn't be noticed. But it turned to look at him with glowing green eyes — an unnatural shade that he'd never seen before. He swallowed. His mouth went dry, and he desperately tried to remember any stories about evil spirits in the forest. The creature almost vanished in the shadows of the trees, seeming to become one with them only to reappear a moment later even closer than before.

The cold was even worse now. It was radiating somehow from the creature. Around them the light kept dimming. He didn't understand. Terror was tearing at his chest, but he didn't know what to do. It came closer. Swinging his axe, he caught the thing in the side and it snarled. At least the thing was solid. The blow barely slowed the creature down. Twisting around, it grabbed the handle of the axe in its mouth, showing those long needle teeth. Dobiemir released the axe and stumbled back. The creature tossed it aside and growled.

His back hit the trunk of an oak. Instinct kicked in. The creature growled and began to charge. He jumped, grabbing the lowest branch and pulling himself up. His feet barely swung up before a paw swiped at him. Dobiemir's arms and legs were cold and heavy, but he forced himself to move. If the thing could climb, he was in trouble. He grabbed the next branch and pulled his shivering body up. His feet slipped, but his arms clenched to keep him in place. Panting and trembling, he found a solid foothold and leaned against the upper trunk of the tree.

The cold sank further and further into his bones. Horrible thoughts brewed in his mind. The thing was trying to reach him; trying to catch him. Would it eat him? What was it? Dobiemir didn't know, but the fear kept him still save for the shivering that he was powerless to prevent. His breath danced on the air, and he longed for the overheating of earlier. The tree shuddered, and he gasped as the creature used its claws and tried to climb the tree. He held on tight and held his breath. Then the shaking eased. A low growl reached him, and he dared to look down once again. The creature was circling the tree, but at least the shaking had stopped. Hope began to flicker to life in his chest, but he dared not move.

Then the creature turned and slinked away. It made no sound as it went, no cry of displeasure or huff of irritation. Dobiemir did not move. He couldn't move. Every muscle ached and twitched against the chill that lingered in every drop of his blood. Yet as the creature vanished into the trees, the world began to warm and brighten.

Dobiemir nearly lost his grip. His once frozen fingers were thawing quickly as the warmth of the sun returned. His mind spun, and black flickered at the edge of his eyes. Keeping a grip on the branches of the tree, Dobiemir closed his eyes and struggled to control himself. He couldn't panic. He was alive. But what had that thing been? What sort of evil creature was spun from shadow and cold? Sometime later, he finally carefully eased himself out of the tree, collected the metal head of his broken axe, and headed for home, eager to return to Slavko.

4

Danger at Home

The morning crunch was over. It was amazingly easy to forget just how packed the bakery got first thing. Bran lamented the day his mother had put in the coffee side of things. Yes, it made more money, but the only thing that made people rushing to work tenser than waiting for their baked goods was waiting for their coffee. At least the bakery was still the main part of the operation, and he wasn't the one responsible for operating the espresso machine.

The bakery was a familiar space, so familiar in fact that Bran knew that it was tied to his very sense of self. When the other mages had first met him, they'd seen glimpses of this place. There was a small seating area out front by the register with a couple of sofas in one corner and several tables with chairs. Located just at the edge of a residential area going into a business district, they rarely had a lot of walk-in traffic that lingered, but it did happen. After twenty-five years, the very dark red brick smelled of bread, cake, and cookies, and Bran couldn't imagine the space ever being anything but a bakery in the future.

But the familiarity sometimes threw him off. Time slipped away from Bran while he was here doing the job he'd been doing for years. Sometimes he found himself reaching for his cane after finishing a task or panicking when he started to walk and realized that his brace wasn't on. He still leaned against the counters more than most people to help support his weight after forgetting that he didn't need to. Having his injury healed was a positive of course, but sometimes there was a strange echo that almost made Bran nostalgic.

Today there was a small trio of people finishing up their coffee and doughnuts at a corner table. Their phones were out and they were discussing their schedules for the day. They'd be gone soon, and a quick clean of the front would be in order. Most of the baked goods were gone from the display cases except for the cakes that were waiting for pickup. Peaceful and predictable.

Bran knew he should enjoy it. School holidays had become messy and crazy times. When he'd started college away from home, he'd been sure that he'd visit often. That had fallen apart. Even when he did come home, part of his focus remained in Ravenslake. It was too easy to worry about the others even when he was home with his mother. Even though his mother knew he was distracted, it wasn't something they talked about.

Part of that was his fault. He hadn't explained the real scope of things to his mother. She knew about magic, knew he could use it and enjoyed watching him use his power around the house. Cleaning was much more fun when you could move the objects with magic. Not easier. It still took energy to move things around and left him tired, but it was satisfying to focus on what he wanted to happen and snap his fingers.

Right now, that wasn't possible. Bran used his hands to pull some of the plates and trays out of the displays and stacked them on top of each other. The other employee on duty right now smiled at him and picked up the cleaning cloth as the last customers filed out. Her long dark hair was tied up in a bun, and her smile reached her brown eyes.

"I'll do the cleanup," she said. "Be back in a moment to do the dishes"

"Thanks, Kayla," he replied. "I've got some things to take care of in the back."

"Hope your mom comes back soon," Kayla said. "We're almost out of stuff."

"Afternoons aren't as busy."

"True, but I'd hate to disappoint people coming in for their afternoon sugar boost."

Taking the trays and plates into the back, Bran stacked them next to the large industrial sink. He noticed with a frown that the floor was a touch sticky and made a note to himself to clean that next. A glance at the bulletin board and then the clock told him what he needed to know.

At this point, baking bread didn't take much of Bran's concentration. He had no real memory of the first time he'd been in the bakery or made bread. It had always been a part of his life, something solid. His hands found the right measuring cups and poured all the dry ingredients together. Then the wet were mixed before being blended with the dry. Familiar and safe. His lips quirked as he considered using his magic as he carried the bowl to the industrial mixer. That seemed lazy; even for him in the summertime.

Glancing into the front, he kept an eye on Kayla. She seemed at ease with cleaning everything up and moving the remaining baked goods onto smaller plates. Everything was running smoothly. That left too much time to think. Bran reviewed his schedule for the upcoming semester. With all the magical threats, school wasn't the highest priority anymore, and he'd accepted that the days of straight As were behind him. Still, he did want to graduate on time. It was too expensive to drag his feet on that issue.

Bran quickly sprinkled more flour across the large worktable by the mixer as he waited. When the mixer finished and Bran pulled out the bowl, taking it back to one of the counters. Picking up the large ball of dough, Bran lightly slapped it down on the floured table. Reaching into the box of flour, he dusted his hands and sprinkled some more over the dough for good measure. He started kneading it, his hands moving on their own through the familiar motion.

"Thank you, Bran," his mom said. Looking up, Bran found his mother in the back doorway. She set a large cardboard box on the counter and reached to a nearby hook for her apron. "I'm sorry you and Kayla were stuck alone. I can't believe that I forgot to restock on cocoa powder!" Shaking her head, she busied herself putting everything away. "I have cake orders to bake, and I forget something so vital. Honestly, I don't know why you put up with me."

"Don't worry about it, Mom," he said. "I'm happy to help. You know that."

His short mother beamed at him, her eyes glowing at the sight of him standing in the kitchen. Every time she was away from him for more than an hour she always reacted happily to the sight of him without his old leg brace. At this point he was starting to doubt that she'd ever not react that way.

"And I'm grateful for that, but I know that you aren't interested in working in the bakery."

"Well, not forever at least," Bran said.

"I'll take over, Kayla should be leaving soon."

Nodding, Bran moved away from the dough and went to the sink to wash his hands. His mother started humming and checked the dough before nodding to herself. At least he hadn't messed it up. His apron was covered in flour, and Bran hung it up on a hook to grab a clean one. Walking to the front, he found Kayla looking at her phone.

"Mom's back," he said. She jumped a little and smiled sheepishly at him. "You can head out."

"Right, sounds good," Kayla said. She smiled, almost batting her eyelashes at him. Smiling tightly, Bran nodded to her. Was she being friendly or trying to flirt? It was difficult to tell sometimes. Those signals seemed lost on him. "Have a nice day, Bran." Straightening up, she called back. "Bye, Jinsung!"

"Goodbye, Kayla!" his mother called from the back.

"Have a good afternoon," Bran said. "We'll see you tomorrow."

"Bright and early."

"The joys of a bakery," Bran replied. "Have to be up early to be ready for opening."

The words were true. His mother's day had always started at 3 or 4 in the morning when he was growing up. Bran had been used to an alarm clock when he was seven. He remembered very clearly waking up, showering, and dressing before walking across the yard to the bakery and eating fresh baked goods and fruit for breakfast. Cereal hadn't been a part of his life until he was in high school. The memory made him smile. Kayla gave him a curious look but didn't ask before she collected her things and headed out.

"She's a nice girl."

Holding back a sigh, Bran looked back at his mother who was watching him with flour-covered hands. "Mom, please don't." Bran shook his head. "I do not have the time or patience for dating right now."

"You're a junior now," his mom said. She was frowning, and her brown eyes were sad. "I know that studying magic is important to you, but-"

"It is," Bran said. He grimaced as his mother's eyes flashed at being interrupted. "But I'm also busy with my friends and projects." Shaking his head, he smiled at his mother. "Besides, if I did start dating, I'd want it to be a local relationship. I don't think I could start dating anyone, even someone as nice as Kayla, only to go back to school next week."

"I suppose." She looked downcast at the news that he still wasn't going to date. Holding back a chuckle, Bran glanced around.

"Did you need something, Mom?"

"What?" She blinked. "Oh yes, I need to run into the house for a moment. I'll be back in a few minutes. Everything is in the oven and should be fine.

"Alright." Bran nodded as he held back a chuckle. In some ways, it was impressive that the bakery did as well as it did with his mother's memory. Then again, most of their supplies were delivered, and they lived across the yard. It limited the area in which she could lose track of things. "I'll hold down the fort."

"Should be quiet, but there might be a pickup," she called back.

Bran doubted it. They were in the doldrums of the day when it came to a bakery. He heard the back door open and close. Bran wasn't sure that his mother had ever used the front door of the bakery herself. Honestly, part of him had always lamented that there wasn't just a second level to the bakery for them to live in. He'd hated shoveling the path between the shop and house and the front of the shop as a kid.

His thoughts were nostalgic today, and Bran wasn't sure what to make of it. Perhaps being home after the chaos and danger of being a mage in Ravenslake, he was trying to fit back into this life. Maybe Jenny and Lance were struggling as well. He wondered if it was like this for Nicki and Aiden. They had grown up in Ravenslake, and surely the events there had altered how they felt about their hometown. He wasn't sure. They never talked about it. There was a lot that they never talked about.

Sliding open the case door, Bran bent over to pull out the empty cookie tray and started reloading it. His mother's fresh chocolate chip cookies always sold well in the early afternoon as people came looking for a jolt of sugar. Outside the hum of traffic echoed softly in the front room. He could hear the ovens and hoped that his mother did indeed finish whatever chore she'd forgotten about before he had to worry about both the front and keeping the bread from burning.

The bell jangled, alerting Bran that someone had come in. Looking up, he saw a man in a baseball cap and a light jacket walk in. Unlike most customers, he didn't even glance at the fridge cake display or up at the prices. The man's brown eyes were dull, almost vacant as he moved forward. Whatever he was on, Bran wanted to stay far from it. Shifting over, Bran smiled pleasantly and leaned against the register counter.

"Hi there, what can I get for you?"

Without a word, the man reached into his jacket. Bran thought he was reaching for a wallet and while frustrated that the man had yet to say or point at anything, told himself to be patient. But the man didn't pull out a wallet, cash wad, or credit card. It was a gun. With a smooth motion, he pointed the gun right at Bran. His eyes flicked up to the man's eyes. There was nothing there, no fear or worry. Nothing.

Panic clawed at him, overwhelming his shock and confusion. Yet, the training that his adventures had given him kicked into place. Without thinking about it, Bran pulled sharply on his magic. The spark of energy in his lower chest flared to life.

Yellow magic snapped forward at Bran's command. Bran dropped low to avoid any gunfire. His knees hit the tile of the floor and he exhaled. Closing his eyes, he tried to see the gun in his mind. Tried to grab it. There was a push against his magic and he shuddered. Focusing the magic was hard. It was pulling and sparking in the air. The gun next to him and the man across the room, he ordered. It helped; the wild tugging eased into a controlled flow, but he didn't dare move.

His eyes opened as there was a grunt of pain. A moment later a swirl of yellow magic deposited the handgun on the mat beside him. Then there was a solid thump. The store went quiet. Slowly, Bran climbed to his feet and peeked over the counter. The man was slumped by the door. Bran's legs quivered beneath him, but he didn't fall. Grabbing the cleaning cloth, Bran knelt and picked up the gun carefully. Wrapping it up in the cloth, he gently put it behind the counter. Then he turned his attention to the stranger. The man's eyes were clearer now. The vacant haze was gone, and he blinked in confusion. Sitting up, he looked around the bakery and then at Bran.

"What? Where am I?"

"...You came in and collapsed against the wall," Bran said. "Are you feeling okay? Should I call an ambulance?" His mouth was dry, but he tried to sound calm. "Do you remember anything?"

The man pulled himself to his feet, grimacing as he stretched. Bran didn't envy him the pain in his back. Shaking his head, the man looked outside, and his eyes widened.

"It's daytime... last thing I remember..." Groaning, he held his head. "Shit, how much did I have to drink last night?"

"Sit down," Bran said. "And I'll get you some coffee."

"Thanks," the man said. "Sorry if I freaked you out when I collapsed. Guess I can't drink like I used to."

Nodding, Bran couldn't think of anything to say. Worry would be too false; his own heart was still beating fast. The image of the man pulling a gun on him was too sharp, too clear for him to muster real sympathy. He had enough empathy to know that it wasn't the man's fault. Swallowing back a rush of bile, Bran made his way behind the counter again. He leaned on it, letting the wood take his weight until the shaking in his legs finally stopped.

Arthur had controlled the man. That had to be it. No one robbed a bakery. Bran looked down at the gun, now tucked beneath the register. He'd have to hide it and take it back to Ravenslake with him. Hopefully Merlin and Morgana would have a better idea of how to get rid of it safely. His heart was still pounding. Fae couldn't come into town; at least, not this close to his house.

This was how Arthur had killed Alex's parents. Bran shuddered at that realization. He'd never given much thought to the truck driver who had hit the Adams. The man had died in the impact, and they'd just accepted Alex's statement that Arthur had been behind it. Yet he hadn't given it much thought. Normally he wanted to understand the how, but in his worry for Alex, he'd focused on her rather than what had happened. That had been an oversight on his part. It should have been obvious. If Merlin and Morgana could change or erase memories by messing with people's heads, then of course there were ways to do much worse.

That man was lucky to be alive. Bran handed him the cup of coffee and received a grateful smile that he didn't manage to return. His stomach twisted, but he walked behind the counter again. A wave of gratitude that his mother had been in the house, that it had been just him in the shop hit him all at once. How could he explain this without scaring her?

His unusual guest was still confused but seemed to have calmed down. After a few gulps of coffee and a refill, he pulled out his phone and began texting people. He didn't seem suspicious and didn't seem to remember anything. Bran took that as a good sign. Either Arthur's control had ensured that he wouldn't remember or his brain was suppressing it all. At the moment Bran didn't care which it was. The sound of his mom coming in from the back was just audible over the ovens. She came out with her apron on and smiled at the sight of the customer.

"Mom, I need to make a call," Bran said. He nodded to the man who was nursing his coffee and looking at his phone with a confused expression. "Man in the corner is... dealing with hangover aftermath."

"Okay, sweetie," his mother said. "Don't take too long. I want to make some cupcakes for after lunch."

Grabbing the gun, still wrapped up, Bran nodded to her and rushed for the back door. He was already pulling out his phone as he went. If Arthur was coming after him, then Lance and Jenny might also be in danger. He sent a quick text to Jenny and Lance, hoping that they'd stay home. Crowded areas wouldn't mean anything to someone under Arthur's control. And who knew what he might try against Alex. Bran's chest tightened at the idea as he brought the phone up to his ear, hoping that Alex would pick up soon. If Arthur was taking over minds, then none of them were safe.

5

New and Lost Connections

The house was full of subtle noises that indicated she wasn't alone. They were the sort of sounds that Alex had grown up with given she had two brothers and a dog. Something had almost always been on somewhere in the house, whether a TV, radio, or computer game. Yet it wasn't the overwhelming noise of the university dorms. Lived in, but not packed. Alex found herself smiling as she came down the stairs of their new house.

Doing a mental check, she remembered that Aiden was helping at the bookstore today, so it was just her and Nicki. Though when she reached the main floor, she recognized the faint music of one of Aiden's games drifting up from downstairs. He'd probably just left it on pause. Shaking her head, she turned her attention to Nicki's voice that she could hear from their dining room. It took her only a moment to find her friend sitting at the table with her tablet set up in front of her. She was talking to someone with an easy-going smile.

"Why are you in here?" Alex asked.

"Wi-Fi is better in here," Nicki said. She shrugged, looking up from the screen. "We may want to get an extender or something. One thing you can say about the dorms is that they had excellent high-speed internet."

"It's how they kept the masses from rebelling," Alex said. She walked around the table, coming into view of the screen and blinking in surprise when she saw who it was. "Oh, hello, Avani," Alex greeted. She found herself smiling over Nicki's shoulder at the pretty Indian girl and wondered what the pair had been talking about.

"Hello, Alex," Avani returned. "How are you?"

"So-so," Alex said. "Did you hear about what happened to Bran?"

"Nicki told me." Avani's smiled faded away, and she shook her head. "I understand that Arthur used a similar method to attack your parents. I'm sorry you had to be reminded."

"It's fine," Alex said. Shrugging, she pulled another chair over and sat next to Nicki. "I'm just glad that Bran's okay and coming back."

"Oh?" Nicki asked. She raised an eyebrow and looked at her expectantly. "When was that decided?"

"He called this morning. I'm not sure what he told his mother, but he was still shaken up," Alex answered. "Said it was best if he was in Ravenslake since Arthur was targeting him. He's really worried about his mother being pulled into this mess."

"What about Jenny and Lance?" Avani asked. "Are they returning?"

"Jenny is on a trip with her dad, but she'll be here in a few days," Alex said. "Lance will be here tomorrow."

"And what if Arthur is targeting your families again?" Avani asked. Her eyes were on Alex, and she frowned a little when Alex stayed silent. "Do you have a plan for that?"

"No," Nicki said. She was looking at Alex in the corner of her eye. "There are blood spells in the towns to keep Sídhe and hopefully Arthur out, but if he takes over someone outside of the blood spell and sends them in there isn't much we can do." Nicki leaned closer to the camera. "Unless you have some thoughts?"

"I'll ask grandfather," Avani promised. "I hate the idea of your loved ones being in danger." Then there was a stretch of silence. Avani was considering them both. "I have a confession," she said.

"What's that?" Nicki asked. Resting her chin on her hand, she smiled. "Unless you're secretly a Demon I think you're probably safe from us."

"I applied to Ravenslake."

Nicki's elbow slid off the table and she banged her knee against the edge of Alex's chair as she suddenly jolted. Holding back a laugh, Alex grinned as she watched Nicki's face turn red and she blinked rapidly at the screen.

"I know I'm not a mage," Avani said. "But I am a magician, and I might be able to help. Jenny and Lance had only a little instruction, and while I can keep giving them advice that doesn't replace a real teacher." Taking a deep breath, Avani relaxed her posture. "I understand that it is sudden, but staying in India while I know the situation just seems wrong. With the portal closed, Shiva is handling the cleanup of violent Demons just fine. There is a limit to the help I can offer from here, but in Ravenslake I could keep working with Lance and Jenny, and maybe help Nicki with some of her projects."

"If you're sure," Nicki said. The eagerness in her eyes was adorable. "But... you shouldn't give up your life over this. Magic sucks you in and doesn't let go."

Turning to look at Nicki, Alex held back a sigh and reached over to squeeze her friend's hand. "If you want to come, Avani, we have no objections," Alex said. "And there is room in the house for you if you don't mind sharing."

"Hell, you might have your own room if Lance and Jenny decide to room together," Nicki said.

"Would you be alright with that, Alex?" Avani asked, suddenly sounding worried.

"Yes!" Rolling her eyes, Alex almost laughed and groaned at once. "Honestly, it doesn't bother me. Yes, I've been involved with Jenny's prior incarnations in other lives, which is a strange thing to have to say, but I'm glad they're happy. Hopefully it will let their souls move on, or at least get out of this cycle or whatever happens."

"Sorry," Avani replied. Giggling, she smiled at them. "I suppose you're tired of those concerns by now. My apologies. You seemed very comfortable with him while you were here. I shouldn't have said anything."

"No," Alex said. "It's fine." Exhaling, she made herself smile. "This place is pretty crazy, Avani, and much smaller than Mumbai."

"It's like a city block in Mumbai," Nicki said.

"You'll have to catch up on a lot of things," Alex continued. "So please don't be afraid to ask questions."

"Excellent," Avani said. "Then I shall make my arrangements to fly to Ravenslake."

"Portland," Nicki corrected. When Avani blinked, Nicki gave her a soft smile. "There isn't an airport in Ravenslake. Portland is where we usually fly out of."

"Uh... then perhaps I'll see if Shiva will open a water tunnel for me." Avani waved her hand dismissively. "The point is that I will be there soon and I'll keep you informed."

"Right," Alex said. Her head was spinning a little. "Sounds good. Let us know if you need anything."

"Well then, I'd better go and take care of some things here," Avani said. She smiled sweetly at them, and Alex could all but hear Nicki's brain turning to mush. "I'll be in touch. Stay safe." Her smile lingered on the screen for a moment before a ding indicated that the call was over and the window vanished.

"I can't believe she's coming here!" Nicki jumped to her feet, almost hitting her knee again. "This is going to be terrible!" She started pacing through the room while Alex watched with amusement.

"Terrible?"

"I've never lived with a crush before." Nicki's eyes widened, and she spun back to Alex. "If Jenny and Lance keep separate rooms then you need to bunk with her. I can't! It would be too weird!"

"We'll see what happens." Standing up, Alex patted Nicki's arm. "But it'll be fine. I think she likes you too."

"You think so?"

"Well, she hasn't been calling me," Alex said. "And I'm the Iron Soul. You're the one she's been keeping in contact with."

"Right... maybe." Nicki flushed bright red, but her eyes were bright with excitement. "We'll just have to see, I guess."

"It'll be nice to have her here," Alex said. She softened her smile. It wasn't fair to tease Nicki about this, not right now at least. "I never saw her use much magic, but she has a good head on her shoulders."

"And access to her family library," Nicki said. "You weren't around, but we talked a lot about enchanting items. She liked my idea of making something to help hide Cathanáil and maybe even Mjǫllnir from non-magical eyes. It would be nice if we could walk around with better weapons than just our daggers. Especially Lance and Jenny."

"Yeah," Alex agreed. She licked her lips, suddenly unnerved at the idea of Lance and Jenny coming back. "I hope they're safe right now."

"I'm sure they are," Nicki said. Reaching over, she squeezed Alex's shoulder. "Bran alerted them, and they're both going to head back soon." Nicki shook her head. "And I can't see them as Arthur's prime targets."

"Why?" Alex asked. "I care about them, and they can't protect themselves as well."

"But they also aren't a threat to him," Nicki said. "If I was Arthur, I'd focus on the mages first and avoid getting you too mad until I had to." But then she paused, and her expression darkened. "Though... I still want to flay him alive."

"Nicki!"

"I do," Nicki said. Her tone was even and deathly serious. "He stabbed you and left Aiden in a coma. But I admit that you have more of a right to kill him than I do."

"Revenge... I hadn't thought about it that way," Alex said.

"Which just proves that you are a better person than I." Nicki shrugged and seemed completely unbothered by it. "I've been dreaming up ways to hurt him. Sadly, he's just hurt us since then. We really need to figure out how to stop him. Not just delay him or foil his plans; stop him. And if he has to die in the course of that, well, I volunteer if you don't want to."

"A few moments ago, you were gaga over your crush," Alex said. "And now you're volunteering to kill Arthur."

"It's not like we can turn him over to the authorities," Nicki said. "When we stop him, we'll be stopping him for good."

"You're right," Alex said. "I know that's true; there's just been a lot of other things to think about."

"I understand, but Arthur wanted the Sword, and now you have it. He and his mother were controlling the Fae, and you destroyed the Iron Chain. Now he's mind controlling humans to kill us, and potentially he'll try to take the Sword that way."

Alex shuddered at the idea. "I hadn't thought of that."

"Which is why I want to figure out a scabbard that will hide the Sword, so it is always with you," Nicki said. Then her serious expression brightened. "Which Avani can help with."

"Hopefully." Alex sighed and leaned against the wall. "You're right about Arthur though. We've cut him off once again, and he'll do whatever he can to get the Sword." Her chest tightened as fear, and a touch of anger, took over. "I don't want to see any of you hurt."

"We'll keep working on defenses," Nicki said. Her tone was gentle, and she touched Alex's shoulder again. "We're all in this together. We'll figure out the next evil plan and keep pushing Arthur and the Queen back. Sooner or later, we'll get our shot, and I don't think that any of us will hesitate to take it." Nicki almost smiled. "In fact, as much as I want to kill him, I'm almost inclined to hand him over to Jenny first. Just to see what she'll do to him."

Alex wasn't sure how to even respond to that. Her smoldering anger made it funny, but she was also worried about what would happen when that moment came. Arthur was a traitor and possibly an outright psychopath, but he was clever enough to fool Morgana and Merlin. Not to mention all of the rest of them. Shame flared in her chest. It was familiar. Arthur had been... amazing, in her eyes. Gorgeous, kind, and smart. He'd been understanding and supportive, but when she'd handed him Cathanáil, he'd stabbed her.

"Stop it," Nicki said. She poked Alex's nose with a serious look.

"Stop what?"

"Stop feeling guilty over what Arthur did," Nicki answered. Giving Alex a stern look, she added, "None of it was your fault. He was a snake and very good at deception. I trusted him too." Nicki rubbed her hands together. "And there are more important things to worry about, like the fact that Avani is coming and this house is a mess. We've got to get our stuff organized!"

Smiling, Alex watched Nicki dash off to clean. In her chest the ache still lingered, but every time her friends reassured her that it wasn't her fault, it got a little easier to deal with. She looked around, eying the stack of boxes next to the kitchen that Timothy had yet to get to. The house was slowly coming together, but Alex now had the feeling that it was about to be become organized and spotless even by Timothy's standards. She just hoped that Nicki didn't run over their house Brownie in her haste. Leaning against the wall of the kitchen, she looked out the window into the backyard.

Still, Avani joining them could be very helpful in figuring out how to deal with Arthur's new strategy. Besides, with all the doom and gloom, watching Nicki deal with her crush would be amusing. She'd always assumed that Nicki was upfront and confident regarding romance. Apparently, that was not always the case. It should be very amusing.

Shaking her head, she opened the fridge and pulled out a can of soda before heading back up to her room. The sugar rush on her tongue when she took her first sip gave her a boost, and Alex turned her attention to the stack of boxes still waiting to be unpacked in her room. The first box didn't take long as she unloaded the extra t-shirts and socks she'd collected into her new dresser. Some old hair ties went into a plastic drawer set, her alarm clock got plugged in, and she set up her computer speakers on the desk.

The next box had books. Old textbooks and a few childhood favorites that she'd brought to college in case she needed to be distracted. Sadly, despite needing them, she hadn't had the time to read them lately. Alex examined her room critically. The full bed would have to go if Avani was staying with her here. If they could replace that with a bunk bed and move it to a wall, then there would be room for a second desk. They wouldn't be able to fit another dresser, but maybe one of them could have the closet and the other the dresser. They'd make it work. Morgana would probably be irritated, but they'd make it work.

Pulling out a few more books, Alex packed them onto the small bookshelf next to the desk. She was quickly sorting some of them when she reached into the box for the next book only to have her fingers brush something glossy. It wasn't a book cover; it slipped away, and she quickly looked down.

They were old photos. Alex didn't even remember packing them with her books for school. The glossy surface caught the light as she slowly turned the stack so she could see them. There were random photos from different vacations and birthdays. In one, she was next to her brothers as her mom held her blonde hair away from the candles of a cake. In another, she and her brothers were crowded together in front of a colorful hot spring at Yellowstone. She flipped through them slowly. Dozens of small moments she'd forgotten about came rushing back.

Tears burned in her eyes. Alex's chest tightened, and a soft sob was ripped out of her. Whatever defenses she'd had against grief was gone. This wasn't for her parents; this was for her brothers. The young men in those photos that she'd never see again. Those men that she'd never have a chance to know. It crashed over her, sending shivers through every limb.

Dropping the photos back into the box, she crawled to her bed and hoisted herself up onto the mattress. Her stuffed dog Galahad was on the pillow waiting for her. Pulling it into her arms, Alex began petting the dog's head with one hand as she turned her face into the pillow. More tears rolled down her cheeks, and another shudder wracked her body.

She missed them. The knot holding back the grief was gone. She'd thought she didn't need it anymore. Alex bit her lip. She'd been fine. Why did this suddenly matter so much? How did a stack of photos hurt like this? Rolling onto her stomach, she buried her face into the soft material and sobbed. Doing her best to muffle the sounds, Alex prayed to anything that could hear her that someday all of this would get a little easier.

6

Weight of Fear

Podlasie Province, Poland 983 C.E.

It was another warm day. Another day when things should have been going well. The crops should be growing as it marched towards summer, and he should be enjoying the warmth. Winter would come soon enough, leaving food and heat as a concern during the long dark nights. Yet, everything was going wrong. Their crops weren't improving no matter how much rain the early spring storms dropped.

So here he was in the forest once again, gathering all the berries and roots he could find. The leather bag across his back already had some long leafy plants and a small basket tied to the bag filled with dark berries. Sweat rolled down his back and his trousers were sticking to his legs. But he kept moving. More and more villagers were taking to the hills, and some were talking about up and moving. It was important to get as much as he could as soon as he could.

Berries could be dried out for winter, the roots would keep for a while, and the seeds and flowers could be stored. Some of the grasses could be dried out for the animals. Already he was calculating how many they could keep alive into winter. Moving forward, he knelt next to another berry bush to check them for ripeness. The bush yielded some more wild dark pink berries, and the weight on his back eased momentarily.

Dobiemir kept moving through the forest. The trees provided some relief from the heat, and the ground was still a bit moist from last night's rain. His foot sank into some mud as he walked out onto a game trail. Glancing down, a long line of tracks made him freeze.

Kneeling, he examined the tracks. They were large and should have been deep in the mud. Yet they weren't. It was like the creature had barely touched the earth. The tracks reminded him a bit of a wolf's in shape, but the toes were a bit too long. Something about them was off. He wasn't sure what, but Dobiemir was certain that they weren't from a normal animal.

A shiver went down his spine and he looked around in alarm. But the sun was shining, and the world was still bright. It had to have been that creature, or something like it. The thing was unlike any normal beast. It had moved too lightly, and too quietly. Just thinking about it made his stomach turn. He eyed the tracks again, trying to convince himself that it was a wolf. That wasn't much better, but at least a wolf was frightening in a tangible, normal way. It or its pack would kill his livestock and they might starve, but at least he understood it. Swallowing, he grabbed his bag and moved away from the tracks. They followed a small game trail that he would avoid.

Gathering the roots took longer than normal. Every sound made his stomach tighten, and he would look around in worry every time. Since he was avoiding the game trail and the tracks, he had to push his way through the underbrush.

Bending over, he dug up the roots of a small flower with yellow petals. It wasn't much, but it was something fresh. Every bulb, every root and all the seeds he could find would help keep them alive. He carefully gathered up fallen pine needles with plans of making tea for Slavko. A few feet away a branch creaked, and he froze in place. Looking up, he didn't dare breathe until he saw a rabbit scampering away. Next time he'd have to bring some snares, but this time he was just too grateful it wasn't that horrible black creature.

"It's alright," he told himself. He didn't dare speak too loudly, but he needed to actually say the words. "It isn't the creature. Maybe it was just passing through."

Dobiemir shivered at the thought of the creature. Just the memory of its strange body put him on edge. The creature had been there and yet, its body had been an icy void in the world. He couldn't explain it. Add to that the cold, its glowing, unnaturally green eyes, and the way it attacked him, and it was a memory that flooded him with fear. Still, he had to be out here. They needed more supplies, and working in the forest now would make winter easier.

Lyubov had always been the one to go into the forest before. His father had taught him what he could and couldn't eat of course, but his wife had been a deft hand at gathering. She'd always somehow manage to collect more, find the best berries, and make the most out of what she found. Hissing at the ache in his chest, Dobiemir kept working even as his hands shook. Lyubov was gone now. He'd lost her. Both he and Slavko had lost her. There was a part of him that was grateful that the child hadn't survived. Without her it would have been impossible to care for the baby, and he would have only grown attached just to lose it in the winter.

Still, he knew that the ache would linger. Even Emond, who had lost four children over the years, had confessed that it never fully went away. Not even knowing that they likely wouldn't live and preparing yourself for the pain made it any easier. It was just part of the weight of life, but he hated it and wanted Lyubov back. She'd have had a good idea of how to turn things around. At least, she would have given him more hope in these dark times.

Something was happening. He wasn't sure what. But he knew that while never perfect, the land here was fertile. There was a reason his tribal grandfather and others had put down more permanent roots here. Now everything was turning. It wasn't just his farm: it was all of them in the area. The animals were acting strangely; always frightened, and the weather was odd.

It had to be that creature. Or creatures, if there were more of them. Dobiemir remembered the terrible cold that had overtaken him. If that always happened, then the creature was damaging plants wherever it went. With that in mind he eyed the ferns and trees. They looked a bit wilted for the warm weather and recent rain. Certainty swelled in his chest, but it didn't solve anything. If that creature was the source of the problems, then what could be done?

The missionaries might be able to help. Their words about the power of their God were impressive, but this creature more closely reminded him of the old stories of spirits that his mother had told him. Maybe the old gods had the answer. He wasn't sure, but Dobiemir couldn't solve it. He was a farmer, and at the moment a poor one. Strange creatures who seemed to be affecting the weather were not part of his world view.

Still, it all made him think of his mother's stories about evil spirits and what happened when the gods were angered. The Christian missionaries had slowly come further and further east. He'd never really concerned himself with the question of religion. If a god or the God could help him, then he'd pray to them. But maybe the old gods of his mother and father were angry. Maybe this was some sort of punishment. Or maybe the spirits were displeased about something else.

The trip home took too long. All of Dobiemir's thoughts about the creature and their problems had put a heavy knot in his gut. Worry for Slavko churned in his chest, and he kept speeding up. However, he also had to be careful not to lose the berries. Looking down the hill towards the village, he wondered if the others had approached the missionaries yet. The last time he'd gone into town a few weeks ago, he'd stopped to pray. Slavko was still ill, and his farm was still struggling. Accepting their words and sympathy was hard. Shaking his head, he made a promise to go and try again. But for now, he needed to get home.

Their home was just as he had left it. A sheep looked up from their field as he passed and nothing looked out of place. Sighing in relief, he shook himself in an attempt to dispel all the worry he'd built up in his shoulders. It helped, and once he felt calm enough for his son to see him he stepped into the house. Slavko was seated cross-legged on his bed with a blanket around his shoulders and a half-woven basket in his lap.

"Father?" His son's frown deepened, and the small boy looked up from the basket he was working on. "Are you alright?"

"Fine," he answered. Moving forward, he put the bag down on his bed and quickly began unpacking the roots and berries he'd gathered. He could feel his son's eyes on him as he stored the various items in separate jars and boxes. "Found some food in the forest."

"Father, is the harvest going to fail?"

Forcing himself to turn around, he knelt by the boy and put a hand on his thin shoulder. "I don't know," he answered honestly. "Things aren't growing well despite the rain, but there is still late summer and autumn for things to recover. I'm just trying to get ahead in case there are problems. If I can gather wood and food to dry out now, then winter will be easier."

Slavko nodded in understanding and Dobiemir smiled in relief. The boy might not completely comprehend his worries, but it all made sense in a way. If this was normal, then they would be alright. It was just the two of them, and while Slavko wasn't strong, there were many things he could do to help as he recovered. Smiling, he nodded to his son, and the boy's face brightened.

But then he shivered. The low light of the house dimmed, and the air turned icy. Slavko pulled the blanket tighter around him as his teeth chattered. Reaching over to his bed, Dobiemir snatched up his blankets and threw them over his son. Then it hit him. His whole body tensed even as his limbs quivered from the cold. With growing fear he reached for his cloak and pulled it on. He debated lighting a fire. There might not be time, and he dared not keep his back to the door. He took a step towards the door and picked up his axe.

"Father? What is happening?" Slavko asked. His voice was still quivering from the cold. "It's so cold."

"I don't know," he answered. "Stay under the blankets."

"But-"

"Stay on your bed and under the blankets."

He inched towards the door, his ears straining for any noise. The animals had gone silent. There were no cries of fear or sounds of running, just total silence. Easing open the door, he looked out cautiously. It was brighter outside, but still far darker than it should have been. Heart pounding and sweat gathering on his palms despite the cold, he stepped to the edge of the doorframe and looked around.

At first he saw nothing. The world was dark and muffled, like a winter day right after it snowed, but he knew it wasn't supposed to be that way. The animals were huddled together in the yard and standing completely still. Then movement in the corner of his eye drew his attention to the shade of some trees along the fields. Something dark was moving towards the house.

It was a different kind of creature. This one was more like a cat, but it was far too large and slinking through the shadows. Its eyes glowed the same sharp unnatural shade of green, and its body was too black. All light seemed to vanish into it — a creature of shadow and nothing more. Gripping his axe tightly, Dobiemir swallowed fearfully. It was coming closer, moving along the patch in the shade of the trees.

Far above them he could still see the sun shining down, but the light was distorted once more. The creature kept moving. It didn't look his way, but he stayed firmly in the doorway. Behind him, soft noises were escaping Slavko as the cold weighed down on him. Was it possible to slay this creature? What would happen then? Would the cold vanish or linger? When the other one had left the area the warmth of summer had returned.

"It'll be alright, son," he said softly. "Just stay still and quiet."

"I don't-"

"Hush!"

He dared not look at his son. He kept his eyes on the creature as it moved past. The air grew colder as it came towards the house. Somehow his heart beat even harder. It was suffocating. The air was too cold to breathe, and he heard a soft, almost pained cry behind him. He still didn't look away from the creature.

It kept walking. In its wake Dobiemir could see leaves trembling and shining as if they had a fresh layer of frost. His heart sank. Whatever had still been growing was sure to be dead now. A different kind of fear filled his chest, but he didn't rush out. The thing was too alien, too strange, and he was alone. Then it moved past the house, not even looking his way. Keeping to the shadows, the thing vanished from view into some trees.

Dobiemir stayed where he was, waiting for any sign of its return. Then the world brightened once more and the chill receded. Air filled his lungs and dizzy relief washed over him. Turning around, he looked towards the bed where Slavko was digging his way out from the blankets.

"Father, what was that? Why did it get so cold?" A lie gathered on the tip of his tongue, but the words wouldn't come. His son blinked up at him, suspicion and worry growing in his eyes. "Was it an evil spirit? Like the sort in the stories?"

Still unable to speak, Dobiemir felt himself nod. He looked back at the doorway and wondered how far that creature would go. It was the second one he'd seen. How many of them were there, and where had they come from? More importantly, how could they stop them before they completely destroyed the harvest?

7

No Rest for Mages

Today was easier than most. Relief and a sense of happiness filled Alex and their new house; her new home. Everyone was safe and sound, and Avani had even joined them. Jenny and Lance had returned safely and hadn't had any problems. While Bran had been attacked, he was back in Ravenslake without even a bruise left. Maybe it was selfish, but Alex was happy that they'd all come back and she had people with her. Every time that Aiden or Nicki vanished to visit their families there had been a sharp sting of pain and regret in her chest.

But now they had a full house. As much as Alex enjoyed sitting in the corner with a book, she had always preferred others to be nearby while she did it. Nicki was helping Avani take her suitcases upstairs and saying out loud that she hoped Avani had enough stuff. While they'd discussed her using a water tunnel, in the end it had worked out just fine for her fly over and drive in with Lance and Jenny. The couple in question were taking their things up to the room that had been earmarked for Lance but was now for the both of them.

"I hope she likes it here," Jenny said. "It's very different from Mumbai."

"It is," Lance agreed. He was following her up the stairs with one of the heavier suitcases. "But she's decided that this is where she wants to bee. She wants to help. I'm grateful for that."

Turning to look over her shoulder at Lance, Jenny gave him a wide dazzling smile that made her boyfriend grin in return. They seemed a touch nervous, but also very happy with the latest development, and as she followed them upstairs Alex couldn't help but smile. The area around the landing was crazy with Nicki helping Avani with her things as Lance and Jenny moved their boxes and suitcases into their room. Alex could already see that the area might become a traffic bottleneck in the future.

"Thank you, Nicki," Avani said. "Really, I can manage if you have other things to do."

"No, I'm great," Nicki said. "Besides, we want you to feel welcome!"

Avani was a very pretty young woman with a clear and warm complexion, long hair, and lovely brown eyes. And Alex was enjoying watching Nicki trying to keep herself from falling all over their newest housemate. Leaning against the railing, Alex held back a smile and watched as Avani nodded in understanding. Alex sidestepped in the doorway so Nicki could bring another suitcase in. Looking up she caught Alex's eyes and looked a touch sheepish for a moment. That might be a good sign for Nicki, Alex decided.

Jenny came back out into the hall, pulling her long dark hair up into a ponytail. She smiled at Avani and turned towards the stairs, but the Indian woman jumped forward and carefully touched her arm to draw Jenny's attention.

"I'm very grateful that you and Lance were able to bring me into town," Avani said. "The landscape was beautiful."

"Yes, the Oregon coast is a lovely area," Jenny replied. "I suppose it was very different than you've seen around Mumbai."

"Very different," Avani agreed. Then she hesitated for a moment. "I hope my moving in didn't put pressure on you to-"

"No," Jenny said. Smiling at Avani, she reached over and caught the other woman's hand. "Don't worry about it. Truly. Lance and I... we've been working towards this for a long time, and when news came that you were coming, we had a serious discussion about everything." There was a calm in her expression and a brightness in her eyes that Alex didn't think she'd ever seen. "It was overdue. We've talked about our past, but never the future. Not really, but we both want to make it work. Long-term." Her smile turned giddy. "Like, marriage in the future long term."

"Did he ask?" Alex stared at Jenny, torn between shock and glee. "Did he?"

"No, not yet," Jenny said. "But he..." Her skin flushed with pleasure. "He did say that when he thought about the future, I was it, and after we graduate he plans on asking me properly." Giggling, Jenny tugged at the hem of her green shirt. "Joked that maybe we'd even go back to Paris for it."

Jumping forward, Alex hugged Jenny, who laughed in return. For a moment, the tension she'd been carrying around melted away, and there was a hum of happiness in her head. Instead of any lingering jealousy from the lifetimes that had been involved with Jenny's various prior incarnations, it seemed that all of her was relieved. Three thousand years of reincarnation, betrayal, and tragedy seemed to finally be on their way to a peaceful and happy resolution. Her head went a little fuzzy as the euphoria of it all overwhelmed her. Alex almost cried: she'd started to forget what happiness felt like.

"Guys!" Bran called up the stairs. "We've got visitors."

He didn't sound panicked, so Alex just shrugged when the others looked at her. "Finish getting the boxes into the rooms," she said. "Then come down. Unless I start screaming, of course."

Jenny gave her a frown of disapproval at joking about something like that, but Nicki's lips quirked up in a smile. Alex winked at Nicki and headed down the stairs to where she could hear voices. It took her a moment to place them as Bran, Morgana, and Merlin. Her happiness drained away a touch. As much as she wanted to believe otherwise, Morgana and Merlin probably weren't here to give them a housewarming gift. They'd already bought the house and furnished it for them.

Merlin and Morgana were with Bran in the living room. Thankfully, they both looked calm. Morgana looked up at her and smiled with a touch of relief. It seemed that Morgana's big sister instincts would never fade.

"Hey," Alex greeted. "What's up?"

"We wanted to check in with Bran," Merlin said. He was frowning slightly. "It is distressing to learn in detail what Arthur can do."

"We already knew he could do that," Alex said. "That's how he killed my parents."

"I confess that at the time I thought it was more likely that he'd paid someone," Merlin said. "I did not consider that Arthur could truly control people."

Alex frowned. Her stomach tightened in a mix of anger and grief. Then she exhaled and told herself to relax. Merlin hadn't seen the driver. He hadn't seen the death of her parents. Of course he'd make assumptions. They'd never talked about what had happened. And that was the core of the problem. If they'd talked about it then maybe they could have had better defenses ready. Instead, they'd been worried about upsetting her.

"Fair enough," she said. Sitting down beside Bran on the sofa, Alex smiled at him and gently knocked her shoulder against his. "I am glad you're back safe and sound."

He smiled in return at her. "I missed you too. All of you."

"Really? I would have thought it was a nice escape from the insanity."

"In a way, but I also had to run five miles a day to deal with all the baked goods my mother kept putting in front of me. She was in full-on mom mode all summer." His smile turned gentle, and he reached over to squeeze her hand quickly. "Besides, I worried about all of you."

Morgana chuckled and said, "Well Bran, you are the most reasonable of the mages."

"Hey!" Alex protested. "I'm plenty reasonable."

Alex was saved from their response to that by the others coming downstairs. Avani hesitated at the back of the group as Jenny, Lance, and Nicki came downstairs. Nicki paused and looked around.

"Where's Aiden?"

"In the kitchen," came a shout. "Helping Timothy with drinks!"

"Ah," Nicki said. She nodded. "Fair enough. I'll just go and help them."

"Hello, Avani," Morgana said after Nicki headed into the kitchen. "Thank you for coming to Ravenslake."

"Of course," Avani said. She was tense even as she smiled, and watched Morgana with thinly veiled awe. "I'm honored to be of service to the mages."

"I imagine that they've brought you up to speed on the situation," Merlin said.

"Jenny and Lance explained what happened with Arthur to me," Avani answered. Her dark eyes lost their spark as anger took over. "And the various enemies that the mages have dealt with. I confess a certain amount of amazement over the complexity of the situation."

"Indeed," Morgana said. "Many forces have been active in a short span of time. Usually, we only have to be concerned with one enemy at a time. At least the situation with the Demons has been resolved."

"And Cathanáil is in our control," Merlin added. "The Iron Gates should remain strong enough to keep the Sídhe forces out. Chernobog and Brekszta are dead and unable to cause trouble. Hopefully, any other Old Ones with delusions of killing us will think twice."

"So, it is just this Arthur and his mother?" Avani asked.

"That seems to be the case," Morgana agreed. "But we shouldn't underestimate them. Arthur knows everyone here, except for you, and has proven that he is willing to kill."

Avani shuddered, but Alex said nothing. Her good mood was draining away rapidly, and she wished that Merlin and Morgana could have let them at least have today to settle in. That was a pipe dream, and Alex knew she should have known better. The older mages had been well aware of when they'd all be home. Bran had come back last night, and Lance and Jenny had given them an estimated time of arrival.

There was the clinking of dishes and glasses from the kitchen. Alex let her head fall back against the thick pillows of the sofa and rolled it so she could see a little further into the kitchen. Nicki and Aiden were carrying platters with drinks out. Alex didn't even know they had platters. That had to have been something Morgana stocked the house with. Along with the matching glasses and small plates. Alex's dishware had been a mixture from thrift stores and cheap box store sets.

Nicki kept her platter much more level as she set it on the coffee table. They had a coffee table. A nervous, almost hysterical laugh started building in Alex's chest. Nicki's platter had tall glasses of iced tea that she quickly passed around before moving to the sofa and sitting by Avani. Lance and Jenny were on the loveseat and started moving over so that Aiden would be able to squeeze in while Merlin and Morgana watched from the other loveseat. Aiden put down the tray with some cookies even as the plate threatened to shake off.

"Timothy made them," he said. "Not sure how he manages it, but he does."

"Baking via telekinesis isn't so hard," Bran said. He shrugged. "I gave it a try while I was home. For me it was more work than it was worth, but when you're Timothy's size I guess it is the best option."

Aiden shrugged and squeezed in next to Lance, who leaned forward so his broad shoulders wouldn't hit Aiden or Jenny. Morgana's eyes scanned the packed sofa, and she smiled slightly. At least she seemed calm, though there was calculation in her eyes.

"We may need to get you a larger sofa," she said. "How is the house otherwise?"

"It's great, Morgana," Alex said. She straightened up and smiled at the older mage. "I know I feel a lot better having some privacy, and knowing that if we're attacked we don't have to worry about the city or other students."

"Plus, it is nice to be in one place," Nicki said. "Honestly, it was overdue."

Nodding in agreement, Morgana folded her hands in her lap and exchanged a look with Merlin. It was one of their silent communication glances. Even after several years of seeing it and memories of it from long ago, Alex still had trouble believing the amount of information they could share in a single look.

"Ambrose and I have been reviewing some of our old records to find ways to protect all of you better. Normally the blood ward would be reliable, but with the Red Caps and now Arthur toying with human minds it can't be depended upon."

She had the attention of everyone in the room. Worry was thick in the air, and Alex knew that everyone was thinking of Bran's report of the attack on his home, as well as the murder of her parents. Morgana took in their reactions, her green eyes darkening with her anger and understanding.

"We believe that we've formulated a new warding spell that can help... deter those who mean harm, for lack of a better word. It won't stop them or prevent the most determined, but it might help."

Nicki nodded in agreement. "It sounds worth a try. Would it be something that could be done at the school or our homes?"

"The school would be difficult," Merlin said, but he looked thoughtful. "The amount of area and bluntly the mindset of some students could cause problems. We don't want to affect too many minds. But your homes are certainly possible."

Avani tentatively raised her hand as if they were in a classroom. When Morgana raised an eyebrow at her, she ducked her head in slight embarrassment. Nicki's eyes went soft and warm. Alex could almost see hearts in them.

"When looking through my family's library I found a perimeter alert spell," she said. "It hasn't been used in years due to the amount of magic that has to be concentrated, but for mages surely that wouldn't be a problem."

"I am not familiar with that spell," Merlin said.

"Oh, it was only created about four centuries ago," Avani said. Alex nearly snorted. The Desai family had a strange notion of time. "But I believe you lay a line outside the house and then link the magic to an object. If something passes the line, then the object changes to reflect that. One of my ancestors had an object that would glow. The problem was that as they weren't mages, the spell ran down."

"Yes... unlike the blood spell which draws power to keep working from the Earth, I can see that something like that would feed off the magic users."

"Unless we can adjust it," Nicki said. "But honestly I'd accept some draining if it meant that we had a magical alarm system. No offense to Timothy, but he did get into Alex's dorm room and almost took out her eye."

"That is a good point," Morgana agreed. "While we couldn't set something like that up at your family's house, a deterring ward and a non-magical alarm system would not be a bad idea."

"Well, my father already has a security system," Jenny said. "I don't know if Arthur would see him as a target, but anything that can be done to keep him safer would be welcome."

"So, what will you need from us to make this ward work?" Bran asked. "Is it similar to the blood spell?"

"It combines the blood spell and an alarm spell that Merlin and I used in the past," Morgana explained. "We developed it in the early Middle Ages... I think." She blinked her green eyes, actually looking uncertain for a moment. "Maybe earlier. It was also during this period that we became confident enough in our magic to start... pushing against human minds."

"That is a dangerous thing," Merlin said. "None of you should try it, but like Morgana said we learned how to push away other minds. We believe that we can link that spell into a perimeter spell."

"It sounds reasonable... I guess," Aiden said. His was frowning, and his dark brown eyes were fixed on Merlin. "But it won't protect our families while they are out and about."

"No," Merlin agreed. "It won't. It has to be tied to a place."

"So even something like a necklace wouldn't work?" Nicki asked. She was frowning now and clutching one of the pieces of her jewelry that her artisan grandmother had made.

"No," Morgana said. "Something like that... I'd worry about the effect it would have on the person wearing it. We can experiment a bit, but don't get your hopes up."

"I wish there was a manual," Aiden groaned. "Seriously!"

"I'm afraid that's not possible," Merlin said. He smiled sadly at them. "What we know is what Morgana and I have discovered over the years. I learned only a few things from my magician mother. She dabbled in magic, but had no natural power of her own."

"And as you children have pointed out, we aren't the most creative minds in history," Morgana added dryly.

Alex stayed still as the others talked. Nicki had more questions about possible adjustments to the warding spell and how to combine it with Avani's perimeter spell. Their voices blended together, making it impossible to keep track of their ideas. Holding back a sight, Alex looked towards the kitchen. From here she could catch the occasional glimpse of Timothy as the Brownie bounced around across the counters. He seemed content enough, and not worried. Alex wished she shared that, but the good mood that she'd been able to cultivate for the day was well and truly gone.

8

New Surroundings

It was a quiet night. A soft breeze carried the sound of rustling leaves down from the hillside, and he could see neon lights in Ravenslake proper reflecting off the lake. The air was crisp, still warm from summer, but carrying the promise of the coming autumn. Years ago Bran would have found it comforting and relaxing. Now it put him on edge. It was the sort of night that might lure you into a false sense of security.

While they had a plan to secure the new house and their homes, it wasn't done yet. Between the memory of the man with the gun and the conversation that afternoon, Bran was finding it difficult to relax. Even as the noise of the others died down, he had found it impossible to sleep. Instead, he'd come outside to check on the perimeter, and stayed for the cooling night air.

He was standing on their front porch and watching the lake. It wasn't much of a view thanks to the other houses, but their new home was a bit higher, and there was a gap in the trees that let him see a good chunk of the lake. Beyond the lake, he thought he could make out the silhouette of the campus library. Drumming his fingers against the railing of the porch, he debated going inside and getting a start on his new textbooks.

It wouldn't hurt to get ahead of things. Their lives were too crazy now to assume that they'd have plenty of time to study.

Except he didn't want to. Bran made no move to go inside. Aiden was asleep, and he didn't want to risk waking up his roommate. The rest of the house was silent and even Timothy had vanished for the evening. Holding back a sigh, Bran wondered if the others were feeling this restless. This on edge. Exhaling slowly, he tried to shrug it off, but the sense that something was coming clung to his shoulders.

He heard the back door open and tensed. Unmoving, Bran listened for any sign if it was someone coming outside or something going in. It was difficult to hear, but he heard the door close with a soft thump and footfalls on the back patio. Relaxing, he slowly climbed down the front steps of the porch and went along the fence to the gate. There was no other sound. The gate opened easily enough, and Bran crossed the lawn to go around the side of the house.

Avani was outside, standing in the moonlight and staring into the forest. For a moment Bran hesitated and debated if he should join her. She was fine, and they were safe enough. Yet some instinct nagged at him to go and talk with their new housemate. After all, she'd left her home and family behind to come and offer whatever aid she could. They didn't have a lot of people scrambling to help them. The poor woman hadn't even had time to unpack before Morgana and Merlin came to discuss the dangers she'd volunteered for.

"Hey," he said. Bran was sure to move with slow and solid steps that made plenty of noise. Avani tensed slightly but quickly relaxed. "Nice night."

"It's a bit cold," Avani replied.

"I hate to tell you this, but it's going to get colder."

"Nicki's warned me." Avani chuckled and looked over her shoulder towards him. "So did all my family when I talked about coming here. Jenny already took me out shopping for autumn gear in Portland after my plane landed." She gestured at the red sweater she was wearing. "She said that there wasn't much selection here."

"Well, college town or not, Ravenslake is a lot smaller than San Francisco or Portland." Stepping up next to her, Bran quickly scanned the trees. "And much smaller than Mumbai."

"Yes, it's strange. Nice, but strange. Everything is so quiet here, and the air is fresh. I never thought of Mumbai as that restrictive." Avani lowered her face in embarrassment. "Honestly, sometimes it feels dangerous. All that open space, not many lights, and the quiet. Does it ever get to you?"

"Me?" Bran shook his head. "No. Portland is pretty large, but my dad liked the outdoors. We went out on a lot of hikes when I was young. Camping a few times too. It's one of the things I like about the Pacific Northwest. You can enjoy life in a city, but the mountains aren't too far away." Then he nodded at the forest. "Then again... knowing some of the things that have come out of the dark after us... it makes everything else a little frightening."

"That's fair." Avani tugged at the turtleneck of her sweater. "I'm sorry if I intruded. It was rude of me and perhaps-"

"No." Bran cut her off and turned to look at her. "You're a magician. You provide a more modern understanding of magic than Merlin and Morgana. They are amazing mages, but they don't really ask why anymore. It's natural to them while you have to study for your magic. That's gives you a different perspective from us which is valuable. Besides, we need all the help we can get. Knowing you're here, teaching Lance and Jenny and helping defend the house makes everything a little easier. Besides, your family knows how to get more out of only a little magic.

I'll be honest: all of us probably throw magic around too hard and too fast."

"I see." Avani was silent for a time, and it was just them and the soft sounds from the houses and the nearby city. "I never thought about what being a mage would be like. Not really? I remember wanting to be one as a child, hearing the stories of what mages could do and their histories. But I never considered the emotional struggle there."

"It hasn't been an easy road," Bran agreed. "Not all bad though. I'm not the broody kind, but there's been problems and complications and things that hurt."

"That hurt? You've been injured?"

"No, not exactly. Has anyone told you about the Iron Chain?" Avani shook her head, and Bran allowed himself to sigh. "Shit. I don't want to have to explain this, but you need to know."

He found it harder to start than he thought it would be. Looking at his hands, Bran forced himself to start speaking. "Not all of the Iron Soul lives have been good people. During the height of the Atlantic Slave Trade, the reborn Iron Soul was the captain of a slave ship. While we don't think he had any real understanding or knowledge of what he was doing, he poured some magic into a chain on his ship. It carried his desire for the slaves to obey him and... well, bound their will to his."

"Are you serious?"

"Afraid so. Merlin and Morgana never knew about it, but the Sídhe Queen, Scáthbás, somehow found the thing. It could bind different magics together, or something like that. It's how she made the human body she possessed part Sídhe like Merlin and Morgana, and she did the same for Arthur." Bran shivered at the statement. He'd never seen it like Alex had, but his imagination was unfortunately happy to provide him with a mental picture. "Then she figured out how to use it and her Sídhe blood to bind the Fae folk, the descendants of the original Sídhe invaders, to her will. She commanded them to kill us."

Falling silent, Bran licked his lips. His chest tightened, and he tried to sort out the words in his head. Most of the time it was just... a fact, an unchangeable reality of what had happened at the back of his mind, but talking about it brought it all forward again. All the emotions that he'd never really processed, that he didn't think any of them had processed.

"You didn't know about the Chain at first, did you?" Avani asked. Her tone was soft. She was trying not to spook him. "When they attacked you?"

"No," Bran agreed. "We didn't know. We thought they'd just sided with her and defended ourselves." He sighed and still didn't look at Avani. "It wasn't a lot... but enough. We killed them in self-defense, but they were under her control. It leaves a bitter taste in the mouth." Nodding towards the house, he finally felt the unease lift a little. "When Alex found out, she did what she could to free them. She broke the spell in the area one night when Arthur was attacking, and then we went to find the Iron Hammer to deal with the rest of the spell."

"And you were successful?"

"Yes, the spell was broken. Alex shattered the Iron Chain and somehow pulled it back to Ravenslake. I don't know all the details, just what Alex shared." He finally looked at Avani and found her giving him a soft, supportive smile.

"That wasn't your fault," Avani said. "You had to defend yourselves. It wasn't like you went hunting them down."

"No, we didn't." Bran nodded and glanced up at the house, towards Alex's dark window. "But it still stings. And the Fae... a lot of them still hate us for it."

"Timothy doesn't."

"He doesn't." Chuckling, Bran shook his head. "Timothy had made it into Alex's dorm room and cut her face. She released him from the spell pretty much by accident, but he was able to provide information. Alex tried to save as many of the Fae under the spell as she could for Timothy's sake."

"That's good."

"Yeah, but not good enough. I don't know. It still bothers me. I'm not sure what to do with it in my head. Most of the time, I'm still not even sure about what magic is or how to best use it."

"But you were taught by the Grand Mages!"

"Merlin and Morgana are human, well, okay they're half human, and pretty good teachers, but a lot has been happening in Ravenslake over the last two years. Things that even they weren't prepared for. All of us have just been doing the best we can, and if that means trying to have some mercy then that's what we do." Staring up at the moon, Bran inwardly grumbled at his sudden brooding. "It makes the rest of it a bit easier."

Avani didn't say anything. He didn't expect her to. He checked the house again. Despite the nice temperature of the night air, everyone's windows were shut tight. The front and back porch lights were on, and Bran expected that they probably always would be at night. Then a high-pitched giggle came out of the trees. Tensing, Bran flexed his fingers and looked around. He couldn't see anything in the backyard. The wind was rustling nearby trees, and the giggle was gone. Glancing towards Avani, he found her frowning and scanning the trees. At least that suggested that he wasn't crazy.

Then there was a rush of giggling — multiple high-pitched voices echoing from the forest. They were familiar. Heart pounding, Bran pulled on his magic, feeling it flash to life. As the yellow sparks poured from his fingertips and surrounded his hands in a golden glow, he heard the giggling increase.

"Shit!" Bran glanced up towards the windows. The others were asleep, and he didn't dare reach for his phone to send a text. "Wake up!" he shouted. The neighbors weren't too close, so hopefully the police wouldn't be called. "Red Caps! Alex! Aiden! Nicki! Get up!"

There was no more time for shouting warnings. Red Caps came jumping out of the tree line, rushing across the grass and leaping onto the fence. The small gray-colored creatures all wore bright red caps. Mythology said the hats were dyed with human blood, and as their long fingernails dug into the wooden fence, Bran completely believed it.

He waved his hands. Yellow bolts formed out of the sparks and blasted forward. The first struck a Red Cap and sent it flying back off of the top of the fence. More hit the Red Caps even as they tried to rush out of the way. It was like a warped carnival game. Small shrieks escaped the Red Caps, but Bran couldn't see them beyond the fence to confirm they were dead. More were coming, now on the lawn of the backyard.

He heard more noise around the front of the house and tensed. Resisting the urge to turn, he sent a wave of yellow energy rippling across the yard. Red Caps squealed and darted out of the way, trying to climb up the fence and the one large tree in the yard. Avani was chanting something. He didn't know how fast her magic could work but wasn't going to risk it. Moving over, he placed himself between her and the Red Caps, eyeing the advancing line.

Crashes from inside caught Bran's attention. He hoped it was the others trying to get dressed and come outside, but he wasn't sure. Red Caps were pouring into the yard, over two dozen at least, and all with sharp teeth and claws. A few were carrying knives. At least there were no guns in sight. Light spread out around Avani's feet, forming a small circle around her. Her hands dropped to her sides and Avani's fingertips moved graceful as if spelling out words. Unfamiliar symbols blossomed into view around her feet, eclipsing the soft glow of the circle. It was exactly what he'd once assumed magic would look like, and he almost smiled.

A Red Cap snarled and rushed ahead of the others only to be suddenly stopped in the air. The outer ring of light flashed, and the creature couldn't move. Its muscles twitched, but it was in some sort of stasis. Shocked, Bran turned to look at her. The circle was bright and spread out far enough to protect him, but sweat was already gathering on Avani's brow. Her eyes were closed in concentration, and there was a slight quiver in her hands. Useful, but it took a lot out of her. Swinging back around, he sent yellow bolts shooting into the crowd of Red Caps.

Several went down with sharp cries. More pressed on, spreading out and hissing. He sent out more bolts. The ring of light vanished, and there was a sigh behind him from Avani. Turning, he caught sight of her slumping against the side of the house. She was awake but unsteady. Bran started to move towards her. He stopped as he realized the Red Caps were closing in.

One of the Red Caps lunged, sharp needle-like teeth revealed in the low light coming from the porch. Bran shoved his hand forward. A wave of yellow sparks swept up the Red Cap and threw it back. Exhaling slowly, Bran focused his attention on the pulse of magic beneath his feet and the warmth in his chest. His father's dog tags shifted against his skin under his shirt, and he braced himself for the next wave of attackers.

Lightning arced through the air and hit the first Red Cap in the hoard. It shrieked and convulsed as it tried and failed to run. His eyes almost closed in relief. Alex was here. More were coming though, flanking the house. Looking towards the front, Bran grinned as small bolts of red and blue shot past him. He was surprised that the others had cleared the rest, but grateful for the reinforcements. Red Caps were falling all over the place, screaming and trying to grab each other. Whatever military precision they'd had was gone, and he moved back.

Then the sky above them began to rumble. Ozone hit his nose and an electric jolt traveled across his skin. Bran's heart jumped. Mjǫllnir. Was she using Mjǫllnir in their backyard? Nicki screamed a warning. Bran slammed his eyes closed and reached for Avani. A deafening crack rattled his bones and the ground shook. The bright light faded quickly, and the back of his eyelids returned to black.

Opening his eyes slowly, Bran scanned the yard. There were still a few Red Caps left, running for the fence and shouting to each other. For a moment he hesitated, but raised his right hand and formed more yellow bolts. As he released them, more blue and red bolts sailed past to strike down the Red Caps. He hadn't been the only one unprepared to let them get away. It was almost comforting.

His eyes dropped to a smoldering spot in the lawn. There were dark lines that looked like more lightning stretched out from the black point of impact. Bran had read about Lichtenberg figures in the past but had never known that they could be so clear on the ground. The strike had burned the grass as the earth absorbed the electricity. It was almost beautiful. The air tasted of ozone even as the rumbling overhead eased. A weatherman somewhere was about to start hating Ravenslake, Oregon.

"That might have been overkill," Aiden said, breaking the heavy silence.

"Warnings, Alex," Nicki said firmly. "Remember friendly fire warnings. Just shout Mjǫllnir or something so we can at least close our eyes."

There was grass on fire in the center of their yard and a dark, scorched ring around it. Nicki stepped forward calmly and flicked her wrist. Her blue sparks turned into a bubble of water hanging in the air. Giggling in pleasure, she looked over her shoulder at Avani. Bran raised an eyebrow as Avani smiled at the display just before Nicki snapped her fingers. The bubble fell to the ground and released the water to extinguish the flames with a splash. Shaking his head, he felt dizzy from the rush of amusement so suddenly after the worry and fear.

"Red Caps in our new backyard," Alex said. "I don't think it was overkill." Then she looked a touch sheepish. "But, yeah, I'll warn you in the future before calling down a lightning bolt."

"Well," Aiden sighed, "this just proves that we need some kind of security system."

"I'll start working on a plan right away," Avani said. Her smile had faded, and she was watching the dusty remains of the Red Caps vanish on the wind. Bran wondered if she regretted coming to Ravenslake yet or not. He didn't ask.

9

Shadows and Strangers

Podlasie Province, Poland 983 C.E.

The village was small but it was the hub of activity. Farmers like him brought in their goods and traded for the items and processed goods that they needed. Today he didn't have much in the way of food, but the chopped wood and a small bag of cooked wildflower seeds had been enough to get him another blanket and some leather. Even with the creatures away from the house, Slavko never seemed to be warm enough nowadays.

The last days of summer hadn't brought any relief, and now into the harvest season he worried about what little food that was still growing. Going into the forest almost every day had yielded more plants and roots to dry and bake, but he'd glimpsed the shadows over and over. Their cold was always sharp and overwhelming. When winter got here, they would surely be unbearable.

"I've seen one of those creatures twice now!" Someone shouted. There were too many people huddled together for Dobiemir to be sure who was talking. "They leave cold in their wake. They're some sort of evil spirits and are destroying the harvest!"

He looked towards the group that had gathered around the mission-ary. The man was pale and seemed frightened even as he listened to them. He was tempted to join them. Shouting out his worries and fears might be enough to help him feel a little better. But the itch to return home in case more of the creatures showed up kept him focused.

"They're black," someone cried. "With glowing green eyes. They're killing off the harvest. The animals are afraid of them. It won't be long before they start killing!"

"Please, calm down," the missionary said.

"Michael, this is your fault! You and that religion of yours! You've angered the gods and the spirits of the forest. They're punishing us."

There was a round of agreement. "It's almost time for the harvest!" another voice shouted. "All summer the crops have been failing, and now there's almost nothing. Winter will be here soon!"

He stopped to listen despite wanting to get home. Unease stirred in his chest, and he found himself worrying for Michael. He took a small step towards the mob and the missionary who was trying to reassure them that God still cared. Passages from Michael's Holy Book followed, which calmed some but increased the anger of others.

"Dobiemir!"

Turning, he found himself being approached by Emond. Walking away from Michael and the crowd, he met his neighbor halfway amongst the livestock and people trading their goods. He couldn't help but notice that Emond had lost a little weight, and the man hadn't had much extra to lose. Looking past Emond, he noted with relief that two of the man's children still looked healthy as they secured some wrapped bundles onto a goat's back.

"Emond, good to see you," he greeted. "Is the family well?"

"We can't complain," Emond said. He almost smiled. "There were a few sniffles not long ago, but thankfully they have passed without any real illness. How is Slavko?" Emond asked. He glanced around for any sign of the boy. "Is he here?"

"No, he's in bed at home," Dobiemir answered. "He's not doing any better." There was more he wanted to say, but the words were too difficult to form.

"You left him alone, with those creatures?" Emond's eyes were wide, and shock took over his face. "Are you-" Then he stopped himself and shook his head. "I'm sorry. I know you would not have if it could have been avoided."

Dobiemir nodded, his mouth too dry to speak, and looked around at the market crowd. Everyone was tense and worried, with furrows between their brows and a defeated slump to their shoulders. He wasn't sure if he was relieved or not that he hadn't been the only one to see the strange creatures.

"Have you seen them?" he asked Emond.

"Yes, only one though. It was getting dark, and something was in the fields. I started to investigate, but... it got so cold. Dobiemir, it was horrible, and then it looked at me. Those eyes are unnatural."

"I know," he said. "I've seen them too. Several times now. A few in the forest and once by the house. In the forest, it attacked me."

"Attacked you?" Emond's eyes widened further. "That's- I haven't heard that from anyone else. How did you escape? Or did you have to fight it?"

"No, I climbed up a tree," he admitted. "It lost interest."

"I haven't gone near the forest in weeks," Emond said. Shaking his head, he shuddered at the idea. "Knowing that they're out there. It's been hard to leave the house just to tend the fields."

"How are your fields doing?"

"Not good, but not as bad as others." Emond frowned. "You're closer to the forest than most. People out that way seem to have it the worst. That's probably why you've seen so many. Are they all the same?"

"I don't think so." Dobiemir frowned and tried to remember the last one he'd seen. As soon as he'd caught sight of it in the forest, he'd climbed a tree and waited until it passed. "They all seem a bit different."

"And you're still going into the forest?"

"Have to collect enough plants to feed the animals," Dobiemir said. "I've already slaughtered one goat and smoked the meat for winter. I need to be able to keep a few alive through winter."

"I understand, but you're braver than I am. I haven't been into the forest since I first heard the rumors. The children have been gathering closer to home. It isn't as much as we'd get in the forest, but we'll get through."

"Good, I'm glad to hear it," Dobiemir said. "It seems that everyone is feeling the effects now."

"Yes. I'm almost grateful that it isn't just us. Then I feel guilty for my relief."

Dobiemir reached out and gripped Emond's shoulder. He understood. He understood all too well, but envy for the good fortune of others was what haunted him. With Slavko ill, he found himself desperately wishing for Lyubov back, even if their child wasn't. They'd lost a son and a daughter before. Slavko had been their survivor, and now...

Shaking off the thoughts, he coughed lightly, and turned back to check on their local missionary. Michael was backing away from the crowd. A nagging little voice told him to intervene and make sure that things didn't turn violent, but the angry part of him didn't care. Besides, two men that he recognized as more devoted converts had moved to flank Michael. The missionary seemed a little more confident and calmer with them there.

"This isn't a good time for missionaries," Emond said softly. "Miloslava took an offering out a few nights ago. She's hoping to honor and appease whatever has sent the shadows. Apparently a few households have done so."

"Well, not everyone is Christian," Dobiemir said. "Do you think that it is an angry god?"

"What else could it be?" Emond shivered and looked towards their farms. "They aren't animals of flesh and blood. Of that much I'm certain. They leave tracks in the earth, but no fur, no waste, and aren't afraid of us."

"Maybe."

"You don't think so?"

"I'm not sure what to think," Dobiemir said. "They don't seem violent... many have seen them and no one has been killed. I'm not sure what that means: maybe they are just scouts or are looking for something."

"Or they're starving us by killing the harvest until we all turn back to their god."

Giving Emond a sharp look, Dobiemir tried to ignore the twisting in his gut. That sort of plan would align with some of the stories he'd been told. Emond seemed to understand his sudden silence and nodded to him before moving off to join his family. Dobiemir inhaled slowly to calm his heart and waited for the nausea to pass. He spotted movement to his right and glanced that way to reassure himself.

There was a strange man and a woman off to the side. They both wore long gray cloaks despite the lack of an autumn chill. He could see only a little of their faces. Both were watching the shouting crowd with thoughtful and serious frowns. A long brown braid hung over the woman's shoulder while the man had gray curly hair. He was sure that he'd never seen them before and they rarely got visitors in their small village.

Still, it wasn't his concern. He had what he'd come for, and it was time to head home. Hoisting the roll of leather onto his back and securing the blanket beneath his arm, Dobiemir set off on the first road towards home. The voices of the villagers echoed behind him, and he wondered if the noise would keep the shadows away. To the west the sun was sinking toward the horizon. The days were growing shorter. He'd need to cut far more wood than usual for this winter if the shadows remained in the area. Surely, light and warmth would keep them away and his son safe.

He kept an eye on the area around the road as he walked. It was a quiet day. He could hear nearby birds and movement in the underbrush, but it was subdued. It was as if the animals were as downcast about the strange creatures as the humans. Dobiemir eyed the graying leaves of the underbrush, which was a sharp reminder that the strange cold of the creatures could be affecting the wild plants and animals just as badly. It would all die together.

Maybe he needed to focus more on hunting and smoking meat. His father had taught him some basic traps, and while he wasn't skilled, surely it was worth the time if it secured a little more food for the winter. Suddenly the sky began to darken, turning the day from afternoon to dusk all in a moment. Dobiemir stopped immediately, his eyes searching for any sign of the shadows, and hoped that they'd just pass by. A chill began to descend over him like falling snow, and he inhaled the now bitterly cold air with a sharp sniff.

Very slowly, he turned his head to look behind him. He could see the village in the distance down by the river. It seemed brighter and clearer than anything around him. It was just near him then. That wasn't as reassuring as he would have hoped, but it should mean that Slavko was safe; unless they'd come from that way. Fear clutched at his heart, squeezing it tighter — the image of his son shivering, or worse, dead under the blankets.

Then, two shadows stepped out onto the road, their coats shimmering in the dimmed daylight. Dobiemir stood frozen, hoping, praying to every deity he could think of that they would just move on. He'd never seen more than one at a time. They were similar, but one was more cat-like, while the other seemed to have the snout of a bear. It made no sense to him. He didn't care. They approached him, sniffing at the air and moving with slow, measured steps.

There was a tree near the edge of the road that looked strong enough to hold him and had lower branches. He debated the likelihood of tossing his pack at the shadows and making it to the tree before they were on him. Dobiemir doubted he could, but began moving his arms to shift the bundle of leather and blankets. His heart was racing now, his blood pounding in his ears so loudly that he could barely hear anything else.

But there was a sound behind him — the cracking of a branch. Both of the shadows stopped and shifted away from him just enough to see beyond him. Dobiemir's knees quivered. His head felt light, and he wondered what was behind him. The shadows growled, but he didn't dare look. The cold radiating from them was cutting into his legs, stabbing into his bones. Lightheaded, it was all he could to stay upright.

Light exploded behind him. It was warm against his back, and a sigh of relief escaped him as the warmth traveled down his aching legs. The shadows snarled and leapt past him, running for something that he couldn't see. Stumbling forward, Dobiemir gulped at the air greedily to fight off the blackness dancing at the edge of his vision. He turned around, almost tripping.

The two strangers were on the road, both still wearing their cloaks. But their hands were bright with strange, unfamiliar light. Around the woman's hands were silver sparks that were twisting together to form a whip. The man was surrounded by green sparks. They weren't running. They didn't seem afraid. The shadows stopped a few feet from them. Swallowing, Dobiemir backed away from the strangers and shadows. His legs were still too sore, too tired to run.

For a moment neither human nor shadow moved. Then they all moved at once. Light exploded around the woman, blinding him. Blinking rapidly, he didn't dare move. His ears strained for any clue as to where the shadows were. As the light cleared and his vision returned, he found the man and woman facing off against the two shadows. Fire whipped through the air around the man, but the creatures kept advancing. The woman shouted for him to run, but Dobiemir couldn't make his legs move. His heart was pounding. It was hard to breathe, and he just wanted to run. But the creatures were closing in on the strangers.

"What does it take to kill these things?" the woman snapped. More light flashed out around them, burning bright spots into Dobiemir's eyes. But it didn't stop the creatures. The light vanished into their pitch-dark bodies without even slowing them down. "Merlin? Any ideas?"

The man waved his hand, and the green sparks rushed forth as beams of light, striking at the shadows, but once more there was no sign of injury. The two shadow creatures snarled and jumped for the man. Merlin waved his hand, and a wave of green sparks caught the monsters and tossed them away. As they hit the ground, the creatures snarled and twisted back to face the strangers. If they felt any pain, they didn't show it, and instead they lunged at the man once more.

"Morgana!" Merlin shouted.

Screaming, the woman snapped both hands out and fire flashed out in a ring, catching both of the shadows, but stopping mere inches from Dobiemir. Gasping, he stumbled back. These people had powers like the gods. Were they gods? He didn't know. Terror and awe kept him in place. Worry hummed through his veins as they launched more attacks. Nothing stopped the creatures. Fire and light vanished into their black bodies, and the cold surrounding them grew worse and worse. Shivering, Dobiemir clenched his teeth together. The pain in his legs was back, worse than before.

"Nothing's working!" Morgana shouted.

"I'll try to contain them!"

The earth beneath his feet trembled. Stumbling to the right, Dobiemir tracked the movements of the creatures as they hissed and snarled. Then slabs of rock shot up from the ground, creating a wall between Dobiemir and the creatures. Another slab sprang forth, next to the first. Then another and another until the creatures were walled in. Sighing in relief, Dobiemir's legs nearly collapsed under him.

"That won't hold them for long!" the man shouted. "Run! Move!"

"Let me try again," the woman snapped. A large glowing orb of light appeared above her right hand, but it did nothing against the cold and unsettling darkness around them. She threw the orb forward, letting it drop into the makeshift pen, but it did nothing. One of the creatures sprang up and began climbing over the wall. "What-"

"My home," Dobiemir gasped. "This way, down the road."

"Morgana," the man said. "Hurry!"

"But-"

"We don't know how to stop them," the man said. "Live today, fight tomorrow!"

"They'll leave," Dobiemir said. "After a while, they just leave!"

He didn't wait to see what she'd say. As she started to turn towards him, Dobiemir somehow made his legs work and began to run down the path. He hoped that his rescuers were following him, but didn't dare look back to be sure. Urging his legs to move faster, Dobiemir prayed that the creatures wouldn't follow. He didn't look back at the strangers. They were running too: he could hear their breathing and footfalls. They'd commanded fire and light and earth, and still hadn't stopped the creatures.

Despite the burning in his chest, they kept running. The snarls behind them faded. New fears began to creep in. What if the creatures didn't just move off this time, but attacked the village or retaliated against someone else? Was this some sort of test from the gods? Or a punishment, and the pair of strangers with him had done something horrible in fighting? Sweat gathered at the back of his neck and across his palms. Still, they'd helped him.

His home came into view, and the cold was fading away. With every stride, the world brightened. Fresh air filled his lungs and a grateful cry tore from his mouth. Tears of relief gathered in his eyes. A sheep in the yard baaed at him as he came to a stop in front of the house. Taking in several deep gasps of air, he turned to face his rescuers, looking at the woman first.

But he wasn't at his home anymore. He was standing on a tall hill with the wind cutting into his skin. The smell of salt filled the air and water stretched out before him past a swamp. The water stretched to the horizon. He'd heard of such a thing but never seen the ocean in person. A strange song was carried on the breeze, voices that made no sense to him.

Then it was over. Backing up, Dobiemir grabbed the fence to keep himself upright. The woman's green eyes were wide with surprise. Yet as her surprise faded, she began to smile at him. That expression terrified him even more.

10

Little Comfort

Jenny's hand kept twitching. Bran grinned but held back a laugh. It seemed that Jenny was having trouble being separated from her phone. He wondered whether Avani would deal with that or if it was something that Jenny would have to train out of herself. Lance, on the other hand, was sitting calmly on the grass of the lawn near the dark lines left over from Alex's latest lightning attack. He didn't seem to be struggling with the basics of meditation, and Bran nodded in approval.

It was a nice day and there were a lot of things that he should be doing, or at the least could be doing. Yet Bran was looking out the back window in the living room of their new house and watching Avani teach Lance and Jenny to meditate. Jenny made another abortive move for her phone.

"Anything interesting happening out there?" Aiden asked. His friend came walking up beside him, his shoes thumping softly against the floor. "Any light shows yet?"

"No," Bran said. "Just meditating, and I don't imagine we'll see any light shows for a while."

"I just hope this helps somehow," Aiden groaned. "Right now, we're just in a holding pattern. I know us getting the sword was good, great even, since it was what Arthur wanted from the start, but..." He shrugged in the corner of Aiden's eyes. "Doesn't seem like enough."

"I wonder if we could boost the blood protection spell?" Bran said thoughtfully. "It feels like we should be able to make it do more."

"Don't forget that Alex was able to infuse the thing with instructions not to hurt peaceful Fae," Aiden said. Leaning against the wall, he joined Bran in looking out the window. "So at least when it is cast the spell has some... malleableness." Aiden shook his head and grimaced. "Not sure how to describe spells. Is that even a word?"

"Malleableness?" Bran repeated. "Not sure, it sounds right though. You could ask Alex."

Aiden just shrugged, and they fell into silence. It was comfortable, and Bran kept watching Jenny's hand twitch. Smiling, he crossed his arms over his chest and tapped lightly on his arm. Next to him, Aiden shifted and glanced his way.

"Penny for your thoughts?"

"Not thinking about anything," Bran replied. He shrugged a little. "Maybe thinking about the blood spell, a bit. Wondering if it can be altered after the fact or what kind of magic it would take." He paused and huffed. "And now that I'm trying to think about it rationally, I'm wondering about how much influence it has since it only has a little bit of blood."

"Oh, I've given up on the chemistry of that," Aiden said. Raising an eyebrow, he looked pointedly at Bran. "I mean the human body only has like, 5 grams of iron in it at most, and it isn't just hanging around as iron."

"I know," Bran agreed. "Iron is too reactive for that. I figure that the iron in red blood cells lets them carry highly concentrated magic. Plus, iron is part of myoglobin in the muscles, which could explain why we feel sore when we use a lot of magic. Even if the iron is in a compound form in our bodies, it is still helping to transmit the magic."

"So, the iron moves magic like it does oxygen." Aiden pressed his lips together but nodded. "It's a solid theory at least." Turning to look out the window at Avani, Jenny, and Lance again, he smiled a little. "I hope this works for them. I worry about them. With the Fae and Sídhe, it isn't so bad since they have their daggers, but what if Arthur shows up or another human?"

"I think Lance would do better against a human," Bran said. "He's tackled Sídhe in the past. He's brave and more... physical than either of us. Besides, I saw Avani use her magic. It was... slow compared to ours and didn't last long. We can't count on those three turning the tide of battle."

Aiden hummed softly, not in agreement or disapproval. Bran held back a sigh and tried to think of something else to turn the conversation towards. Yet they hadn't had the chance to see new movies or shows or read any new books lately. The realization made him frown, and his stomach tightened uncomfortably.

Then Aiden's phone beeped, and his friend quickly pulled it from his pocket. "Sorry, time for me to head to the shop."

"Are you helping out through the school year?" Bran asked.

"No, Mom and Dad... well, they don't completely get it, but they know that I can't always be around."

"How are they taking it?" Bran asked. "Are they still doing okay?"

Aiden stopped, his jaw clenched and his shoulders tense. "Not really, but they can't change it." He grimaced. "There's a reason none of you have been invited back for a BBQ. They know it isn't your fault, but... it's not easy. I still think Alex had the right idea telling them the truth, but living with the truth is hard."

Nodding, Bran watched Aiden head for the stairs. His shoulders were slumped now, and Bran regretted asking him. Sometimes, he worried that he was weaker than the others, that his desire to be able to go home and pretend there wasn't danger meant that he couldn't take it. Then again, as much as he tried to keep those aspects of his life separate, Arthur seemed determined to have them collide.

He had nightmares where his mother had been in the shop, or that there'd been other customers. If he hadn't been alone, he might have been forced to use his magic and reveal them all to the world. In an age of cell phone cameras, secrets were hard to keep. He didn't trust himself enough to do the memory tricks that Merlin and Morgana had used in the past. If his mother had been there, she would have seen the potential danger. She'd have to understand that magic wasn't just... there, it had a purpose and strings attached that he'd never told her about. Worst yet were the dreams where she'd been hurt or killed.

Moving away from the window, Bran shook his head. A sudden chill spread over his skin and nausea took over. Rationally he knew that he should tell his mother, but he hadn't. Logic and maybe even wisdom broke down when he thought about it. There was a folded-up flag that his mother still looked at almost every day. The dog tags he wore under his shirt served as a reminder of both his father and the danger of being a soldier. His mother deserved to know, but fear took over whenever he thought about telling her.

Footfalls on the stairs made him look over to watch Alex coming down from her room. She still seemed half asleep, but her gray eyes focused on him quickly. Smiling softly, she walked over and peered out the window. Bran couldn't identify all of the emotions that washed over her face as she found Jenny and Lance working on magic.

"So, they're really doing this," Alex said softly. A soft exhale escaped her before she looked towards him. "Any luck so far?"

"No," he answered. "Aiden and I were watching earlier. He had to go to the bookstore."

"Okay."

She just kept watching out the window, her lips tugging up into a smile when Jenny tried to reach for her phone again. It was nice to see her smile again, but Bran's thoughts wouldn't leave him alone enough for him to enjoy it. Shifting uneasily, Bran grimaced when Alex turned to look at him again.

"You okay, Bran?"

"Yeah... I just...." Looking up at the ceiling, Bran second-guessed himself before pressing on. "Look, I have a question, but you don't have to answer." He waited for Alex to nod even as her eyebrows went up curiously. "How did you decide to relocate your brothers?" Bran asked. Alex's whole body stilled, and her eyes went wide. Bran wished he could take back the question. Still, he desperately wanted the answer. Pushing forward, he exhaled and asked, "Does it help? Knowing that they are safe and away from all this?"

"Yes," Alex said carefully. She was weighing her words even though her eyes were still wide like a deer caught in headlights. Turning to look out the window, Alex's mouth opened and closed a few times. "I miss them. Desperately, sometimes. I think about calling them and wanting to check on them, and then I remember. But yes, it helps knowing that they are away from this. Knowing that Matt doesn't remember that I exist and doesn't have to worry about me while trying to take care of Eddy. He's strong, but knowing that Mom and Dad were murdered and that their killer was still after me, trying to finish law school, and taking care of a grieving teenager... it was too much. It was causing him pain."

Her eyes were sad, but there was steel in them. Wistfulness; wanting to know what might have been. He understood that but didn't say it out loud. People saying they understood rarely helped, but listening might.

"I worry about my mother," Bran said. "I've never told her the whole truth because after what happened with my Dad, I know she'd struggle with it. I don't want her to worry, but now I don't believe that she'll be safe." His mouth was dry, and his throat tightened. "I'm wondering if I should... you know."

"I understand wanting her safe," Alex said softly. "But you're all she has Bran; you can't take that from her." She swallowed, and her eyes tracked a speck of dust in the air as she avoided looking at him. Bran stayed still and didn't take it personally. "If my mother... I wouldn't have done it. I wouldn't have taken one of her children from her. But my brothers-I already cost them our parents-"

"That wasn't your fault, Alex," Bran said quickly. Reaching over, he took her hand and squeezed it. The blank expression remained on her face. "You didn't cause it."

"They were killed because Arthur wanted to hurt me." Then she shrugged, as if he couldn't see tears starting to gather in her eyes. "And I'm working on forgiving myself for that. I wonder if it would have been better to do the memory thing before, but... selfishly I'm glad that I got to have a few more years seeing them."

"That's not selfish," Bran said. "You cast the blood spell, Alex. You did what you could to protect them." Sighing, he squeezed her hand again, now for his comfort. "And I'm wondering now if I should ask Morgana to relocate my mother." There, he'd managed to say it. "She'd be safer."

"Don't be in a hurry to give her up," Alex said. "It hurts. Even knowing that my brothers are alive out there hurts. I can never see them again. And Even if I saw them, they'd have no idea I was their sister. Everything that

I was to them is gone. But they still have each other and their whole lives ahead of them. It would be different for your mother."

"But it still happened. Everything you lived through with your brothers still happened."

"Yes, it still happened." Alex shook her head. "I'm sorry, Bran. You asked me a clear question, but I'm not sure how to answer it." Turning towards him, she finally met his gaze. "Do what you think is best. But know that you can't take it back. I do think I made the right decision, but it hurts." Her gray eyes began to cloud up with tears, and her lower lip trembled. "It was hard, and I miss them." Alex's voice went higher and softer with barely restrained sobs. "I miss my parents, and I can't even talk to my brothers about them."

"So... why?" The question felt too harsh, but the ache in his chest needed something.

"I've gotten used to waking with the names of the dead on my tongue and tears in my eyes," Alex said. "I dream of those long gone almost every night. Guilt that isn't mine builds up in my chest, and I didn't want Matt and Eddy to join that parade of loss." A dark laugh escaped her. "That was oddly poetic wasn't it? Apparently, I'm a maudlin sort of writer. If I ever actually manage to write anything down."

"I'm sure you will one day," Bran said. "Though I'd suggest writing all this as fiction."

She laughed; it was a brittle sound, like it had been ripped out of her. "Not this. I wouldn't want to write about all of this. It keeps turning into a sad story. But at least I kept my brothers from dying." Alex smiled and shook her head. "Morgana keeps hinting that she might be able to reverse it if I wanted. But I'm not changing my mind. I want them safe."

"People die all the time; there is no guarantee that nothing will happen to your brothers," Bran reminded her carefully. "You can't... count on this keeping them safe. If you do go and try to find them in the future, Alex, there's no guarantee that something else wouldn't have happened."

"True, life is random and dangerous. I know that, trust me," Alex said. He didn't like the knowing way she was almost smiling; it was sad and resigned. "Some friends and family have died in my wars, but many have died to natural causes and at young ages by our standards. You're right that something could still happen to Matt and Eddy, but at least it won't be because I was their sister." Then Alex fell silent for a long moment, lost in thought while Bran lingered at her side. "I am sorry though; Matt and Eddy vanishing might have been what spurred Arthur on to attack you."

"Why attack me?" Bran asked. "I'd have figured Lance or Jenny would be better targets. They have no magic."

"Yes, but he may still think that they'll betray me somehow," Alex said. Tapping a finger against the windowsill, Alex studied Jenny and Lance. "I'm not sure what kind of belief Arthur has in forgiveness and people moving on. He may figure that I'm keeping instruments of my own doom close to me."

"Wow, you are a maudlin sort of writer," Bran said, searching for some levity. Alex's lips turned up into a smile, and she gave him a mock stern look. "Just agreeing with you, Alex. And you might be right. Part of the problem with Arthur is that we only knew the mask. I keep trying to predict him or figure out what I'd do, but..."

"But we just don't know him," Alex said. "Sometimes he's reasonable and strategic, but other times he grandstands and lashes out."

"I wonder if being made artificially half Sídhe messed with his brain development," Bran said thoughtfully. When Alex looked at him curiously, he shrugged. "I mean, Merlin was born that way, and Morgana was made that, but she was at least a little older and that ritual was done mostly by Sídhe magic. I wonder if something about the Iron Chain made it unstable."

"Maybe, but maybe the Chain had nothing to do with it." Alex frowned and glared at the horizon. "I don't remember a lot about Medraut, but I do remember him killing me. He wanted power and thought that I was destroying the valuable bronze trade. He wasn't completely wrong about that, but he just didn't value the human lives involved. He didn't care that the Sídhe were taking humans, including children, as slaves. And he was good at hiding his real allegiance then too. All it was ever about for him was taking over the area and having the bronze trade under his thumb. My- Arto's presence and fight against the Sídhe changed that."

A shaky sound escaped Alex and she shook her head. "I never saw it. Looking back, there were hints, but I didn't see it. And I didn't see Arthur either. Apparently, I'm a horrible judge of character." She laughed; it was a fragile sound that slid down Bran's spine. "I let him get close again! Back then, he killed my father, but this time he got both my mother and my father."

"Alex, don't talk like that." Bran reached uncertainly for Alex. Was he supposed to hug her? He wasn't sure how to react. Guilt and grief were flickering in Alex's eyes. "Medraut was a piece of shit and betrayed his family. Lives, real people, mattered more than his position, and he couldn't see that. That wasn't Arto's fault. And in this life, Merlin and Morgana were fooled too. That's not your fault."

She nodded a little, but her eyes were getting glassier. She swallowed. He recognized that swallow. Something had tipped over the edge. There was guilt over making her cry even as a rational part of him said that maybe this was good. Tears escaped Alex, and a dry sob echoed in the small room.

Wrapping his arms around Alex, Bran pulled her close and gently rocked her. Soft sobs reached his ears and his heart twisted. Words dried up in his mouth and he settled on making soft sounds to reassure her. Alex's legs gave out. He carefully lowered her to the ground. Bran brought one hand up to gently hold her head.

"It'll be okay," he whispered. "It's okay to miss them. You love them, and you protected them. You have us, Alex. We're your friends. We're your family."

Alex hiccupped at the words, but her sobs calmed a little. Still tense, Bran tried to figure out if that had been the right or wrong thing to say. He wasn't sure. He wasn't going to get an answer to that one right now. Instead, he slowed his breathing and tried to calm his mind as he focused on comforting Alex.

11

Living Situation

Living with so many roommates was a new experience for Alex. She'd had her own bedroom her whole life and had never had to share her space until freshman year. In fact, she'd asked her parents to let her have a single dorm room, but they'd thought a roommate would be good for her. And of course, she'd ended up with Jenny, who was the reincarnation of a past incarnation's wife. That hadn't been a terrible housing situation, but the circumstances had been rough.

Nicki had been a much easier roommate. Of course, they'd had separate bedrooms and only shared a common area. They had worked out a bathroom schedule fairly easily and were able to stay out of each other's way. But in a house with herself, Nicki, Jenny, Avani, Lance, Bran, Aiden, and Timothy, it felt like they were edging into Brady Bunch territory. They had two full bathrooms and had set up a rough schedule of who showered when to make sure there was hot water for everyone and toilet access at all times. There was also a toilet and sink in the basement laundry room that helped matters.

They were lucky in that everyone had their own space and an unspoken rule about privacy had taken hold. Timothy had taken over one of the kitchen cupboards and seemed very happy with the doll furniture that Jenny had bought for him. It was weird, but it worked. To Alex's surprise it had been Lance who had broken down and called a 'house meeting' one week into them all living together to set up a chore wheel. Timothy was fantastic, but it wasn't fair to expect their friendly Brownie to do everything. Again, weird, but it worked.

Still, it was an adjustment. Living with so many people was new to all of them. There were moments when they got in each other's way in the hallways when multiple people wanted to do laundry and occasional arguments over what to eat. None of that surprised Alex, and she had faith that they'd all adjust.

It was Avani that surprised her. Alex wasn't sure how to feel about the late addition. Alex liked her certainly, and there was a warm, happy feeling at the back of her mind when she thought about the magician. That was probably Lokpal, who was so thrilled to know that his family had lived on happily. Alex understood: she imagined that she'd feel the same way if down the road she learned that Matt or Eddy had children. Avani was clever and enjoyed the same sort of books and movies as Nicki, Aiden, and Bran. Plus, she'd brought some media from India that she enjoyed sharing and translating when necessary.

Yet, she also could sit and talk about fashion and makeup with Jenny without it being a strain. While well-mannered and a touch older than them, she navigated her way through the group smoothly. She was friendly with everyone and had quickly adjusted to the realities of living with Timothy. Nicki's behavior around her continued to be amusing. It was made even funnier by the fact that at first Nicki had been calm and flirty around Avani without any problem. It seemed that the more Nicki liked someone the more tongue-tied she became.

Despite all this, Alex found Avani's presence a little irritating. She knew rationally that she was being silly. Avani was loyal to the Iron Realm and had a great deal of respect for her as the Iron Soul. It was a hint of jealousy, and Alex knew it. She wasn't Jenny's closest friend in the group now. They were close, they had a connection, but Avani enjoyed online shopping with Jenny while she didn't. Nicki spent a lot of time focused on Avani and Aiden enjoyed talking with her and teasing Nicki about her crush.

The countdown to the start of classes weighed on the group. Alex was torn between relief that she'd have something to occupy her days once again and dread of something going wrong. Without a family to visit or a job, summer had dragged on. Even her favorite books hadn't helped entertain her that much. Their newcomer had provided a temporary distraction, but Alex was beginning to get used to her and the new smells that came out of the kitchen on Avani's nights to make dinner. Avani was pleasant and not as worn down as the rest of them. As she grew more comfortable and her manners became less practiced, Alex had to admit that she was nice to have around, even if was still a little irritating.

"What are you doing?" Nicki asked. She looked at Alex as she lounged sideways in an armchair. "Other than destroying the new furniture."

"We can fix it with magic," Alex said. "So that's hardly a problem."

"Alright, that's a fair point, but please tell me you aren't brooding."

"I'm not brooding," Alex said. "I was just thinking about things."

"Things?" Nicki raised an eyebrow and Alex raised one right back.

"Don't give me the eyebrow of expectation," Alex said. "I can do it too. And if you must know I was thinking about Avani. It's different having her here is all."

"Ah, she and Jenny are out shopping again." Nicki sounded far too understanding. "Jenny loves you Alex, in a platonic way of course. But it's probably nice having a real buddy again. Her relationship with the cheer squad never really recovered from the rumors about her causing Arthur to leave. He was one of the quarterbacks."

"Who probably used magic," Alex grumbled. "Freshman don't make varsity as the quarterback."

"You're probably right," Nicki agreed. "But that's not the main point."

"I like her," Alex said firmly. "I do; you don't need to worry about that. It's just different, and I have too much time to think... maybe I am brooding." Shaking her head, Alex groaned. "I need classes to start. I need something! Maybe I should have gotten a job."

"Not a good idea if you might have to run out at any moment," Nicki said. "Aiden and I at least work for family members who understand our need to vanish suddenly."

"I know." Alex sighed and slumped down further in the armchair. "I'm just bored, I guess. Jenny and Avani are out shopping. Lance was going to the gym, and the boys are downstairs doing who knows what." Bumping her head against the upholstery, Alex ignored Nicki's soft giggle and shook her head. "Enough whining. Are you happy living here?"

"It's an adjustment," Nicki said. She gave Alex a soft and warm smile. "It always is, but I think it will work out."

"Plus, you get to see Avani every day," Alex said. That did it; Nicki blushed and then winced a little at her reaction. "I remember you calling dibs." Nicki's blush deepened, and the redhead groaned. "And you blush a lot more nowadays. When you first called dibs, I was expecting slightly more... assertive behavior."

"I know," Nicki groaned. She dropped her head into her hands and groaned even louder. "It was easier when I first met her. Avani was gorgeous and knew about magic, but the more I get to know her the more... she's just-"

"Use your words, Nicki," Aiden said. Alex turned in the chair to find Aiden watching them with a smile. She wasn't sure when he'd come upstairs. "I don't think I've ever seen you shift behavior like this." His tone was kind and curious as he strolled over to sit down in a chair. "What's up, honey?"

"Avani's just even better than I thought at first," Nicki admitted. She sank into herself and looked at the ground. "She likes a lot of the same things as me, is creative and wants to try new things with magic, has a sharp sense of humor, and is beautiful. I mean, she's even more beautiful every time I see her! How does that work?"

"Wow... you really like her." Alex smiled gently and reached over to put an arm around Nicki's shoulders. "For what it's worth, I approve, and I think Lokpal does too."

"That doesn't help," Nicki mumbled. "But thanks. I just need to regain my courage and ask her out. But she's even a grad student while I'm still an undergrad! It's not fair! She's just better-"

"Do not finish that thought," Aiden said. His voice was stern and serious as he stared Nicki down. "Do not. You are good enough for her. Yes, she's a bit older and further along in school, but you're smart and have a lot in common with her."

"Maybe," Nicki said. "But India isn't exactly the most gay-friendly place in the world. Even if Avani liked me..."

"First, Avani is from a big city," Alex said. "They are usually more progressive. Two, her family has already met you and liked you. Three, you're a mage, so while yeah you two can't have kids the normal way, but still, I bet they'd like having a mage in the family, and four like I said I totally approve, which has to count for something."

"I'm not trying to marry her," Nicki mumbled. "I just want to ask her out, but what is there to do in Ravenslake that she can't do in Mumbai?"

"Stargazing," Bran said. Everyone looked up to find him lingering in the doorway. Shrugging, he offered them a sheepish smile. "Sorry to burst in, but maybe stargazing. Mumbai is a big city which means it has a lot of light pollution. I've seen Avani looking at the stars a few times now. If you got a tracker and some red lights, maybe a picnic basket, you could stargaze. Just be sure to do it before it gets too cold at night."

Nicki gaped at him, blinking with wide eyes. Then she jumped up and rushed forward to hug Bran. He made a sound of surprise while Nicki shifted from foot to foot in her excitement.

"Bran, you are a genius!"

"Not sure about that," Bran said. "If I was, I'd know a lot more about how magic worked."

"Good idea, man," Aiden said with an approving nod. "Though, have you ever been on a date? Aren't you asexual?"

"I am, but I'm not aromatic," Bran said. He sat down in one of the armchairs, his body suddenly a little tense. "There's a difference." Smiling at Nicki, he added, "I can appreciate romance."

"Seriously," Nicki said. "That's a nice idea. It provides a topic to talk about, but it is also romantic and something different. I like it." Vibrating in her chair, Nicki's whole-body language changed and the last traces of her blush were gone. "I'll- I'll ask if she'd like to after I do some reviewing of the constellations," Nicki said. "Should I be clear it's a date or just play it as friends?" She looked between all of them eagerly. "Bran?"

"I'd say be honest," Bran said. "But I'm not exactly an expert."

"I'm with Bran," Aiden agreed. "We can't afford misunderstandings among us."

Nicki looked a bit nervous again, but Alex nodded in agreement with Aiden and Bran. She hoped that this went well for Nicki. The front door opened with a soft squeak that no one was in a hurry to fix. It served as an alert that someone had come in. Cheerful voices rolled over Alex, and she relaxed as she recognized them as Avani and Jenny. The pair appeared a moment later carrying bags from their shopping trip.

"Oh," Jenny said. "Hello, sorry if we interrupted."

"You didn't," Nicki said. "We were just hanging out." She smiled at Avani, managing somehow to keep her blush at bay. "Did you two have fun?"

"We had a nice afternoon," Avani said. "Jenny did her best to give me a tour of campus before we went shopping."

"I know only a few of the buildings." Jenny looked a bit put out. "So I wasn't much help."

"It's a very nice campus," Avani said. "I love all the open green space and trees."

"So, how is your master's set up going? Everything squared away?" Nicki asked. "Are you excited for classes?"

"Yes," Avani said. She smiled warmly at Nicki, causing the redhead to blush a little. Walking further into the living room, she set her bag down next to a wall and then took a seat next to Jenny. "I've got my schedule and I think everything is sorted. I'm also a little nervous. I'm comfortable learning in English, but I haven't written a great deal in the language. The essay focus of some of my classes is a little concerning."

"Don't worry," Bran said. "You speak English beautifully. I'm sure that you'll write without a problem, and we'll be glad to proofread for you."

Everyone nodded in agreement and Avani looked touched. "Thank you."

"I'm just sorry that you've had to adjust your schooling to be here," Bran said. "I'm sure it isn't what you had planned."

"No," Avani agreed. She nodded a little but didn't seem concerned. "But I don't have to even take classes, after all. I could have just come over, and I would have been glad to help. Taking classes, even part-time, is just a good way for me to blend in. Besides, while the class offerings aren't as diverse as I would have had in Mumbai, I do not doubt that Professor Cornwall's history classes will be interesting."

"They will be," Alex said. She exchanged a glance with Jenny and smiled. "Morgana can be a bit... intense. She'll try to scare all the students in the first class."

"Well, she doesn't have time for people to act up," Avani said. "Being a college professor and a mage must be difficult."

"Thankfully, most of the nasties in Ravenslake attack at night," Bran said. "And the professors avoid scheduling any classes after three just to be on the safe side during winter."

"Most," Avani said. "Not all. Merlin told me about those Shadows." Everyone shivered, and Jenny curled closer to Lance on the sofa. "I'm sorry, I didn't mean to upset all of you."

"Chernobog was a difficult opponent," Aiden said. "But... honestly, it's everything that happened around him that puts us all on edge."

"Arthur." Avani nodded in understanding. "Yes, I'm sorry."

"Don't be," Alex said. "It happened. You didn't cause it, and now that you're here, you need to understand what happened with him." She straightened up and took a deep breath. "This is overdue, but do you have any questions for us? About him? About what happened?"

The others were looking at her. Bran's worry was most obvious, but Jenny was picking nervously at her nails. Alex pushed down the wash of grief and guilt that was trying to rise in her chest. This was necessary, and Avani deserved a chance to learn what she felt she needed.

"I-I... what was he like? I mean, what did he pretend to be like? It is difficult to understand how he fooled the Grand Mages." Alex thought she heard the 'and you' at the end of the question.

"He was... charming," Alex said. "Seemed brave and understanding. When all the magic stuff started happening, Arthur comforted me when I was upset. I had a crush on him even though he was dating Jenny."

"He looked the part," Aiden added. "Tall, broad shoulders, and charismatic. If you were looking for a reincarnated hero, it made sense to look at someone like that."

It was Jenny who spoke next, her voice surprisingly strong given the topic. "Arthur was smart," she said. "We started dating in high school. That meant that when he and I came here, he was involved with the girl that Merlin and Morgana recognized as Arto's reincarnated wife."

"He's a planner," Bran said. "Though, it's hard to say for sure how much was him and how much was his mother. But he was able to play a part for over a year, and we were all fooled. Looking back now, there were moments where there were hints, but nothing that gave him away. Even if he wasn't the mastermind behind the scheme, he made it happen, and he was willing to live that lie to get what he wanted. We can't lose sight of that."

"So, he's intelligent," Avani said. "Driven, manipulative, and has magical powers."

"That sums it up," Alex said. "He dropped the act when I- I handed him Cathanáil. Cyrridven had thrown it to me, and I used it to kill Chernobog, but even then, I still thought that he was the Iron Soul." Shaking her head, Alex met Avani's eyes. "I'm sorry. That was what led to the Sword opening the portal near Mumbai and causing all that trouble."

"That's not your fault." Avani's voice was softer now. "We can't see the results of our actions. You did what you thought was best based on what you knew to be true. Now you know the truth and can act accordingly." Then she smiled more brightly and clapped her hands together. "Since all the mages are here, why don't we get back to work on those spells! I know I'll sleep better once we have them in place."

Avani's sudden shift made Alex blink, but then she smiled. Lokpal's affection bloomed along with a rush of pride. Breathing a little easier, Alex nodded in agreement. In the corner of her eye she saw Nicki grin. Maybe this new situation could work out. Bran was right. She didn't have her brothers anymore, but she wasn't alone. She just had to remember that.

12

Letting Them In

Podlasie Province, Poland 983 C.E.

These strangers were impossible. Upon meeting their eyes, he saw strange things. Not frightening in and of themselves, but his sight was taken from him and the familiar fell away. Every instinct urged him to flee, to hide from them and shelter his son. And yet they'd held back those Shadows. Those things had been a thorn in his side, in everyone's side, and the very idea that someone could fight them made something unknot in his chest. Then again, the sterner side of himself reminded him that they hadn't killed the things.

Panting softly, Dobiemir looked behind them. There was no sign of the creatures. Birds were singing in the nearby trees and the sun was warm on his skin. It was too good to be true, but he grabbed onto the peace. The strangers were watching him in silence, giving him time to gather his thoughts. Turning to look at them both properly, he fought back the urge to not meet their eyes. But he did. Nothing happened. There weren't more visions, and he breathed out a sigh of relief.

The man had slight wrinkles, especially around the eyes and mouth, which was reassuring. His curly hair was a bit sweaty. Dressed in a tunic, pants and a cloak, he had a pack slung over his shoulder and looked very normal. The woman was much the same but with intense green eyes, long dark hair and only a few wrinkles. She was clearly younger than her companion, but it was hard to know by how much. Something about them didn't belong, but Dobiemir wasn't sure what it was. Perhaps it was just based on what he had seen.

"Are you gods?" he asked softly. His knees trembled. Surely he should bow, but he feared falling over. "Have you come to punish us?"

The woman, Morgana, scoffed. Her lips curled down disdainfully and her nose wrinkled up at his suggestion. The man, Merlin, was calmer and offered him a gentle smile.

"No, we are not gods," Merlin said. "And we have come to help. Those creatures are magical in nature, and we were drawn to them. We are here to protect you and your village."

"Oh." It wasn't what he wanted to say, but it was the word that escaped him. Relief set in followed by worry. If beings such as this had come here then what were those Shadows capable of? "I- thank you."

"What is your name?" Merlin asked.

"Dobiemir."

"It is a pleasure to meet you, Dobiemir," Merlin said. "I am Merlin, and this is my companion, Morgana. As you no doubt noticed, we have magical abilities." Dobiemir nodded, unsure of how else to respond to that. "And you had visions when you met our eyes, did you not?" Again, he nodded, but it was more hesitant this time, and Merlin's smile widened. "That means that you are a mage as well."

"A mage?"

"A person with magical abilities," Morgana said. Her tone wasn't as sharp as he'd been expecting. "You have the power to call on the natural magical energy of our world and are charged with defending it."

"Defending-" He started to shake his head and looked back at his small home. "I can't. I can't be involved in this. My son is ill; my wife is gone. He needs me. I can't be fighting Shadow creatures. Normally they leave us alone. I mean, yes, they kill the harvest and frighten the animals, but they don't usually attack."

"Usually?" Merlin asked. His brown eyes were old, very old, and having those eyes focusing on him made Dobiemir nervous. "How do you mean?"

"They... one attacked me, but it was only once. I climbed a tree, and it lost interest."

"Scouts," Morgana said. "That one must have sensed your magic. You're a potential threat."

"But-"

"Maybe," Merlin said. He gave Morgana a stern look. "We don't know enough about them to be sure, but they are a threat to your village."

"Do- do you know what they are?"

"We've never seen anything like them before," Merlin confessed. "We sensed a rise in magic in this area and came to investigate. We've come across them in the area before today, but I fear we know little more than you."

"Fire and light don't work on them," Morgana snapped. "Creatures of bound shadow and ice, and fire and light don't work!"

"We'll figure it out," Merlin said. He placed a hand on Morgana's shoulder. "Just be patient, old friend."

Morgana looked at Merlin with a hint of disapproval, but she did seem calmer. They both turned their attention back to him. Dobiemir swallowed, unsure of what came next. His eyes jumped back to the road, and then he looked over at his house. It still looked in order. The animals in the yard were calm and paying them no mind.

"I need... my son." He gestured back towards the house. "Uh, I need to check on him."

"Of course," Merlin said. He smiled softly and nodded in understanding.

Dobiemir hesitated to let them come into the house but knew there was nothing he could truly do to stop them. Merlin was watching him with an almost kind and patient smile. Morgana's gaze was far from gentle, but there was a hint of understanding and maybe even approval in her eyes. He didn't understand it. He didn't understand any of this, but he wanted to check on his son.

"Come in," he said. "Uh, if you like. It's small but warm. And safe. So far, the creatures have never entered a home."

"That's interesting," Morgana said. She raised an eyebrow thoughtfully. "I wonder why? Some aversion or just luck on the part of the locals?"

"Or perhaps whatever has created them has no interest in the day to day lives of the people," Merlin offered. Dobiemir didn't like any of the suggestions.

Despite his reservations, he led them into the small house. It was dark with the window covered by a thick blanket. The whole space was warm but musty, as he'd hesitated to let any cold air in. Everything was still tidy, the shelves filled with the wrapped and stored food that he'd been collecting. A row of earthen pots and jars held roasted seeds, roots, and jerky. Baskets along the walls held long grasses that were drying out for the animals come winter.

Slavko was lying in bed. His eyes were closed and he was mostly under a blanket. Still, some of his dark hair was visible. For a moment, Dobiemir stared at his son's chest. It didn't seem to be moving. Then, thankfully, there was a soft rise, and Dobiemir's shoulders slumped with relief.

Creeping forward, he forgot about the strangers behind him and sat on the edge of the bed. He carefully felt his son's forehead. It was too hot once again.

"How long has he been ill?" Morgana asked. Her voice was soft and gentle. "The boy?"

"Over a season," Dobiemir replied. "His mother and brother passed… not long ago. It's just us now."

"Poor child," Morgana said. She moved closer to them, not bothered at all by the mess. "If you'll allow me, I might be able to help."

"What?" Dobiemir blinked at her in confusion. "I don't understand."

"Magic exists to protect this realm," Morgana explained. She took a small step closer, minding the baskets and jars along the wooden wall. "But it can also be used for other things. Including healing. I may be able to ease his illness."

"I… alright."

Standing up, Dobiemir moved away to give Morgana room. She sat down on the edge of the bed and carefully drew back the blanket. Slavko didn't move and just kept sleeping. His breathing was shallow. This was a stranger, a woman he didn't know, and yet he was letting her near his son. Dobiemir couldn't explain his actions. He'd seen what she could do, and if she could help his son, then he would happily take it. The woman's hands moved slowly, and she kept looking at him. Maybe she understood his hesitation.

Morgana's hands glowed as she touched his son's forehead. The man Merlin, put a hand on Dobiemir's shoulder. A frown marred Morgana's elegant features, and the silver glow brightened further. Slavko's eyes were still closed and he was huddling under the blankets. Then his skin began to darken, the pale shade fading into something stronger. Dobiemir swallowed a gasp and Merlin's hand on his shoulder tightened.

"Morgana is very capable," Merlin said. "She's always been better at healing than I." The older man almost sounded irritated about that. "Not sure why, but every mage has different strengths." Merlin smiled gently. "She has a soft spot for children. Morgana knows how difficult life can be for them."

There was more to it than that, but Dobiemir's focus was on his son. The glow faded into his son's skin, and Morgana smiled. Slowly, she eased back from the boy and made room for Dobiemir to see him. Moving forward, he almost tripped on a half-woven basket. His son was breathing better. His forehead wasn't as hot, and as he was checking the boy shifted closer to him, shrugging away some of the blankets. Everything stopped. Dobiemir breathed in deeply, almost faint at the sudden rush of air. His eyes closed. Too many emotions were rising and mixing in his chest. It wasn't safe. But happiness and relief were strongest — a lump formed in his throat. Dobiemir struggled for a moment.

This couldn't be real. Yet it seemed to be. But he'd probably wake up from a strange dream and it would be morning. There would still be those strange Shadows and a failing harvest. Slavko would still be ill. But maybe it wasn't just a dream. He opened his eyes. Morgana was watching them with a sad little smile.

"Thank you," he said softly. The words weren't enough. "I- I don't understand, but thank you."

"The boy isn't completely healthy," Morgana cautioned. Her tone was gentler now. "I'm unsure of the source of his illness, but I was able to give him strength. It should help."

"It's nice to have a chance to help in a small way," Merlin said. He was smiling brightly at Morgana, and even she seemed to be struggling not to look pleased. "I know that today has been a shock, Dobiemir, but as you can see, magic has its uses. You have the potential to be a mage, and there are never many of us. You know the area and the people. If we are to discover the source of these strange beings, then we will need your help."

"I..." Slavko stirred in his arms, shifting closer to his chest. The boy made a contented sigh. "I'm sorry, but I have my son to worry about and the harvest. These creatures have all but destroyed the supply of food for winter as it is. I have to focus on making sure we'll make it through the winter."

Merlin nodded in understanding but looked pleased. "That is something that we can help with. While our magic exists to defend the realm, it can be used for a great many things. While not my strongest talent, I do know how to encourage plants to grow."

Dobiemir stared at him. He'd heard the words, but... "Are you sure you aren't a god?"

Morgana laughed and tossed her long braid over her shoulder. "I suppose it depends on what you consider a god. Many would think of us as such."

"Morgana," Merlin scolded, without any real sternness.

"Immortal and with great power." Morgana turned towards the doorway. "Close enough for most. I'm going to go and check the fields for any clues. We need to understand what these things are."

Merlin sighed as she left, shaking his head. Then he turned back to Dobiemir and said. "We aren't truly immortal. At least, we don't think so. It is a test neither of us have any interest in performing." Then Merlin sat down on the bench. "Now, I know that this must all be very alarming, but I need you to tell me everything you know about these creatures. Are there any habits they have, anyplace they're seen most often? Anything could help."

"I- I'm not sure." Closing his eyes, Dobiemir tried to focus on the memory of that first Shadow creature. "The first time I saw one, I was in the woods. It attacked me, so I climbed a tree. It was pitch black. The world dimmed, and it got cold, just like you saw. After a while, it just moved off and left me alone. I've seen a few since then. They just seem to patrol areas."

"Interesting," Merlin said slowly. "They may be looking for something or merely scouting the area." He hummed softly to himself for a long moment. "Tell me, do you have any local legends with something like this? Anything in your area that is similar to the creatures?"

"No," Dobiemir said. "I mean, there are the stories about spirits of course, and the gods, but nothing like these Shadows."

"Who is the chief deity in the area?"

Dobiemir blinked at the odd question but pushed on. "Lately the Christian god has gained followers. Some are blaming the missionaries for the creatures. They're saying it is a punishment for not honoring their gods."

"Which explains your question to Morgana and I," Merlin said. "But is there anyone specific?"

"There are several local gods who watch over the valley," Dobiemir said. "Svetovid, Lada, and Veliona are well known throughout the whole area."

"Anyone that stands out?"

"Well, some stories say that Belobog visits the area. He is probably the most famous," Dobiemir said. "He is thanked for the good things that happen. He's a god of light and good."

"I'm familiar with him," Merlin said. Dobiemir almost asked what that meant. Merlin and Morgana had such power, had they met a god? "Though... I've not heard anything from him recently. That could be the problem."

"Wait, you think this is Belobog's doing? But why? He's one of the friendliest gods to humanity!"

"I'm not sure," Merlin said calmly. He held up a hand and motioned for Dobiemir to be silent. He quickly obeyed: he owed them that much. "But gods can become ill. It is an ugly but very real thing. If Belobog is in the area then checking on his condition would be a wise first course of action. If we are to understand what these creatures are, then we must learn their source."

"You said that you've seen them before?"

"Yes, but not until we came to this area," Merlin said. "Thankfully, they are only in this region."

"Then why did you come here?"

"Morgana is rather talented at scrying," Merlin explained. "It is a form of magic that allows her to see or at least become aware of problems in other places. She routinely checks for troubling signs and caught a glimpse of these creatures. It was simple enough to learn that we needed to come east."

"Where are you from?"

"A good distance to the west," Merlin said. "I fear that in truth our first homes are long gone." The man's eyes glazed over and a wistful smile appeared on his features. It made him look younger. Then the older mage shook himself. "I understand your worries Dobiemir. Truly, I do. But you are a mage, and you can help your homeland. Please, consider letting us train you to use your magic. You'd be much better equipped to protect yourself and your child. There are many things that we can help you achieve."

"Why do you need me?" Dobiemir asked. "You both have so much power! I'm just a farmer."

"You are a mage, and thus you should be trained," Merlin replied. There is something in the tone of his voice. Dobiemir didn't think it was much of an explanation, but it was enough for Merlin.

"Father?" Slavko called.

Dobiemir looked down and smiled. The boy was waking up and rubbing his eyes. Slavko began to sit up, and Dobiemir let him, though he stayed close. The boy's coloring was far better than it had been in weeks. Slavko spotted Merlin watching him and blinked in confusion.

"How are you feeling?" Merlin asked kindly.

"I..." Slavko twisted around to look at his father. "I'm feeling much better, Father."

"Good," Dobiemir said. Putting an arm around his son, he smiled. His muscles almost protested the movement. It had been far too long. "That's good, son." Slavko's gaze returned to Merlin. "This is Merlin," Dobiemir said. "He's... he's a friend."

Merlin smiled at him approvingly. Dobiemir wanted to tense, suddenly very worried about what he was in for now, but Slavko was breathing easily. The boy was sitting up and honestly looked bored just sitting in bed. It was more than he'd had since the loss of his wife.

13

Semblance of Normal

Wanting to be normal was such a cliché that part of Alex's brain rebelled fiercely against it. As a child who had loved all sorts of books, she'd always wanted magic and grand adventures to be real. She'd disliked the notion that you grew up, got a job, and that was it. Sure marriage and kids were an option, but only a lucky few would get to really go out and see the world.

Now her life was exciting, and she had magical powers, but there was a bubbling pit of resentment beneath it all. At least it could make for some useful writing fodder. Tapping her fingers softly on the edge of the desk, Alex blinked her eyes and fought back the urge to sleep. She was back in class: everything was as it should be, and that should have been a relief.

This was normal and reasonable, and so much harder than she remembered, which was stupid. She'd been in class since learning she was a mage. That had been Halloween of freshman year, and she was a junior now. This shouldn't be this hard. Resisting the urge to shift in her seat or tap her feet, Alex focused on the professor at the front of the room.

What class was this again? She'd checked the room number on her schedule, and it was one of the usual English lecture halls, so she wasn't in the wrong place. But really, which class was this? It was one of the upper-level classes. She'd been excited to have more of them now and be done with the basic stuff.

Now, there was just a nervous tension. There were things to do. Nicki had been working on designing some kind of scabbard for Cathanáil. Merlin and Morgana had been over to discuss some of Avani's family spells with her. Yet, they didn't seem to be getting anywhere. More Red Caps could attack at any time, or Arthur could do something much worse. They were in a holding pattern, and she was supposed to pay attention in class.

Reaching up, Alex rubbed a knot at the back of her neck. It helped a little, but the nervous twitch was still there. Others around the classroom were also having trouble focusing. She saw a few videos playing on tablets and laptops, a few discreet headphones, and not so subtle checking cell phone maneuvers.

Alex's eyes jumped to the doorway. The room had two of them on the right side of the lecture hall. There were three large windows on the left side that were open to let in some air. She'd chosen a spot in the back and could see the whole room. Nothing was out of place. Alex sighed, holding back a groan. She wanted to focus, wanted to get back into the swing of classes and wanted something else to work on. The first essay would either be a blessing or a nightmare, depending on what happened next with Arthur.

Turning her attention to the students, Alex eyed all of them carefully. They'd done the whole stand up and introduce yourself thing that some teachers still liked to do when classes had started on Monday. Not that she remembered their names. No one was out of place though. No one was paying her any attention, so hopefully, Arthur didn't have his fingers in someone's head as a spy. Still, the thought was distressing, and she took in each of her classmates carefully, trying to memorize something about them.

It wasn't working. She was in the back. They were all just backs and clothing, nothing that would be distinct. Alex held back a groan. She was being ridiculous. This was paranoia and nothing more. Still, she was bored, and her eyes fell on a girl with long black natural hair pinned up with small buns. It was really pretty, and Alex stared at the small ribbons holding everything in place.

There was a flutter, a strange sensation right between her eyes that made Alex bring a hand up to rub at the spot of skin. It wasn't painful. The girl she'd been watching shifted in her seat and shook her head a little. Nothing else. But then, Alex caught strange almost echoing words.

'God, this book is so boring.'

The words were clear as a bell in her mind. Alex hadn't thought them, but there they were, fully formed. Holding back a yelp, Alex dropped her eyes and gripped the edge of her desk. The flutter faded quickly, and she focused on counting her breaths. The professor was still talking and no one was looking at her. At least she hadn't drawn attention to herself like she had the first time she'd met Merlin.

Glancing around, Alex checked that no one was watching her. She started to reach for her phone before hesitating. Class would be over soon and this wasn't an emergency. There was no need to alarm the others just yet. Pulling her hand back, she folded her hands on top of the desk and her open notebook. The urge, the itch to contact the others was there, but this wasn't dangerous.

She hadn't been paying attention. That was the bottom line. Alex swallowed and risked a glance at the girl she was sure she'd heard the stray thought of. The girl looked fine and was writing something in a notebook. The boy next to her had a video playing on his laptop and was slumped in his chair. Everything was normal. No harm done.

As the worry faded, guilt and frustration took its place. She had to be careful. There were reasons why none of the mages drank alcohol. No matter how much Alex had wanted to explore that fabled oblivion in the aftermath of her parents' deaths, the dreams of her past lives and, well everything: a mage out of control was a danger. Gritting her teeth, she stubbornly looked back towards the professor. He was pacing across the front of the classroom, talking about the first few chapters of the book.

She'd read it, Alex knew that she had. But she couldn't remember a single character or word. Well, she suspected that the word "the" was probably in there. You could usually count on the word "the" to show up in a book. Alex inwardly groaned. Clearly, she was going to need more coffee in the mornings if her brain was fighting this badly against school.

Taking a deep breath, Alex opened her eyes a little wider and read the notes on the board. It helped, and she typed them into her tablet. Maybe a notebook would help. She'd heard that physically writing things down helps memory and focus. This wasn't the time to start failing. She'd kept her grades decent even while dealing with the reality that she was a mage and then Arthur's betrayal. It was important. It had been important to her parents that she have a college education. They'd lectured her and her brothers about it for years. There was a reason that their life insurance policies had been so large: they'd wanted to be sure she and her brothers went to college no matter what.

Alex wasn't sure how Morgana had dealt with that money. There was a probably an account somewhere with her share, and the rest had been sent with her brothers. Maybe all of it had been sent with her brothers. She needed to check on that.

Her eyes jumped back to the girl she'd accidentally mind read. Still nothing. No signs of discomfort. She seemed to be focusing on the professor without any trouble. The boy next to her was still watching a video. At least she wasn't the only one struggling.

Telling herself to breathe, Alex made a point of dropping her eyes to her desk. It was an older model and honestly a bit too small for modern college students and all their gear. Listening to the professor's words, Alex did her best to ignore what had just happened. Maybe she was wrong and was just imagining things because of how tense she was.

But Alex didn't believe it. That was too easy, too normal, and her life just wasn't that way. Normal wasn't her. Still, she stayed in her seat and didn't look back at the girl. Time passed slowly, but finally people began to pack up and give their professor a hint. Some more reading was put up on the board, but Alex didn't look at the words. She told herself that she'd check the syllabus later. Everyone stood and made for the doorway. Alex lingered despite the urge to get out and let the crowd clear out a little first. The professor nodded to her and Alex tried to give him a smile in return.

The long corridor of the building was full of noise. Students' shoes against the wooden floors echoed off the brick walls. Someday they'd probably switch the floors out with tile or carpet, but it hadn't happened yet, no matter how much abuse the floors took. Then again, Alex inwardly told herself, college students quickly got over wearing heels and dressing up within the first few weeks of freshman year. Jenny didn't even bother with it that much anymore despite having an impressive shoe collection.

Catching sight of Bran in the flow of students, Alex maneuvered her way past the people chatting in small groups and through the press of bodies. Some were in a hurry and others were just in her way. Finally, she was close enough to call out his name. Bran turned quickly, scanned the crowd, and stepped out of the flow of traffic when he caught sight of her.

"Hey, Alex," he greeted as she reached him. "You okay?"

"Why are you in this building?" Alex asked. "Do you have classes here?"

"Yeah, I've got an introduction to literature class in here." Bran shrugged a little. "You're right that this isn't my usual area. Well, not since freshman year 101 science lectures. They usually keep us locked away in one of the science buildings."

"Introduction to literature?" Alex repeated. "I thought you'd finished your general education requirements."

"Most of them, but it seems that I made a mistake in one of my classes. I read most of the books already in high school so it shouldn't be a big deal. Though, it's been a while since I wrote a non-scientific essay. Literature is all about symbolism and other..." he trailed off while Alex gave him a look. "Right... sorry, shutting up now."

Chuckling, Alex nudged his shoulder with her own. "It's not your thing. I get it." Sighing, she leaned against the brick wall and watched more students go past. "How's your day going?"

"Fine, nothing special," Bran replied. He was studying her intently. "What happened, Alex?"

"I think I read someone's mind during class," Alex confessed softly. "It was strange, and I wasn't trying to. I was struggling to focus and then suddenly it was like... I don't know, I slipped." Alex struggled for the words but then nodded. "Yes, slipped into a head for a moment. I heard something very clearly and then pulled out. I'm pretty sure she was okay though." She shook her head and a shaky laugh escaped her. "It was unexpected. I wasn't trying to. Feels weird to have suddenly pulled that off without even trying."

"...Good," Bran said. He looked a touch overwhelmed by her sudden rush of information but recovered quickly. "Well, we do know that Merlin and Morgana can alter memories. To do that, they'd have to get into someone's head." Bran looked torn with a smile trying to creep over his face. "What was it like?"

"Weird, but not bad," Alex said. "It wasn't clear, like it always is in the movies. I only got a short thought."

"That makes sense," Bran said. "People don't think in clear sentences. It's a jumble of different electrical signals that cascade into each other." He finally gave into the smile and grinned at her. "Honestly, I'm surprised that you even got words. I would have expected something visual."

"All I know is that I don't want to make it a habit," Alex said. "Though..." she trailed off thoughtfully. "It could be useful. I'm sure that Arthur will try something again, but if we could read his mind then maybe we could learn something."

"Except that Arthur can't come into Ravenslake," Bran pointed out. "And I doubt he'll spill his plan to whatever poor human he enslaves next."

The word enslaves made Alex shiver. It was a sharp reminder of what Arthur could do, but also made her think of a ship and a cargo hold full of people. It seemed that some things would never completely go away.

"True," Alex said. "Yet I can't help but think that he'll show himself again."

"I can believe that." Bran nodded in agreement. "He's arrogant and wants to be seen, wants us to know what he can do. In that regard, he's a rather cliché villain."

"I suppose he is."

"Sometimes I'm surprised that he didn't just stay with us," Bran said. "We thought he was the Iron Soul; he was the most important of us. I wonder if he ever considered letting the charade go on longer."

"Probably not," Alex said. "Cyrridven seemed to know. I don't know how, but she threw the sword to me before she died. Merlin probably would have been suspicious about that."

"And Arthur probably wouldn't want his position on the basis of a lie."

"Oh, I'm not sure about that," Alex said instinctively. Then she sighed and groaned. "Sorry, that might have been Arto talking. I'm not sure anymore. There are moments that Arthur's like Medraut, but then there are lots of times when he isn't."

"He's a reincarnation, just like us," Bran said. "He probably doesn't remember." Alex looked up at him sharply, but he nodded to reinforce his point. "He probably doesn't, Alex. At best, he probably has a few scattered visions from dreams. Most of what he knows or think he knows probably came from the queen."

Alex shivered as her stomach turned. "Yeah, who is his mother and lover. God, that's so, so..."

"Creepy," Bran provided. "But it's a way of controlling him. If you had to make yourself human and had access to the soul of someone who had been loyal to you, but probably wouldn't remember it, it figures that you'd do everything you could to keep control."

"Please don't say it like that," Alex snapped. "With the 'you.' I could never do something like that."

"Of course not," Bran agreed. "You're a good person." Alex's expression must have betrayed something because Bran frowned at her. "You are, Alex. You proved that, no matter what your former lives did, when you went back for those children."

"You like to bring that up. I'm sure all of you would have."

"Maybe," Bran said. "But then, everyone hopes that they'd be brave in times of trouble. Doesn't mean that they are." He put a hand on her shoulder and smiled. "Come on, let's see if we can find the others for lunch." With a smooth motion he pulled out his cell phone and started texting the others.

The crowd was fading away; most of the students were already heading out to either their next class or the food court. Bran pushed himself off the wall and gave her an expectant look. They headed down the stairs and outside into the fresh air. Sunshine warmed her skin, and Alex rolled her shoulders, trying to shake off her earlier melancholy.

"You're tense today," Bran said.

"It's just been an odd day. Not bad, just odd."

Bran's phone beeped, and he smiled. "Come on, Nicki and Aiden are already in the food court. We can grab something and join them."

Following Bran, Alex found herself still scoping out the other students for any sign of danger. When they reached the main food court the sheer number of people made her stomach tighten. But there was no Arthur. He couldn't come to Ravenslake, so there should always be a limit in how many people he could control. Bran spotted Nicki and Aiden and pointed them out to her before moving into the food court to order something.

Alex didn't feel very hungry, but she headed for the grill and ordered a burger. There were more and more people coming in and ordering. She moved off to the side to wait and avoid getting knocked over. No one seemed all that worried. It was only the first week and spirits were high. Tests and quizzes hadn't started yet. It was raw energy and nervous looking freshman.

Then her food was up, and she went to join the others around the small square table. It was a tight fit with the tables around them filling up and people trying to navigate. Noise filled the tall space, and more and more students were coming in for lunch. Yet, surrounded by the others, Alex found herself finally relaxing a little.

"You okay?" Nicki asked. "You're wound up tight."

"Do you find it hard?" Alex asked. Bran, Aiden, and Nicki all looked at her with small frowns of confusion. "School, I mean. Focusing on it when you know what you do now."

"A bit," Aiden said. His fork with the slightly off-smelling sushi was almost to his mouth. "But it makes for a nice distraction. I can focus on the absolute reality of engineering and lose myself in that a bit." Then he looked at Bran. "That reminds me: that free corner we've got in our room, can I have that? I need to build a project this semester."

"Sure," Bran replied. He smiled a little at Alex. "I'm about halfway between you and Aiden. I enjoy having class and homework to focus on, but I find myself being distracted by questions about physics and magic. And I can't find out the answers. It can be frustrating."

"I try not to think about it too much," Aiden admitted. "Started driving me crazy." He shook his head. "And honestly, unless we have a chance to examine the physical laws of the other worlds, it's always going to be elusive. I understand the theory in play. The idea that the physical laws conflict makes sense to me, but I mean, is there a limit? Or do certain worlds make it worse?"

"That's a good point," Bran said. His eyes brightened, and he grinned excitedly. "The world where the Old Ones come from isn't as based on matter. They're bound up energy, but not bound all the way to matter... it would make sense that interaction with their world is worse."

"They are the ones that go mad," Nicki said. She was smiling in amusement and had an eyebrow raised. "And banish people here."

"And then you have the dragons," Aiden said. He mostly ignored Nicki. "They can't die properly. I mean... it's like the electrical signals that keep their brain running can't shut down. Of course, their bodies may not work like ours, so who knows what's going on there."

Alex exchanged a look with Nicki. Her lips were curling up into a smile and she found herself holding back a laugh. Nicki rolled her eyes dramatically and shifted her chair a bit closer to Alex. Leaning closer to Nicki, Alex let the boys' conversation fade away and listened as Nicki went over her plan for asking Avani out.

14

Central Battlefield

Central Diner was loud and busy with staff all but running between tables and rowdy college students. The classic restaurant was full to the brim, and even the brightly colored red seats along the old-time soda counter were full. Bran smiled lightly. They weren't the only ones out celebrating the end of the first week of school. Hurray, they'd all survived. Good for them, but for him and his friends, that was a bit more literal.

Thankfully, they'd arrived a bit later in the night and managed to get one of the corner booths that could hold their large group. Jenny and Lance were in the middle with Lance's arm over her shoulders. Avani was next to Jenny on the left with Nicki next to her and Aiden at the end of that side. He was on the other side of Lance and Alex was at the end of their side. Any more additions to the group and they'd have to start stealing chairs.

"Is it always this loud here?" Avani asked. She was looking around with a fond smile, taking in the old 1950s décor. "I can't hear the jukebox."

"Sorry," Nicki said. "First Friday night of the school year. This is a favorite place for off-campus eating. They have really good..." Nicki trailed off and then paled. "Uh, shit, are you cool with us eating burgers? I swear that they have other things!"

"It's fine," Avani said. She smiled gently and nodded. "I don't eat beef, but I don't mind you doing so."

"Oh," Bran said slowly. He blinked and then smiled sheepishly. "Sorry, I forgot that cows are sacred to Hindus."

"That's not your fault," Avani said. "Besides, the atmosphere here is great! Very classic American. Almost doesn't seem real."

"Well, they do play it up here," Alex said. She was smiling and looking calmer than Bran had seen her in a while. "Still, they do have good food. It's one of those places where they only make what they can do a good job with. I do recommend the fries."

Avani took the suggestion when she ordered a chicken sandwich with a side of fries. Bran easily settled on a burger and fries like the others. He'd never had the chicken sandwich and hoped that it was good. They settled comfortably into a conversation about classes and the semester ahead. They were juniors now, except for Avani. Unlike freshman year, they didn't have any classes together. There were no group projects or sharing notes or whining about shared professors. Food came without much fanfare, and Bran pushed the tomatoes that had been mistakenly put on his burger to the edge of his plate.

Despite not feeling hungry when he came in, Bran plowed into the burger and didn't even feel bad about it. Aiden, Lance, and Nicki were laughing about some new cartoon show that was good, and Avani seemed interested. Jenny was shaking her head and glancing at Lance with a fond smile as she scrolled through something on her phone. It was calm and peaceful. Alex was smiling, and Bran allowed himself to focus on the conservation.

Suddenly the front door opened so fast and hard that a high-pitched squeak filled the diner. The door hit the wall with a crack, and everyone turned to look.

"There's something outside!"

The shout made their table freeze in alarm. A young woman, probably another student, was stumbling inside with a young man right behind her. Their eyes were wide and almost panicked. One of the waitresses hurried over to them, trying to calm the girl down.

"There's something out there!" The girl screamed again. "Small and hiding in the dark. Lots of them. They were laughing and tried to grab us!"

Bran felt Alex move and grabbed her hand to keep her in the booth. If they left now, it would draw attention. People were staring at the young woman. Then the noise broke out. Other people started standing and moving towards the doorway.

"Shit!" Bran swore. "We can't let them see what's out there."

"Probably Red Caps," Nicki growled. "But if we-"

Avani shifted in her seat, clasping her hands tightly together and lowering her head. Bran frowned, but he and the others piled out of the booth. The noise level was even worse, and the waitress was saying that she'd call 911. Then the air shimmered throughout the diner. There was a faint hint of gold in the air, and the noise of the crowd became muffled.

Twisting around, Bran looked back towards Avani. Her head was still bowed, but he could see her lips moving as she chanted something too softly for him to hear. Then the diner went silent and still. Frowning, Bran turned to look around. People were frowning and blinking at each other. The pair of people who'd come running in were standing still.

Bran's eyes turned to the waitress. She was peering at the phone on the counter, holding the receiver of the old-fashioned landline in her hand

and blinking in confusion. Patrons were silent and dazed. The couple who had come in shouting swayed and the young woman had to lean on the wall. A waitress hurried over to help the young man keep the young woman on her feet.

"Sorry," he apologized. "She... uh..."

"Sit down here," the waitress helped the young woman over to the counter. "I'll get you some water."

"Do you need an ambulance?" the waitress at the phone asked. "I can call one. You looked ready to fall over!"

"No, no, I think I'm alright." The young woman smiled and nodded. "Some water please. I'm not sure what happened."

"We were outside and..." the young man frowned, but pushed forward. "Your legs started to give out."

"I'm fine, Derek. Really. Just give me a second."

After another beat, the other patrons seemed reassured that the young woman was okay. Their conversations resumed and their started eating again. There was a lingering sense of 'that was odd' in the air, but Avani's spell seemed to have misdirected things just enough to prevent all out panic.

"I think..." Bran whispered. "I think Avani took care of it."

"That's amazing," Nicki gasped. She leaned across the table. "Avani, are you okay?"

"Yeah." Avani blinked rapidly and looked exhausted. "But hurry, it won't keep them from noticing a problem outside. It only wipes away their immediate concerns.

"Lance, Jenny, stay with her," Alex ordered. "Come on."

They moved quickly to the front door, and Bran looked around in awe. Avani's spell was amazing! It packed more of a punch then he would have expected, but then again maybe it was just the sort of spell that a family of magicians would need in a big city. Cool air hit his face as he stepped outside with the others. They weren't immediately attacked by Red Caps, and Bran flexed his fingers as he called on his magic. The magic in his chest pulsed in time with his heart. He tugged softly on the connection, letting the small flame burst to life.

Yet Central was much the same as ever. It wasn't completely dark yet, but the neon signs had already started coming on. Bran scanned the shops, restaurants, and bars that filled the lower levels of the buildings. Twilight was closing in on the town, but it wouldn't be dark for a while. Red Caps weren't happy in the light any more than other Fae species. Moving forward, he looked into the alleyway along the side of the diner. It was dark. The usual lights that illuminated emergency exits and dumpsters were out.

"What do you think?" Nicki asked. "It's probably a trap."

"Probably," Aiden agreed.

Alex walked forward. She ignored their soft protests and turned slowly to examine the brick walls. There was still enough light that they could see most everything, but the alley was full of shadows. Sunset was here, and no sunlight could reach between the buildings now. Bran moved forward a few steps with Nicki and Aiden alongside him.

"I think we need more light," Alex said. She looked back toward the alley. A few people were still visible on the street, but none of them were looking their way. "Bran?"

He nodded, but didn't look at Alex. There was scratching against the walls, but he still didn't see anything. Too many spots were too dark to be sure of anything. Sparks flared in Bran's hands, spinning together in a heartbeat to form a glowing yellow orb. The yellow faded, leaving white light pouring forth. Small eyes gleamed in the light of the orb. A small mouth opened to reveal rows of needle-like teeth. Bran's breath caught.

He'd seen Red Caps dozens of times now, but they always frightened him. Low giggling echoed around them, seemingly coming from everywhere at once. The eyes he'd been watching vanished back into shadows, and he heard scratching along the dark walls as the things moved.

"I'll hide the fight," Alex said softly. "We can't let people see."

Bran wasn't sure what she was going to do, but Alex moved back near the opening to the street. The move surprised and worried him. Her hands glowed dark gray, and a strange wall appeared between her and the street. It wasn't solid, but rather a slight distortion to his eyes that rippled with hints of wrought iron gray. He didn't know if it would work, but Avani's spell was certainly proof of concept. Alex was a bit out of breath, and Bran started to move back towards her. No one on the street seemed to be reacting to them.

A snarl behind him made Bran spin on his heel. Small figures were leaping out at them from all sides. There was no panic. He was calm as he shifted his fingers. The magic flowed easily from his chest through his hands. It was easier now. So much easier than when they'd started. Pushing his hand forward, Bran's magic crashed forward like a wave and knocked the sudden rain of creatures back. There were over a dozen.

Bolts of red and blue showered down into the frenzy as they flew back. One then two then three were struck and dissolved into dust. Nicki said something behind him, but it was difficult to understand as the Red Caps snarled. Another volley of bolts cut down their numbers again, but more were coming out of the shadows and advancing. All were dressed in bright red hats that were supposedly dyed in blood and stitched together out of rags. Some were carrying extra weapons while others simply held their sharp talon-like nails forward. Some were just baring their teeth.

A group of four were running along the ground, rushing at him with knives at the ready. Yellow magic flared around his hands, and Bran sent it spinning at the group. It collided with them, sending all four slamming back into the wall. Small cries of pain escaped them, but those didn't bother him. A yellow glow held all four of them in place, pinned to the wall. Bran turned his hand, extending one finger. Glowing bolts of magic blasted forth from his finger. They collided with the Red Caps in rapid succession, turning the creatures to dust.

Two more came jumping through the air, vaulting off an electrical box. Bran brought his hand up, catching the pair in a wave of yellow and leaving them hanging in the air. They kicked against the air as if it would free them. One started moving like it was trying to swim. Bran's chest lightened for a moment before a fireball exploded around the creatures. Blinking, Bran shook himself. These were Red Caps; they were vicious. Not amusing. They weren't under the power of the Iron Chain. He needed to remember that.

More were coming. They were splitting off into small groups, and a few were by themselves, crawling across the alley walls. Their twittering words and giggles surrounded them, echoing off the walls and creeping up Bran's spine. He and the others grouped up in the center. Catching sight of a couple heading for Alex, Bran sent a volley of bolts straight at them. A bolt of lightning erupted from Alex's hands, striking and killing one of them. The other caught a bolt in the shoulder and screamed before a second bolt finished the job.

There were fewer and fewer. Ice swept up to trap two in a corner. A fireball exploded to his right and took out a couple. The shadowy corners of the alley were going silent. Bran's heart was beating steadily, rather than racing. His limbs didn't ache, and he realized, with surprise, that he was getting better at this. He caught two more Red Caps and pulled them off the ground. Two well-aimed icicles sailed through the air and killed them.

Looking around, Bran saw only one Red Cap left. It had no weapons and was looking around frantically. A raspy call escaped it, but nothing came to help it. Nicki kicked her right leg forward, catching the Red Cap and sending it flying back against the dumpster. The metal rang, and Bran grimaced. Aiden didn't hesitate, and a well-placed fireball destroyed the creature, leaving a lingering scent of smoke on the air and a small scorch mark on the side of the dumpster. They were all still, listening for the sound of more. It was quiet in the alley, and Aiden sighed in relief.

"Someday we're not going to fight in an alley," Aiden muttered.

"Don't complain," Bran said. "It's easier this way. Unless you want another incident that involves the whole town."

"Don't even joke," Nicki said. She was looking around carefully. "I think that's all of them." Nicki turned slowly and held out her hand. Another light orb formed as her blue magic spun together. She tossed it forward, but rather than hanging in the air, it moved around and illuminated the corners of the alley as Nicki moved her finger. "I'm not seeing anything."

"Me neither," Aiden agreed. Shaking his head, he motioned towards the scattered clothing, knives, and other makeshift weapons. "We should deal with those."

"On it," Bran said. Waving his hands, he sent his magic forth to scoop them all up. Nicki turned and opened the closest dumpster. "Uh... yeah, I guess that will have to do." Curling up his nose slightly, Bran floated the mess of objects over and dropped them into the dumpster. "Do you think that's safe?"

Nicki stood on her toes and peaked in. "One second," she said. Nicki waved her hand and sent blue sparks flowing into the dumpster. Bran couldn't see what she was doing, but she nodded to herself. "There, I broke them apart a bit and wrapped some of the other trash around the pieces. Not perfect, but it should do the trick." Laughing slightly, she shrugged. "It isn't like this is prime dumpster diving territory."

"No," Aiden said. "That's always the giant one they put by the dorms at the end of the year."

"I've found some good stuff in that one," Nicki agreed. When Bran gave her a doubtful look, she grinned. "Seriously; two years ago I got a perfectly good working scanner and printer. It's all about what people don't have room for and know their parents will replace for them. There's a reason I collected for the thrift stores last year. Too much good stuff was being thrown away."

Looking towards Alex, Bran noted that she'd barely moved during the fight and had stayed silent. The odd shimmering wall was still in place, and he walked towards it. Everything on the other side was distorted, like an old swirling window. Alex had caught her breath and smiled at him as he stopped beside her.

"How'd I do?" she asked.

"Good," Bran said. "And good idea."

"Seemed like the right call on a Friday night," Alex said.

"Yeah," Nicki agreed. "But you can stop now. I think we got all the evidence." The magical lights vanished, and Alex nodded. Then the wall was gone, and the noise of the street rolled over them. "Huh, you must have blocked out the noise too," Nicki said.

"I didn't mean to." Alex shrugged a little but looked surprised herself. "Must have done that part subconsciously. I just wanted a wall that would keep people out and from seeing us."

"A spell to keep the noise separate would make sense then," Bran said. "After all, if someone heard fighting, they'd try to come into the alley." Smiling, he nodded towards the doorway. "We should probably reassure the others that we're alright."

"And check on Avani," Nicki added. She looked behind them at the alley and shuddered. "I wish the Red Caps would stop doing this."

"Yeah." Alex dusted off her hands and shook her head. "Me too. But I doubt they will. Come on, let's get inside. I need something sweet."

"That chocolate chip cookie with ice cream did look yummy," Nicki said. "I haven't had that one before."

"Really?" Aiden asked. He blinked and looked confused. "I thought you had."

"No, I usually go for the cake, but that sounds a bit heavy right now." Nicki's cheeks reddened, but it wasn't because of the neon lights. "I wonder if Avani will want to share it."

"Ask," Bran said. It was hard not to tease her, but he kept himself under control. Turning to Alex, he asked, "What about you?"

"I'm not sure, maybe some pie." Alex hummed and smiled. "Yeah, pie."

The door jangled as they opened it. Some people had left after they'd gone out, but Jenny, Lance, and Avani were all still in the booth. Avani looked up as they came in and visibly sighed in relief. She looked tired but was still sitting upright. The waitresses glanced their way but didn't stop them as they returned to their seats. Alex grabbed her basket of food eagerly but then frowned. She looked over at the waitresses and then down at the burger.

"Alex?" Bran asked. "Is it too cold?"

He put a hand on the bun of his burger. They weren't icy, but the temperature had dropped while they'd been distracted. Holding his breath for a moment, he reached inward for the spark of magic. It was thrumming and felt strong. Despite the battle, there was no aching in his muscles. There was also no feeling of guilt for the death of the Red Caps.

"Don't tell Morgana on me," he said. Alex looked at him in surprise, and he quickly checked that no one was looking. Snapping his fingers, he sent a spark of yellow magic into Alex's burger and then his own. "You earned it. That was an impressive cloaking spell."

Alex smiled, and Nicki huffed, looking down at her burger. She then elbowed Aiden in the side and nodded pointedly at her food. Aiden rolled his eyes but followed Bran's example. Small red sparks floated across the table to heat everyone else's food. Humming in approval, Nicki picked up her sandwich while Avani laughed in amusement. Jenny shook her head, and Lance hid a smile in one of his hands. As he bit into his now warm burger, Bran spotted Nicki plucking the dessert menu from the little condiments rack on the table.

A shadow fell over the table. Someone had come up right next to them. Bran looked up, expecting one of the waitresses. Instead, it was a tall man with messy brown hair and dark bags under his eyes. He was dressed in normal clothing, but they were stained in places like he'd been wearing them for days.

"Uh... are you okay?" Alex asked.

The man looked right at her. "Don't get overconfident, mages," he said. His voice was low and raspy. "I know you have the Sword. I'll be coming for it. Do you really think you can protect the world? You can't even protect yourselves." A nasty little smile twisted up the man's face, but it didn't reach his eyes. "You couldn't even protect your families."

Alex started to move. Bran saw dark gray sparks around her hand and grabbed her arm, pulling it under the table. The man laughed, the sound disconnected and off. People were starting to look at him. A waitress was coming over. Groaning, the man's eyes rolled back, and his knees buckled. On the far side of the table, Aiden moved to catch him, but the man's head hit the edge of the table. Blood spilled out onto the floor as he slumped unconscious at their feet.

15

Searching for Shadows

P odlasie Province, Poland 983 C.E.

Dobiemir knew this was dangerous. The forest was dangerous, and these strangers were dangerous. Yet here he was, showing them the paths where he'd most frequently seen the Shadows. Merlin and Morgana were taking it all in stride. They said that they'd never seen creatures like these before, but it was obvious that they had experience with battling others.

They'd explained things. At least they seemed to think they had. It was still too much, and Dobiemir couldn't quite make things fit. Reality, his reality, had been turned over too many times for him to be sure of his footing in the universe. They weren't gods, so they said, but he had a healthier son at home and was helping them hunt for vile creatures. It was all very confusing.

He'd let them stay at his farm last night. There wasn't room in their small house; not with all the food he'd been trying to stockpile. But Merlin had calmly waved his hands and made a small hut out of slabs of rock that ripped right up from the ground. It had been horrifying and thrilling all at once. Slavko had, of course, asked dozens of questions about the strangers and what was going on. Dobiemir wasn't even sure anymore just what the mages had told his son. Today it all seemed like it should have been a dream.

He'd come out of his own home this morning to check on the fields and animals and spotted the stone hut. Slavko had been awake and healthy, eagerly offering to help with chores. It hadn't been a dream. It was all real, and as grateful as he was for his son's renewed strength, Dobiemir was at a loss.

So here he was walking towards danger with the two strangers. Around them the forest was humming with life. He could hear creatures moving in the distance and heard birds chirping. It was reassuring, and yet not reassuring enough. Merlin and Morgana had power, but Dobiemir worried that they were poking at a beast that was beyond them. Kneeling, he plucked a few mushrooms from the ground and eagerly stowed them in his bag.

"I did tell you that we could help with food," Merlin said gently. The older mage was looking down at him with an indulgent smile. "You don't need to do that."

"Let him, Merlin," Morgana said. "Surely you remember a time that you faced the fear of famine. Gathering food is a difficult habit to break."

Merlin frowned at her back as Morgana moved ahead of them on the small game trail. "When were you ever in a famine?"

"That's hardly what you should be focusing on now," Morgana said. "Besides, making plants grow takes magic, and that can be exhausting. Then you eat more to recover. It is still helpful, but gathering is much safer."

"Fine, fine," Merlin said. He looked at Dobiemir and chuckled. "There is no arguing with her." He paused and glanced at the bag Dobiemir was carrying. "And I suppose that she isn't wrong."

Watching Merlin move forward on the trail, Dobiemir shook his head and tightened his grip on the bag. He took a deep breath and followed the pair further into the trees. Beneath their feet, dried pine needles cracked softly, and he jumped as a deer ran past.

"No sign of any Shadows," Morgana said. "Do you think we frightened them off?"

"I doubt it," Merlin said. His light-hearted tone was gone. "We were forced to run. They may not have followed up, but I doubt we scared them."

"Maybe... but depending on the intelligence behind these things it may want to avoid mages altogether."

"Possible," Merlin agreed. "Still, I'd like to know for sure. Unless your scrying has revealed anything?"

"I'd tell you if I'd learned something," Morgana said. "But it's just dark when I try to look. I can't see anything."

"Darkness and shadows," Merlin said. He shook his head. "I don't like this. Something new after all this time. I don't like something new showing itself in the realm."

"I don't know how much help I can be," Dobiemir said weakly. "Maybe I should go home?"

"We may need you," Merlin said. "You know the area. If something is off, even a little, you have a much better chance of noticing than us."

"But I can't fight them," Dobiemir insisted. "I'm not sure what to do."

"For today stay behind us," Morgana replied. She almost smiled at him. "We can teach you to use magic once we know more about what we're dealing with. You have the potential. We told you as much. Did you think we were teasing?"

"I'm not sure..." Dobiemir hesitated. "Things are tense... the missionaries and everyone is afraid right now. I'm not sure using magic is wise."

"You've got a good mind if you noticed that," Merlin said. "You're not wrong. It's why we were merely watching in the village. We only stepped in against the Shadows because they were going to kill you."

"But I still would have seen you."

"That can be fixed." Merlin smiled at him, a secretive and pleased smile that Dobiemir didn't understand. "Don't let fear of the villagers stop you. This area has fallen under some sort of dark influence, and you are a mage. You are meant to fight it back."

"I'm not so sure," Dobiemir replied. He hoped he sounded calm, but his heart was jumping at every little sound. "I'm not a brave man."

"Bravery is not a simple thing," Merlin said. "It is complex and determined by the situation. I've met many brave people, cowards, and those who were only out for glory and wealth. Most of the brave men never felt brave. That was why they were."

"I don't understand," Dobiemir said. Then he shook his head. "There's much I don't understand about you, but you talk in riddles."

"He does," Morgana agreed ahead of them.

Merlin chuckled and looked towards Morgana fondly. "I suppose she would know that better than most." Looking at Dobiemir, Merlin smiled warmly. "Tell me more about yourself, Dobiemir."

"There isn't much to tell. You've met my son; he's my only surviving child. I was born in this village. My grandparents settled here not long before that. My grandfather had been part of a roaming tribe in the past but hoped that farming would be easier." Dobiemir patted the bag on his side. "His son, my father, taught my sister and I to find food in the woods. I'm better than most of the others around here. My wife had a talent with the animals that I lack."

"And farming is your trade?"

"I can do some other things, basic woodworking and such."

"Blacksmithing?"

"No, not that. I've never tried."

"I see," Merlin said. "Well, I could teach you. Though I'm uncertain if these creatures are affected by iron. Many are."

"I've heard that from the stories."

"Yes, many of the Fae are known to your people," Merlin agreed. "But what of your childhood? Your sister?"

"She died years ago," Dobiemir said. "There were others, but I only remember her." Shrugging, he ignored the fact that he couldn't remember her face. There was only a vague memory of dark hair and eyes like his own and a pretty smile. Even the pain that he remembered being present when she passed was muted. "It happens."

"It does." Merlin looked around carefully, though his pleasant demeanor didn't change at all. "Anything else?"

"No, I'm not that interesting," he insisted. "These things are the only exciting thing ever to happen here. What about the pair of you? You must have exciting stories."

"Many," Merlin agreed. "Some far darker and more frightening than others. The reason I believe this is an Old One gone mad is that we've seen that before. They didn't create living Shadows, but they made the dead walk."

"Dead... walk?" His heart stopped at the very thought, and his feet almost slipped out from underneath him. "How? Why?"

"She was tormenting humans," Morgana answered. "She was crazy. That's something you need to understand. When the Old Ones begin to lose themselves, they don't necessarily have plans that make sense. Sometimes they're lashing out and just trying to make others hurt like they hurt."

He nodded slowly when she glanced at him for confirmation that he'd heard. Suddenly it was difficult to swallow, and the fear was back. He was so small compared to them. How could they walk in a life such as this? These Old Ones were deities, creatures of fearsome power, no matter how Morgana and Merlin might dismiss them. He was tempted to ask how the missionaries' God fit into all of it, but the stories of that God spoke of power that was horrifying to imagine. If such a thing was real, he didn't want to know for sure.

"I'm sorry," Merlin said gently. Dobiemir blinked and focused on the mage rather than his thoughts. "This is a lot to take in, but thank you for helping us."

"You helped my son." That was the core of all of it. "And I suppose that these things are dangerous. It isn't safe for them to just be running about."

Merlin nodded in agreement. Dobiemir was certain that the man was amused by his answer. There was understanding in his eyes. He wondered if Merlin had ever been married or had children. It was tempting to ask. He didn't.

The temperature suddenly shifted. It grew colder. Not sharply, but it was noticeable. Looking around in alarm, Dobiemir tried not to think too hard about what he was going to do if they found any Shadows. Merlin shifted closer to him and caught his eyes with a serious gaze.

"Calm yourself, Dobiemir," Merlin said. "I will keep you safe."

"Thank you." He swallowed and kept moving. "They don't seem to have a den or anything like that."

"But they must come from somewhere," Merlin said. "Either on foot or by magic. Have you ever seen a figure near them?"

"No, no one. People run when they are nearby." Merlin hummed thoughtfully and nodded, indicating that he'd heard. Dobiemir didn't think the statement had been helpful, but Merlin wasn't distressed. "What are we looking for?"

"Signs of an encampment," Merlin said. "Or signs of decay... well, that isn't helpful with these creatures. I am still unsure if they are a creation of something or from another world. Either is possible, but magic has not greatly increased, so I don't think anything has found a way into our world."

"I don't understand."

"No, I suppose not. I fear that there is a great deal of history between Morgana and myself. Far too much to ever bother you with. But our world has defenses. They are all but impossible to breach. That which is in our world that does not belong here, came here long ago. Nothing new enters the Iron Realm."

"Something made it colder," Morgana said. "But I don't see any Shadows."

Merlin looked up into the sky and hummed thoughtfully. "The sun has gone behind some clouds, but that doesn't seem enough for the chill."

"No." Morgana nodded in agreement. There was a curious spark in her eyes, almost excitement. "This is something else. We might be close to something."

She pushed on. The tree branches above them grew thicker, and as the world darkened Dobiemir wasn't sure if it was the sun being kept out or something else. He hoped it was just the thickness of the forest, almost started to pray before thinking better of it. If he hadn't been sure who to pray to before, he was even more conflicted and confused now.

They followed the game trail around the hillside. Dobiemir frowned and examined the trees around him. It was foolish to think that he knew the forest well. He didn't, and this was farther now than he usually went.

Glancing over his shoulder, he reminded himself that he just had to head down the slope of the hillside to return home. Here the trees were taller and closer together. Everything became even darker as the sun was blocked out. Dobiemir shivered and looked around nervously.

It was quiet and still. Even the wind seemed to have died down. They were approaching a steep cliffside of rock that cast a shadow across the area. Looking towards Merlin, he found the old mage examining the area thoughtfully. Neither he nor Morgana spoke, both slowly surveying the area. Nothing came. There were no Shadows suddenly leaping out, but something felt off. His eyes met Merlin's, and the old mage nodded cautiously. He gave Dobiemir a pointed look that he translated as 'stay close.' It was a suggestion he was glad to take.

Morgana eventually moved forward, and Merlin followed her leaving Dobiemir trailing along behind them. As still as the forest was, Dobiemir was sure that all the animals would hear his heart beating. Fear was creeping up along his spine. It whispered in his ears and made his footfalls distressingly loud.

Then he caught sight of a dark patch slightly ahead of them. For a moment, he held his breath before realizing that it wasn't a Shadow. There was a hole in the hillside, almost hidden in the shadows of the trees. Shivering, Dobiemir wrapped his cloak tighter around his shoulders. He wasn't sure if the temperature was truly changing or it if was his fear.

"Dobiemir, do you know this cave?" Merlin asked.

"No," he answered quickly. "I don't usually come up this far." Frowning at the cave entrance, he searched his memories. "I'm sure I've not seen it before."

"Have you been here before?" Morgana asked. "Even some time ago?"

"I don't know," Dobiemir said. "I'm not sure."

The mages exchanged a look before inching closer to the cave entrance. Dobiemir stayed back, eying the cave uncertainly. This area was vaguely familiar, but it was possible that he'd missed the cave before. It wasn't easy to access, and the thick trees made this section of the forest very dark. Dobiemir stayed back and waited for them to tell him what to do. Nervously, he checked the nearby trees and found one that looked sturdy with low branches.

A low growl made them all stop. Merlin's hands began to glow a bright leaf green and silver sparks shimmered around Morgana's right palm. The mages slowly turned and surveyed the area. It took Dobiemir only a moment to see it. The darkness itself seemed to shift. He gasped and pointed, opening and closing his mouth, struggling to form words. In the shade of a tree, the darkness was stretching and twisting. Then it started to move, pulling out of the darkness like it was stretching fabric. A long snout appeared, and glowing green eyes snapped open. With a tug it pulled loose, the shade transforming and snapping into the shape of legs and a torso.

The Shadow was moving slowly. It was large and vaguely catlike all the way down to its ears. Its fur was pitch black with a strange shimmer, and its eyes glowed green. The thing released a soft hiss that made Dobiemir's heart jump into his throat. It was watching them, focusing on Merlin and Morgana. Like it knew them; knew what they were. Shivering, Dobiemir fought to ignore the cold and moved towards the tree. Another low growl made him jump — another patch of shadow near another large tree had started shifting. A shape pressed at it, pushed against the shadow against the stone of the cliff.

"Get up a tree," Merlin ordered.

Dobiemir spun and grabbed the lowest branch of the tree he had noticed earlier. It wasn't much, but it was enough to help him get a grip. Catching the next branch, he pulled his feet off the forest floor just as a snarl cut through the silence. Everything was darkening; it was worse than the twilight. Behind him a light flared to life, but he didn't look back. The cold was sinking into his shoulders. His skin tingled and tightened. Nonetheless, he grabbed the next branch and went higher in the tree. More snarls and growls reached him. He wanted to look, but fear tore at his chest. Tears pricked at his eyes as a sharp, throbbing pain from the cold filled his head.

Collapsing against the trunk, Dobiemir let his teeth chatter and attempted to wrap his stiff arms around the middle of the tree. More Shadows were creeping out of the darkness towards the mages. He wanted to shout, but his lips weren't working. Merlin and Morgana somehow hadn't collapsed. The magical fire between them kept burning, filling the air with warmth and light, but it was fading as the Shadows came too close.

"Morgana, I think the fire is making them stronger!" Merlin shouted. "Look at them, look at the light. They're absorbing it!"

"Then what do you want to do?!"

More Shadows were coming forth, pulling out of the darkness surrounding the cave and dragged it forth into the world with them. Dobiemir's breath danced in the air as his chest tightened. They were surrounded by Shadows. His eyes went back to the cave, to the strange and unfamiliar entrance. The cold was seeping out into the world from there. There were six Shadows now, all circling Merlin and Morgana, growling and eyeing them with gleaming eyes. Then, in the pitch blackness of the small cave mouth, Dobiemir saw a pair of large, unnaturally bright green eyes open wide.

16

Waiting Room

Alex hated the Ravenslake hospital. It wasn't because it was dirty or a bad hospital or anything like that. Nothing good happened here. Just the smell took her back to when Aiden had been in a coma, and she'd been reeling from learning that Arthur was a traitor. She'd been trying not to cry or shut down. Those first few hours were a blur, but the sharp smell lingered in her memory.

The nurse at the desk kept giving them odd looks. They hadn't brought the man in themselves. After he collapsed, an ambulance had been called, though Alex had put pressure on his head wound while they waited. They weren't family, they didn't even know his name, and yet all of them were waiting for news. Alex's head fell back against the boring white wall as they waited. They hadn't been given any real information, but the man wasn't dead yet.

He was probably getting an MRI or something to check for brain damage. At least, Alex hoped so. She didn't know what the combination of mind control and a head injury would do to a person. Tapping her fingers on the arm of the waiting room chair, she held back a sigh. Jenny was across from her, leaning against Lance and tapping away on her phone. Aiden and Nicki were in a corner while Bran and Avani were talking softly.

There was only one other man in the waiting room. He'd been there before them. A nurse came over to talk to him, and the man eagerly followed him back towards the patient rooms. They were alone, but no one rushed to speak. Closing her eyes, Alex listened to the whispered suggestions of her previous selves. No one had any real ideas, but the gist was that sitting in silence wasn't going to help.

"Did anyone notice anything about him that could help?" Alex asked.

"He came into the diner just after you left," Jenny said. "I was watching the doorway. The waitress talked to him, and he was waiting for a seat at the counter I think."

"That does sound right." Lance nodded in agreement. "I remember thinking that he was a mess. The waitress didn't look happy with him. He went back to the bathroom for a moment, I think."

"Okay," Alex said. Exhaling, she was sharply aware of the frustration building up in her chest. "We don't even know who the guy was," Alex groaned. "I mean, maybe they'll tell us, but I'm not sure how much it is going to help."

"His name is Austin Parker," Lance said softly. They all looked at him, and he smiled a bit sheepishly. "I checked his wallet while the waitresses were panicking. He's from Las Vegas, according to his driver's license. There wasn't a cell phone in his pockets." Lance ducked his head a little as they all stared. "I didn't have a chance to write anything down. Didn't want the paramedics freaking out on me."

"Vegas?" Jenny repeated with a frown. "That's a long way off... then again, he looked ragged, like he hadn't slept in a couple of days."

"Maybe he hadn't," Bran said softly. They all looked towards the main desk again. "I hope he'll be okay. Exhaustion, head trauma, and magical possession if we want to call it that can't be easy."

"How was the guy who came to your bakery?" Lance asked. "You said he seemed fine."

"He did, but I don't think he was far out of town. Maybe even lived in a suburb. It's not like cities around here are compact and easy to protect."

"True," Alex said. "We always focus the blood protection spell on our homes... so some areas are still going to be outside of it." Guilt tugged at her, but it wasn't important right now. "And if Bran's right, then that man wouldn't have been affected for long."

"While someone from Vegas who came all the way here would have been under Arthur's control much longer," Jenny said softly. "Do- do we know how this works? I mean, does he give them instructions and that's all or is he with them somehow? The message seemed like it was in the first person, but it might have been more like a recording."

"That's a good question," Alex replied. Exhaling deeply, she slumped back into a chair again. "And I hate to say it, but I preferred the recorded message to the idea that he could watch us."

"He didn't try to lash out," Bran said. He sounded calm. Alex was both grateful for that and agitated by it. How could he be calm? "He got right next to us, but didn't try anything with magic. Maybe he can't."

"His last puppet pulled a gun on you," Lance reminded him.

"Trust me," Bran said. "I remember. I'm just trying to wrap my head around this. The last man... it was different. He was more of a zombie; this guy seemed to be a vessel for Arthur. When the guy in the bakery woke up, he didn't remember anything. He didn't even really understand that anything had happened. There was no message from Arthur. It was just an attack."

No one spoke for a long moment. Alex shivered at the reminder of what Arthur had been trying. Maybe he'd been confident that it wouldn't work. Maybe it had just been another taunting message, but the idea of just how close he'd gotten... He could have hurt Bran, or killed his mother or someone else or forced Bran to expose magic. Or maybe he'd made sure of the timing. Maybe it was all just a game to Arthur. Alex's head ached, and she nervously licked her lips.

"So, is this the first time he's contacted you?" Avani asked softly.

"No," Alex growled. "He's called me a few times. I suppose he didn't want me hanging up on him this time." Pulling out her phone, Alex checked all her recent calls. Nothing new or unknown had come through.

"Not to mention it lets him show off his power," Bran added. He was staring at the fish tank in the waiting room. "Lets him build himself up as the villain I think he is in his own mind."

"Yeah," Aiden murmured. "He is a special sort of arrogant crazy."

Nicki was fidgeting in her seat. She kept shifting closer and closer to Aiden, who was staring off into space. If he noticed Nicki's odd behavior, he said nothing. Swallowing, Alex stood up and stretched her arms and legs. Bran caught her eye and tilted his head towards Nicki. She nodded quickly, silently assuring him that she had noticed.

"There's no reason for all of us to stay here," Alex said. "Nicki, Aiden, you two can head out."

"You sure?" Aiden asked. He blinked up at her, his eyes quickly coming back into focus.

"Yeah; plus, I can't imagine you like being in hospitals much nowadays," Alex said. The attempt at a lighthearted tone didn't work well, but Nicki's shoulders relaxed. Aiden smiled slightly and nodded. "We'll let you know if anything happens tonight. I don't expect it to," Alex said.

Aiden opened his mouth to say something, but then glanced at Nicki. Nodding, he forced a smile and rolled his shoulders to stretch. "Yeah, okay," he agreed. "Just let us know if you need anything. I suppose I'll get some homework started."

"We'll see you later," Bran said.

"I won't booby-trap the door to our room," Aiden promised.

Standing up, Aiden dramatically offered his arm to Nicki. She raised an eyebrow at the display, but Alex caught the small smile on her face. Looping their arms together, Nicki glanced back at Avani but didn't stop Aiden from leading her out of the waiting room.

"I'm glad we had some cars at the diner," Bran said. "Otherwise tonight would have been a real pain."

"We live too far away now to walk everywhere." Alex shrugged and slumped down in her seat, trying to find a comfortable position.

"Do you think Nicki and Aiden are safe going home?" Avani asked softly. She glanced towards the doors they'd vanished through with a frown.

"They'll stay close together," Lance assured her. "They've known each other a long time. Try not to worry."

"Lance is right," Alex agreed. She smiled at Avani, feeling a curious little jolt of happiness at Avani's worry for Nicki. "They're basically brother and sister. They'll probably play a video game or something or at least stay close in case of trouble."

"Good," Avani said. She nodded and tucked a strand of dark hair behind her head. "That's good. Nicki seemed very upset."

"She was just reminded of when Arthur hurt Aiden," Bran explained. "That was a hard period for her. For all of us, but especially for her. I think it's affected how she views hospitals."

Avani nodded slowly. Alex looked over at Jenny and met her friend's eyes for a moment. But they didn't speak. They all sank into that strange limbo of waiting. They'd already turned down the television, but images were still playing out. None of it was of any interest. Jenny's phone beeped, and Lance looked down at it, smiling at something.

"Did someone call Morgana and Merlin?" Alex asked. She honestly couldn't remember.

"I did," Bran said. His voice was gentle and patient.

Giving him a grateful smile, Alex nodded. "Thanks, we'll need to bring them up to speed." She rubbed her forehead in a weak attempt to stop the growing ache behind her eyes. "Hopefully they can learn more."

"You probably could as well," Bran said. "If you weren't so tired." At her confused frown, he nodded to her hands. "Headache?"

"A bit."

"Could be that cloaking spell you did. None of us have really used magic like that before."

"Maybe," Alex said. "Or it could be old-fashioned frustration."

"Also possible," Bran said. "But if you need to go and rest, I'll stay until Morgana gets here."

"No." Chuckling softly, Alex shook her head. "No, let's not put Morgana into an overprotective warpath. If she comes and I'm not here it might not be pretty."

"Fair point," Bran agreed. "You three can go if you want."

"I'll stay," Avani said. "I'm a bit tired after the confusion spell, but my nerves are on edge." Avani shook her head and Alex noted that her hands were trembling. "I won't be able to rest. I'd rather stay with you."

"We'll stay," Lance said. "It's not fair for you to have to stay here alone."

Smiling, Alex nodded. The sentiment warmed her chest. It was easy to worry about Lance and Jenny, to tell herself that they didn't belong in the middle of this. And then one of them would come up with a clever idea, make a needed observation or make her feel less... alone wasn't the right word. Disconnected, maybe. Alex frowned at the direction of her own thoughts before deciding that was probably it. What with magic and living with mages, a magician, and a Brownie, it was easy to get swept up in things. Jenny and Lance were at least still mostly normal.

Footfalls in the hall made Alex turn her head. She recognized the stride and the click of the shoes. Sitting up in her chair, Alex stretched her arms and yawned before shaking her head to wake herself up. Morgana strode into the room, her long hair flowing behind her due to her speed. Then she came to a stop with her eyes checking over each of them in turn, starting with Alex and instantly going back to her when finished.

"Nicki and Aiden left," Alex said. She shrugged a little, trying to dismiss it as unimportant.

"Yes, I can imagine they would be uncomfortable here," Morgana said. Her green eyes softened for a moment, and Alex relaxed. Of course, Morgana would understand. "How are the rest of you?"

"We're fine," Lance answered. "No one got hurt."

"What happened, exactly?"

"There were Red Caps in the alley," Alex answered. "So, we went outside to check it out while Lance, Jenny, and Avani stayed inside the diner. We took care of the Red Caps and came inside. We were all back at the table when this stranger came up and started talking to us like he was Arthur. Then he collapsed and hit his head."

"I see," Morgana said carefully. Her voice was tight with anger and worry. She glanced back at the door. "Ambrose is finding out what he can from the nurses and doctors."

"Yeah, they haven't told us anything," Alex said. "Which I do understand; we aren't the guy's family, but-"

"We need to know," Morgana agreed. "Especially given that to do this, Arthur would have needed to interact with the man. This isn't something that can be done over the phone."

Alex wasn't sure if that was reassuring or not. Her stomach turned at the idea of being able to track Arthur down. Morgana crossed the room and sat down next to her.

"What did he say?" Morgana asked. "Exactly?"

"Uh, he didn't say anything specific. It wasn't a supervillain monologue or anything like that. He told us not to become too confident. Said that we couldn't protect ourselves and couldn't protect the world." Alex didn't look at Morgana. The memory of Arthur's barb at her parents' murder stung too much. "Nothing detailed."

"He may be trying to scare you," Morgana said. "Or testing his abilities. If he can control people, then that opens up some new possibilities for him." Morgana's expression tightened. "You said that Nicki and Aiden headed back to the house?"

"I'm not sure," Alex said. "Probably, but-"

"Call them. Tell them to keep an eye on Cathanáil and Mjǫllnir," Morgana ordered. "If Arthur can control someone or even program someone like this, then he might be able to use them for missions."

Nodding, Alex dug out her phone. There was a flutter of panic growing in her chest. She didn't think that Arthur had the sword. The man had collapsed, and he hadn't had it. If Arthur had been able to get it from the man before he came to the diner, he probably would have gloated. But maybe this was some kind of distraction. Hitting the speed dial for Nicki, Alex waited impatiently for an answer. Maybe a text would have been better, but she wanted, needed to hear Nicki's voice.

"Hey, Alex," Nicki greeted. "You okay?"

"We're fine. Still at the hospital. Morgana says to keep an eye on Cathanáil and Mjǫllnir," Alex said. "They're in my room. She's worried that Arthur might try to steal them."

"Oh," Nicki said. "Yeah, that makes sense. Can't believe we didn't think about that. We're on our way now. I'll text you when we get there and check on things."

"Thanks."

The call ended, and Alex exhaled, looking over at Morgana. "I hope you're wrong."

"I do too," Morgana agreed. She was frowning and drumming her fingers on the armrests. "I should have thought of that possibility earlier. We need to work on those spells. Ideally, make an alteration to the blood spell so that even someone who is controlled couldn't come close."

"It could be possible," Alex said. "I've changed it before."

"Yes, you have," Morgana said. "We'll work on it, Alex."

"It feels like that's all we ever say."

"Magic is complex," Morgana said. "It is one thing to conjure a fireball, and another to provide a standing pool of magic with specific instructions. Of course, it takes more time, energy, and planning. I promise you that Ambrose and I are working on it. We want you safe, and we want a solid foundation from which to fight Arthur and Scáthbás.

Pressing her lips together, Alex held back a sigh. That made sense, but she didn't like it. Moments like this just highlighted why school was a waste of time. If they could just have focused on the magic, then they'd have surely had something set up by now. Morgana gave her a warning look. The older mage probably knew exactly what she was thinking. Putting a hand on her shoulder, Morgana guided Alex down into a chair and sat next to her.

"Patience," Morgana said. "I know that's rich coming from something as old as I am, but patience. We don't want to risk the integrity of the blood protection spell because we rush ourselves. You saw the power it can contain even after centuries in Glastonbury."

"Fair point," Alex said. It was, but she was still irritated. It did seem that you could never argue with Morgana.

"Just focus on this for now," Morgana said. "We'll figure out the spell."

At least she didn't say that it would all be alright. Morgana knew better than that. Alex knew that plenty of her lives had been tragic. Her phone beeped, and Alex quickly checked the latest text message.

"Aiden and Nicki are back at the house. All's quiet and the hammer and sword are still there."

"Good." Morgana exhaled, and her shoulders eased. "That's good to hear. And I suspect that Nicki will spend the evening working on the spell."

"Very likely," Avani agreed. "She is very creative and very driven."

"Yes." Morgana smiled in amusement. "Even when she first learned about magic, she wanted to know all about making magical objects. Of course, iron is usually used for holding magic, but she does have a lot of interesting ideas."

"I'm looking forward to seeing what she creates." Avani's smile was softer now, and Alex sat up with interest. In her chair, Jenny was smiling knowingly, and Lance just looked amused. "She showed me some of her ideas the other day. She has a notebook full of things she wants to make and ideas for how to bind the magic using symbols."

"Nicki is very creative," Morgana agreed. Even her green eyes had a twinkle in them now. "I confess that the sort of enchanting that Nicki wants to do is something that Merlin and I lack the talent for. Iron is what we always turn back to for enchantments. The best we've managed is the slight cloaking spell on your dagger scabbards, but even that isn't absolute."

"Still," Alex said. "There are some things that I wouldn't mind her figuring out how to make. There are some neat old myths about the scabbard used with Excalibur."

"True, though I doubt there is any spell in the world that could be placed into leather to make the bearer invulnerable. Though I'd be glad if there was."

Then they heard footfalls, and everyone went quiet. Jenny was still looking at her phone, but her posture was tense as they waited to see who it was. Merlin walked into the waiting room, his shoulder slumped and his eyes tired. The conversation was completely forgotten. Jumping to her feet, Alex inhaled sharply and braced herself. The others all moved closer. Morgana was the calmest and set a hand on Merlin's shoulder.

"Did you learn anything, Ambrose?" Morgana asked.

"They don't expect the man to live," Merlin replied. Shaking his head, he glanced towards the nurse's desk. "They believe it was a brain aneurysm." Merlin shifted and looked at each of them. "He was brain dead upon arrival here. He's hooked up to life support now. They are waiting to speak with his family about potential organ donation." At their horrified looks, Merlin held up his hands in a calming gesture. "I can't say for certain if Arthur caused this or aggravated an existing problem."

"The man did look exhausted," Lance said softly. "I doubt that helped."

"Yes," Merlin agreed. "But the fact remains that whatever Arthur did is unstable."

"You and Morgana have affected minds before," Bran said. "And tonight Avani-"

"Oh god," Alex gasped. "Avani cast a spell to confuse everyone in the diner. Two people had come in, and we had to go and-"

Morgana grabbed her arm, and Merlin put his hand on the top of her head. Both of them gave her gentle smiles. Almost on reflex, she started to relax a little.

"It's okay," Avani said quickly. "My family has used it many times. It helps us stay hidden. There are no aftereffects you need to worry about."

"She's correct," Merlin assured Alex. "You shouldn't worry. I have controlled minds in the past without ever having problems. Our ability to go unnoticed and gather medical information that shouldn't be released to me, for instance, is an example of using magic on the brain."

"Keep in mind that Arthur might have caused this on purpose," Morgana said. "Just to alarm you. He knows that you don't want people hurt, so this could be him lashing out at you."

"And we don't know everything about Arthur's magic," Merlin added. "He is part Sídhe like Morgana and I, but he isn't loyal to the Iron Realm. The source of his magic... how it works and the way it affects things are still a mystery to us."

"It's probably tied to mine," Alex muttered. "Through the Iron Chain."

"That is a possibility," Morgana said. She squeezed Alex's shoulder. "But we can't know that for certain."

"There's nothing more we can do here tonight," Merlin said. "You children have done what you can for this unfortunate man."

"Is there nothing we can do?" Alex asked. "I mean, the Chalice could help him."

"No," Merlin said. His eyes were stern. "Alex... he's in the hospital surrounded by doctors. There's already been one miraculous recovery here in Aiden. We have to be careful. Besides, I doubt the Chalice could restore brain function after this."

"But if he's on life support-"

"Alex," Morgana said. "Our responsibility is to the Iron Realm. We have to be careful," she said softly. "It would be too risky. We'd have to hide from the doctors since none of us are supposed to be there, hide from the cameras and hope that the Chalice worked."

"But we can!" Twisting around, Alex glared at Morgana. "We can help him. We should."

"We don't know enough about what Arthur did to him," Merlin said. She'd never heard his voice so cold before. "I don't want to risk triggering something worse."

"Worse for him?" Alex scoffed. "I'm pretty sure it can't get worse for him. He's brain dead."

"No. Worse for us, for you," Merlin said. "Arthur knows the legends about the Chalice. If I was Arthur, I'd try to find a way to destroy it. If the Chalice, a concentration of magic, gets close to that man, who knows what will happen."

"Do... do you think he's done something like that?" Alex asked. "That helping that man would be a trap?"

The expression on Merlin's face answered her. Lowering her eyes, Alex swallowed. A little voice argued that maybe they were wrong, maybe they were giving Arthur too much credit, and that fear shouldn't stop them from helping. But her side began to ache, a phantom pain from her sword slicing through her gut. She didn't answer. She didn't know how to answer. Morgana sighed and said something to Merlin that Alex didn't pay attention to. Bran took her arm, and she felt Jenny squeeze her hand.

"Come on," Bran said. "Let's go home."

"But-"

"I don't know," Bran said softly. "I don't know, Alex. I'm sorry."

Nodding, she fell silent and let the others guide her out to Lance's truck. It was a tight fit, but they all piled in and headed for home. Leaning her head against the window, Alex watched the buildings go past while guilt and, strangely, a little relief churned in her chest.

17

Salvation Within Creation

When Alex finally pulled herself out of bed the next morning, she had a pain in her neck and shoulders, as well as a sense of lingering guilt. Torn between wanting to know what had happened to Arthur's victim and worrying that it was better to leave it alone, she took her shower and detangled her hair. The others were up and moving, judging from the footfalls in the hallway and the voices drifting up from downstairs. It wasn't as soothing as she'd hoped it would be.

Still, Timothy and Aiden were in the kitchen making waffles in a pair of waffle irons that Alex hadn't even known were in the house. The dining room table was covered in food, and most of the others were already eating; only Nicki was missing.

"Morning," Bran said. There was an empty place next to him. "How did you sleep?"

"Not great," Alex confessed. Sitting down, she reached for a bowl of scrambled eggs and dished up a helping. "But I did sleep."

"Good," Bran replied gently. "I know last night was hard." Shaking his head, he sighed. "And the more I think about it the worse I feel, even as I realize that Merlin and Morgana were probably right. If Arthur could find a way to use our desire to protect others against us, then he would."

"Could we not talk about it?" Alex muttered. "I can't this morning."

"Right, okay," Bran agreed. "Sorry."

"So, where's Nicki?" Alex asked.

"Still in her room," Jenny answered from across the table. "She was up pretty early this morning, but hasn't come down yet."

Aiden frowned as he brought a plate with two more waffles on it over. "Really?" he asked. He pushed one of the waffles onto Alex's plate. Nodding her thanks, Alex ate a mouthful of eggs. "No one has seen her?"

"I knocked on her door," Jenny said. "Told her we were making breakfast, but she said that she'd eat later."

"I hope she's not in crazy art mode," Aiden grumbled. He put a hand on Lance's shoulder. "I'm going to go and check on her. Can you keep an eye on the waffles?"

"Sure," Lance said. He started to stand up before faltering. "Uh, what do I do?"

"Timothy knows." Aiden gestured into the kitchen. "Just give him a hand."

He vanished upstairs, and Alex exchanged looks with the others. Then she heard voices from upstairs and relaxed. Nicki was fine; she was just on an art kick. That wasn't an issue. She poured syrup on her waffles and quickly cut a piece to eat. The hot, crispy texture was glorious with the sweetness of the syrup, and Alex sighed happily.

"Yeah," Jenny agreed. She was smiling, and with her hair half up in a bun looked happier than Alex had seen her in a while. "They're really good. I'm going to enjoy the days when Aiden cooks. Of course, Bran's baking could get dangerous."

"You could always join me on my runs," Alex offered. She was pretty sure that Jenny wouldn't and enjoyed watching the other woman's eyes widen. "I know Morgana and Merlin would be happier if I didn't go alone."

"Thanks for the offer, but no. I couldn't manage it freshman year, and I'm not delusional now." Jenny reached for the bowl of eggs. "I like the weight room, and it isn't as cold."

"Fair enough," Alex agreed. She considered that option for a moment.

Noise from the stairs made Alex look that way. Thanks to the wall, she couldn't see Nicki or Aiden, but they came into view a few moments later.

"I'm fine!" Nicki shouted. "I'm better than fine! I had a breakthrough last night!" Her hair was piled up on her head in a messy bun, and her eyes were bright as she bounced into the living room. "Oh, waffles... yeah, okay, I'll eat, but then we need to have a meeting. A group meeting to talk about what comes next." She grinned at Alex and waved before scooping up the last waiting clean plate and heading into the kitchen. "Guarding your weapons gave me time to think. I've never really looked at Mjǫllnir or Cathanáil before, not closely." Nicki's grin turned almost menacing. "It was very helpful for a project I've been stuck on."

Looking towards Aiden, Alex searched his face for any signs of worry. He just looked amused and a touch annoyed. Not a new thing then. Alex frowned. She hadn't seen this before, and she and Nicki had lived together. Strange that even now there were new things to learn.

"Leave her be," Aiden said. "She doesn't often lose herself in a project, but it happens."

"I don't remember it," Alex said.

"She did have her own room," Aiden replied. Shaking his head, he watched Nicki sit down at the table. "I'll get some more eggs. Anyone need anything else?"

"No," Avani said quickly. "I'm full. It was a wonderful breakfast, Aiden. Thank you."

"Be sure to thank Timothy," Aiden said. "I swear that he did most of the work."

"Have you eaten?" Alex asked, suddenly aware that Aiden hadn't been sitting with them. "I mean, you helped out and haven't eaten yet."

Aiden laughed and smiled at her. "Let's just say that there was a lot more bacon originally. I'll have the last waffles that come out. Don't worry."

They finished breakfast with Nicki talking excitedly to Avani. All of her nervousness was gone in the rush of energy. Alex had a bad feeling that there were empty soda cans up in Nicki's room. That she had seen before. Avani was smiling gently and nodding. Jenny caught Alex's eye and grinned. Biting her lip to keep any teasing remarks at bay, Alex gathered up the plates of those who had finished as Aiden sat down with a stack of two fresh waffles.

Timothy was sitting on the kitchen counter, happily munching a corner of a waffle with a tiny bowl of syrup beside him. There was a small half scoop of eggs in the bowl, and Alex wondered just how Timothy ate. Did he have tiny forks somewhere or was it all by hand?

"Thank you for breakfast, Timothy," she said. "It was very good."

"Aiden did the waffles," Timothy replied. His dark eyes were gleaming. "He makes good waffles."

"Well, we'll have to keep stuff for the batter around then," Alex said. "I'll take care of the dishes."

Timothy started to protest, but Alex quickly filled the sink with water and started to scrub. It was tempting, very tempting to let the Brownie do everything, but it was almost nice to wash the dishes. A simple task that she knew how to do. For a little while, she didn't have to think about anything. The others brought in plates to her as they finished breakfast, and Alex could hear things moving in the living room.

"Come out when you're done," Aiden called. "Nicki wants to talk to us."

Raising an eyebrow, Alex put the dishes in the drying rack and then remembered that they had a dishwasher now. She snorted and reassured herself that she wasn't the first to forget that fact. Drying off her hands, she rejoined the others only to stop in the doorway in disbelief and amusement.

Nicki was being dramatic. She'd pushed around the furniture in the living room to create a circle of sofas, an armchair and a small table. Sitting in the chair, Nicki had a serious expression on her face and a blank notebook and pen on the folding table in front of her. The lack of furrows between her eyes and the fact that her arms were placed on the armrests reassured Alex that this wasn't a crisis mode meeting.

"I suppose you're wondering why I called all of you here today," Nicki said. Aiden snorted. Nicki ignored him. "We need to talk. A serious talk about where we want to take our magic and how to get there."

Glancing at Avani, Alex found their newest team member frowning slightly in confusion. Strangely, Avani's reaction didn't deter Nicki. That was almost a miracle, but Nicki seemed to have pumped herself up for this. The caffeine followed by sugary syrup probably hadn't hurt.

"Okay," Alex said. "I'll bite; just what do you mean?" She took a seat in a chair next to Jenny.

"For starters, let's all acknowledge that Merlin and Morgana are good mages." Nicki leaned forward slightly in her chair. "They are masters at using their magic, have faced a lot of enemies, and dealt with the changing centuries with dignity. I'm not trying to say that they're bad mages with what follows."

"They're resistant to using magic in new ways," Aiden said. He was leaning with his hand under his chin and looking unimpressed. "We know that, Nicki. They're adaptable but pretty damn stubborn."

"And while they say that they're open to trying new things, not much experimentation has really been done," Nicki said. "I think we've got enough control to try things now. We've got our own space. It's time to stop just thinking about what we want to try and make it happen."

There was a long pause. No one seemed sure what to say to that. Alex knew that Nicki was right, but the idea of trying something completely new was daunting. Judging from Nicki's expression, Alex guessed that her friend understood. Nicki had talked about a lot of projects, thrown out a lot of ideas, but nothing had happened. Maybe that daunting fear was universal amongst them.

"Where do you want to start?" Avani asked.

"With the blood spell and protection options," Nicki said firmly. "You said it yourself that you'd sleep better once we had it in place, so let's get that done." Picking up her notebook, she poised the pen above the paper. "Now, at your home, you had protections woven into the place with what looked like words. Were they special in any way?"

"No." Avani shook her head. "You can use any symbol or word. As I told you in Mumbai, the important part is that the word or symbol means something to you; that it helps you visualize your power."

"Exactly," Nicki said. She was starting to smile a little. "I suggest that we design a magic circle to use. We keep pushing our magic to Alex, but maybe a guide for all of us to focus on would be more useful rather than placing that whole burden on Alex. And maybe using symbols would let us add more... utility to the blood protection spell."

"It's a reasonable thought," Bran said slowly. "Visualization is always the hardest part of trying anything new."

"Maybe not a magic circle, exactly," Alex said. The others looked at her and Alex fought back the urge to squirm. "Remember when we were first learning magic and blacksmithing? Merlin had me create a small symbol, or maybe I made it myself, I don't remember, but the point is that we poured magic into those. We used them to make the Iron Gates."

"I remember," Nicki said.

"Yeah and iron holds magic better than most things, so I'd say something like that needs to be the base," Alex said. "A triskelion. Maybe using it as a hub of sorts for controlling the spell." She paused and looked at the others, expecting hesitation or doubt, but Bran was nodding thoughtfully, and Nicki was smiling.

"I think that sounds solid," Nicki said. "We've been puttering with what symbols to use, but the triskelion is a strong one for magic. I'm a bit concerned about the whole 'hub' thing, but given your ability to affect magic and sense it at a distance that could work."

"Yes, if Alex and all of you pour magic into the iron then it could be a battery for the spell," Avani said. She grinned in approval at Alex. "That's one of the largest problems we have with spells. A protection spell could fail if you lose focus." Bringing up her hands, Avani moved them awkwardly in front of her. "You need something that would hold the magic together; seal it to the area with a purpose. If you could do that, then I think it would work."

"And if we do that, do you think you could link it around the house?" Bran asked. "I know that sounds strange, but-"

"It's..." Alex licked her dry lips. "It's a bit different? Honestly, the idea reminds me a bit of the Iron Chain, but I think it is the most likely option to work. I've seen threads of magic, and I know that things can be connected like that. We'd need something, though. If you all start working on the symbols or words you want around the house, then I can go to Merlin's and create the central hub."

"We'll want something in the doorways," Avani said. "And the windows."

"They have iron in them," Nicki said. "Merlin and Morgana reinforced all the portals with iron."

"That will help, but that won't stop things like the Red Caps," Avani said. "But it could make the perfect link to the central magical battery. If we could carve something into the metal, then that would be the spell right there!"

"Simple enough," Aiden said. He rubbed his hands together gleefully. "I'll just do some welding-"

"That's not necessary," Bran said. He was smiling even as he gave Aiden a look. "We should be able to reshape it slightly with our magic."

"Yes," Alex agreed. Thor's voice rumbled at the back of her mind. For an instant, she saw a large finger moving across the metal of Mjǫllnir to create a symbol. "That isn't very hard." There was genuine optimism on everyone's faces. "Okay," Alex said. Relief filled up her chest and she smiled. "That's a plan for this house at least. Nicki, you and Avani work on the details of what we want to do with the metal. Plus, think about how we can recreate this in other locations. We can't pull out door frames everywhere."

"Maybe the old horseshoe over doorways trick," Aiden said. "That could do it if you set up the horseshoe to hold the magic. It may not be perfect, but it would be something that a Fae usually couldn't touch, and with a bit of magic maybe it could even repel Arthur and Red Caps."

"Good," Alex agreed. "That makes sense. At least it's worth a try." Standing up, she stretched out her arms. "I'm going to brush my teeth, and then I'll head over to Merlin's to work on the main hub."

"Wait!" Nicki jumped up, almost tripping over the coffee table. "I need to give you something first!" She bolted for the stairs only to stop sharply at the bottom. "Uh, is it okay if I go into your room really quick?"

"Okay..."

Alex blinked as Nicki grinned and rushed up the stairs. Turning back to Aiden, she waited for him to say something. He just shrugged.

"She doesn't get like this often," he said. "Not since sophomore year of high school at least. Her Gran forbade her from using energy drinks. This is a special state brought on by inspiration, lack of sleep, and caffeine. Thankfully, she loves to sleep."

A few moments later Nicki returned. A long leather scabbard with small symbols engraved into it and an odd belt hanging from it was in Nicki's right hand. In her left, she was gingerly carrying Cathanáil.

"Nicki?" Aiden asked. "Oh..."

"I- I made this for you," Nicki said. "It's been a work in progress for a while, but things clicked together last night when I was guarding the weapons." She laughed a little. "It was almost painful actually. Plus side though, magic makes hardening leather a lot easier." Thrusting both her hands forward, Nicki nervously smiled at Alex. "Put the sword into the scabbard," Nicki ordered. "I think...I think I'm onto something, but I need to make sure." Closing her eyes, Nicki exhaled, and a soft blue glow surrounded her hands. "I think it's ready."

The tiny marks on the leather scabbard glowed bright blue for a moment, but only a moment. Nicki was holding her breath as she handed it to Alex. The smooth leather felt odd to Alex's fingertips, but she tightened her grip on it. Cathanáil hummed in her right hand as she carefully lined up the sword with the mouth of the scabbard. Everyone was holding their breaths, and Alex almost laughed. This was just another experiment, not a life and death battle. She slid the Sword in. Nothing happened.

Jenny gasped. Alex looked at her friend to find her and Lance blinking and shaking their heads. They looked worried and startled and happy all at once. Glancing at Avani, she found a wide smile on the woman's face, but she also looked surprised. Alex looked back down at her hands. The sword was still there, snuggly in the scabbard.

"I can't see it," Lance said. "The Sword just vanished. I mean... I know it's there. I see Alex's hands, so I know that's where it has to be, but..."

Nicki clapped her hands, making a happy squealing sound. "Oh brilliant! Okay, okay, question time. Can you see the scabbard?"

"No," Jenny said. "Both the Sword and scabbard vanished. I saw Alex putting the sword in, but then there was nothing there."

"Yeah," Lance agreed. "And it's weird. I mean, as I said, I see her hands, but I'm sort of aware that they look... a bit off?"

"Magic is hiding something that you know is there," Aiden said. "Could be that the magical invisibility isn't perfect or that your brain is trying to compensate."

"Whatever it is, it's giving me a headache." Lance closed his eyes and rubbed them.

Alex pulled the Sword an inch out of the scabbard. "Do you see it now?" she asked Jenny.

"No."

She pulled it out a few more inches; her arms were now clearly positioned in the unsheathing motion. "Now?"

"Still nothing," Jenny said. Lance opened his eyes and nodded in agreement.

Drawing Cathanáil fully free of the scabbard, she watched the light glint off the iron as Jenny and Lance both nodded.

"I see it," Lance said.

"Yeah, it appeared once it was completely out," Jenny said. "At least you know it doesn't have to be all the way in all of the time."

"And the scabbard too?" Nicki pressed. "You saw them both at the same time; it didn't appear before the sword?"

"No," Lance answered. He gave Nicki a soft smile. "Looks like you got them synched up on the first try. Well done, Nicki."

Exhaling slowly, Alex slid Cathanáil back into the scabbard and ran a hand over the hard leather. This was good. At least, she thought it was. Now she could keep Cathanáil with her, and only mages would be able to see it.

"Avani?" she called. "Could you see it?"

Nicki turned towards the magician with interest. Avani frowned slightly and pressed her lips together.

"See? No, but I was aware of it. There was this slight glow in the air where I think it was." Her expression brightened. "That's actually a surprise to me. I'm not a mage; I was sure that I wouldn't see anything different."

"You may not be a mage, but you are attuned to magic," Bran said. "It would make sense that your brain would be harder to fool."

"Nicki..." Alex touched the hilt of the Sword and looked up at her friend. "This is amazing... truly."

"I've been working on it for a while now," Nicki confessed. A soft blush appeared on her cheeks. "It wasn't coming together very well. I was working on smaller scabbards for our daggers first, trying to improve on Merlin and Morgana's spell work, but after India it seemed more important to make it work for Cathanáil. But I needed something better than the old sheaths." Then she shook her head. "I put the same symbols on the baldric- uh, the shoulder belt, so it should stay hidden too."

Alex didn't know what to say. After last night it was beyond a relief knowing that she could have the sword with her. Her throat tightened up and her mouth went dry. Tears stung Alex's eyes, and she looked down as she awkwardly pulled on the scabbard. It was a bit strange, holding it in place as she fumbled with the small metal buckle of the strap.

"Well?"

"It fits," Alex said. "It'll take some getting used to." The weight of the Sword was comforting against her back, but it was odd. Even through her shirt, Alex could feel a warm hum of magic radiating into her body. "Feels good."

Smiling at Nicki, Alex hoped that she understood. Her friend nodded and stepped forward to hug her. Alex didn't mind the scent of leather that was still clinging to Nicki. She understood the source. Stepping back, she grabbed the banister of the stairs and grinned at the others.

"You guys work on the spell; I'll go and make us that hub. Or try to at least." She glanced back to Nicki. "And make sure that she takes a nap. She's earned it."

18

Holding Back Shadows

Podlasie Province, Poland 983 C.E.

Dobiemir clung to the branches of the tree. Ice was creeping over his skin, yet his fingers were beginning to burn as he held on for his life. The Shadows were circling Merlin and Morgana. Their long bodies were all a little different, but all of them had sharp teeth and claws. Regret filled him. How could he have come out here with them? Gratitude should only go so far.

Yet Slavko's health was better. It might be enough for the boy to survive on his own. A loud snarl and sudden vibration made him look down. One of the Shadows was clawing at the tree he was in. Panic gripped him, squeezing tightly around his heart. Its green eyes narrowed, almost angrily. He tried to open his mouth to speak, but the cold robbed him of breath.

"Dobiemir, run!" Merlin shouted. "Get away!"

"He won't make it!" Morgana snapped. Her voice quivered with rage. Magic flared around her, and for a moment Dobiemir hoped that she might deliver them from the situation. "Fight, Merlin!"

Silver magic exploded around them, lighting up the area and pushing back some of the Shadows. It didn't stop them and the creatures rushed back in. Merlin's green magic struck at a few more Shadows. The sparks scooped them up and threw them hard against the side of the hill. Rocks shook, and the eyes in the cave narrowed. The Shadows kept standing up.

"This isn't working." Morgana opened her hand and light surrounded them.

"Stop using light," Merlin scolded. "We know that doesn't work. The earthen wall held them back for a while the other day."

Morgana nodded and opened her palm. Silver magic gathered together to form three small orbs. Flicking her wrist, Morgana sent them jolting forth. They lengthened in the air before striking one of the Shadows. It convulsed backward. The dark fur of the creature shimmered and its legs collapsed underneath it. Not dead, but down.

"The magic is helping!" Merlin called. "Don't use fire or light! Just focus on the magic itself!"

"That's not helpful!" Morgana shouted back. But she created more of the small bolts and launched them.

More Shadows were injured by her wave of attacks, but it only knocked them down. They all stood moments later and snarled, marching forward again. While the attacks could harm them, it lacked killing force. Dobiemir frowned and curled his nose. There was something: a stray thought at the edge of his mind, but he couldn't catch it. One of the Shadows looked up at him and then started clawing at the trunk in the exact same spot. Another round of magical bolts pushed it back. His eyes jumped back to the cave. He tried to peer in, but no light seemed even to reach the cave. There were only the glowing eyes, but they didn't illuminate anything around them. It was just a hole of blackness. He couldn't even see a hint of a shape. Was it humanoid or something like these creatures? Beneath him, the branch creaked. The layer of ice on it cracked, and he sprang back to grab the trunk.

The ice had slowed. The dryness in the air stung at his skin, but he hoped it meant that there was no more water to turn to ice. Looking back at the mages, Dobiemir hissed as the Shadows closed in. Suddenly vines burst out of the ground. Dobiemir's eyes widened with shock and glee as they twisted around the legs of the Shadows. They fought and tried to pull away. A few lowered their mouths and began gnawing on the vines. There were flashes of silver, and more vines began to spring up from the ground and coil around the creatures. A snarl echoed out of the cave, and the eyes flashed brightly. But whatever was inside did not come forth.

"Dobiemir," Morgana shouted. "Come down!"

Hissing in pain, Dobiemir wretched his fingers open. The cold clung to his skin and was sinking into his bones. It was difficult to move. He sucked in sharp, pained breaths every time he moved his leg. As he slowly climbed down the tree, he waited fearfully for a Shadow to grab him or for his limbs to fail. His feet touched the ground just before his arms gave out. Stumbling back, he gasped for air as Merlin caught his shoulder to steady him.

The Shadows were pulling and chewing on the vines. More magic was swirling around them and into the ground to make more vines, but they were withering. Dobiemir could see the dull brown color of dying plants creeping up the vines inch by inch.

"We need to go," Merlin said urgently.

The older mage pushed him back the way they'd come. Stumbling forward, Dobiemir grabbed one of the thick tree trunks to stabilize his aching legs. Then he pushed himself towards the next. Maybe it was just in his head, but with every step, the world seemed to be growing a little warmer. He could still hear snarling and looked back.

Merlin and Morgana were slowly walking backward, their hands glowing as more and more vines burst out of the ground to bind the Shadows. He couldn't see into the small cave any longer, but Dobiemir was sure that the eyes were narrowed in anger. Still, nothing was coming forth, and the Shadows were now in a small cluster by the cave as the vines dragged them back.

Stumbling forward, he kept trying to put more distance between himself and the Shadows. Hope was beginning to grow in his chest. They might make it back home from this foolish trip. A loud growl made him look back. One of the Shadows had finally torn free. Merlin shouted something just before more vines ensnared the Shadow. More were pulling free. The pounding of his heart grew faster and faster and filled his ears.

Morgana spun around and waved her hands. The silver sparks of her magic rushed forward and solidified into a wall of ice. It pushed out with a strange crackling noise, forming almost a circle around the Shadows before colliding up against the hillside. Behind it, Dobiemir could just barely see the shapes of the Shadows and hear their howls of protest. The wall seemed to be holding. He turned and kept moving. Following the game trail, he kept an ear out for the Shadows or any other threat. His feet were steady now even as his heart thumped wildly. Merlin seemed to know the way ahead of him, and Dobiemir trusted the mage to get him home.

With every step, it was easier to keep his balance and breathe. The ice was fading, and the sounds of the Shadows were growing faint. Swallowing, Dobiemir noticed his hands were shaking, and he rubbed them together nervously. Their group moved quickly, and this time he didn't stop to gather useful plants he spotted. Overhead, the tree canopy was thinning as they came closer and closer to the village. Flickers of sunlight overhead nearly made him cry in relief.

Then, finally, the trail finished curving around the hillside and sloped downward. Things here were familiar, and he could see evidence of recent woodcutting. Sunlight caressed his skin, helping to dispel the last effects of the unnatural cold. Running out into the road, Dobiemir gasped for air. The sun was warm on his skin and harsh on his tired eyes. Tears of relief pricked at him. His knees quivered, but thankfully he was able to stay upright. Morgana and Merlin came closer, and he finally turned his attention to them. Both looked tired. There was lingering fear in their eyes, and Morgana's hair was a mess from the trees. She spun back to the forest, silver magic dancing around her fingertips.

"I don't think they'll follow," Merlin said. He was glaring into the trees. "Those were guards. The Old One was in that cave and didn't want to be disturbed."

"Then it shouldn't be sending out those Shadows and frightening the locals!"

"I don't understand either," Merlin said. Stepping forward, he put a hand on Morgana's shoulder. "The wall was an excellent idea, Morgana."

"I was afraid that they'd just snuff out a fire wall," Morgana said. Then she frowned slightly, watching the trees quizzically. "Though... I thought they'd have destroyed the wall much faster than that. I'm not even sure if they did."

"What are you thinking?" Merlin asked. There was a hopeful note in his voice that made Dobiemir straighten up and listen closely.

"I'm not sure," Morgana admitted. "It just seems strange that such cold creatures of darkness wouldn't absorb magic in the form of ice. I wasn't thinking clearly. I just wanted something to hold them, and I've never had your talent in shaping the earth." Morgana flexed her fingers and rubbed them carefully. "Now I find myself wondering if ice made by magic is... harmful to them?"

"Ice," Merlin repeated. "It sounds impossible, counter-intuitive, but we have tried light, fire, earth, and even more raw magic with little luck. You may be onto something. Next time we encounter them, let us both try ice."

"Next time?" Dobiemir croaked. He coughed to clear his throat. "You're- you're not going back there, are you?"

"I fear that we may have to," Merlin said. Shaking his head, he moved closer to Dobiemir. "I'm surprised that we got away." The remark made Dobiemir shudder. "That was an Old One, but it is far gone. Leaving it in this area unchecked could be devastating for the environment and your people. You saw how quickly the plants nearby were dying."

"We escaped because it didn't want to strain itself," Morgana said. "That's what these Shadows are for. It's experimenting with its powers now that it has turned into something new. It's studying the area, studying us." Morgana's agitation was apparent. "Even if we're right about the ice, that thing has power. I could taste it in the air."

"I agree." Merlin nodded to Morgana. "We can hope that it doesn't mean harm, but even if it does not intend to, it is causing it. The Shadows did seem to act as scouts, and now as guards. We need to prepare ourselves and learn more." Turning back to Dobiemir, Merlin smiled. "But for today, I suggest that we return to your home and rest. There is nothing more to be done now."

Blinking at the mages, Dobiemir repeated the words silently to himself. That was it? How did they recover so quickly from near death? Morgana sighed and nodded down the road towards his home in a silent demand for him to start moving. Slowly, Dobiemir began putting one foot in front of the other. His bones still ached from the cold, and his skin was dry, but he relished the sunlight with each step. Merlin and Morgana fell into step behind him. Guarding his back, he realized with a jolt. His stomach tightened, and he sped up a little just in case.

No one was out near the forest. They were alone on the narrow road. Dobiemir couldn't blame anyone for avoiding the area. Honestly, he never wanted to go near the forest again himself now. His fingers tightened on the strap of his bag. Somehow, he'd held onto it, but he was already wondering how much of it was still useful after being near so many Shadows.

They didn't speak the whole way back to his farm. He kept waiting for Merlin or Morgana to say something, anything, but neither of them did. Seeing his home almost made Dobiemir's knees give out. It looked the same as always, with no signs of trouble. Slavko was in the yard near the animals, moving chopped wood up against the house. The boy turned and caught sight of them. A smile lit up Slavko's face, and the boy climbed over the fence and rushed towards them. His smile faded as he came closer, and he slowed.

"Father?" Slavko asked. "What happened?"

Moving closer to his son, Dobiemir put his hand on the boy's head and played with his fine hair. His son was barely past his hip and still had more growing to do. His hand dropped to his son's shoulder, and he pulled him closer. Thankfully the boy didn't protest and pressed himself closer to him.

"We had a bit of a scare," he said. The words were hard to form. Holding back a shiver, Dobiemir pushed away the memory of the glowing green eyes. "That's all. We're fine."

"Yes," Merlin said. "But at least we know the area now, and that those things can be stopped."

"They can be delayed," Morgana corrected. "That's hardly assured victory, Merlin. Though it is nice to have some ideas."

"Father?" Slavko was looking up at him with fear growing in his eyes. "Are you alright? You weren't hurt, were you?"

"I'm fine," he promised. "They never touched me. Morgana and Merlin protected me."

His son turned and smiled at the two mages. Morgana blinked in surprise before a softer expression took over her face. She nodded to Slavko as Merlin smiled openly. The moment was over quickly, and Merlin sighed, turning his attention back to Dobiemir.

"You need to learn," Merlin said. He offered Dobiemir a warm smile: he clearly felt none of the worry that was plaguing Dobiemir. "You are a mage, and these things and what is in that cave are unlike our prior enemies."

"We need help," Morgana agreed.

"So... just the three of us?" Dobiemir asked. "What can I do?"

"We'll teach you," Merlin said. Dobiemir wanted more information. "We'll teach you to use magic, but we'll also see who we can call on for help."

"Do you think that's wise?" Morgana asked. Frowning, she looked back towards the forest. "This is an Old One. We don't want to risk any siding with him."

"He's powerful," Merlin said. "And we have no idea how to fight him. We need help, and other Old Ones may have ideas." He sighed and glanced towards Dobiemir. "Besides... only one mage in the area. The odds aren't in our favor."

"Fine," Morgana groaned. "But be mindful. The last thing we need is a group of Old Ones deciding now is the time to take over the realm."

Judging from Merlin's expression he didn't think Morgana's concern was serious, but the words made Dobiemir worry. He tightened his grip on Slavko, and the boy looked up at him. Those green eyes flashed in the front of his mind. Something was in that cave, and it hadn't liked them being nearby.

"Father?" Slavko called. "What's going to happen?"

"I'm not sure," he admitted. His chest constricted at the words. "I'm not sure, son." Looking back towards the forest, he thought that it seemed darker than usual. Like even the leaves were dying off. "I'm honestly not sure, but I'll look after you. I'll keep you safe."

"I know, Father."

He wished that he had his son's faith in him. The boy gave him a smile before running off to feed the animals. Dobiemir watched him, allowing his eyes to follow his son's stronger movements. Slavko climbed over the fence and tugged the bundle of wrapped hay to the goats' trough without collapsing. His son smiled as the animals moved closer and pushed his hair out of his face. Slavko was out of bed and able to help on the farm. The cough was gone, but... Shaking his head, he turned back to Merlin and Morgana only to find them watching him. There was something in their eyes. Something that he almost recognized, but it was gone too quickly.

"So... how do I use magic?"

19

Forging Something New

Merlin's workshop was hot and dry. Even having the windows open did nothing to help circulate the air, and as much as Alex wished she could cool down, she knew better than to lower the temperature using her magic. The furnace was humming, filled with red-hot coals that shimmered to her sight as the heat created ripples in the air. A thin bar of iron was beginning to glow orange, and Alex readied herself with the tongs.

Pulling it out, she quickly turned to place it on the anvil. In one smooth motion she shifted the tongs to her left hand to hold the hot metal in place and picked up Mjǫllnir with her right hand. The Iron Hammer thrummed in her hand, sending pleasant vibrations down her arm that were strangely soothing. She inhaled slowly and held the air for a moment as the magic in her chest sparked to life. It rushed down her arm and into Mjǫllnir. With a practiced motion, Alex began to hammer the piece of hot metal, lengthening it a little bit further.

Once that was done, she put it back into the fire. Two finished pieces were waiting next to the furnace, glowing softly with stored magic. Alex wasn't completely sure what she was doing. It was hard to focus. Alex's mind kept jumping around even as she hammered the iron band into a spiral shape using a combination of the anvil horn and magic. A soft shimmer flowed over the surface of the cooling iron.

Heat rolled out of Merlin's furnace and over her skin. Alex had stripped down to a light tank top and had her hair bound up on her head. She still had Cathanáil on her back. The weight resting against her spine made it easier to breathe. Its soft hum filled her ears, forming a soft melody when mixed with the smash and clash of the Hammer. It wasn't the sort of thing that Alex had found comforting before, but it was now.

Safety. Keeping that word in mind, Alex pushed more and more magic through Mjǫllnir. Her dark gray magic flickered over the surface of the Hammer, and the triskelion design lit up with a bright blue glow. Like lightning. Thor's magic dimmed slowly to the same shade as hers. Moving quickly, Alex heated the ends of the coils in the furnace, pushing a little more magic into them as she did. Putting Mjǫllnir down, she arranged them on the worktable in the proper formation to make a triskelion, but even with the heated ends they didn't seal together as she would have liked.

After a moment of debate, Alex decided to forgo the welder. She'd have more precision with her magic. Extending her pointer finger, Alex heard it crack slightly after so long gripping tools tightly. The dark sparks of her magic appeared quickly enough. With a quick flick of her finger, Alex focused the magic into the center of the triskelion shape. There wasn't any resistance. The metal swallowed her magic and heated up immediately. Biting her lower lip, Alex leaned forward and stared hard at the metal, urging it into the proper shape. If she could have used Mjǫllnir to push more magic into the shape, she would have. The ends of the three pieces melted further, turning hot orange and joining together.

Alex pulled back and ended the stream of magic. The metal began to rapidly cool. She just hoped that she hadn't hurt the workshop table.

Then again, she decided as she looked around, none of the old tables were in good shape. Half of them had deep burn marks and the other half were covered with unfinished projects that were gathering dust. Merlin's hobby of blacksmithing had taken a hit when they'd entered his life.

Looking over her shoulder, Alex noted the top of the safe. The Chalice was in there, tucked away and hopefully safe. Tightening her fingers on Mjǫllnir, she allowed herself to wonder about Arthur's victim for a moment. Only a moment. Guilt welled up, and she closed her eyes to breathe. The heat filled her nostrils and throat. She should ask Merlin and Morgana what had happened. But she knew that if there had been good news, they would have shared it.

Shuddering, Alex walked over to one of the side tables and picked up another iron ingot. It was hard not to sink into her guilt and fears as the metal heated up, but Alex did her best to stay focused on her task. She pulled the iron out with the tongs, picked up Mjǫllnir and got to work lengthening and narrowing the piece. With every swing of the Hammer and crash of iron to iron, more gray sparks were pounded into the metal.

Once it was thin enough, Alex bent it over the anvil horn and started to curve the metal. Reheating it a few more times and pounding out more of a curve, Alex kept glancing at the triskelion to gauge how much more she needed. After the fourth time she gave up and pulled the mostly complete circle out of the fire. It cooled rapidly in the air, and Alex carefully brought it to the triskelion. Setting it down, Alex waved her right hand and commanded her magic to pick up the triskelion section.

The triskelion floated into the air, and Alex grinned. Flicking her left hand, she pushed out some more magic that scooped up the circular piece. As they floated in the air, Alex fit the two parts together and forced the last bit of the circle to finish curving around the triskelion seal. Picking up Mjǫllnir, she grit her teeth and tried to keep her focus as she hit the metal two more times in hopes of putting a bit more magic into the symbol. A few well-placed streams of magic welded the edges of the triskelion to the circle and secured the design. Letting go of her magic, Alex caught the iron seal and set it to the side. With a grateful sigh she wiped her forehead, feeling both relief that she was done and a bit of pride that she'd managed it in only a short time.

It wasn't all that impressive. The magic finished seeping into the metal, leaving the surface as dark wrought metal with a few visible tool marks. Alex reached out and called on a little more magic. Dark sparks sank into the metal, and with a soft flicker, the last tool marks were smoothed out. Straightening up, Alex studied it for a moment. There was a soft glimmer in the metal. It was barely there. She was confident that only mages would see it, but hopefully it would be enough to power their spell.

The triskelion was almost perfect. This time she'd managed to get all the coils about the same length and the curves the same size. A longer and thicker band of iron surrounded the triskelion, nestling it in a circle. Alex was reminded of the metal artwork that she'd seen in home décor shops in the past. Smooth and elegant. It was a far cry from the first one that she'd made. Alex frowned. She'd given that one to Arthur not long after they'd first met. Now, Alex wondered what had happened to it.

Pulling off the apron, Alex flinched and groaned. She hadn't stretched before starting. She never did. Sighing, Alex carefully flexed her sore fingers and rolled her back. The muscles protested but loosened a little bit. A glance at the finished project made her feel a bit better, and she started cleaning up.

Her sweat had dried and the furnace had started to cool when Alex caught movement out of the corner of her eye. Out the window she saw Merlin crossing the back lawn. Alex held back a sigh. She'd known that he'd show up sooner or later. Wiping off her hands, she set Mjǫllnir on the table next to the door. It opened a moment later and Merlin stepped inside, his eyes widening slightly. Green magic was shimmering around his hands, but it vanished a moment later.

"Alex? What are you doing here?"

"Working on a project. You did say that I could use the forge whenever I needed," Alex answered. Looking over her shoulder at him, she smiled and shrugged. "Nicki was in a creative zone and we made a plan that we're going to try. Avani's family has spells that can be used as alarms, but they run out of magic. Since I know that magic can be linked together, we're going to use Avani's spell, but power it from a central location. I've put a lot of magic into this symbol that we can hang on the wall inside." She picked up the symbol and held it up for him to see. "Pretty good huh? Made it in one go."

"I see..." Merlin trailed off as his eyes landed on something over her shoulder. "Is that Cathanáil on your back?" Merlin asked. His voice was almost alarmed. "You really shouldn't be walking around with that! If someone sees you and calls the police-"

"Only mages can see it," Alex answered. She set aside her work and turned fully to Merlin. She couldn't help but grin. "Nicki figured it out. Only mages can see the sword and scabbard. When the sword goes into the scabbard, both vanish from sight. We tried it in front of Jenny and Lance. It was great! Even Avani can't see it."

"I- I... are you certain?" Merlin's expression was dubious and hopeful as he narrowed his eyes on Cathanáil's hilt.

"Positive." Alex reached up to her chest and opened the buckle. The scabbard started to slip off her back, and she quickly grabbed it and swung it in front of her. "Take a look."

Merlin moved closer and bent down a little to study the small markings engraved into the leather. "Interesting," Merlin said. "She's used triskelions: that isn't surprising, but she's also used some unfamiliar symbols as well."

"I haven't looked," Alex admitted. "But you did say once that symbols were just a reflection of what we wanted." She examined the markings herself. There were several small triangles that joined at their tips to form a circle. That didn't make sense to her, but she had a suspicion that it came from a book or something. "She's been working on it for a while, but finally got it. We have a non-iron magical item now." She wasn't sure what to make of Merlin's expression. He still didn't look like he believed it. "It works, I promise. I'll try it out tonight downtown in one of the parks if you like. If anyone asks, we can say it's for a play or something, but if it works Merlin, then I could keep Cathanáil with me all the time."

"That would be good," Merlin agreed slowly. His fingers were still brushing over the surface of the scabbard. "Are you sure that it works?"

"I doubt that Lance and Jenny would lie about it vanishing," Alex said. Her temper was beginning to flare, but she held it in check. "Come on; you know that Nicki has been interested in magical items since day one."

"That's true." Then Merlin chuckled, but Alex noted a shadow of worry in his eyes. "I never truly thought that she'd manage such a thing. The question will be how long it lasts."

"What do you mean?"

"There have been other magical items over the years," Merlin said kindly. "But unlike iron, they eventually fade."

"So, I'll keep putting magic into it," Alex said. "Besides, I think that it might be getting some power from Cathanáil. The sword has been humming all morning. A sort of pleasant hum."

Again, she had no idea what Merlin was thinking as he looked at her. Then he exhaled and nodded, suddenly looking much older. Alex braced herself for something more, but then he started to smile.

"You children have surpassed all my hopes for you," he said. His voice had gone soft, and almost sad. "So creative. You work so well together. So eager to try new things." Reaching out, he put his hand on the top of Alex's head. "And you, Alex, one of the best incarnations of the Iron Soul yet. I know that Arto would have adored you. He'd be proud to be a part of you." Then he dropped his hand off of her head.

"Uh, thanks."

They stared at each other for a moment, Merlin watching her with searching eyes. Alex tried to gather her courage, but the words kept sticking in her mouth. With a soft cough, she moved away from Merlin and grabbed her open bottle of water from the table, keeping the scabbard clutched in her other hand. The older mage was still watching her as she took a drink.

"So," she finally said. "Any news from the hospital?"

"I'm afraid his family is coming to say their final goodbyes. The story is that a brain problem made him act erratic and come to Oregon. I believe they've agreed to organ donation." Merlin made a thoughtful hum. "You're angry with me."

"I- I don't know," Alex said. She looked towards the safe again. "I want to help. It doesn't feel much like we're heroes if we don't. I went back for those kids, but I didn't help that man because I was afraid that you were right about it being a trap."

"I'm sorry if I was harsh," Merlin said. "How you children view all this and how Morgana and I view it is different. Sometimes I am sternly reminded of that. We... we are old, and worry about different things. That

Chalice is an invaluable tool, and I hesitate to risk it. Still, I understand your desire to help."

"Thanks, but that doesn't make it better," Alex said. "If nothing else... even if we didn't use the Chalice, we should have tried to help with normal magic."

"Perhaps, but I still worry that Arthur might have plans for that," Merlin said. His tone was soft. "This is war, Alex." Then he smiled a little at her. It was a brittle smile. "Forgive me for not greeting you earlier." Rubbing his eyes, Merlin fought back a yawn, and Alex stared at him. "If you need anything-"

"I'm fine," Alex said. "I was going to head home with this." She gestured to her creation. "We'll let you know how the spell goes."

"Perhaps Morgana or I should-"

"Rest, Merlin," Alex said. "You clearly didn't sleep last night. We'll be fine. It's just an experiment. We're not brand-new mages anymore."

To her surprise, Merlin nodded in agreement. The shadows in his eyes were darker now. He gave her another fragile smile and turned to leave the forge. Alex stared at him. Something had just happened, but she didn't know what. Her eyes dropped to the scabbard, and she tried to remember the past conversations about enchanting. Nicki had always been curious, but nothing had ever really happened with it. Now that she thought about it, Merlin and Morgana didn't really have any magical items. Merlin had a triskelion pin that he wore at the university that she thought might be magical. Morgana had a necklace, but Alex didn't think that was magical. Was this really so different? Had Merlin's staff been enchanted or just a good method of channeling his magical power?

Moving to the window, Alex watched Merlin cross the lawn and head into the house. His reaction left an uneasy feeling in her gut. She didn't know what it was, but Arto's voice whispered his concern at the back of her head. Frowning, Alex tried to understand just what was going on. Arthur was being creative and vicious with his magic, and they were finally making some progress. Swinging Cathanáil and its scabbard back over her shoulder, Alex quickly fastened the strap once again.

Shaking her head, she turned back to the forge and picked up the now cool iron symbol. The metal glowed where it touched her hand, and Alex smiled. She had a good feeling about this. It was just what they needed to seal the magic in place. Picking up Mjǫllnir in her left hand, Alex tucked the seal under her arm and headed for the doorway. She and the others could worry about explaining everything to Merlin and Morgana once this was done.

20

Raising the Alarm

Bran was optimistic. He hadn't been optimistic in a while. Knowing that Arthur was still out there and expanding his repertoire of magic left a bitter taste in his mouth. Most of the time, it all came down to distracting himself from worrying about Arthur. Classes, homework, and projects could keep him busy. But today Nicki's excitement was infectious, and Avani's confidence that they were onto something had created a pocket of hope in his chest.

Avani and Nicki were running the show. In her excitement and slowly approaching caffeine crash, Nicki was behaving almost normally around Avani. Except for the moments when she trailed off and clutched her coffee to her chest like a zombie. Then Avani gave her indulgent smiles.

"Put your phone away," he hissed at Aiden.

"Don't take this from me," Aiden whined. He was tapping on the phone like he was typing something, but it was definitely pointed at Nicki, who was yawning and blinking at Avani with big doe eyes. "She'll be grateful at her wedding."

"Not with those bags under her eyes," Bran said. Reaching over, he plucked the phone from Aiden's hand and ignored his cry of protest.

"Don't be mean, Aiden. Just think of the damage she could do if she turned against us. I, for one, do not want a prank war in this house."

"It wouldn't be that bad! Could even be good for morale."

"Nicki just made a magical scabbard that hides Cathanáil. Do you really want to see what she'd come up with for revenge?"

Aiden did stop in consideration and looked over at Nicki. With a slight pout, he sighed and nodded. "Fine. Spoilsport." Grabbing his phone, he put it in his back pocket quickly. "And for your information, Nicki did say that the scabbard drew magic from the sword."

"She thinks," Bran corrected. "That's an assumption, but seriously, Aiden: be careful tickling a slumbering dragon."

Aiden rolled his eyes but smiled. Shaking his head, Bran left his friend to his tasks. He was pretty sure that Aiden wouldn't do anything too stupid. And if he did, he could honestly say that he'd tried to warn him. Nicki would probably allow him to make Aiden sleep in the living room during the fallout so that he could stay in their room.

Kneeling at the side of the house, Bran pushed back the branches of one of the small shrubs that hid the house's foundation. He inhaled slowly and gently pulled on the spark of magic flickering below his heart. A jolt of heat spread down into his gut and up his spine. Yellow sparks appeared around his right hand, and Bran reached into his pocket to wrestle out the small sheet of paper. The symbol combined a triskelion with a vector mandala. Extending his index finger, he focused his magic on the concrete of the foundation and deliberately carved the symbol into it. It was slow work, and his hand shook as he moved his finger, but the magic knew what he wanted and kept the mandala perfectly symmetrical.

Smiling, Bran eyed the symbol with satisfaction and a bit of curiosity. He hadn't given the whole visualization aspect of magic enough thought if it could compensate for uneven human movement. He stood up and checked on the others. He saw Nicki at the other end of the foundation on this side and figured the others were spread around the house at this point. At least they didn't have any neighbors too close by to wonder what they were up to.

But someone was coming up the drive on a bike. He should have tensed up, but Bran doubted that Arthur would ever travel on a bike. His sense of importance demanded at least a motorcycle. With the helmet he couldn't get a good look at the rider until the bike came to a stop and he walked towards it.

"Hello, Aisling," he greeted.

Aiden's sister took off her helmet and climbed off the bike. The teenager offered him a small smile. Her dark brown hair was much shorter than before, now only hanging to her shoulders. Those familiar piercing brown eyes searched him for a moment, making him almost uneasy. She was taller than the last time he'd seen her, and Bran searched his memory trying to remember how old she was. He knew that the age gap between her and Aiden was at least five years.

"Hey, Bran," she said. "It's been awhile."

"Yes." He tried not to shift awkwardly. "It has been. How are you?"

"Fine."

"High school going well?"

"As good as it ever can," Aisling said. Then she glanced around the front yard. "Is Aiden here?"

"He's around here somewhere," Bran replied. Turning around, he looked for Aiden, but he was still out of sight. "Uh, give me a second to track him down."

"Are you going to use a spell?" Aisling asked. Her eyes lit up a little, a lot like Aiden's did when he discovered a new combo in a game.

"No, afraid not. He's just around the house. I was going to walk around."

"I'll come," Aisling said. "It's not like I'm going to see something magical and blow the secret."

Something in her voice gave Bran pause. It was tense, almost afraid, and he studied her for a moment. Aiden hadn't said anything about problems in the family, but maybe he just wasn't ready to talk about it. Nodding, he smiled again and gestured for Aisling to follow him. They went around the back. Aiden was kneeling on the ground beside the back door. Red magic surrounded his hand, and he was looking at a sheet of paper that Bran knew had the same symbol as his.

Aisling started to move forward, but Bran put his arm out in front of her. "Let him finish," he said. "There's magic around him."

It only took another moment for the red magic to vanish from around Aiden. He stood up and stretched his arms. Then he blinked in surprise as he turned and spotted them. There was a flicker of near panic in his eyes, but he quickly smiled.

"Hey, Sis. What brings you out here?"

"I wanted to talk to you," Aisling said. She walked towards her brother. "Haven't had a chance in a while."

"I know, sorry about that." Aiden smiled bashfully. "Moving into the new place and resuming classes has been a bit rough. You know what they say about junior year."

"Not really," Aisling said. "Freshman in high school, remember?"

Bran sighed in relief. At least he'd gotten the high school part right. Barely.

"Well, you'll learn." Aiden walked over and opened his arms to his sister. She rolled her eyes but didn't argue with hugging him. "It's good to see you though. Are Mom and Dad here?"

"Nope, just me. I rode over on my bike."

"Great," Aiden said. He stepped back from her. "So... what's up?"

"I was going to ask you that," Aisling replied. She nodded pointedly to the foundation where about half of one of the symbols was visible.

"Oh, nothing, we're just-"

"I'm not an idiot you know," Aisling said. Her tone was calm, but the undercurrent of anger made Bran look back at Aiden's sister. His friend was blinking at her in surprise. "Something is wrong... isn't it?"

"Something has always been wrong," Aiden replied. "I told you, Mom and Dad about what happened."

"Yeah, but you said that he was gone." Aisling was watching her brother carefully with sharp eyes. "He's coming back, isn't he? Arthur?"

"Maybe." Aiden sighed and crossed his arms over his chest. "We aren't sure what's going to happen. The Iron Gates are solid and keeping the realm closed, and the problem in India has been resolved, but Arthur is still out there. We have something he wants, or at least something that he used to want."

Bran's eyes jumped over to Alex, who was trying to act like she wasn't listening. Cathanáil was still on her back, safe in its scabbard with its hilt glittering in the sunlight. But Aisling couldn't see it.

"Aiden, you told us about what happened," Aisling said. "But you never talk about it now. Mom and Dad are really worried. They've been worried, but don't want to push you away. You've been avoiding us."

"Hey, come on! I'm home a lot, and I'm still helping at the bookstore. I'm not avoiding you."

"You don't like talking about magic."

"Look, what happened put me in a coma. That was hell for you guys. I don't want to bring up bad memories or hurt Mom and Dad."

"We know that this isn't your fault," Aisling said. She looked ready to shout at him but then took a deep breath. "Sometimes... I wonder what it is like. Being a mage, having magic. I envy you that." Aisling shrugged, a soft blush coloring her cheeks.

"Don't, seriously. The novelty wears off fast. Some of it is still cool, but the whole saving the world thing is scary."

"So, there is danger."

"Like you said, Arthur is still out there. We think he's going to try something." Aiden gestured to the symbol he'd carved into the concrete foundation. Aisling knelt to get a closer look at the small triskelion. "These symbols are magically tied to an alarm system. We're experimenting with new spells to keep us safer. I promise that we're trying to stay safe and do what we can." Aiden dropped down next to his sister and wrapped an arm around her. "I'm sorry if I seem distant, but when I'm home with all of you, I just want to be Aiden. I just want to be your brother and Mom and Dad's son. I want to forget about all of this for a while."

In the corner of his eye Bran saw Alex flinch. His chest tightened and he turned away from the siblings. He hadn't called his mother in over a week. Now he was certain that it was overdue. Aisling stepped closer and hugged her brother again. Tense silence surrounded them until Aisling patted her brother's back. Smiling, she walked over and hugged Nicki, who looked both pleased and uncertain of what to do with the teenager.

"Good to see you, Aisling," Nicki said. "Staying out of trouble I hope?"

Aisling shrugged. "Still learning to navigate high school. Give me a few more months and we'll see where I'm at." Turning to look at the gathered group, Aisling's gaze settled on Avani and she smiled. "Hello there, I'm Aisling Bosco, Aiden's sister."

"Uh, right," Aiden said. "Aisling, this is Avani Desai. She's from India."

"I'm a magician," Avani added. "It is a pleasure to meet you, Aisling."

"A magician? So, you can use magic?"

"Yes, but not like your brother can. I have to use formulas to summon magical energy. Still, it is a long tradition in my family." Avani's smile was warm, and Aisling smiled in return, finally allowing some of the tension around them to fade.

"Do you do lessons?" Aisling tilted her head curiously.

"Aisling!" Aiden scolded.

Avani just laughed. "I'm working with Lance and Jenny right now. Once I've settled into school and they've managed a bit of progress then perhaps you and I can talk."

Bran rolled his lips together tightly to keep from laughing. Aiden's expression was interesting. It wasn't full-on panic, but he was definitely unsure of how he should feel. On the one hand, Bran was sure that Aisling would have a talent for magic. Her insight was... unusual. Glancing down at his legs, Bran smiled and remembered the first time he'd met Aisling. She'd been sure that he wouldn't need his leg brace forever.

Aiden dusted off his hands and looked at Avani eagerly. "How many more symbols do we need, Avani?"

"I think that should be enough," Avani said. Her words were cautious as she moved slowly around the back of the house. "There are many symbols now, and we've got them around all the portals, but they are also discreet. I think this should do."

"You're doing magic," Aisling said to Aiden. "I want to see. I've barely seen you do anything."

"We're testing a protection spell," Aiden said. He rolled his eyes at his sister. "And I'm not your entertainment."

Aisling grinned smugly, opening her mouth to say something only to blink in surprise. "Whoa," Aisling said softly. Bran turned to look at the girl: she was pointing into the trees beyond the yard.

A moment later a bell chimed somewhere in the air around them. Out of the corner of his eye he saw a flash of dark gray at the edge of the foundation. An instant later he realized that it had been one of the markings.

"That's the alarm!" Avani shouted. The bell chimed again. It was soft and yet rang in his ears all the same.

Running to Aisling, he spotted figures moving in the trees. They were almost as tall as humans and dressed in long coats with hoods over their heads. He relaxed and touched Aisling's shoulder as they came closer.

"It's some Fae," he said. "It's okay. They won't hurt us."

Glancing at Alex, he found the blonde frowning slightly as she peered at the advancing group of Fae. They were close enough now that Bran could see their pale hands and some silver, almost translucent hair. All of them still had their heads down to avoid the sun. He began to move forward to go and meet them in the trees. Alex grabbed his arm and shook her head.

"No... stay here. Everyone."

"Alex?" Nicki called. She was looking between Alex and the Fae.

"I just... there's something off," Alex whispered. Then louder, she added, "Lance, Jenny, Avani, why don't you give Aisling a tour of the house?"

Bran braced himself for an argument from Aisling. But instead, the teenager turned and looked hard at Alex. Then she slowly nodded and all but ran to the back door. Jenny and Avani were right behind her with Lance placing himself firmly between them and the Fae. They headed inside, and Aisling only stopped for a moment to look curiously at the approaching group.

There were five of them in total, and Alex stopped at the edge of the shade. "Hello," she greeted. "What can we do for you?"

One of the Fae beckoned her closer without a word. Alex stayed put, and Bran moved forward. They all did. In the corner of his eye he saw some of the symbols still glowing softly, and the bell sound was still chiming. The Fae drew back at their approach and Alex waved her hand, gesturing for them to stop.

"What's going on?" Alex asked. "Why are you here? Do you have news about Arthur?"

"Yes," one of the Fae said. "Please, the sunlight is too much. Come closer."

"We won't harm you," Alex said. She stepped forward, and Bran did the same. The Fae retreated further. "They won't harm you," she repeated.

"We want to speak with the Iron Soul alone," another of the Fae said.

"I'll tell them everything afterward," Alex said. "That's just how it works. Please, just tell us what you came here for." She looked into the trees behind them. "You could have just driven up, you know. Or called."

"This cannot wait."

"Then stop waiting," Alex said. Her right hand was twitching slightly. "Tell me what you need."

The Fae looked at each other. Their hoods still hid their faces, but their behavior had put everyone on edge. Bran flexed his fingers, feeling his magic gathering. They shouldn't be enemies. The blood protection spell kept any Fae creatures who meant harm out. But Arthur was experimenting with magic, and this group was acting strangely.

Sunlight reflected off metal. A knife was slashing through the air at Alex. Throwing his hand forward, Bran released a wave of yellow magic, and made the air ripple. The knife was knocked to the side by a few inches and the Fae were thrown back. They scrambled to their feet, swaying and fighting to regain their balance. Alex turned towards them, her right hand grasping at the side of her neck. He couldn't see if she was hurt, but her eyes were wide and fearful. He hadn't thrown the knife off target enough!

Grabbing Alex's shoulder, Nicki pulled her back from the Fae as Aiden conjured fireballs in each of his hands. Bran wanted to look back and check on Alex but he kept his focus forward. If Alex was hurt, Nicki would tend to her. The Fae started to draw weapons, including a few more knives and three guns. His hands moved before he even thought about it. Yellow sparks spun around the Fae and pulled the weapons from their hands. One tried to grab a gun as it was carried away. A fireball collided with its chest.

The floodgates opened. Bran pulled the weapons towards him, un-willing to let the Fae even attempt another attack. Three red bolts blasted past him, striking one Fae and pinning it to a tree. The thing groaned, clawing at the bolts as the magic sank into its body. A moment later it began to fall apart into dust. Its cloak and clothing fell to the grass with a soft thump.

Lightning flashed past them. Bran's heart jumped. Two more Fae were caught in the lashing electricity and collapsed to the ground as dust and empty clothes. Then a long blue shard of ice hit the last one in the chest. It gasped and fell to its knees. Wide violet eyes looked up at him before they turned to dust. Stepping forward slowly, Bran searched the trees, but there was no sign of any more Fae waiting in the shadows.

"How the hell were they here?" Nicki demanded.

"I'm not sure," Bran answered. He knew Nicki wasn't really expecting an answer and he turned to check on her and Alex.

There was a smear of blood on Alex's neck, but thankfully no sign of a wound any longer. Thank goodness Nicki had reacted so quickly. Alex's hand was grasping Cathanáil's hilt as her gray eyes scanned the trees. Swallowing, Bran exhaled and turned back to the piles of clothing.

"You okay, Alex?" Aiden asked.

"Yeah: one of them got me, but it wasn't very deep," Alex said.

"Still," Nicki said. Her voice was thick with frustration. "They got close because we figured they had to be on our side."

"Must have been some of those that sided with Arthur." Now Aiden's voice was angry. "How did they get through?"

Kneeling, Bran examined the nearest pile of clothing. He didn't see any additional weapons, but he carefully picked up the hooded coat. Something tumbled free from the shirt when he moved it and hit the grass with a soft thunk. It was a medallion of some kind. Picking up the small round amulet, Bran carefully turned it over in his hand. It was made of bronze and an unknown symbol was stamped into the metal in the center. He wasn't the best judge, but it looked well crafted.

"Drop it!" Alex ordered.

He did as she commanded on reflex and dropped it on the ground. Alex and the others moved closer to him to inspect the medallion. Aiden stepped around him and kicked at the other piles until he revealed one with each pile. One for each Fae.

"Don't touch them," Nicki said.

"Alex?" Bran asked.

"They're magic," Alex said carefully. She knelt beside him and leaned over the medallion. "I don't know the symbol, but I can see the magic.

It's... I'm not sure. Sort of knotted up in the metal. The bronze doesn't want to hold it, but it is."

"Some kind of protection against the blood spell," Nicki suggested. "They shouldn't have been able to make it through."

"No, they shouldn't have," Alex agreed. "Arthur has done something... made something new now. He's trying to break through our defenses."

Bran frowned as he examined the medallion. Not even a full inch in diameter, it didn't look like anything special, but it did give him an uneasy feeling. Reaching into his pocket, he fished out the slip of paper he'd been using earlier and picked up the medallion. There was no thrum or hum. Instead, it felt cold to his touch. Bran wasn't sure what to make of that or Arthur's latest action at all. What was the point? And had it been just luck that he sent them today when they were working on the new protection spell?

21

Strange Allies

Podlasie Province, Poland 983 C.E.

Nothing bad had happened for over a month. Merlin and Morgana had kept their promise and helped his crops grow. In truth, it was one of the better harvests he'd had in some time. Slavko seemed stronger than he'd ever been and grew a little better every day. For the first time in several seasons, Dobiemir's boy was growing taller and a bit broader.

The extra food had been a blessing. The animals were healthy and he had stores of food ready for the onset of winter. He'd been careful in the village with trading some of his harvest for goods and raw materials. People were still fearful and whispering about the shadow monsters, but they hadn't been seen for some time. The reprieve was welcomed by all, and thankfully everyone had been able to save a little of their harvest. Still, Dobiemir was using his excess food to buy new tools that he didn't need yet to share the food around quietly. Directly giving it away was tempting, but would bring far too many questions.

Late in the evenings he thought he heard something in the distance, a whisper coming down from the hills. But whatever was in the cave hadn't come forth. Sometimes, he allowed himself to imagine that maybe it had been a dream. Sitting in the sunshine just outside his home, it was easy to imagine that the being of dark and cold was just a nightmare and forget about it.

Merlin and Morgana hadn't forgotten. The pair of mages trained him in magic, telling him a bit about previous battles they had faced and the importance of magic to the realm. Nothing helped. He had yet to conjure even the smallest spark. To his surprise, it was Merlin who was growing impatient with him while Morgana remained calm and gently encouraged him to try again. Slavko tried to watch as much of the lessons as he could around his chores. Dobiemir felt it was a shame that his son did not have such power. Then again, if Slavko had that power, then Merlin and Morgana would wish for him to fight that creature in the cave.

Stepping out of his home and into the morning air, Dobiemir stretched and looked around. The sun was creeping above the horizon and he could hear the animals waking. Looking around, he spotted Morgana walking down the trail that she and Merlin had worn from their small earthen hut to his own home.

"Good morning," she greeted. A yawn escaped her and Morgana glared at the rising sun for a moment. "Merlin has gone to check the perimeter of the forest."

"Alone?"

"He was confident in his ability to flee should a Shadow appear," Morgana assured him. "Though, I do get the sense that he'd like to give that ice idea a try."

"But you don't want to go into the forest yet?"

"We hope that the Old Ones will come soon," Morgana said. "Merlin and I... we don't dare go alone again. That thing would be ready for us."

"Strength in numbers," Dobiemir said thoughtfully. He nodded in agreement. "That might be the key."

"Yes, but I worry why none of the Shadows have returned." Morgana toyed with her necklace and glared up into the hills. "Did he learn what he wanted to know? Is he gathering strength?"

"Maybe it left," Dobiemir suggested.

Turning to look at him, Morgana raised an eyebrow and smiled in amusement. "Do you believe that, Dobiemir?"

"No." Looking down at the ground, he couldn't help but notice that there was still a strange chill clinging to the soil. "I know it's still nearby."

"Yes," Morgana said. "It's far enough away and keeping the Shadows near it that the land is not suffering as much, but it is still suffering. I believe that it is merely preparing defenses. As much as I want to confront it... Merlin and I will need help."

"What... is there anything else I can do?" Dobiemir looked down at his hands. "I'm sorry that I'm not very good with magic."

"You're a farmer at your core," Morgana said. "A provider and a father." Something in her tone was warm, almost wistful. "There is nothing wrong with being that. But your desire to remain only that holds you back." He lowered his eyes and Morgana was silent for a moment. "You are not the first mage that Merlin and I have trained. There have been many at this point. Problems such as this... somehow, there is almost always a mage nearby waiting for our guidance. The Iron Realm is strong and seeks to protect itself."

"It sounds alive."

"There is some kind of awareness behind it all," Morgana agreed. "But beyond that, I cannot say for sure what it all means. Merlin and I were born or created differently than other mages so that we can continue to train other mages and lead the fight. Some of the Old Ones have a fragile bond with the Iron Realm, but even that is beyond words to properly explain."

"What if I can't use my magic to help?"

"Then hopefully some Old Ones will aid us," Morgana said. "Before this mad Old One grows too strong."

Dobiemir didn't like that answer. It felt too weak, too dangerous. Swallowing, he closed his eyes and exhaled slowly. Morgana had told him about the spark of magic he could find within himself. She'd described it in several different ways, but thus far none of it had helped. Perhaps she was right about him. Maybe at the heart of things, he didn't want this power. He just wanted to look after his farm and keep his one surviving child alive. There was nothing wrong with that, but he needed to be more.

"Do not punish yourself," Morgana said. "Besides, Merlin is building the forge. Maybe working with iron will help you connect with the Iron Realm. If nothing else, it will be a valuable skill for you." She smiled. "And once this is over, you will have the benefit of a forge on your land, and Merlin and I's little stone hut."

"It would make for a good place to store food," Dobiemir agreed. "If I dug it down a little more, that would make it even better."

"Good; make plans for when this is over," Morgana said. "But for now, close your eyes and try to connect with your magic."

Rather than arguing or poking at more things that he didn't understand, Dobiemir nodded and closed his eyes. The sunshine was still warm on his skin, but the conversation had dulled his enjoyment of it. It wasn't difficult to slip into the dim awareness that Morgana had guided him towards. In his chest he could feel something, but it remained out of reach.

After a little longer he gave up. Morgana didn't argue with him. Instead, she just nodded to him and watched as he went off to join his son. Slavko was in a talkative mood. He frequently was nowadays. They fixed up the yard fence for the animals, and he examined the crops that his son had harvested in the coolness of the morning. The routine was comforting, even as Slavko asked questions that he didn't have an answer for.

"Father!" Slavko jumped up from where he'd been kneeling and pointed off down the road. "Look!"

Turning quickly, Dobiemir braced himself for an attack. But there were no Shadows. The sun remained shining, and instead he saw three figures walking up the road. None of them were familiar. There was an old man in a gray cloak who was using a walking stick. His companions flanked him on either side. One a man a little younger than him and a young woman.

"Slavko, go get Morgana," he said. Something about the three of them tugged at his instincts. In the light of the sun, they were a little too bright. "Hurry."

"Who are they, Father?"

"I'm not sure," he said honestly. "Now go."

The trio kept coming towards him as his son dashed off to fetch the mages. Nothing in their posture was hostile, and for a moment he thought that they might continue past. But the old man stopped and turned towards his house and farm with a thoughtful look.

"This is the place," he said. "There is a great deal of magic in the air."

"Hello," the woman greeted. "I am Sif. This is my father Odin and my brother Baldr." She gestured to each of the men in turn, the older one being identified as Odin and the younger as Baldr.

"Hello." He swallowed, suddenly aware of sweat gathering on the back of his neck. What was he supposed to say or do right now?

"Are Merlin and Morgana near?" Odin asked.

"Morgana is," he answered. His voice squeaked a little. "My son just went to fetch her. Uh, Merlin should be back soon."

"Thank you," Odin said.

Sif was a tall woman with golden hair hanging over one shoulder. A glow beneath her skin marked her as something else. She wasn't human, and neither were her companions. The old looking man had only one eye and wore a gray hat and cloak. Dobiemir thought he'd heard stories of a god like that. The younger man bore a strong resemblance to Sif with golden hair, bright eyes, and a face too clean and free of scarring to be human.

The sound of people moving behind him was a relief as they stared at each other. Looking over his shoulder, Dobiemir was grateful to find not only Morgana coming, but Merlin rushing along beside her. Merlin looked a little out of breath. He must have just returned when Slavko fetched Morgana.

"Odin," Merlin greeted with a nod. "Thank you for coming." Then with a slight smile, he turned and gestured towards Dobiemir. "This is Dobiemir."

There were some looks exchanged. Silent questions were answered without anyone saying anything, and leaving Dobiemir once more in the dark. Swallowing back a protest, he reminded himself that he just wanted to return to a peaceful life. If Merlin and Morgana felt that keeping certain details from him would help with that, then he was going to be grateful. Slavko made a curious noise, but Dobiemir put his hand on his son's shoulder.

"Slavko, you have chores to do," he said softly.

"Aww, but I want to hear!"

"No, go do your chores."

"Father-"

"Slavko."

The boy huffed, but there was no fire in it. He'd be forgiven soon enough. Then his son walked towards the animal yard: very slowly, but he went. Sighing softly in relief that his son wouldn't get any more tangled up in magic than he already was, Dobiemir looked to Merlin and found that the old mage was watching him with a smile. There was a wistful expression on Sif's face, but she said nothing.

"Thank you for coming," Merlin said. "I fear that an Old One has become corrupted. They are in this area."

"An Old One?" Baldr asked. "You're certain?"

"Very," Merlin replied. His face turned cold and stern. "Nothing new has entered our world recently. Magic remains at a low level, so the conflict is limited. Yet something powerful and twisted hides in the nearby woods."

"Do we know who it is- was?" Sif asked.

"We aren't sure," Morgana answered. "There are many local stories of deities, but a regional lord of light seems to be missing. Belobog."

"Belobog?" Horror filled Odin's voice. "But he's..."

"Father?" Sif asked.

"He came through with me. We were exiled at the same time. I haven't spoken to him for some time, but we used to-" Odin shook his head. "This is distressing news. He has been in the Iron Realm a very long time. I hope that you are wrong, Morgana."

"If you were friends, then perhaps, he will speak with you," Merlin said.

"Friends is too strong a word," Odin replied. Nonetheless, he nodded in agreement. "But I will do so. If we can reach him, then maybe we can help reverse what has happened to him?"

"What about saving him like Shiva?" Sif asked. "You said that he had been corrupted and had an artifact?"

"Yes," Morgana said. "He was, and the Iron Soul Lokpal entrusted the Iron Trishula to Shiva, but I fear we've not been successful in contacting him." The other Old Ones exchanged looks and Sif frowned. "The distance is... very great, and our magic is limited right now."

Dobiemir didn't understand this. He'd seen the pair do amazing things and breathe life back into the land. Yet they were speaking as if their power was nothing. Merlin caught his expression, and his features softened. Reaching over, Merlin gripped his shoulder gently.

"Magic is a force created by the intersection of two worlds that should not meet," he said. Dobiemir's eyes widened as he tried to make sense of the words. "There is always some magic in the world because of those who live here." Merlin nodded at the three Old Ones, and Sif smiled at him. "But it is not at its strongest. To you, it is very impressive, but there are limits on what we can achieve. I'm not sure that I would risk traveling all the way to Shiva's land to speak with him without more power to call upon."

"So, what are you going to do?" Dobiemir asked. He was almost afraid of the answer.

"Odin, I know that you have come some distance," Merlin said. "But if you are willing, I would prefer to examine the Old One as soon as possible. We have been giving it distance, but I fear he will only grow stronger."

"I agree," Odin said. "It pains me to think of another one of us going mad, but if it has happened, then we need to address it and quickly."

"Father," Sif said. "If it is Belobog then it won't be easy to stop. He's been here as long as you have." No one said anything in response to Sif's observation. Merlin and Morgana shared another worried look. "Is there a plan?" Sif asked. She glanced his way.

"We will inspect the area," Merlin said. "Then withdraw. There is no reason to fight today. I warn you; this Old One has created strange manifestations of its power. Shadow creatures that draw in heat and light. Baldr, you must be careful around them. All of you should be careful," Merlin said. "We don't know how they might affect you physically. Magic used against them does have some effect, and we believe that cold and ice may be their weakness."

Then, to his surprise, Morgana put a hand on his shoulder. "Will you come, Dobiemir?"

"Me? But I can't use magic."

"Not yet," Morgana said. "But perhaps today will mark the day that you do. Besides, you are a native of the area. You know far more about Belobog than Merlin or I."

"I-I'm not sure that's a good idea."

"You're a mage," Sif said. Her voice was almost sad. "It's your responsibility."

"We will keep you safe," Morgana promised.

"I'm not a warrior."

"No, but you are a mage," Merlin said.

Dobiemir once again had the feeling that something had been decided without him. Looking at the mages and the three new arrivals, he debated with himself for a moment. He didn't want to go. He wanted to stay with his son.

"I'm not sure what I can do."

No one answered him. Merlin just gave him a soft smile and nodded towards the forest. "It's up that way. It won't take long to reach it."

They started walking. Dobiemir inhaled and opened his mouth to argue. To say something. Nothing came forth. He exhaled in defeat and looked towards his home. Shaking his head and grumbling under his breath, he rushed into the small house to grab a shawl. If they were going near that thing again, then it was sure to be cold. For good measure, he grabbed a knife and secured it on his belt and picked up a leather bag. Calling out to Slavko, he promised that they'd be back soon and rushed to catch up with the others.

"Have you heard from Cyrridven?' Sif asked Merlin. She looked back towards him as he came up to the back of the group. "Is she coming to help?"

"I've tried to summon her," Merlin said. "But thus far, she has not responded. There has been no sharp rise in magic to wake her."

"Yes," Sif agreed. "I suppose she would be asleep for a while."

"And what of you?" Morgana asked. There was a sharpness to her tone that made Dobiemir's eyes widen. "I trust that you will be cautious."

"We will be," Sif promised. Her lips quirked, but she didn't seem insulted. "You may recall that we went into the waters for over a century not so long ago."

"I suppose that is true."

"It's been eight hundred years, Morgana," Sif said. "I wouldn't have thought that seeing us was so distasteful."

"It isn't," Morgana replied. "I just don't-" Morgana stopped herself and shook her head. Sif kept pace with her and briefly touched Morgana's shoulder.

There was history here, history he didn't know. Again, Dobiemir considered going home. How could they think that he belonged here? Yes, he was a mage. At least that was what Morgana and Merlin believed, but he had yet to use any magic. That flicker remained out of his reach. And now there were these new beings who had known them for many years. Why was he even here? Why would the world have even bothered to create another mage like him when it already had Merlin and Morgana? There was no answer for him. He didn't ask the question and just kept walking up the trail with the others into the hills.

Magic in the Metal

Arthur was ahead of them. Again. Alex wanted to be surprised, but that disquieting feeling at the back of her head was resigned. He was always ahead. Arthur was a snake. No; that was unfair to snakes. He was something worse — something parasitic that ate its host from the inside out. Arto's memories proved that. She'd hoped that in his new life Arthur was too arrogant and wild to play long games and fool them.

They'd been wrong. She held the bronze medallion in a bandana that Nicki had retrieved for her. The others were talking around her, mostly in the kitchen. Everyone left her alone. She hadn't moved from the armchair since Aiden had all but dragged Aisling back to the Bosco house, and Nicki had called Merlin and Morgana. The symbols on it didn't mean anything to her. They were vaguely familiar. She assumed they were Sídhe in origin and helped Arthur create the item.

"Alex?" Bran called. He sat on the sofa near to her, leaning forward to peer at her. "You okay?"

"I'm angry."

"I know, but-"

"I'm angry at us. We keep making assumptions about him. Thinking that we know what he'll do. We don't. Arthur is too... changing."

"Mercurial," Bran offered. "Adaptable."

"Yeah. I guess I thought he was a classic villain after the whole mono-loguing thing he did when he-" Alex cut herself off and swallowed. "Stabbed me. I've seen parts of his past, and I don't understand him. What makes him tick and act the way he does."

"You may not know the most important things," Bran said. "We don't know much about him, Alex. Does he have memories of his prior life? How did being trapped in an Iron Gate affect his soul?"

"And we're never going to get those answers."

"There's no one on standby to give exposition in real life."

Snorting, Alex felt herself smile and glanced out the window. Aiden would be back soon. Merlin and Morgana were certainly on their way. Merlin had promised to check on the safe hiding the Iron Chalice before coming over.

"What do you think about the medallion?" Bran asked. "You said the magic was knotted."

"Yes," Alex said. She narrowed her eyes at the gleaming metal. "Something is anchoring the magic to the bronze."

"Maybe your blood." Alex looked up at Bran sharply. "Arthur took a bunch from you. In theory, he had a reason. Probably to let him use the sword, but without the sword he might be using it in his magic."

"Maybe." Alex held the medallion up a little higher and examined the way it caught the light. "I don't see anything like that, but then again, I have no idea what it would even look like."

"Bronze is cast, right?"

"Correct. It has to be heated and poured into a mold," Alex said. "It's what was common before iron took over. Arthur might even remember it from the old days."

"The old days?"

"Uthyrn, my father, ruled over a tin and copper trading system," Alex answered. The words slipped out without her paying attention. "Medraut was his heir. I don't remember him spending much time with the craftsmen, but he probably at least knew the basics. Merlin taught me some of them before I learned to use iron."

"I see." Bran's voice was cautious and guarded.

"But imperfections in bronze can't just be removed. It has to be melted down and recast," Alex continued. "I'm not sure what adding blood would do to the metal." Then she frowned and brought up her free hand, wrapping the medallion in the bandana. She tried to flex the metal slightly. "It is a bit soft, though. Arthur could have quenched it in my blood. It's possible, but we can't prove it."

"If he did, then he will eventually run out."

"Maybe." Alex set the medallion, still in the fabric, on the table. "I'm tired of making assumptions. We thought we had something, but-"

"We still do," Bran countered. "The alarm went off, that odd chiming sound. It alerted us to harm. Even if Arthur can send Fae into Ravenslake, we do at least know that we can be forewarned." He pointed over to the side of the room where Alex had hung the large metal triskelion. "It isn't reacting to Timothy. It works, Alex. Today was still a step forward. We can go to sleep at night knowing that at least we have a warning system."

Pushing on the armrests, Alex stood up and quickly moved across the room. The metal triskelion gleamed in the sunlight coming through the windows. Reaching out, Alex ran a finger over the metal. Arto's memories and voice had quieted, but now there were whispered suggestions from the others.

"We'll need to make more," Alex said. "If Arthur can get through the blood protection spells now then your families aren't safe." She heard the sharp intake of breath from Bran behind her. "They aren't his priority, but we need to be sure. Tomorrow I'll go back to the forge. We can use water tunnels to get the protections laid quickly."

"And our families?" Bran asked. "The alarm might warn them, but then what?" Alex didn't answer. She didn't know how to. "Maybe you were right," Bran said. "Your brothers. Maybe you had the right idea. Arthur doesn't seem to care much about Lance or Jenny, but their families are vulnerable if he decides he wants to hurt them."

His voice was fearful. Alex didn't turn around. Bran was the calm one, the one who didn't panic. She didn't want to see that falling apart. Closing her eyes, she pulled on her magic. It flared to life in her chest and more energy rushed up through her feet. For a moment, she just let it linger in her veins, wrapping her in warmth and a sense of safety. Then, she pushed a little more magic into the metal.

Shimmering lines of magic appeared to her, uncaring that her eyes were closed. She could see the magic connecting, linking with the small symbols throughout the house. Power radiated outside of the house, forming an aura, a halo. All of it was visible, with hints of the different colors of their magic flickering in and out of her sight.

They formed a web through and around the house. Alex relaxed and exhaled. At least this part of the day had gone according to plan. Bringing up her hand, Alex carefully touched one of the strings connecting the seal to the symbols, providing a constant flow of magic. It hummed against her skin and brightened, pulling a bit more power from her.

"Are you seeing the magic?" Bran asked.

"Yes," Alex said. "I can see it. Our protection spell is good." She chuckled and shook her head, lowering her hand back to her side. "I wish I'd tried to see the protections at the Desai house."

The slam of a car door made Alex turn. She saw a humanoid form moving, surrounded by a halo of silver. Morgana was here. Opening her eyes, Alex moved toward the front door and pulled it open before the professor could even knock.

"You know, you're the owner," Alex said. "And we don't even pay rent, so you could probably just come in when you want."

Morgana's lips quirked into the start of a smile. "I will if I feel it's necessary, but I do know the value of privacy."

Stepping to the side, Alex let Morgana into the house. "Fair enough. I can at least report that our alarm spell did alert us to the Fae."

"But?"

"I'll go over that when Merlin gets here," Alex replied. "It'll be easier to only do this once."

Morgana nodded and touched her shoulder. The she sat down on one of the sofas, crossed her ankles and folded her hands in her lap. The slight frown lines around her eyes betrayed her worry. Her eyes kept jumping over to the new metal symbol on the wall with curiosity. Alex went into the kitchen and pulled a glass out of the cabinet. Timothy was pacing on the counter, not doing anything, but his nervousness was apparent. Smiling at him, Alex poured Morgana a glass of iced tea. Timothy didn't say anything. Nicki stumbled in and groaned as she reached for the coffee maker.

"Need more coffee," Nicki groaned. "Now... maybe magic will..."

"Don't use magic on the coffee maker," Alex said. Nicki whimpered, and Alex bit her lip to hold back a laugh. "Timothy, will you give her a hand?"

"We'll make a new pot," Timothy promised. He walked over to Nicki and patted the top of her pinkie with his tiny hands. "Just give it a few moments."

Retreating to the living room with Morgana's drink, Alex glanced at the door again. She'd feel better once Aiden returned. Then again, he might not want to leave his family alone right now. These medallions complicated everything. The blood spell wasn't going to be enough anymore, and their alarm system, while useful, wouldn't protect the Boscos or Nicki's grandmother. They'd need to adjust the spell.

"I can hear you thinking," Morgana said. "Breathe, Alex."

Handing Morgana her drink, Alex obeyed the order and took a deep breath. It helped, but it wasn't the solution. A knock on the front door made her jump before she realized that it would be Merlin. She rushed to the door and opened it to find the English professor protectively carrying a brown bag. Alex shivered as she felt the familiar hum of the Iron Soul's magic.

"Are you all alright?" Merlin asked. His eyes were wild as he looked past her into the house.

"We're all fine," Alex promised. "They cut me a little, but Nicki took care of it right away." Nodding towards the living room, Alex kept talking before Merlin could keep asking questions. "Aiden is taking Aisling home: she had stopped by for a visit, but he'll be back soon. Morgana is in the living room. Can I get you something to drink? Coffee? Water? Ice tea?"

"Uh, coffee… if you have some."

"Nicki and Timothy were just making a fresh pot," Alex said. She looked down at the bag. "You brought the Chalice?"

"You didn't give me much information, but it didn't seem wise to leave it with only a safe for protection."

"Fair enough. Go sit down. We'll join you in a moment."

Merlin blinked at her, almost suspiciously, but nodded and headed into the living room. Alex heard him greet Morgana and sighed in relief.

Bran came up the stairs and caught her eyes. His shoulders slumped slightly, but he nodded and headed into the living room. She went back into the kitchen where she found Avani pouring a cup of coffee for Nicki.

"Merlin would like one too," Alex said.

"I'll take care of it," Avani said. "Jenny and Lance are upstairs."

They were already at the bottom of the stairs as Alex moved to go up and fetch them. Jenny gave her a soft smile, leaning forward to kiss her cheek quickly. Lance offered her a smile of his own, reassuring Alex that he didn't mind Jenny's casual affection. There was a quiver of emotion in the back of her mind, but Alex wasn't going to address that today.

"We'll figure it out," Jenny promised.

They gathered in the living room without much fuss. Only Aiden was missing, and Bran had his phone out, making Alex believe he was probably texting the final mage of the group. Avani had given Merlin his coffee and Nicki was slumped next to Avani with her own mug. Timothy was on the coffee table, making sure that no one else needed anything. The bag with the Iron Chalice was on the sofa between Merlin and Morgana.

"Alex, what happened exactly?" Morgana asked.

Alex gestured at the medallion that was still on the table. "We had just set up the alarm system. It started going off, sounding like bells chiming to all of us, I think, and there was a group of Fae in the forest. We- I assumed that they were allies, since the blood spell hadn't destroyed them, so I got close. One of them pulled a weapon and attacked me. Nicki pulled me back and healed me while Aiden and Bran took care of most of them." Pausing, Alex licked her lips and tried to remember any important details. "Where each Fae had been, I saw a knot of magic. That's how we discovered the medallions in the piles of clothing left behind. We gathered them up using cloth, so we didn't touch them. They all look the same. The others are in a towel in the kitchen."

Morgana nodded and leaned forward, pulling back the fabric of the bandana to expose the bronze metal. She hummed softly, pulling out her phone and taking a photo. Merlin was eyeing it thoughtfully, but with much more suspicion.

"It's bronze," Merlin said. "Not iron. The marks are familiar to me, but I don't know if they say anything."

"I recognize them," Morgana said. Her lips were pressed tightly together, and her back was taught as a drawn bow. "They're Sídhe letters. Nothing too specific. Similar to the scabbard actually. They are markings for protection against magic. To turn back an enemy's power."

"Great," Nicki growled. "Copycat."

Morgana raised an eyebrow at Nicki but almost smiled. "As I said, similar to the scabbard, but that is an old form of magic. Iron is superior because it holds not only magic but intent. It will do what its creator wanted it to, even if they were not fully conscious of their desire."

"And now Arthur is using magic in bronze," Merlin said. "Creative, but it won't hold the magic for long. I suspect that the magic will erode quickly."

"Alex?" Bran turned to look at her. "Is there less magic now?"

Blinking in surprise at the question, Alex focused her gaze on the medallion. She closed her eyes and tugged gently on her magic. It rushed up her chest, and she slowly pushed it outward. Rather than a stream of power, she whispered for it to spread out. The magic did so and quickly illuminated the forms of her friends. On the table was still a knot of black, but it was smaller, and even now she was aware of its magic fading.

"Yes," she said. Opening her eyes, Alex sighed in relief. "It's being tugged at, for lack of a better word, by our magic."

"Good," Merlin said. "At least these medallions won't work long in Ravenslake. Still, it could be a problem. Arthur is vicious when he wants to be and has already assembled small armies of Fae creatures before."

"Yeah," Alex said. "But... look, Merlin, Morgana. We don't know much about Arthur's magic, or how he even has magic. We keep thinking about his magic like ours, and maybe that's wrong." Looking up at Morgana, Alex gave the older mage a soft, apologetic smile. "I hate to ask, but how did you become what you are? You've never really provided details."

"I was combined through a magic ritual with the Changeling that had been left in my place when I was stolen," Morgana said. "To be blunt, I do not fully understand myself how the ritual worked, but I assumed that the Síd magician who performed it was able to summon enough of his magic to Earth."

Merlin made a sound of surprise. "It was done in the Iron Realm?"

"Yes," Morgana answered. She looked at him curiously. "It only now occurs to me that you never asked."

"When I first met you, Morgana, Arto was my concern. You were not my priority. In fact, I saw you as the greatest threat to him," Merlin replied. He sounded a bit embarrassed and irritated. "There just... it didn't seem important. I knew what you were, but the details..."

"I don't know the details." Morgana sighed and looked back to Alex. "I'm sorry. The reality is that we know that the Sídhe have magic for the same reason we do. Magic is generated when their laws of physics clash with ours. Not all Sídhe can use magic. At least, it never seemed that way. Thousands of years ago, many of the invaders had at least some limited control over their power, but then again, they were better trained and prepared for entering our world."

"This is interesting and all," Nicki said. "But Arthur has never been off of Earth. His half Sídhe nature comes from the Queen playing Frankenstein. So, he shouldn't be getting magic from the clash of physics."

"Plus, the Iron Gates are still in place," Alex added. Sinking back into the armchair, she tapped her cheek thoughtfully. "So where does he get his magic? It is really from his Sídhe half, or is it tied to the Iron Realm because of the Iron Chain?"

"The Iron Chain is destroyed," Bran said. "So that might not be it."

"Maybe, but the effects could still linger," Alex said. Then she groaned. "I don't know. I saw her make him! But... I don't know. He was made using Fae flesh, but they haven't got magic anymore. And the Queen possessed Arthur's mother, so how would she have known that Arthur was a mage?"

"He might not have been," Merlin said. "We're trying to unravel something that we might never understand."

"The Queen used a piece of an Iron Gate to fuse Medraut's soul into Arthur," Alex said. "Maybe that could be part of his magic." She shook her head. "Then again... maybe the clash of physics is just a part of Arthur's own body." Glancing at Merlin and Morgana carefully, Alex really hoped that she wasn't horribly offending them. "Part of his creation might have been... more unstable than the pair of you."

"Maybe," Morgana said. Her tone was careful and even. "But Merlin is right: understanding the how isn't important. Not really. I know the mystery is difficult, but the critical question is how do we deal with this. Arthur and his mother are seeking ways to attack us here. These experiments might be merely harassment now, but if they do figure out ways to bypass the protections of iron, then things could get much worse."

"You mean the gates?" Bran asked.

"Maybe," Morgana said. "Arthur and the Queen potentially have allies waiting in the tunnels. The Sídhe civilization was one of expansion and conquest. I worry about how political fractioning and stagnation has affected them. They've proven that their lust for slaves hasn't vanished since the Iron Gates were first made."

More questions without answers. Alex closed her eyes. A headache was making itself known, creeping up the sides of her skull and settling behind her eyes. She listened. Nicki had more questions and suggestions. Aiden came home not long after. Morgana and Merlin had the sense to express their relief that Aisling was alright. At least it all made Alex feel better about her decision with her brothers. Then, she pushed her magic at the medallions once more and watched the last traces of Arthur's magic vanish. At least, there was that. They could work with that. Tonight, they could brainstorm and worry, but tomorrow she was going back to the forge.

23

Stalking the Enemy

She was dreaming again. Alex had become too familiar with the hazy way that the world appeared when she was dreaming. Sounds echoed just a little too much and colors were a bit strange. It was enough to reassure her that she wasn't in danger at the moment. Small flickers of memories played out around her, but they were random, leaving her floating through random images.

For a moment the familiar stone tunnels of the Sídhe stretched out in front of her. Alex swallowed as the memory pressed down. She wondered how the children she'd saved were now. Strange to think that it hadn't been that long ago, and yet it felt like decades. Walking forward slowly, Alex eyed the neatly fit stones that indicated she was deep in the tunnels. Were they still intact like this beyond the Iron Gates, or had the magic of the Iron Realm ripped them down?

The tunnels began to fade, the clear lines of the cut stone and their textures turning to smoke. It all blurred together into an empty gray backdrop. People appeared in the distance and walked toward her, some smiling and greeting her with old names and others frowning sadly. Her emotional reaction to seeing the faces of long-gone loved ones had dimmed. She'd had these dreams too often now for them to cause more than a bittersweet pang.

Around her the scenery changed once again, turning into a dark stormy sky. A ship's wheel appeared before her, and a mast and riggings beyond it. Back on the ship then. Alex sighed and steeled herself for the smell that was going to come. The ship rocked and rolled on the waves beneath her feet, but even this faded quickly. Nothing was tangible. She was just drifting through an odd mixture of memories in her subconscious. This wasn't helpful.

"I'm dreaming," Alex said out loud. The words echoed around her. She braced herself, ready to have faces appear and call to her in different names. "This is just a dream. If you want to show me something useful that would be better."

Around her, the cloudy gray background shifted. Closing her eyes, she inhaled slowly. In her chest was a flicker of magic. It rose slowly and danced over her skin. Alex didn't know if she was just imagining the feeling or if she was really using her magic. But this was a dream, and she wanted control. Walking through sad memories wasn't going to help.

Her magic hummed in response. It was comforting, reminding her that she had power here. For a moment Alex was left floundering in the mists. What should she do now? What was the next step? Dreams could be useful. After all, she'd seen her future in dreams, but her past wasn't what she needed to know more about right now.

"I want to see..." she trailed off. Swallowing, she ignored the request to see her brothers. Her gut told her that this was more than a normal dream. Alex couldn't remember the last time that she'd had a simple dream. If she used magic to reach out to her brothers then maybe Arthur would detect it and find them. "Arthur," she decided. "I want to see

Arthur." Her stomach twisted at the request, but Alex pulled on more of her magic. "Show me Arthur."

The gray nothing trembled. New shades of gray began to swirl in the distance, finally breaking up the bleakness. New colors appeared, dropping in like wet paint on a canvas, exploding out to form shapes. Red and black took over with hints of brown and yellow beginning to appear.

Walking forward, Alex became aware that the world around her was becoming more solid. The texture of a worn industrial brick wall beside her became clear and sharp. Reaching out, she tried to touch it but felt nothing. Her hand didn't vanish through the wall. She was just disconnected. With resignation, Alex rubbed her fingers together. She thought that maybe she felt that, but wasn't sure. The colors and texture, the details, expanded. Then she looked around.

She was in a room with a few high windows. It was dark outside, and large lamps hanging from the ceiling lit the room. A hardwood floor stayed silent under her bare feet as she walked. Bookshelves lined one wall and plush armchairs were set up near a small end table. It wasn't homey, but it was lived in. She turned to look at the far side. There was a kitchen with an island and a doorway leading into a dark bathroom. At the right corner was a hat stand and a heavy wooden door that Alex assumed led out. Scanning the kitchen, Alex looked for anything that indicated where she was. There wasn't any mail in sight, and the laptop on the island was closed up. She reached for it, but her hand didn't connect with the hard plastic.

The sound of a door opening made Alex turn quickly. Her eyes darted around for cover, and she moved into the shadows behind the island. She recognized Arthur at once as he stormed inside. He'd grown his hair out long enough that it was now tied back with a band. His blue eyes swept through the room but didn't settle on her. This was a dream... or something similar to it, Alex reminded herself. She wasn't really here.

Then another person came in. It was Scáthbás, but she looked far more exhausted than the last time Alex had spied on her. She braced herself for Scáthbás to notice her somehow, but she didn't. Instead, the woman tore off the long coat she was wearing and threw it angrily at Arthur. He caught it and moved to hang it up on the metal hat stand by the doorway.

"Mother-"

"That was a failure! An utter failure! If we can't deliver on some of our promises soon, the Red Caps will desert us!"

Blinking in surprise, it took Alex a moment to fully process what had been said. Scáthbás' hair was a mess of tangles, and the woman was running her hands through it frantically as she paced. Heeled boots tapped loudly on the hardwood floor as Alex crept closer and closer to them. She was ready for some sort of magical attack, but nothing came.

"Mother, please calm down," Arthur said. He sounded calm but worried. The familiar tone gave Alex pause. He'd talked to her like that, a long time ago. "This isn't helping."

"We need the sword!" Scáthbás snarled. "We've tried attacking the Iron Gates, but they draw power from the world around them. Their decay takes too long. I can't wait another three thousand years for them to fall apart!"

"We'll get the sword," Arthur promised. "The medallions worked, Mother!" Arthur's nose curled up with frustration. "The Fae I sent walked right into Ravenslake."

"Yes, but they were killed, and the medallions were found," Scáthbás said. She reached up, grasping Arthur's face gently with both of her hands. "Arthur, darling, you must be cautious. Yes, this was a victory in your magical ability, but you tipped your hand. The mages will know."

"That won't save them," Arthur huffed. He pulled away from Scáth-bás, shaking his head. "I can make more, while their precious blood spell won't be enough now."

"Allied Fae of the Iron Soul live in Ravenslake," Scáthbás said. "The blood spell has been altered by the current Iron Soul to let them pass. You're assuming they can't alter it again."

"Alex isn't that creative."

Flinching, Alex gasped at the rush of hurt in her chest. Then she viciously stamped it down. Caring about what Arthur thought of her was stupid. Beyond stupid. Yet there was a little part of her that was still hurt by his dismissal. Then anger took its place.

"She's still alive," Scáthbás said. She raised one perfectly arched eye-brow, and Alex shuddered with how much she looked like Morgana at that moment. "You tried to kill her, but she lived."

"That was Aiden's fault. He interfered-"

"And according to the Fae who are loyal to their Queen, she and the other mages have successfully dealt with Demons in India and at least one Old One."

"Two," Arthur grumbled. "She did kill Chernobog."

"Yes: a feat that even Merlin and Morgana couldn't manage when he turned." Scáthbás sat down in the armchair and eyed Arthur carefully. "Please tell me that you aren't emotionally compromised."

"No!" Arthur shook his head. "Not in the way you mean. There are just moments when she reminds me of Arto, and I can't help but want-" A low growl escaped him, and Alex blinked in surprise.

"There are more important matters." Scáthbás shook her head. "The medallions worked, but you should have had them steal the sword. Instead, the mages know what you're trying to do because you were impatient to show off."

"It wasn't like that."

"No? It seems like that to me. You failed to make any real impact on the mages, so you insult the Iron Soul to cover your failure. It makes me wonder if you really know anything about this Alex Adams like you claim to."

"We'll get the sword, Mother," Arthur said. "And I want the Hammer too. If we can destroy the Chalice that will be a victory for us."

"Yes, but once again, you've given the mages warning. Your attack this summer did nothing except warn them, and now this." Scáthbás touched Arthur's cheek again, running her fingers over his skin. "It almost makes me wonder if you're even trying to help me?"

"What?" Arthur's eyes widened and looked legitimately shocked. "Mother? How can you even say such a thing?"

"This human body is growing older." Scáthbás shrugged and looked up at Arthur coyly through her lashes. "And you did enjoy the company of two of our enemies."

"Jenny and Alex weren't anything special."

Scáthbás gave him a look, once again raising her eyebrow, but she seemed pleased. "Things will be different once we open the way and my people join me. It will be delicate, Arthur. I do not doubt that in my absence, others have tried to take and hold my throne." She laughed, a soft and sweet sound that had no business coming from her. "But I know the Sídhe. They'll be divided. I had strength and conviction that the others lacked. I will regain control!"

"Why do you want to bring them here so badly?" Arthur asked. "They're not loyal to you; not anymore. Just leave the Iron Gates and rule over the Fae here who have sided with us. The Red Caps like having license to kill, and most of the others are tired of hiding from humans."

"That's not enough."

"Then we could ally with the Demons or use some magic to release a nuke or something!" Arthur rocked on his feet and rubbed his hands together, a spark of excitement in his eyes.

"No!" Scáthbás' tone was harsh and cold. "No, I do not want the Iron Realm itself damaged! We need it."

"You keep saying that, but won't explain," Arthur said. "We can take this world! Even the greatest weapons of the humans could be dealt with easily enough-"

"You are but a boy," Scáthbás sneered. "There's much you don't understand, Arthur."

"Is this about the homeworld again?" Arthur asked. "Mother, you've told me about it. So, one world died."

"It wasn't one world!" Scáthbás glared at him, her fingers curling into tight fists. "Think, boy! Why do the others come here?"

"The Old Ones are exiles."

"Yes, but no new Old Ones have come into this world for centuries," Scáthbás said. "They are either very old or were born here."

"The Iron Gates-"

"Even before the Iron Gates, it had been some time since Old Ones came here. And when the Iron Gates fell, there were no signs of any openings to the world of the Old Ones."

"That doesn't mean that it's dead," Arthur argued. "Really, Mother, you're being paranoid. The government probably just changed."

"And the Demons?" Scáthbás asked. "No Arthur; something is wrong. We need Earth, and we need a way to open the Iron Gates. I must release the Sídhe into this world. We will conquer it and be safe at the trunk of the Tree of Reality."

Watching Scáthbás, Alex couldn't help but notice the hope in the woman's eyes. It wasn't the greed she was expecting. Taking a step forward, Alex moved to examine both of them a little closer. Then a sharp pain made her stop. Her chest ached. A dull fire was spreading through her body. Alex closed her eyes and focused on her magic. It was pulsing, but weakly. Stretched too thin. Opening her eyes, she looked around. The colors were beginning to vanish and bleed together. Small pieces of her surroundings were flickering, like a glitching video game.

"Mother?"

"I know this to be true, Arthur," Scáthbás said. "I have dedicated my life to ensuring that the Sídhe spread. These three thousand years have delayed the process too long. My-our kind must be secure."

"The Iron Realm will try to reject us."

"It tries to reject them all. Sídhe, Fae, Old Ones, and Demons, but they live. Without the mages, the Iron Realm can't fight back." Scáthbás inhaled slowly and relaxed in her chair. "Get me the sword, Arthur."

Panting, Alex swallowed and focused on Scáthbás. The woman's face gave nothing away. It was calm and cold, almost like a statue. Arthur was staring at her, waiting for something. She glanced between them, wishing she could understand what they were thinking. If this was real, as she believed, then maybe it could give her a clue about what happened next.

"I don't want to fight with you, Arthur," Scáthbás said. With a tired air, she leaned her head into her palm. "I'm tired. We will speak later, but leave the mages be for the time being. We need a plan: an actual plan to take the sword."

"We'll send in multiple groups. One will distract them, and the other will steal the sword," Arthur said. His voice was distant, almost echoing now with distortion. "It was easy enough-"

Scáthbás held up her hand to silence him. "My darling, that's enough. It's late, or rather early, and the human frailty in us needs rest."

Arthur was frowning still. Between his eyebrows, wrinkles were forming as he pouted. Scáthbás didn't look at him, but Alex was certain she knew Arthur was still there. Then he bowed slightly to Scáthbás, backing away from her. His fingers curled into fists, but he turned and marched towards the door. Nothing more was said, and Alex felt the burn of her exhausted magic growing worse and worse.

Scáthbás stood up and made a brief effort to smooth down her hair as she moved across the room. With an exhausted sigh, Scáthbás opened a large wooden cabinet to reveal the bottom side of a mattress. Around Alex, the world was becoming hazier as the former Sídhe Queen pulled down the bed and smoothed out the blankets. Moving towards the doorway, Alex hurried after Arthur, but the ache in her chest was growing worse. Reaching the door, Alex's legs started to collapse.

Heat rolled through her arms and legs. Sharp pains radiated out from her muscles. Suddenly she gasped and found herself looking up at a dark ceiling — her room. She was in her bedroom. Inhaling slowly, Alex held it for five long seconds before releasing it. Carefully, she flexed her legs. They moved, but the muscles protested the action.

Groaning in pain, Alex curled into a ball and rolled onto her side. Her fingers tightened into her blankets. Shifting her cheek further into the pillow, Alex struggled to muster the energy to get up. She needed to write down what she'd heard. Needed to try and regain some magic. Whatever she'd done to watch Arthur and Scáthbás had worked, but it had been difficult. Maybe she'd slipped past their defenses. That almost made her smile.

Sitting up, Alex reached blindly to the side of the bed. Her stuffed animal Galahad was almost knocked off the table, but Alex caught him. She hugged the old stuffed toy tightly. The soft lingering scent of her childhood home was gone now, but the memory remained. Exhaustion weighed her down. After a few minutes like that, Alex swung her legs out of bed and reached for her phone. Maybe it had only been a dream, but her chest still burned slightly from using too much magic, so she was going to be safe and make a note of everything that she'd heard. With any luck, some of it would be useful.

24

Not His Life

Things were moving fast now. Dobiemir wondered if that was how life went for mages. Days of everything being quiet and then suddenly everything moving all at once. As they moved deeper and deeper into the forest the world grew darker and darker. Plants were dying all around them, and a few showed strange signs of frost damage. It shouldn't have been possible in the summer, but it proved that the strange being was still here.

Focusing on his breathing as they walked, Dobiemir could feel a soft pulse inside his body. It might have been his heart and blood, but he was hoping it was his magic. If there was ever a time where he needed it, it was now. He shouldn't have come. Merlin and Morgana were wrong about him: he wasn't a mage, and that was becoming more and more apparent as they went on.

Then there was a sound ahead of them. A branch snapped and there was a soft cry. He froze. The others came to a stop ahead of him. Swallowing, Dobiemir leaned to the side just enough to peer around Baldr's wide shoulders. He was ready for the sight of Shadows coming towards them. Dobiemir braced himself for the onslaught of cold. But it didn't come. Something else was coming towards them.

It was a woman, but unlike any he'd seen before. Her skin was darker than his, almost the same shade as bronze. Her long dark hair had small glowing droplets of water scattered throughout, and a glowing circlet illuminated her face. She wore a simple gown that in the shadows looked blue, but he wasn't sure as the material was strange and much smoother than anything he had ever seen. Green eyes met his, and Dobiemir gasped as a strange vision gripped him.

A thick mist surrounded him. It clung to his skin and clothing, and yet the air was too thin. Voices were speaking in the distance before one word began to be repeated loudly. He didn't understand it, the word meant nothing, but more voices were chanting it now. Suddenly light exploded in front of him, forming an archway of stone and metal. Strange symbols on the doorway glowed and the light filling the opening twisted and churned like dirty water. The voices kept chanting, and then he was being pushed towards the light.

"It's alright," Morgana said in his ear. Baldr was holding his arm to keep him upright. "It's alright. Inhale," she ordered. He obeyed. "Good, now hold it in for a moment and then exhale."

Swallowing, Dobiemir followed her instructions a few more times. Then he carefully looked back at the woman. She was leaning against a tree and seemed a bit shaken herself. Nonetheless, she gave him a soft smile. When she started to turn, Dobiemir's eyes widened. At her side, hanging from a belt was a sword. It had no scabbard but instead what looked like a small trickle of water holding it in place. Blinking, Dobiemir tried to understand what he was seeing for a moment before giving up.

"Uh, thank you," he said to Baldr.

"You're welcome." Baldr didn't even look at him; instead, he was watching the newcomer with a hint of fascination.

"Cyrridven?" Merlin called. He stepped towards the woman. His eyes were wide and disbelieving. "When did you-"

"Yesterday," she answered softly. Turning her head, she looked up the hill. "I arrived in a lake a few miles that way. I've been on my way to see you." Leaning against the tree, she gave their small group a grateful smile. "I'm glad that you came upon me."

"I'm sorry," Merlin said. He stepped towards her and offered her his hand which she happily took. "I had not considered the lack of standing water nearby when I called to you."

"You called to me from a river alongside a village," Cyrridven laughed. "I did not want to frighten the poor humans. But I also... felt drawn to these woods, so the lake seemed the best choice." Then she smiled and looked to the Old Ones. "Odin, Sif, Baldr." She nodded to each of them in turn, her strange circlet illuminating her face and the nearby trees.

"I don't think I've ever seen you so far from water," Morgana said dryly. "This feeling drawing you in, do you think it was Belobog?"

"I do not know," Cyrridven answered. "It is possible, Morgana. Belobog and I have long known each other." Then Cyrridven stepped forward towards him. "I am sorry, young one. I'm afraid that my connection with the Iron Realm is so strong that mages often Connect with me the first time we meet. As you likely gathered, my name is Cyrridven."

"Dobiemir." He straightened up, reassured by her kind smile. "My name is Dobiemir."

"It is always a pleasure to meet a mage of the Iron Realm." She nodded deeply to him. "I am sorry that your life has been disturbed by the darkness growing in this forest."

"It's... it's alright," he answered. "It hasn't been all bad. My son was ill, but Merlin and Morgana have helped me."

"You have a son," Cyrridven said. Her voice was soft, and her smile widened. "I am grateful to hear that they were of aid to you." She turned slightly to look at the two mages in question. "They have good hearts, though I fear that sometimes they fail to connect with those they meet."

Morgana grumbled something and Merlin blushed, suddenly looking very bashful. Smiling despite himself, Dobiemir almost started laughing at the strange situation. But his eyes were drawn back to the hilt of the strange sword. The odd pulse beneath his skin grew stronger, making him shiver. Questions about who she was and how she had found them dried up on his tongue. The feeling beneath his skin was distracting, itching, and unpleasant.

"The sword," Morgana said. Her eyes jumped over to him. "What do you think?"

Dobiemir blinked as Cyrridven looked at them. She smiled again but shook her head. "No, I don't think so," she said. Morgana blinked at her and Cyrridven moved over to join her. "He is not a warrior, is he?"

"No." Morgana sighed softly, but her eyes were gentle. "I suppose not."

"We were on our way to investigate the cave that we last encountered Bel- whatever is in the woods," Merlin said. "Do you wish to-"

"I shall be fine, Merlin," Cyrridven said. "I prefer to stay in the water, but it is no more necessary for me than it is for Sif. I am a bit weaker in terms of my power without access to water and my awareness of magic is dull, but it does not harm me."

Merlin didn't seem reassured by the words and kept looking down at Cyrridven's bare feet. She wasn't bothered and instead gave them all a soft calm smile. Morgana chuckled and nodded towards the path.

"Come along then, Merlin," Morgana said. "This has already been a strange enough day, but we still have a task to complete."

The older mage nodded, but once again offered his arm to Cyrridven. She took it, and the pair followed after Morgana, leaving Dobiemir with Odin, Sif, and Baldr.

"Well," Baldr said. "This day has been... odd."

"We did know she might be coming," Sif said. They started walking. "I have never seen her away from water, though."

"I have," Odin said. "But not for a very long time. I hope that this does not bode poorly for our enterprise."

"We should have thought of it," Sif said. "Dobiemir, when we return to your home, would you object to us making a pond or a well of some kind? In case Cyrridven requires it."

"I- uh, no," he answered. "That would be fine. There's an empty and rocky patch of land not far from the house. It's never been good for planting: that might be a good spot."

Sif nodded in agreement, her eyes lingering on him for a moment before she walked a little faster. Odin kept pace with her and called to Merlin. Staring after them, Dobiemir looked at Baldr. The Old One was watching him with an almost pitying look. Anger flared in his chest. He knew he didn't understand what was happening here, but none of them were bothering to explain.

"Don't," Baldr said. "Just... don't, Dobiemir. This isn't the life you want, so be grateful that they aren't pulling you in."

Baldr shook his head and followed the others. Dobiemir's chest tightened. Part of him wanted to object. He was a mage too, even if he couldn't use his powers. Surely that meant something. Yet, he had Slavko, and Baldr was right. This wasn't really what he wanted. Shaking his head, he pushed away the odd emotions. They wouldn't help him today. Right now, they were only a distraction. Speeding up, he passed by Baldr and fit himself into the center of the group, hoping to overhear something that would provide an explanation.

They weren't helpful. Cyrridven was uneasy walking on the ground and leaned heavily on Merlin, to Morgana's amusement. The comments from the others made him believe that she was usually in water, but how that was possible, he didn't know. Morgana stayed close to him, and every time a branch shifted she took a defensive posture. Nothing came, but the air kept getting colder. He wanted to ask, but the words wouldn't form. Merlin and Cyrridven had gone silent. She kept looking back towards him, her hand brushing the hilt of the sword.

Hesitation filled her eyes. She wasn't sure. Someone else was as uneasy about this as he was. It was almost comforting. Dobiemir wanted to go home and think it over. Today had started normally, but now there were new strangers to contend with and not enough information about any of it. But Merlin was walking forward with long, determined strides.

They came to the cave far too quickly for him. Dobiemir hung back with Sif and Baldr as Odin slowly moved forward. Dobiemir's breath danced on the air, and he shivered as the cold sank in again. Silver sparks surrounded Morgana's hand as she watched for Shadows. Dobiemir swallowed. It was difficult. Fear clawed at his chest, urging him to run, but he stayed still.

"Belobog?" Odin called. He moved towards the cavern with slow, measured steps. Baldr stayed close to Sif, but Dobiemir could see the siblings watching with worried eyes. "Belobog, it is Odin. Are you there? Is it you?"

Bright green eyes suddenly appeared in the cavern. The terrifying chill swept over the area. The cold turned brutal. Out of the corner of his eyes Dobiemir saw the long shadows of the trees begin to twist. With a trembling hand he pointed to them, and Morgana nodded quickly.

"Belobog, stop this!" Odin took a step back. "Old friend, please try to listen. Try to remember!"

A roar spilled forth. The green eyes flashed, and the shadows turned and twisted. Shapes began to pull forth. Morgana threw her hand forward. An icicle struck the nearest half-formed Shadow. It yelped and collapsed. Odin stumbled back and hurried to Sif and Baldr. Dobiemir looked at Merlin, but the older mage was glaring into the cave. Green magic flared around his hand, and Dobiemir's eyes widened.

Someone grabbed his arm and pulled him back. All of his limbs protested. Suddenly, the stark cold really hit him and he started shivering. Sif was pulling him away. Merlin and Morgana were shouting something. It was a mess. He couldn't see the others. Shadow monsters were appearing all around them out of the shadows of the trees. Glowing green eyes were everywhere he looked — dozens of pairs coming closer and closer. Sif kept pulling. Or maybe Baldr was pushing. There was noise behind him. He looked back to find patches of ice on the ground. Merlin and Morgana were throwing strange spears made of ice and orbs that shimmered with frost. There was something beyond them. A large figure was reaching towards them out of the cave, made of darkness and those glowing green eyes.

"Keep moving," Sif ordered. "Stop looking back. This went poorly. Keep moving. We need a real plan."

Then they stumbled out into the light. Sif released him, and he took a few steps away from her. Inhaling a deep breath, Dobiemir suddenly became aware of the blackness that had been creeping into his vision. It started to clear, and he took another breath. Merlin and Morgana came out of the trees, Morgana still facing the cave.

"They don't seem to be following. At least the ice worked," she said. "But there were so many of them. He's gotten stronger."

"There were dozens," Odin agreed. "I've never seen anything like those."

"The ice works," Merlin said. "That's something."

"And we confirmed the worst." Morgana looked over at him. "Dobiemir, are you alright?"

"Fine."

"We shouldn't have taken him there," Morgana said. She looked at Merlin. "He needs more training, and we need a better plan."

"At least we know who we are dealing with."

"That thing is Belobog," Cyrridven said. Her eyes were downcast, and grief filled her voice. "I fear that we have lost him."

"Belobog?" Dobiemir repeated. Shaking his head, he fought off the haze trying to roll in. "But... he's the God of Good. He's one of the few that truly defends humanity and-"

"No longer, I fear," Cyrridven said softly. "I'm sorry."

"I... I don't understand." Dobiemir shook his head. "How does this happen? Why does this happen?"

"This is not our world," Cyrridven replied. Her voice was soft, sad, but rang of finality. "Belobog did not take the proper precautions... or perhaps he grew tired. That also happens."

"Yes," Merlin agreed. "We've seen that before."

"So, what can we do?" Dobiemir asked. "Against him? These creatures? What do we do?"

"He lives," Morgana said. "And thus, he can die. Do not lose sight of that." Moving over to him, she put a hand on his shoulder. It didn't help his rising panic. All those Shadows could come forth at any moment to destroy everything nearby. "We will deal with Belobog, Dobiemir."

"Let's just call it Chernobog and be done with it," Dobiemir growled. "He's not the good god anymore! If we have to fight him, then at least fight him as he is now." His head ached, and the cold was receding slower than usual. Even now, the muscles in his leg ached and were twitching. "I don't understand what it is you want from me? If the gods are real then surely-"

"Nothing is certain," Morgana said. "And don't call them gods: they aren't deserving of that title." Her voice was sharp and icy. "They're powerful, but they aren't gods."

"You don't believe in the gods?" Dobiemir asked softly. His eyes jumped to Odin and the others. "Are you a Christian then?"

"No." Morgana snorted, but then took a deep breath. "Dobiemir, they are beings from another world. I know that means little to you, but they are. But the longer they stay in our world, the more... challenging it becomes for them. Over time, many go mad. Belobog has gone mad. I believe that when you called him Chernobog, you were very accurate. What was once good and sane has been twisted into something far uglier."

"Uglier... that thing." Dobiemir shivered at the mere memory of the cold. "It was like a living nightmare."

"Yes, very distressing in appearance," Morgana said. "And much stronger than I would have expected. He might even be stronger now than he was before. Then again, he isn't holding anything back now." Morgana shook her head and turned to Merlin. "But that's not the real issue. We need to find some way to stop him."

"Perhaps Shiva could help," Merlin said carefully. "He has the Trishula. Lokpal was able to restore him with it. Maybe we should try to reach him again-"

"Shiva wished to be saved," Morgana said. Her lips curled into a slight sneer. "Lokpal told us the story, Merlin. Even near the edge Shiva did not wish to harm him. Chernobog is past that point. And that plan would require us reaching Shiva!"

"We haven't the power to destroy him," Merlin said. "At least, I don't think so. He's... very powerful. Those shadows of his are impressive. Fighting him and them at once will be a challenge."

"He was one of the first to enter your world," Cyrridven said. "He's held off the madness for so long, but it has finally taken him. I confess that even I had begun to believe that he would never fall. He kept to himself, but tried to help the humans that crossed his path."

"Yet he never became an ally of ours," Morgana said.

"No," Cyrridven agreed. "He didn't. Belobog disliked conflict, and you mages are constantly finding it."

"Part of our mission in this world, I'm afraid," Merlin quipped.

Dobiemir swallowed. Belobog wasn't a god that his parents or grandparents had worshipped much, but he was a figure of good. Thanking him for the good things that happened in a year was custom. But lately there had been nothing good to be grateful for. This madness that had infested the god might be the reason for that.

"So, because he's gone mad bad things are happening?"

"The Shadows spring from him," Merlin answered. "But... the gods do not have the power over your lives that you think they do. Nothing has that much power."

Dobiemir didn't believe that. But he didn't argue with Merlin. The pair of mages had great power: it made sense that they did not fear any of these great and terrible beings. But his power was nothing compared to theirs. He had a child to worry about. He would not be risking the wrath of something by speaking so against it.

"I can reach out to Shiva," Cyrridven said, returning to the original topic. "But last time I sought him out, he had started to sleep near the island. Other Old Ones have joined him in the area and follow his example. Even if he cannot help, then perhaps they can. I suppose it depends on the Demon population's behavior. And not all Old Ones are willing to communicate with mages."

None of it made sense. Their words meant nothing. Shaking his head, Dobiemir pulled away from Morgana's grasp and looked at the trees again. They were still. Almost too still. There wasn't even a breeze.

"Are you alright?" Merlin asked.

"I- I'm unsure," Dobiemir said. A strained laugh escaped him. "Life wasn't easy before you arrived, but at least I understood it better."

"I'm sorry."

"No... ignorance had its own dangers, I suppose," Dobiemir said. "And my son is healthier now. He grows stronger and has hope for the future. That's the point of it all. I'm a parent and I must try to give him a better life. I'm frightened, but if fighting Chernobog is the way to do that then I will."

Merlin was staring at him. The old mage's eyes were soft but proud. Dobiemir wasn't sure of the source of the look, but then Merlin's smiled widened.

"Ah... it is you then," Merlin said softly, almost to himself. "You are a good man, Dobiemir, I am grateful that we found you here."

"I haven't been of much help," he protested. "The villagers won't-"

"They are frightened and torn between beliefs," Merlin said dismissively. "I doubt that anyone could have won us their support. Honestly, we're lucky that they haven't sought to drive us off."

"That has happened? To you and Morgana?"

"Many, many times," Merlin answered. "We travel a great deal. Sometimes together, sometimes apart. Always moving and trying to learn as the world changes. It isn't an easy life, but there are times when I know that it is worth it."

"I've never been more than a few miles from my village," Dobiemir said. "I was born here. I'm not sure I'd like to leave."

"It was different when I was young," Merlin said wistfully. "In my day there was much more travel and trade. People went much further for events, trade, and even peace talks. But the world changes." He shook his head and looked towards the trees. "As do the beings in it." Walking forward, Merlin offered his arm once more to Cyrridven. "Come, we need to rest and regroup."

They walked past Dobiemir. Cyrridven offered him a gentle and worried look. Odin and Baldr nodded to him before following. Sif and Morgana waited, giving him a moment to recover. Closing his eyes, he tried to sort it all out, but it was too much. Too noisy and loud. Holding back a sob, Dobiemir found the urge to run returning. But then Morgana put a hand on his shoulder once more and gently pushed him forward on the path towards his house.

25

Into the Furnace

Anger was an unpleasant emotion, but when hammering out numerous metal bars as quickly as possible, it was a useful one. She'd gotten up with the sun and stopped only long enough for Timothy to give her some toast before coming to Merlin's. The old mage had come out in a rush when she started hammering. He hadn't stayed, still half asleep, but he'd checked on her a few times before the others dragged themselves over.

Lifting Mjǫllnir, Alex brought it down on the band of narrow iron. The tongs in her left hand glowed slightly, carrying the magic from her hand into the iron as she held it still. Her thoughts were chaotic, but her magic was easily sinking into the metal. Mjǫllnir's soft glow kept catching her attention out of the corner of her eye.

Beads of sweat were rolling down her neck. Even the bandana holding her blonde hair out of her face was getting damp. She glanced up, noting that Cathanáil was still leaning up against a worktable, safe and sound. Nicki was also leaning against the table, lingering next to the sword almost protectively. Straightening up, Alex shoved the metal back into the furnace and walked around to the other side where Aiden was pulling out another piece of metal.

"Take a break soon," he said. "Please."

"Soon," she promised.

She didn't have long. It didn't take much time for the metal to cool and reheat. Taking a deep breath to regain some strength, Alex slid the iron over the horn of the anvil and started hammering. Under the force of Mjǫllnir the metal began to bend. Alex shifted Mjǫllnir in her hand, turning it so that she was using the small hammer face and began tightening the coil. This part was slower work. More precise, but it also gave her more time to focus on pushing as much magic into the metal as possible.

The others gave her space to work. She didn't need them there, but she was grateful for the company. It was one of those days where she didn't know how to feel and didn't want to be alone with her thoughts. The churning mix of emotions and whispers was annoying, and only her need to work kept her grounded. Panic was trying to take over, and her mind was clawing over every detail that she remembered from the dream. None of it seemed helpful on the surface, but the information was frightening in other ways.

Another spiral was done, and Alex backed away from the furnaces long enough to use her magic to seal the pieces together. Aiden jumped forward to help, creating a tiny hot stream out of the tip of his pointer fingers. He looked so pleased with himself that Alex laughed.

"There's two done," Alex said. Setting Mjǫllnir down on a rolling tool bench, she wiped her eyes clear of sweat and dried her hands. "Wish I could wear gloves."

"Me too," Avani agreed. "It doesn't look right... you being so close to so much heat without gloves."

"Dulls the magic too much," Alex said. "I need full contact with Mjǫllnir." Rolling her shoulders, she looked over at the waiting pile of iron that Merlin always kept at the ready now. "But that takes care of two houses. Three to go, unless you want one for your family, Avani?"

"We already have alarm systems," Avani said kindly. "I'm confident that our home is secure from the Fae."

"I don't know," Nicki said. "Those Demons were able to attack. It might be worthwhile for us to go there and set up a blood protection spell."

"True: Arthur is going to look into who you are," Bran said. "And the Fae aren't common in India."

"You make a fair point," Avani agreed. "But my family has defenses. Let's worry about yours first."

"Right." Alex nodded and grabbed the nearly empty water bottle. She downed the rest and tossed the it back on the table. "Back to work."

"So, you're just going to make more of the symbols?" Jenny asked. She was sitting on the edge of one of the work tables, holding an iced coffee and nervously twisting the straw.

"That's the plan," Alex said. "Make them and use water tunnels to get around quickly. We'll get them installed in everyone's homes and hopefully discourage Arthur."

She was aware that the others were nervous. Both furnaces were going, and Bran and Aiden were switching out to help her keep the process moving. If they pushed, and her magic held out, then hopefully she could make them all today. They had classes tomorrow, but with Morgana's help, maybe they could take care of all the houses in a few days.

"This isn't going to fix the issue," Avani said. "The alarm is great, but it won't stop the Fae with Arthur's medallions."

"I'm hoping that he'll only send Fae with those after us," Alex said. The words were true enough. "And maybe I can boost the defenses of the blood spells around the houses." Even that didn't really fix it. People had to leave their homes. They had jobs and shopping and lives. "We'll do everything we can. I promise."

The others exchanged worried looks. It made Alex wonder if her speech was slurring or if her hair was greasy. Still, no one said anything. She moved toward the pile of iron. The edges of her vision were spotty, and she shook her head. A dull ache was beginning to set into her muscles and chest. Alex grit her teeth. Maybe she'd overdone the magic in the first two, but they'd need it. Bran caught her arm and Alex blinked. She had started to fall and hadn't noticed.

"You need to rest." Bran's green eyes were stern as they met her own. "Let us give you some magic Alex. If you're determined to do this, let us help."

"I don't trust another hammer," Alex said. "Mjǫllnir is the best hammer." Her speech was a little slurred. The words were ridiculous. Best hammer. She giggled. Bran nodded and pulled her over to the table. "It has the most magic. Thor made it."

"We know, but you're not made of metal. You need something to eat." He looked up, and Aiden nodded.

"I'll go and raid Merlin's kitchen," Aiden said.

"Where is Merlin?"

"He said something about going with Morgana to check the Iron Gates," Aiden said. "Something about a dream Alex had."

"Yeah." Alex didn't look at them. "Had a dream. Emailed Morgana and Merlin about it."

"And?"

"I don't know. I think it was real." She shrugged and glanced towards the furnaces again. "There's a lot to worry about. The Queen still wants to open the Iron Gates, but Arthur is more interested in conquering with the Fae."

"And you're only telling us now?" Nicki asked. Her expression was dangerous, still part feral from lack of sleep.

"I woke up and wrote it down," Alex explained. "You were all still asleep when I came here."

They all exchanged looks. Aiden was still by the doorway and looked confused. Nicki turned to him and pointed towards the house. Nodding, he jumped into action and headed for the house. Sighing, Alex turned towards the iron and prepared to pick more up.

"No," Bran said. He grabbed her hand and pulled it down to her side, keeping a tight grip on it. "Just wait."

"I need to finish these," Alex protested. "We need to secure your family homes."

"And we will." Bran's hand began to glow, and Alex looked down. She could feel the magic fluttering against her skin. "Just... let us give you some magic. Aiden will be back with some food soon, and then you can tell us what to do to help. I get that Mjǫllnir is your hammer and the seals are strongest when made with it, but tell us how we can help."

"Magic," Alex admitted. "That would be good, and helping run the forges. And Aiden can finish assembling the things after I shape them. They should have enough magic then."

The statement got her soft looks from the others. Alex both loved and hated those looks. Bran's slow transfer of magic was helping. She didn't even have to pull or focus on it. Her body was so exhausted and starved for magic that she was absorbing it like a sponge. The fog in her head was clearing a little. She'd been stupid to drive out here this morning. She'd been in no condition for it.

"Better?" Bran asked.

"A little." Alex inhaled slowly. Things were clearing a little. Enough that she was embarrassed. "I'll wait a little. You're probably right."

"Good," Nicki said. "So, what is this about the Queen? What is she up to?"

Closing her eyes, Alex focused on the flow of magic from Bran. He wouldn't be able to do it long, but she suspected that Nicki would take his spot when needed. The dream was hazy, but Alex could remember enough.

"I saw Arthur and Queen. It sounded like they'd been trying something and it failed. They didn't discuss the details, but Arthur was angry that she was still focusing on opening the Iron Gates. It was weird: I always thought he wanted that too, but it didn't sound like it."

The door opened and Aiden came in bearing a plate of sandwiches. Carrying them over to her, he gave her a firm look. Alex chuckled and obediently picked up a ham and cheese sandwich. It was the best thing she'd ever tasted. Bran snorted softly, and she knew that he was judging her.

"Let me know when you need to swap out," Aiden said. Bran nodded, and Alex felt a little rush of relief and happiness.

Taking another bite of her sandwich, Alex looked towards the furnace and the finished symbols. There was still a lot of work to do, and she should be focusing on that. But now her mind had some fuel, and she couldn't help but think more about the dream.

"Every villain is the hero of their own story," Alex said.

"Pardon?" Nicki asked. Leaning closer, she gave Alex an uneasy smile. "Did you say something?"

"Yeah, something I've heard before." Alex stared down at the sandwich. She wanted to eat more, but suddenly her jaw tingled in a subtle threat of illness. Ideas in her mind were trying to reorganize into something coherent. "Every villain is the hero of their own story. The Queen... she is afraid of something. Of whatever made her homeworld die. She thinks it's part of other branches." Alex forced herself to take another bite, chewing slowly this time.

"That's silly though," Aiden said. No one agreed, and his shoulders slumped. "Isn't it?"

"No; I mean, I don't know if that's true," Alex admitted. "But she is certain of it. That's why the Sídhe embraced conquest, even if they all aren't aware of it."

"How could they not be aware of it?" Jenny asked.

Nicki frowned at her and raised an eyebrow. "Seriously? You think we're always aware of why our government pushes for something? You add a monarchy structure and propaganda to that, and maybe you could pull it off. Push forward and leave the dying world behind. Jump to world after world until people forget. How long has this been going on?"

"I don't know," Alex said. "Morgana said once that the Queen hadn't been in power long. I don't think she started the conquest thing, but if she discovered the truth, that might have been what spurred her into seizing absolute power for herself. She sees herself as delivering her people."

"Delivering her creepy, child snatching, murdering, and raping people," Aiden snarled.

Alex shivered, remembering too clearly the sight of the Queen kissing Arthur despite being his mother. Her stomach turned, but she pressed on. "Different species," she managed. "Different cultural rules. No matter how gross they are to us."

"Yeah," Nicki agreed softly. She shuddered and didn't look happy about it. "Add maybe centuries of warfare to that and ... well, you get the Sídhe as we know them."

"So, they want to get into the trunk," Aiden said. He slumped into a chair, throwing one leg over an armrest. "I get that they might die if they don't get here, but we still have the issue of the physical differences. Opening the way could have bad repercussions for Earth."

"True," Nicki said. "Only a few lived in our world. The modern Fae are their descendants. Their presence means that there is always a little bit of magic, just from fighting them off, but I have no idea what the whole population would cause."

"Plus, the Fae have adjusted to living around humans," Aiden said. "I'm not saying that's right, but I doubt the Sídhe and humans would mix well."

"And maybe it's natural," Avani suggested. Her voice quivered a little, and Alex grimaced in sympathy. The poor woman had been pulled into the deep end. "Life and death go hand in hand. Shiva is the destroyer because death is necessary for life. While frightening, this may be a natural process, and the Queen is simply afraid of the natural order."

"Maybe not," Bran said. He had a thoughtful expression on his face. "The Tree of Reality takes the form of well, a tree. But unlike what most people think, most of the mass of a tree comes from the air — about 90% in fact. So maybe thinking of Earth as the trunk and base is wrong. It's the core, but external energies and changes to the system would come into the trunk not from the bottom but from the branches. I suppose it could be a natural process, but that's not necessarily good for us either if it is spreading."

"Now I'm worried," Jenny said. "I think I understand what he's getting at."

"If something is happening then we need to care about it," Bran said. "The trunk won't survive without the branches."

"So, if the Queen is right and this is a far-reaching issue, then we have a real problem," Alex said. She looked up at Bran, hoping for him to smile and reassure her. Instead, he nodded. "Shit. That's not another problem I want."

"But this has been going on for thousands of years," Aiden pointed out. "It's hardly mission critical."

"Except that no mage has been paying attention to it for thousands of years," Bran said. "At least not as far as we know. Merlin and Morgana admit that they haven't been everywhere. We know about some of Alex's lives, but I doubt we know about all of them."

"No, we don't," Alex said. Closing her eyes, she inhaled slowly and replayed some of the faces that had appeared to her in the past. The line of people who had greeted her when she touched Arto's skull. "Not even close. And without something pulling the memories to the forefront, it's hard to sort the flashes into any kind of order."

She opened her eyes to find the others were giving her sympathetic looks. Alex didn't like it, and it didn't help anything. "So, what do we do? How do we deal with this? Are there ways to check on the other branches? Maybe this is a Sídhe branch only problem, and it isn't an issue for us beyond refugees trying to get in." Grimacing, Alex sighed. "I wish I hadn't described them that way. Now I feel horrible for not trying... something to help them."

"I know," Bran said softly. "But we don't know what letting them all here would do to Earth. They are all made up of molecules from other worlds, whole other universes. Matter cannot be created or destroyed, but more keeps entering our world. I worry that at some point... there's going to be more consequences to that than our world releasing energy." He looked at the ground and sighed loudly. "After all, it's not a culture or a government saying they don't belong here, it's the physical world around us flinching at their existence. I understand Merlin and Morgana not hunting down all the Fae, but maybe they should have. Maybe they are just making things worse; corroding the world." Rubbing his eyes, Bran finally sat down. "I don't know. Sorry, but I don't know."

"So, we have to keep the gates closed," Nicki said. "But... it might be worthwhile to see if we can learn more about the other branches. If something is happening in them then maybe it is important to us. For the health of the whole weird interconnected universes system that we're stuck being a part of."

"Great," Alex sighed. "One more thing to worry about."

Nicki moved closer to her. Alex braced herself, and sure enough, Nicki touched her shoulder a moment later. Raising an eyebrow, she looked up at Nicki and forced a smile.

"Ignore me; I'm just whining."

"You've mastered Morgana's eyebrow," Nicki said. "You okay?"

"Just... frustrated. Thought we were ahead and now we're not. With Cathanáil concealed in a scabbard, I was feeling... not optimistic, but not dreading Arthur's next move. Now that's gone."

"He's a bastard," Nicki said. "We should call him The Bastard. Capital T capital B."

"That doesn't solve the current problem."

"No," Nicki said. She nudged Bran's shoulder and pointed to where he was still holding Alex's hand. "I'll recharge her for a bit. Finish your sandwich, Alex, and we'll finish these iron symbols. And soon we'll get The Bastard."

Bran released her hand and moved to the side. With a smile, Nicki grabbed her hand, and Alex felt the tickle of magic increasing. Maybe it was her imagination, but it was a little easier to think now. Then again, she didn't like any of the conclusions they were coming to. Swallowing another bite of sandwich, Alex held back a shudder and prayed that she would keep the meal down.

26

Waiting Game

Bran liked magic. At least, he liked the general principle of the thing. As a lifelong geek and lover of fantasy, he enjoyed a thrill every time he used his magic to move anything. Of all the mages, he'd managed to have the most useful natural form of magic. True, the first manifestation was just based on personal talents and quirks, but he had used it usefully outside of battle first. As pretty as Nicki's water and ice sculptures were, they had limited use in day-to-day life. So, yes, in general, he liked having magic.

He enjoyed being able to do small tasks or play with it from time to time. It grounded him. Bran wasn't sure if it was like that for the others, but sometimes he'd just sit down and let the magic fill him up. Meditation had been a key part of learning how to use it, but he wasn't sure if the others still meditated. Alex probably needed it, but she wasn't going to let things go quiet and look around inside. He could understand her hesitation: in Alex's case, who knew what she'd find there.

Yet there were aspects of magic that bothered him. It wasn't even the fighting and the complications derided from it that bothered him the most. In light of what had happened to Alex's family, he did admit to having some fears for his mother, but at the end of the day he doubted that he was Arthur's greatest priority. Learning about magic had led to questions that were so much bigger than him. Even now, almost two years later, he still didn't have his answers, and every fight seemed to bring more questions. His injured leg had been healed, and he'd relearned moving without his brace, but he'd also seen friends hurt and learned he was a reincarnation. But even that wasn't the worst part of it all.

The worst part was trying to understand magic. It aligned just enough with what he understood about physics to taunt him. Magic was definitely some form of energy. It was used to create and affect the world around them, so there was no question that it was energy. In general, it was some sort of potential energy that seemed to be stored in the Earth itself and generated based on specific changes to the Earth. Once a mage called it forth, it transformed into kinetic energy based on how they used it. He gave objects movement while Alex released lightning bolts and they could all use it to speed up the reproduction and repair of cells.

When there was too much contact with the physical laws of another universe due to an incursion, more magic was generated, and when everything was at relative peace and equilibrium, there was less magic generated. That much he understood. While he wasn't sure how to measure it and couldn't reveal it to the public even if he did, he understood it.

Visions were a bit harder. He'd seen a glimpse of the future once and the past several times, but maybe that came down to something on the quantum level that wasn't yet understood. Maybe the science of another hundred years would know about magic and have explained it to the point that it wasn't really 'magic' anymore but was a form of energy named after someone. It just wouldn't be him, and Bran could admit that having to be silent bothered him a little.

However, he didn't understand the why of it all. There were moments, many moments, when something seemed to direct events, and yet physics didn't have a ringmaster. Why were certain people born mages and not others? Sure, he and the other mages had been drawn to Ravenslake, but only Aiden had been born there. And they'd been born years before the Sídhe broke through the Iron Gates, so it was like something had known.

He supposed it could be related to the idea that everything was happening all at once and human perception gave time order, but he'd never really believed that theory. There were a few other fringe theories that explained pieces, but not all of it. Not without something directing. Or maybe he was too limited. Maybe he was trying to personify a force of energy that operated unlike anything that humans had ever looked at before.

Part of the problem, part of his frustration, came down to Merlin and Morgana. While in general they'd done a pretty good job of staying up to date in an ever-changing world, they didn't bother with trying to understand magic. How they could see the rise of electricity, the automobile, and modern medicine and not need to know was beyond him. But even Aiden, the engineering major, was giving up and just embracing it.

Maybe that was the smart choice. It wasn't like anything was ever going to sit down and give him the answers. Merlin and Morgana had grown used to not having the answers and never getting to know what had led to current events. He supposed that maybe sometimes that was just what happened. In a time before smartphones and even written records you couldn't count on learning what had happened somewhere else.

But he still wanted the answers. Why had Lance and Jenny been reborn time and time again? Why had he been reborn to help Alex and not another incarnation of the Iron Soul? Or had he been reborn before and didn't know it? Was it because the Iron Chalice was going to be found this time and they needed him? But what had known that? It all came back to the nature of magic and the question of if there was an intelligence behind it.

Groaning, Bran rubbed his eyes and stood up slowly. His mind was too noisy, too busy for meditation today. Alex was gone with Morgana working on establishing defenses at Jenny and Lance's houses. Officially she was sick with the flu this week. But that left him in Ravenslake worrying. He sat down at his desk and booted up his computer. He needed something in his life that he could solve, that he could figure out and put to paper. Magic was not that thing.

Time ticked on. He stopped studying and called his mother to check in with her. There was no special news, but it was nice to hear her voice. Alex hadn't revealed the order that she'd be visiting their homes to put up the alarm system and hopefully, with Morgana's help, some extra protection. Bran's eyes began to ache, and he closed the laptop with a sigh.

"This isn't working."

"What isn't?" Aiden asked, looking up from his desk. "What's wrong?"

"I'm on edge," Bran replied. Tapping his fingers against his desk, Bran sucked in his lower lip and looked around. "Can't shut my brain down."

"Well, I've got homework if you'd like to give me a hand with that."

"Sorry, electrical engineering isn't my thing. I'll get out of your hair though."

Grabbing his phone, he headed upstairs and took a quick look around. Timothy was humming to himself in the kitchen and tossing items into the large slow cooker, probably making dinner. The Brownie noticed him and gave a quick wave before going right back to slicing up carrots.

Someday Bran would have to study how Timothy managed everything he did.

Settling down in an armchair, Bran glanced up at the clock that had already been on the wall when they arrived. Not that it meant anything. Morgana and Alex probably wouldn't be back tonight. They'd probably stay in a hotel somewhere to recover their magic and then do more houses tomorrow. One of Nicki's books was sitting on the end table, a second-hand science fiction novel, and he picked it up. There was no bookmark so he started reading, resting his phone on his leg where he could easily keep track of it.

Jenny came home about half an hour later and blinked at the sight of him in the living room. "Hey," she greeted. "Lance home yet?"

"Uh, I'm not sure. I've been downstairs."

Jenny pulled out her phone and tapped the screen a few times. "Yeah, he's upstairs." Slipping the phone into her pocket, she smiled. "How were your classes?"

"Fine, nothing unexpected. Yours?"

"Good, good," Jenny said. She was distracted and looking towards the stairs. "I've got several group projects this semester, which are going to be so much fun, and special projects for broadcast practice." Sinking into an armchair, Jenny sighed. "You know the worst part?"

"That you have a prize-winning story and can't share it?" Bran smiled at her and chuckled. "Same boat. Well, not a story, but magic and proof of the multiverse would make my career as a physicist. Straight to Ph.D. for me."

"But it's not safe for the people we care about."

"No, it isn't. Some days I think that it would probably be okay, that Merlin and Morgana are paranoid, but then I watch the news and am reminded of how horrible people can be."

"Yeah... it makes me wonder about my major," Jenny admitted. "These upper-level classes... maybe I'm not cut out for journalism. So much of it is about ratings and views now rather than just the truth. Then again... I'm helping hide a big secret."

"Just because you're going to school for it doesn't mean that you've got to go into that career." Bran folded his hands across his chest. "You could always take after your dad and go to law school. Understanding the journalistic process wouldn't hurt there."

Jenny's nose curled and her eyes went distant. Bran recognized the expression and braced himself. "Arthur was doing political science. He talked about going to law school." The bitterness in Jenny's voice shocked Bran for a moment, but only a moment. Shaking her head, Jenny sighed and schooled her features into a smile. "It doesn't matter. Have you heard from Morgana and Alex?"

"Nothing yet."

"I hope it goes well," Jenny said. She tugged at the hem of her long blue shirt. "I can't... my father- I don't even know how Morgana is going to explain any of this."

"Yeah." Aiden grimaced. "And they sort of have to, what with the alarm. It does no good if no one pays attention."

"Except that my father doesn't know about magic," Jenny said. Bran's eyes widened, and she shrugged, throwing her arms out. "What? I don't have magic to show him! I told him that Arthur went off the deep end and turned violent."

"So... Alex and Morgana are going to have to go over everything with him?"

"Or... or make him believe that it is part of the normal security system," Jenny said. "And to be fair, we do have a very good security system at the house. Daddy is a lawyer." Snapping her fingers, Jenny nodded and headed for the stairs. "I'm going to call them. It's better if Daddy never has to get involved in all this."

Setting his head against the backrest, Bran nodded slightly in agreement. He could certainly understand that viewpoint. Hopefully Alex would remember that he'd never told his mother the whole story about things either. He debated calling Alex to remind her, but with Jenny already calling it seemed like putting too much on Alex. This wasn't fair. She was trying to protect all their families without help. Yes, they couldn't draw attention to themselves, but it still sucked. The front door opened again, and Bran twisted around to find Nicki coming in. She kicked off her sneakers by the front door and pushed her sunglasses to the top of her head.

"I have to do a group project," Nicki announced. She dropped her bag onto the sofa and glared at him as it if was his fault. "A group project! You know what that means!"

"You doing all the work and cursing out the one person who doesn't even pretend to help or make excuses?"

"Exactly!" Nicki huffed and glared at him. "You're not even going to let me vent, Bran? That's low. That's cruel."

"We do have other concerns," Bran said dryly. He glanced over at his phone — still no calls. Nicki's posture relaxed.

"I'm worried too," Nicki said. "But Alex really wanted to get this done. Waiting until next weekend would have driven her crazier, and we can't all miss classes without drawing attention."

"I know," Bran said. "And Morgana is with her. She won't let Alex overdo it, no matter what arguments she makes."

"Exactly, it'll be fine."

"I thought you were worried."

"Of course I'm worried, that doesn't mean that I'm not confident..." Nicki trailed off and groaned. "Alright yeah, I'm trying not to freak out. I mean, what if the Queen is right about the Tree of Reality? What can we do? Are we supposed to do anything? It's freaking me out."

"Alex was going to talk with Morgana: she knows a lot more about the Sídhe than any of us."

"Maybe," Nicki sat down next to her bag. "Is that my book?"

"Uh, yeah, sorry. It's been a bit hard to focus this afternoon."

"I get it." Nicki nodded and looked out the window behind him. "Avani should be back soon. Why don't we do a movie night or something? Maybe it will help us relax."

A sudden change in the lighting of the room caught his attention. It took him a moment to realize that the flashing of blue light was coming from the wall. Turning quickly, his eyes widened as they landed on the metal symbol hanging on the wall.

"Nicki!" Jumping up, Bran shoved his feet into his sneakers without bothering with the laces.

"Oh shit!" Nicki snapped. "Aiden! Get up here!"

Then the bells began to chime. Bran looked towards the doorway as the strange musical sound echoed around them. He had no idea where the noise came from but didn't care. Nicki nodded and moved closer to him.

"At least the alarm system is working," Aiden said as he reached the main floor.

"That's great," Bran said. "But we can't just let them tear up the outside of the house or go after the neighbors."

"Do you think it's more Fae?" Aiden asked.

"Red Caps!" Timothy shrieked in the kitchen. Bran raced to the doorway and looked in. Timothy gripped his small hat and pulled it down fearfully. "They'll rip us apart! Alex is gone!"

Something raced past the window. It was too quick for Bran to see it clearly, but it was much too small to be a Fae. He frowned and looked towards the clock. It was too early for sundown, and yet the Red Caps were already attacking.

Bran looked at Aiden and Nicki. "How do you want to do this? Try to blast them from inside or go outside?"

"We can lay down some cover fire," Aiden said. "But those things are fast, and we don't want them losing patience and trying to draw us out by hurting someone else."

"Right," Bran agreed. "Okay, I'll stay near the front door and use telekinesis to help with crowd control. Aiden you focus on range. Nicki mix it up as best you can."

"What's going on?" Lance asked. He and Jenny were rushing down the stairs. "Is that the alarm?"

"Yeah," Aiden said. "You stay inside."

"Where's Avani?" Jenny asked. "Is she here?"

"No," Nicki answered quickly. "She's still in class. You two stay together. Alex will kill us if something happens to you while she's gone."

"Be safe!' Timothy shouted. "Remember iron doesn't bother Red Caps!"

"Which is why they are the worst," Aiden said. "The absolute worst!"

They all took their positions, the three non-mages inside and Bran, Nicki, and Aiden going onto the porch. Alex's absence was distinct, a void in his gut as he summoned his magic. His heart rate increased, and the spark below his lungs leapt to life. Holding back a shiver, Bran kept his eyes on the trees but saw nothing.

"There were some around the back," Nicki said softly. "There's more cover from the trees there."

Bran nodded, and they slowly moved towards the back of the house. It was quiet. There was none of the laughing that he'd come to associate with the little psychotic Red Caps. They'd just made it to the backyard when a blur of movement out of the corner of his left eye made Bran spin around. Magic flared in his hands just as metal flashed in the light. On instinct he threw his head to the side. A knife slammed into the side of the house and bounced off the metal siding.

"Oh, they did not," Nicki growled. She opened her hands, summoning her magic and casting blue light all around them.

The Red Caps took that as the signal. They came running out of the shadowy patches, all wearing bright red hats. Bran shook himself, trying to dismiss the tangle of thoughts all centered around almost being stabbed with the knife. Pulling on his magic again, he felt the spark ignite and shoved the magic forth. A wave of yellow energy rolled forward, sending the Red Caps on the lawn flying with small shrieks of pain and anger. Grimacing, Bran looked towards the nearest neighboring home. Nothing yet. Hopefully there wouldn't be any problems.

"Any idea how Alex cast that notice-us-not spell?" Aiden called.

"No details, I guess she just really really thought about it," Nicki said. "God, that sounded stupid!"

"You can't visualize everything," Aiden said. A fireball flashed to life in his hands and he tossed it into a group of Redcaps.

They caught fire and one instantly dropped to the ground, rolling around to put out the flames. Aiden groaned as the fire started to spread. Bran held back a sigh and glanced towards Aiden, debating if Aiden would take him putting the fire out personally.

"That didn't work," Bran said.

"I got it," Aiden huffed.

Aiden reached out his hand as red sparks swirled down his arm. The flames started twisting up from the ground, swirling into a small spinning vortex. Bran looked at Aiden in surprise. His friend's hand was shaking, but his expression was pure concentration. Eyes widening, Bran watched as it floated off the ground and spun around in a circle, catching all of the Red Caps. There were small shrieks, but those quickly faded. Nicki was cheering. Bran didn't know how to react. On the one hand, he was very impressed, but on the other, he was vaguely disturbed.

There were only a few survivors. Bran threw a hand forward, focusing the magic into one point on the nearest Red Cap's chest. The yellow bolt connected with the Red Cap, killing it instantly. He moved on, pushing another magical bolt at the next one he spotted. They were splitting up, moving all over the place. Cold hit his arm, and he looked sharply to the right. Part of the lawn was frozen, and there were three small frozen figures, like something from a cartoon. Nicki stalked forward. Bran couldn't see her expression, but anger and violence were telegraphed with every step. Then the ice shattered, breaking apart the Red Caps.

Everything was still and silent. Closing his eyes, Bran strained his ears and listened. If Alex had been here she could have spread out her magic to check. He didn't understand how she did it. The low ache in his chest warned him against trying.

"I think we're done," Aiden said.

"Arthur's got to know that Red Caps won't do the job," Nicki was glaring at the trees. "So, what was even the point of that?"

Bran didn't have an answer. Maybe it was a numbers game, and Arthur figured that sooner or later a Red Cap would get lucky. Or maybe it was part of something else. Part of some larger plan. He didn't know and his stomach twisted into a knot. He didn't know.

27

What He Wants

P odlasie Province, Poland 983 C.E.

Dobiemir felt something as he brought the hammer down on the iron. There was a warmth beneath his skin. Illusive, but there. If he could just grab it then he would be able to do more; do what Merlin and Morgana did. He raised the hammer and slammed it down again. The hot iron shifted at the impact, widening and flattening under the pressure.

A jolt of pride raced through him. It wasn't pretty. That much he knew; but it was working. He was doing it. Iron wasn't too easy to come by, but if he could master this, or at least learn it decently, then it was one more thing that could help him and his son survive. Dobiemir flexed his fingers around the handle of the hammer.

He fell into the rhythm of the work. In theory, it was simple, but there were so many tiny things. The angle of the hammer mattered when trying to shape the metal. He had to mind the temperature and texture of the metal. The work was soothing. Being a farmer was a lot of work and waiting. This was solid, he could hold it in his hands.

Dobiemir wasn't even sure what he was working on. It was slowly taking shape as he kept hammering. The heat in the small forge was thickening, pressing down on him. Outside the warm sun was beating down on the small earthen hut that Merlin had created in only one morning. The stone furnace channeled the heat just right and didn't use as much fuel as he'd feared. A small selection of tools hung from hooks to his right. Where Merlin had acquired them, Dobiemir didn't know, but he was grateful to have been spared the expense.

Pounding the metal again, Dobiemir noted with surprise that it was flattening into a remarkably even circular shape. Maybe he would make it into a pot. Even if he lacked the skill to make it attractive, it would still be useful. Merlin had started his lessons with simple daggers, but Dobiemir had little interest in weapons. When this was all over he'd restrict himself to making tools and goods that he could trade for materials.

Putting the iron back into the fire, Dobiemir rolled his shoulders and considered taking off his shirt. His sweat was making the material stick to his back uncomfortably. The thought of a stray coal hitting his bare skin was enough to make Dobiemir keep his shirt on. His muscles were beginning to protest. This was a different kind of work — a different kind of movement and motion. His arms were strong from carrying supplies and cutting crops, but this was something else.

It was still difficult for him to be sure of the temperature and how long to let the metal heat up. Merlin was a good teacher, but he'd made it clear that experience was the key. There was a 'feel' to the metal that he had to learn for himself. At least this was proving easier than magic. Pulling out the iron, Dobiemir thought it might still be a little cool, but hammered it a few times anyway.

Sweat trickled into his eyes. Dobiemir grunted and put the cooling metal aside. His eyes stung, and his body ached. Time to rest. Setting the hammer to the side, he brought up a hand and wiped his face. That didn't help much: he'd have to remember to bring a rag out to the small forge. Turning around, he almost stumbled back into the furnace. Morgana was leaning against the side of the doorway watching him.

"Morgana? Is something wrong?"

"You have a talent for working iron," Morgana said. Her voice was soft and wistful. Turning to look at her, he noted that Morgana's gaze seemed far away. "That's not surprising."

"Why isn't it?"

Morgana blinked. It took her a moment to recover, but then she smiled at him. "You're a working man. Good with your hands and unafraid of toil. You're patient, and you're willing to let things take some time to get right. Those are very good traits for when you work metal."

Dobiemir didn't believe her. There was something else. There was always something else. A secret that all the others knew and understood, but no one shared with him. Shifting awkwardly, he started to move his hand but thought better of it. Morgana straightened up and stepped into the furnace. It was tight, but it meant that he could leave now if he wanted to.

Stepping into the doorway, Dobiemir leaned outside and inhaled a deep breath of fresh air. Even the light breeze was enough to cool his skin instantly. The change was so sudden that he shivered a little but gloried in it.

"Blacksmithing is hot work," Morgana said. "Don't worry. You'll build up endurance to the heat."

"Do you smith?" he asked. Turning back to Morgana, he found her examining the tools critically. "Merlin never said."

"I know how to work iron," Morgana answered. "But Merlin is much more skilled than I. It is better that you learn from him."

He nodded absentmindedly, looking towards the fields to check on Slavko. His son was lounging in the sunshine outside of the animal yard.

There was no sign of Merlin or any of the Old Ones who had taken to visiting his home at odd hours in the day. Cyrridven had come out of the small pond that Baldr and Merlin had built up behind the house last night for a brief time before returning to the water. Somehow, this was his life now.

"You're pushing magic into the iron," Morgana said. She reached towards the rounded piece of metal he'd been working on with a glowing fingertip. "Watch." A soft light appeared from the metal. Dobiemir blinked in surprise, but there it was. A faint purple hint that was brighter than the rest of the metal. Morgana smiled, and the glow grew brighter, bathing the forge with color. "You don't have full control of it, but your magic is responding to your thoughts. I've seen this before."

"I- how am I doing it?" Dobiemir blinked, not believing his eyes, but the glow was still there.

"What are you thinking about?" Morgana drew her hand away, and the glow started to fade.

"I don't know. Nothing special." He shrugged even as he kept staring at the metal. The glow was gone now. "My son, what happens next, that night in the forest. It's all sort of jumbled together."

"Hmmm." Morgana studied him for a moment. "Your magic could be responding to your worry for Slavko, in light of Chernobog being so close." Tilting her head, Morgana raised an eyebrow. "So, the question is, Dobiemir, what is it that you want from magic? It is yours to command, to achieve what you need."

Dobiemir's eyes jumped to the flattened round shape. What was it going to be? What did he want it to do? He hadn't been thinking about anything like that, so what was possible now? Morgana stayed silent, just watching him process this. There was a sharpness to her gaze. It took him a moment to recognize it, but there it was — that same searching look that she frequently gave him. That Sif, Odin, Merlin, and Baldr all gave him. They were looking for something and not finding it.

Anger and frustration started brewing in his chest. Bitterness licked at his heart like flames around a pot. He hated it. Dobiemir struggled against the growing storm of emotions for a moment. But he was tired, sore, and tired of the looks.

"I'm not stupid," he said. It was hard to meet Morgana's gaze, but he did. "I know there are things you aren't telling me."

"You're right," Morgana said. She held his eyes, looking much calmer than he felt. "There are things that you haven't been told. I'm not sure you really want to know them. You're special Dobiemir. Special as a mage as well as a man, but you have a life. You have a son. Merlin and I... we agreed that if we can deal with Chernobog, that you don't need to get pulled into the greater scope of magic."

"You think that's best?"

"I think you'd prefer it."

"I don't feel like that is a real answer."

"When this is over, Merlin and I will move on. I'll scry once more and make sure that there are no other problems that we need to address. But you... you can stay here at this farm with your son. You'll still have some access to magic. You can make your life a little easier and live in peace."

"And that's what you want?" Dobiemir asked. She didn't answer, and he sighed. "I just... I feel lost, Morgana. There are these holes in my understanding, and no one is filling them in. And there's something more powerful than I can imagine in the forest, just waiting and growing stronger while we try to think of a plan."

"I'm not sure that's wise," Morgana said. "Merlin and I... we've put a lot on mages in the past. We're trying to be smarter, kinder about the mages we meet. You have a child who needs you."

"My ignorance won't protect Slavko." Dobiemir swallowed, suddenly chilled at the thought of something happening to his son. "Or me," he added when Morgana raised that damned eyebrow. "But it might get me killed."

Morgana studied him for another moment. Then she stepped out of the forge, leaving the furnace to cool behind her. "No, I suppose it won't. Your soul is ancient," Morgana said. "You don't remember anything from life to life, but I'm sure you are the current incarnation of the Iron Soul." She shook her head when he opened his mouth to speak. "It doesn't change who you are, but it explains why you are here." A soft chuckle escaped her, and Morgana smiled sadly. "The Iron Soul is always where they are needed. Always. No matter how much time passes, Merlin and I always seem to find a mage nearby."

"I... that doesn't mean that I have the same soul. Mages are supposed to protect the world."

"Yes," Morgana agreed. "But I'm sure. I scryed for the current Iron Soul when we became aware of the danger. And we found you. I'm confident that it's you. But that's just it, Dobiemir. You will die someday and be reborn again to fight when needed. I suppose that seeing you with your son, a peaceful man trying to live a peaceful life, that Merlin and I just wanted to let you have that."

"Why? Why does that matter so much?"

"The Iron Soul doesn't always survive."

The words stung. They caught in the air and struck like a cold wind. Exhaling, Dobiemir felt a rush of worry and relief. It shouldn't be surprising. This was dangerous. He'd known that something horrible and dangerous was going on the moment those Shadows appeared. Yet, hearing Morgana say the words still had an impact. He wasn't sure why. Maybe it was something about his soul.

A laugh escaped him. "The Iron Soul?" he repeated. "I'm not sure how the Christians would feel about that."

Morgana smiled, but she was still watching him carefully. Her hand came up and toyed with her necklace as she waited for him to say something. She expected questions, but he didn't know what to ask. The idea that he somehow kept returning to fight with magic was strange. Besides, it wasn't him. He couldn't remember anything. Maybe they were wrong. Maybe Morgana and Merlin just saw what they wanted to see. His eyes were drawn to the three spirals that formed her necklace. It was familiar, yet he couldn't put his finger on it. Morgana lowered her hand and frowned at him.

"Dobiemir? Are you alright? Do you have questions?"

"That symbol," Dobiemir said. He pointed to the necklace around Morgana's neck. "The spirals, what is it?"

"We call it the triskelion," Morgana answered. Her long fingers came up to touch it softly, tracing the symbol. "It has other names, but it was an important symbol in our homeland. We see it as the symbol of magic. It represents a unity of different forces."

"So that's why you both wear it."

"Yes. You've also seen it on the sword that Cyrridven carries. Several items carry that symbol. As I said, to us, it is a symbol of magic."

He nodded; that made sense he supposed. "Is Cyrridven Merlin's mother?" he asked. "They seem... they seem very close."

A chuckle escaped Morgana. Her smile widened, and her eyes sparkled with real amusement. Then her expression softened and turned more thoughtful. A soft sigh escaped her, and she looked out into the distance for a moment before turning her attention back to him.

"No, she is not his mother. His mother was human. Very human. She was not even a mage, though she did have some ability to call on and use magic from what he has told me. Cyrridven was his teacher though, when he was much younger. They remain... close. Even after all the years we've spent together, sometimes I think she still knows him better than I do."

"Oh." He grimaced, internally groaning at his response. Was that all he could say? "I'm sorry?"

Morgana chuckled and shook her head, almost fondly. "Thank you, Dobiemir, but it's alright. Merlin and I trust each other now, but we haven't always been close." Folding her hands in front of her, she glanced back into the forge. "Is there anything I can help you with? The others are checking the area for Shadows."

"No," he said. Shaking his head, Dobiemir grasped at the frayed edges of his thoughts. "No... I think that I'll keep working in the forge. What you said about what I wanted... I think that maybe I understand."

"I hope so," Morgana said. She gave him one more searching look. "You are a good man, Dobiemir. A good father." Then she turned and walked towards the hillside.

Dobiemir watched Morgana walk away. He didn't try to stop her. He didn't want to stop her. Something like fondness warmed his chest. It might have been gratitude. There was something in her words, something in her gaze that was softer and kinder than he understood. Yet, Dobiemir was sure that it wasn't really about him. This Iron Soul... it didn't matter. Not really. Morgana was right; he was a farmer. He was a simple man and all he wanted was to keep his son, his only remaining family, safe from the monsters.

Nothing else mattered. He searched the yards and smiled when he found Slavko. The boy was sitting amongst some of the goats and weaving a basket. He was lucky that the goats were occupied with other food or else they'd be pulling the reeds out of his hands. His boy's skin had a healthy glow, and he was growing again. That was enough. That was more than enough.

Turning back to the forge, Dobiemir picked up the odd metal piece he'd been working on. There was a faint glow still visible in the iron. Running a finger over it, Dobiemir thought he felt a jolt in his chest. Like a pull. Exhaling, he gave Slavko one more look and headed back into the forge. If this was the key to his magic and ending this threat, then it was time to finish it. Now he knew exactly what he was making.

Adding some fuel to the furnace, Dobiemir inhaled the warming air. The taste of charcoal filled his mouth, but he embraced it. Looking at the round iron piece he'd already made, Dobiemir began to plan the next steps. Something fluttered in his chest, a tiny spark that he thought might just be his magic. Closing his eyes, he tried to pull on it like Morgana had described during lessons. Nothing happened, but he felt a little bit stronger, and a little more certain of the future.

28

Returning Home to Questions

Pulling out her key, Alex quickly unlocked the front door and pushed it open. They hadn't lived at the house that long, and yet the smell of it enveloped her at once. There was a soft smell of books carried in by Aiden and the various collections they all had. An earthy undertone of clay and leather mixed oddly with the small hints of make-up products, electronics, and cooked food.

A few pairs of shoes were stacked up by the door underneath a bench. Someone had hung up a row of hooks, and jackets for the cooling autumn weather had already been hung up. Alex was pretty sure that the hooks hadn't been there when she left, but everything was a blur. She blinked, trying to gather her thoughts. Setting down her duffle bag, Alex maneuvered her shoulder bag around Cathanáil and hung it on a hook.

Someone was moving up the stairs from the basement. Alex wasn't worried but stopped to see who it was anyway. The footfalls were fast and excited, so she guessed it was probably Aiden. He came upstairs a moment later, his brown hair a bit of a tangled mess.

"Alex." Relief filled Aiden's face, and he grinned at her. Stepping forward, he opened his arms, and Alex obeyed the silent demand for a hug. His arms wrapped around her and squeezed. It felt nice, and she relaxed into the embrace. "Welcome home. I'm glad you're safe."

"I'm fine," Alex promised. Aiden released her, and she stepped back. "We'll do your parents' house tomorrow. Right now, I need food." She headed for the kitchen with Aiden on her heels.

She made it into the kitchen only to find Bran drying off his hands next to a rack full of clean dishes. He offered her a soft smile which widened when Alex stepped forward to get another hug. It was nice to come home to people that were glad to see her.

"How did things go?" Bran asked. "Any problems?"

"Things went fine," Alex answered. Opening the fridge, she bent over and looked at the various leftover options. Someone, probably Bran, had made some kind of fried rice. She could see peas through the plastic and smiled. That sounded good. "Jenny's house went smoothly. I'm afraid that Morgana had to use a bit of magic on her dad so he didn't notice that we were messing with his security. But at least he knows to take the chiming seriously." She took the container out and pushed the fridge door shut. "Bran, your Mom was weird about it. Morgana told her that some nasty faeries had moved into the area and might sense your magic."

"You didn't tell her about Arthur?"

"I know you don't want her to know. I think that's the wrong choice." Alex walked to the microwave and put the leftovers inside. "But it's your choice. I'm not going to cause family drama."

"I know," Bran said. "I know, I should tell her. I'm working on a plan."

"A plan," Aiden repeated. He smirked a little. "I wonder how long that will take."

"Don't start, Aiden," Bran sighed. Aiden offered him a soft smile and a shrug.

"My house has been prepped," Aiden said. "Whenever you're ready."

"Let me rest tonight," Alex said. "I need some sleep."

"Yeah... you look tired," Bran said. "Nightmares?"

Alex blinked, a bit surprised at the bluntness before chuckling. She shouldn't be. Bran was more than willing to be blunt when he thought it was important.

"Yeah, I had some nightmares. Nothing that I think was real," Alex said. "Just repeats of that vision of the dying world."

"Did you talk to Morgana about it?"

"I tried, but she's in that stubborn mode of hers." Shaking her head, Alex opened the microwave and pulled out her food. There were some forks in the drying rack, and she plucked one out before heading to the dining room. Aiden and Bran followed her, like little ducklings. "Sometimes she and Merlin are so unwilling to change their minds. She didn't want to talk about the Queen or anything she remembered from the Sídhe tunnels. I get that it was a long time ago and she was a child, but I got the sense that she was avoiding it."

"So, she doesn't think that there is anything wrong with the Tree of Reality?" Bran asked. He and Aiden sat down as she did around the oval wooden table.

"Nope," Alex said. "I mean, she's open to the idea that worlds could die and maybe the Sídhe world did, but she doesn't believe that it could affect Earth."

"Damn," Aiden huffed. "Those two can be so stubborn."

"They're used to things; they've had a long time to become set in their ways," Alex said. "Honestly... given how old they are, I still feel the need to give them a lot of credit for their adaptability."

"But this could be a real issue!" Aiden raised his voice, and Alex heard something overhead. "I think we're onto something!"

Holding back a sigh, Alex shrugged and started eating her food. Aiden started pacing. She understood his frustration, but today she was a little too exhausted to do anything about it. Noise on the staircase drew her attention, and she smiled when Nicki came into view. The redhead was grinning. Alex quickly put her fork down and stood up. Nicki all but jumped her, wrapping her arms around Alex and pinning Alex's hands to her side.

"Welcome home!" Nicki released her and tucked a strand of Alex's blonde hair behind her ear. "I hated knowing you were out there without us."

"I had Morgana," Alex replied. "Speaking of which, she was going to run home and shower, but she'll be here soon. She was going to bring Merlin."

"Is that a good thing or a bad thing?" Nicki asked. Her glee had faded into worry.

"I'm not sure. I tried talking to her about the Queen, but Morgana... she doesn't like to think about it."

"So, we have to convince Merlin of the threat to the Tree of Reality," Bran observed.

"We'll get through to him," Nicki said firmly. Alex held back a sigh and resumed eating. "Any more dreams?" Nicki asked gently.

"No," Alex answered. They didn't seem to believe her: all of her friends were giving her dubious looks. "Nightmares," she conceded. "But nothing that seemed useful. I'm sure that I could see them again if I tried... at least I think so, but I'm not sure how to try. Scrying usually doesn't work. I know that Morgana has tried to find Arthur that way numerous times. She told me a bit about that."

"So... was it awkward?" Nicki asked. "I mean, thanks for working on it obviously, but was it weird?"

Shrugging, Alex finished chewing. "Wasn't much time for it to be weird."

The others were exchanging looks again, and Alex properly studied them. Everyone looked okay, but three were missing. There was no sign of Jenny, Lance, or Avani. Straightening up, Alex stopped chewing.

"They're fine," Bran said. "Jenny, Lance, and Avani are upstairs doing magic lessons."

"Oh." Alex exhaled and took another bite of food. "Okay."

"You sure you're okay?" Nicki was frowning at her with narrowed eyes.

"Just tired," Alex said. Shrugging, she tried to keep eating, but her appetite was slipping away with everyone watching her. "And worried. I didn't like being away from town. Without you guys there, it was like I had to keep looking over my shoulder. It was just off."

Scraping up the last bite, Alex smiled as she noted that her friends looked oddly pleased. Nicki was smiling again and chuckled a little at her. Turning around in her chair, Alex looked into the kitchen as she realized that someone else was missing.

"Where's Timothy?"

"He said something about checking inside the walls." Bran gestured all around them, looking vaguely alarmed. "He's concerned that there's enough space in the walls for Red Caps to get in."

Maybe she had missed something. That was fair. The others had missed her failed attempts to talk to Morgana about a subject that Morgana didn't want to talk about. Swallowing the last bit, Alex took the empty container and spoon back into the kitchen and dropped them in the sink.

"I'm going to go up and check on them," Alex said. "Uh, Merlin and Morgana will be here soon. It won't take Morgana long to get Merlin moving."

"No, it won't," Nicki agreed. "I'll make up some tea."

"Thanks, Nicki."

"I'll make sure that the living room is clean," Aiden said. Bran nodded in agreement and followed him.

That left Alex with Nicki. Her friend caught her hand and squeezed it for a moment. "I'm glad you're back," Nicki said. "It didn't feel right for us either, you being out on a mission without us."

"I was only gone a day and a half."

"But you were gone. Without us."

Moving quickly, Alex hugged Nicki, making the redhead laugh. Nicki had to adjust the teapot that she'd picked up, and Alex heard a clunk as Nicki put it down on the stove. Inhaling slowly, Alex enjoyed the soft, quiet moment. Her knees quivered, and she sank into the sense of safety. But it didn't last, and Nicki squeaked a little when Alex put a little too much weight on her. Standing up, Alex felt her cheeks heating up, but Nicki just gave her a soft look.

"They're up in Avani's room."

Heading upstairs before she proved herself any more of a basket case, Alex stopped briefly to pop her head into her room. Mjǫllnir was still on its stand on the wall, and Galahad was on one of her pillows. Everything was where it was supposed to be. Everyone's homes outside of Ravenslake were protected, and nothing bad had happened at home. Tapping the wall, Alex furrowed her brow thoughtfully and nodded. That was good, but it didn't make her worries go away. She headed to Avani's room.

Alex stopped in the doorway and stared in surprise. Avani's bedroom furniture had been pushed against the walls to make an open space in the center of the room. She, Jenny, and Lance were sitting in a small circle with an unlit candle between them. Blinking, Alex couldn't help the stray thought that suggested this was something out of a weird teen movie. Biting her lip, she held back a laugh and sternly reminded herself that she didn't know what went into ritual magic.

None of them seemed to have heard her, but she didn't move. Leaning against the doorway, Alex flinched as Cathanáil hit the doorframe. Avani's eyes opened, and she looked towards Alex, but Lance and Jenny didn't move. Concern for the pair took over, but Avani gave her a reassuring smile. She lingered for a moment, watching and waiting for something to happen. There was nothing. No new magical glow around Lance or Jenny. Nothing that shouted magic.

"Light the candle," Avani whispered.

The sudden words made Alex jump, and Cathanáil's hilt scraped against the doorway again. Yet Lance and Jenny remained still. A flame suddenly appeared on the wick of the candle, and it began to burn happily.

"Open your eyes and exhale," Avani instructed.

Jenny did so first. She looked down and saw the burning candle. Her face lit up, and she clasped her hands together.

"Nice," Alex said. Not that she knew what had gone into that, but it was the first bit of magic that she'd seen the pair do. Lance grinned as he caught sight of her. "I'm back."

Jumping to her feet, Jenny rushed forward for a hug and Alex chuckled. It was easy to accept the hug, letting it ground her. The old whispers about Jenny and her former lives were silent. Lance climbed to his feet, and once Jenny released her, extended his hand. Taking it, Alex grinned when Lance gave her a quick one-armed hug.

"Welcome back," he greeted.

"Alex!" Nicki called from downstairs. "As you predicted, Merlin and Morgana just drove up!"

Shrugging, Alex turned towards the door, but Jenny caught her hand before she made it into the hallway. "How did it go?" Jenny asked. "My Dad; did you arrange things like I suggested?"

"Yes." Alex smiled indulgently. "It went fine, Jenny. Just like it did the first three times I texted you back." Lance chuckled, fighting back a full laugh. He winked at Alex right before Jenny spun and pouted up at him. "Are you coming downstairs?" Alex asked, moving towards the stairs.

"We'll be right down," Avani promised.

Morgana and Merlin were already seated in the living room when Alex came in. Sitting on the sofa wasn't very comfortable due to Cathanáil, but Alex was getting used to it. Aiden was handling the tea, and she sat down next to Bran on the sofa.

"Morgana brought me up to speed," Merlin said. "Well done on the alarm system."

"It doesn't solve the problem," Alex said. "But hopefully it will help." When Aiden offered her some tea, she shook her head. "Arthur might try to use hostages to get Cathanáil."

"I doubt it," Morgana said. Blowing softly on her tea, she looked towards the staircase as Avani, Lance, and Jenny came down. "Arthur seems... detached from normal human emotions. I'm not sure that he'd believe you'd give up the Sword for a human, given what you know of him."

There was a hint of warning in Morgana's voice of what would happen if Alex ever did give him the sword. She doubted that Morgana would ever consider any trade worth the risk. Alex didn't respond to the words and stayed still on the sofa. Bran shifted slightly, making their legs touch. Hopefully, it would never come to that. Morgana sounded far more certain of the outcome than Alex felt.

"We need to learn what Arthur's goals are," Merlin said. "The Fae we've been in contact with have no new information. Arthur and the Queen have stopped contacting them and seem to be only in contact with those who already pledged to help them."

"So, I use my magic and try to spy on them again," Alex said.

"I'm amazed that you were able to see them that time," Morgana said. Her green eyes narrowed on Alex, carrying a hint of irritation and a warning. "We've tried looking at them, but the Queen always repels us. Her magic, her power, is stronger. Far stronger than it should be, likely due to the Iron Chain." Holding back a grimace at the reminder of the Chain, Alex dropped her gaze for a moment. Morgana sighed. "You probably only managed because she was exhausted."

"There were signs of someone trying to damage one of the new Iron Gates," Merlin said. "It was unsuccessful, of course." He chuckled for a moment but quickly turned serious. "Those two events are likely connected, but pushing yourself; pushing your magic to spy on her, could be dangerous. Arthur's Fae won't be able to break down the Iron Gates, not without Cathanáil."

"But we need to try something," Alex said. "The Queen seemed... desperate. Doesn't that make her even more dangerous? She wants Cathanáil."

"And we need to be cautious and make sure that she doesn't get it," Morgana said. "The new security measures are good, especially in light of Arthur's medallions."

"What about the Tree of Reality?" Aiden asked. He crossed his arms and studied the older mages. "What do you want to do about that?"

"Aiden... You children are jumping to conclusions," Merlin said. Shaking his head, he tapped his left fingers on his knee. "There is no evidence-"

"That's not true!" Alex snapped. Fisting her hands, Alex did her best to keep her voice calm. Anger wouldn't sway Merlin or Morgana. "The Demons spoke of a Darkness that frightened them into coming to our world again, and I've had visions of the Sídhe's dead world."

"Maybe there are world's dying," Morgana conceded. "But that doesn't mean that the whole Tree is doomed. Tree branches die, and new ones are born. That's natural."

"Okay," Bran said. "How do we check that then? You both have told us about the Tree of Reality, but how do you know all that? I mean, how did you learn?"

Merlin and Morgana exchanged a weighted look. Then they spoke rapidly in their ancient language. Pulling on her magic, Alex focused on the words and willed them to be translated. But the older mages finished talking too quickly. Morgana raised an eyebrow, clearly guessing what Alex had been trying.

"Some mages... some beings..." Merlin said slowly. His expression was cautious and guarded. "In the past, beings with magic looked beyond our world. It stretched their magic to the limit, of course. Magic, our magic, is part of the world, and it... shifts if exposed to the outside."

"But it still works?" Bran asked.

"Yes: magic is generated by different physical laws interacting after all, and beyond... well, there is... it is difficult to explain." Merlin waved his hands in frustration, and Morgana sighed.

"We know that not all the worlds in the Tree of Reality are part of the same universe because of the different physical laws," Morgana said. "At least, we don't think so. I suppose they could be different dimensions, shadows of our universe or something like that, but that isn't the issue here. The issue is that the worlds in the tree share a connection. A strand of energy, of some greater magic, that transcends all of them. It acts like a river, flowing through our world and branching out."

"Which is why you can't jump between branches usually," Merlin said. There was something about the usually that tugged at Alex's memory. For an instant she had a vague memory of strange holes in the sky and beings falling through them. "The Sídhe had to conquer several worlds and come through them to reach our world. They'd never gone to the homeworlds of the Old Ones or the dragons for instance. They can't get there except by following the energy trail."

"But it is possible to look outside the energy trail," Morgana said. "Cyrridven did it, long ago, and saw the branches spreading out from Earth."

"And she told me," Merlin said. "And cautioned me not to try. The attempt was difficult. She didn't talk about it, but I get the sense that the experience was part of what opened her so completely to the Iron Realm."

"I tried once," Morgana confessed. "It was almost impossible to push through into the void between worlds with my magic. Looking back now, I know it was foolish. But that method is how we are aware of the other worlds. You can't see them in detail. All we know has to come from visitors. Thus, the furthest worlds are complete mysteries to us." Morgana then fixed her weighty gaze on Alex. "Do not attempt to force your sight beyond our world, Alex. And leave scrying for the Queen to me. We have far more experience in navigating the potential dangers."

Still frowning, Alex reluctantly nodded. In the corner of her eye, Alex saw Bran watching her intently. She took another sip of her tea and tried to pay attention as Avani proudly announced that Lance and Jenny had done their first bit of magic. The others gave congratulations, even Morgana, but she still never took her eyes off of Alex. It was already clear to Alex that Morgana didn't expect her to listen to her command.

29

Desperate Measures

The house wasn't quiet, but it was calm. Music was drifting up from the living room, and she was aware of the locations of the others. Sitting on the floor in her room with Bran seated across from her, Alex had to admit that she felt safe. Her eyes scanned her room, landing on the closed door and then the photos of her family she'd put up on the shelf above her desk. Twisting around, she checked on Cathanáil and Mjǫllnir in their displays by her bed. Everything was where it was supposed to be.

She righted herself, facing Bran again, and rolled her shoulders. Controlling her breathing, Alex tried to relax her muscles. It was difficult to let go of the tension. She'd just become used to it. Even her stretches this morning before her run hadn't done much to help. Bran shifted a little closer to her, and their knees touched, reassuring her that she had help.

"You sure about this?" Bran asked. "Morgana didn't want you to try scrying for them."

"I know," Alex said. "But Morgana and Merlin are being stubborn. Something is going on with Scáthbás. She's scared about this Darkness. If it is the same issue the Demons had, we need to know what is going on."

"You don't trust Morgana to be reasonable about it?"

"No, I don't." Alex closed her eyes. "I... I sometimes remember what she was like, long ago. Scáthbás did a ringer on her. Scáthbás raised her and sometimes... I don't know." Alex shook her head and squeezed her eyelids tighter together. "I don't know. I need to check for myself. Merlin and Morgana don't know everything."

"Okay." Bran's voice was soft and understanding. "Okay, that's fair. You know them best. Probably better than they give you credit for. Just promise me that you'll have me nearby when you do this, or at least someone with magic. Just in case something happens, so that we can feed you some extra power."

"That's fair." Alex opened her eyes and gave Bran a grateful smile. "You're right. That's a good idea. No reason to be stupid about this."

They joined hands. There was a tingle against Alex's skin. Like static electricity. A shudder rolled up her spine as the first traces of Bran's magic started to flow into her. Closing her eyes, Alex focused on gently pulling the magic into her chest. There was another tingle, but in her mind's eye she could see the yellow magic turning a dark gray color.

Scrying was still a weird thing for Alex. She knew that it was about sending the magic out to find something, but the details were hazy. It made her wish that they had the Iron Chalice to fill with water and use, but it was currently with Merlin. That was a conversation that she didn't want to have.

"Okay," she said softly. "I'm going to try and focus on Scáthbás."

"I've got a mirror if you want to try that," Bran said.

"No... last time I saw them was in a dream without a medium. I want to see if that works."

Bran didn't argue. Maybe it wasn't a good call, but he'd had visions without using other objects before too, so it was possible. The issue was control. But they were in the area. Probably, at least. If they were messing with the Iron Gates- Alex shook herself softly and concentrated on Scáthbás.

Her eyelids were pressed tightly together, so tightly that the blackness began to shimmer with color at the edges. In her chest the magic hummed, and Alex commanded it to spread out slowly. At first, the outlines of her furniture and the yellow burst of color that was Bran appeared to her, burning their images on the backs of her eyelids.

"Scáthbás," she whispered. "Scáthbás."

Her hair shifted. A soft breeze swirled around Alex, cooling her skin and freshening the air. The outlines of the world vanished as the magic shifted wildly. It pulsed, forming long strands that stretched out into the distance. A jolt in Alex's stomach was all the warning she got before the magic pulled her after it in one direction. She was falling.

There was red all around her — gleaming red lines across the ground that ended suddenly as she fell. The outer edge of the Blood Spell, she realized as the landscape turned hazy and green. A thick line of blue marked the river. There were faint outlines of trees and hills, but it blurred as she moved. The magic didn't let up. It kept pulling her, dragging her where she'd wanted it to go. Scáthbás, Alex chanted in her mind. Scáthbás.

Then she stopped. Her feet were both against the ground and tucked under her. There was a faint wind and stillness at the same time. Splotches of color surrounded her, slowing gain more hue like an unfinished impressionistic painting. Everything came together gradually. The splashes of color formed distinct shapes, and Alex stayed still, waiting to see what magic would reveal. Energy was still rolling down her arms and creeping up the back of her neck.

It was a forest. Thick evergreens filled the space around her on a steep rocky hillside. It tugged at Alex's memory as she examined the nearest rock face. There was a pile of rubble from where part of the mountain had shifted and sent rocks falling. She was sure that wasn't familiar, but she was certain that she'd been here before.

Alex turned slowly, only to stop after moving a few degrees. Two figures were hiking towards her, the long shadows of the trees obscuring them until they came a few feet closer. Arthur and Scáthbás. Arthur was in the lead, wearing jeans, a Ravenslake University t-shirt and a knife on his belt. Scáthbás was dressed in functional clothing, jeans and hiking boots with her blonde hair up in a crown braid.

They came up close, almost walking through Alex. The rocks had shrunk the flat area, but there was enough space that Arthur shrugged off the backpack he was carrying. Without a word he pulled out a bottle of water and shoved it at Scáthbás. She took it and drank down several gulps. Her dark red lips curled into a frown as she glared at the hillside. It was familiar, and Alex furrowed her brow, trying to figure out where they were. Birds were singing up in the trees and sunlight was streaming down over the rocky hillside.

"It's buried a bit," Arthur said. He marched forward, pulling on a pair of leather gloves and began to pick up and push rocks out of the way.

"The mages might have done that to avoid human meddling," Scáthbás said. She was looking around carefully at the trees. "Arthur…"

"What?"

"Do you feel… never mind. The Gate must be interfering with my magic."

Alex's head snapped towards the rocks, and she flinched as iron bars were uncovered by Arthur. He shifted back from the metal. Alex looked around again. She couldn't remember which Iron Gate this was, but it was up in the hills. They were just far enough out of the town that the blood spell wouldn't affect them.

"Maybe," Arthur said. He looked around carefully, glaring into the trees, but his gaze didn't stop on her. Alex sighed in relief. She was here and yet not once again. Whatever excitement that she would have felt was overshadowed by worry. "Come on, let's give this a try. We had to come far enough to get here."

"What a pity," Scáthbás said. "This was one of the proper tunnels. Though they were never so poorly made in my day."

"That didn't stop them from being barred by Arto," Arthur said. He sounded smug, and Scáthbás glared at him. "It's true, and you know it."

"Arthur, I don't want to have this fight." Scáthbás sounded tired, and the look she gave Arthur was almost pleading. There was no domination in her posture or tone. "You agreed to come and help me attempt to break the Gate."

"The Iron Chain is broken," Arthur said. "And even when it was intact, you didn't have enough of a connection to the Iron Soul to break their spell."

"Arthur," Scáthbás growled. It was the sharp tone of a tired mother, and Alex stared. "Just come on. Stop whining. This isn't the time."

"Fine."

Arthur lurched forward to the edge of the rocks. He kicked one and glared at the rubble. Frowning, Alex studied the pair, trying to sort out what was happening between them. Scáthbás stepped forward beside Arthur. He tugged off his right glove and shoved it into his back pocket. Joining hands, they both closed their eyes and lifted their free hands towards the Iron Gate. The remaining rubble quivered. Black sparks encircled Arthur's hands, but there were also flickers of gold mixed with them.

The iron bars that made up the crisscrossing gate shook. Stunned, Alex watched and braced herself. Arto's voice started shouting. Thor growled in frustration, but she just stared. The bars shook and quivered, glowing the dark gray color of her magic. Her eyes jumped back to Arthur and Scáthbás. The air around them rippled. Scáthbás' face twisted with pain. Her body shook, and Arthur snarled something before releasing her hand and catching her as she started to fall.

All the magic vanished as quickly as it had appeared. Checking the Iron Gate, Alex found it still standing. Magic radiated off of it, pouring out into the surrounding forest. Whatever they'd been trying to do hadn't worked. Walking forward, Alex reached out and touched the Iron Gate, wrapping her fingers around one of the bars. It warmed in her grasp, and she gazed into the blackness beyond. The Sídhe tunnel was gone: the stones had collapsed inward, blocking the tunnel mere feet in.

Turning, she looked back at Scáthbás. The woman's face was pale, her wrinkles suddenly standing out. She stepped closer. There were faint dark lines on Scáthbás' neck and she was breathing hard. Arthur was staring at her with impatient eyes. There was none of the fondness she'd seen in the past, only frustration.

"Alex!' The voice cut through her magic. Around her, the world dimmed and faded in and out like a glitching image on a computer. "Alex!" It was Bran's voice. "Alex? Can you hear me?"

Exhaling, Alex allowed the magic to retreat. It swirled back into her chest, and she was falling again. Hands grabbed her arms as the forest collapsed into black. Someone was holding her still. Another voice was telling her to breathe.

"Alex?" the voice called again, softer this time. She recognized it as Nicki's. "Alex? Can you hear us? Are you alright?"

"I'm fine," Alex said. Her words slurred a little. Forcing her eyes open, Alex inhaled slowly. "I saw them."

Nicki groaned. "Morgana is going to be pissed at you-"

"Tattle on me later," Alex said. Shaking her head, she climbed to her feet. Nicki moved to stop her, but Alex avoided her grasp and slipped out the door. "It was in real time. I'm sure of it. They're still near the Iron Gate! We could catch them!"

"Alex!" Bran called. "Wait! What happened! What did you see?"

She kept moving. The feeling was coming back into her legs, which she was grateful for as she hit the top of the stairs. Bran and Nicki were behind her. Frantic words filled her mouth, but Alex wasn't sure how to start explaining. Patting her pockets, Alex realized that she'd left her wallet and keys upstairs.

"Cathanáil," she said. "Bran, I need Cathanáil!"

"Alex," Nicki called. She came down the stairs and caught Alex's arm. "What is going on? Bran started shouting when you started convulsing!"

That was unexpected to hear, but Alex dismissed it. There were more important things. "I saw Arthur and Scáthbás," she said. "They're nearby. We have a chance to get them. We need to move. Just trust me."

"What do you want to do?" Nicki asked. Her voice was softer now, almost resigned, but her eyes were clear and focused. Awaiting orders. Alex almost smiled.

"I want to catch them," Alex said. "It was just the two of them. No Red Caps or Fae guards."

"Can we drive?" Aiden asked. He was waiting near the bottom of the stairs and frowning.

"I... I don't know," Alex admitted. "I'm not sure where they were exactly. They were at an Iron Gate, trying to break it down. Up in the hills-it was close to the river and near the edge of the Blood spell."

"Do you have enough magic to find it again?" Bran asked. He came back with Cathanáil and the scabbard in his hand. Alex took them gratefully and slipped the sword into its proper place on her back. "You're the guide right now."

"They were hiking," Alex said. "At least some of the distance, but I don't think we have a lot of time. A water tunnel. There was a river nearby, and I think a stream not too far." She vaguely recalled the blur of color and hoped she was right. "We can get there if we use a water tunnel."

"Alex..." Aiden sighed. "Morgana is going to kill us."

"We can go to the lake," Nicki suggested. "But it's the middle of the day."

"Bathtub," Bran suggested. Everyone looked at him, and he shrugged. "It isn't impressive, and we can't just leave water standing in it like the Desai pool, but it could work."

Eyes widening, Alex wondered why she hadn't thought of it. That was so much better than driving or having to go to Merlin's house. He'd ask questions, and there wasn't time for that. Alex twisted around and rushed back up the stairs to the full bathroom. She tripped, but Bran caught her before she hit the floor.

"Slow down, Alex!"

"There isn't time!" Alex protested. Glaring at Bran, she waited for him to release her arm.

"Nicki, please start the tap," Bran said. "Alex, you just used a lot of magic. You need to let us help."

Nicki leaned over and opened the water tap. The bathtub began to fill with water and Alex almost laughed. This was a far cry from dignified, but it just might work. Bran's grip slowly eased when she didn't try to do anything stupid.

"We're going to get wet," Nicki complained. "No way around wet feet this time."

"We almost always get a little wet," Aiden said. There was a long pause. "...I'm going to ask. Are we trying to capture them, or kill them?"

"If you have a shot, take it." Alex didn't look at the others. "We've killed Fae and Red Caps. This isn't any different."

Extending her hand, Alex glared at the rising water, mentally urging it to fill the tub faster. Her fingers tapped against the wall nervously as her breathing increased.

"Alex?" Bran asked. He let his hand drop away. "You okay to try this?"

"We need to try," Alex said. "Uh... someone text Merlin and Morgana."

"They're going to be pissed," Nicki said. But Alex heard the beeping of her phone.

"What's going on?" Avani's voice asked from the hallway. "Uh... are you going to make a water tunnel in the bathtub?"

Turning to look at Avani who was lingering in the doorway, Alex started to laugh. It burst out and quickly took on a hysterical note. Aiden and Bran were both frowning at her while Nicki was eyeing her carefully with thoughtful eyes.

"I'm fine," Alex gasped. "Uh, yes, Avani. I had a vision of Scáthbás and Arthur nearby. We're going to try and find them. close up the place until we get back."

"Alright," Avani agreed. She took a step back from the doorway. Even her calm tone didn't disguise the worry in her eyes. "Just... be careful."

Extending her hand towards the tub, Alex closed her eyes and tried to envision the scene. There was no water at the gate, or even that close by. Frustration welled up in her chest. Her magic flared angrily, threatening to lash out at the lack of direction. Then someone took her hand. Magic fluttered over her skin. The panic and desperation in her chest eased a little. The spark in her chest grew stronger, and Alex exhaled, letting the magic spin together. Feeling a thrum through her limbs, Alex relaxed and focused.

Hearing the water move, Alex pressed her eyelids together and pushed out her magic. Her right hand dropped to her side only for someone to take it. Judging from the smaller size of it, the hand belonged to Nicki. Splashing echoed through the room. Pushing out more magic, Alex softly mouthed the name Scáthbás. Her magic pulled, tugging at her grip and into the distance.

More magic entered her body, sinking into her even faster than she was releasing it. Her eyelids stung, and her throat tightened. Her friends didn't let go. Squeezing their hands in return, Alex smiled when the lines of magic led into the hills. It wasn't the same as before. She was still standing in the bathroom and listening to churning water. The magic found Scáthbás and Arthur moving down a hill towards the stream.

Opening her eyes, Alex pulled her hands away from her friends and swung them forward towards the tub. Waves of water were scooped up by dark gray sparks. The water began to spin in midair, faster and faster. The clear water took on a hint of brown and dark gray. Flashes of color appeared in the center, and Alex stepped forward. She put one foot up on the edge of the tub. Nicki reached around her and turned off the tap. Extending her hands back, Alex inhaled when Nicki grabbed her hand.

"We're here," Aiden said behind her. "We're going with you."

Propelling herself forward, Alex stepped up onto the edge of the tub, but only for a moment. She all but fell into the tunnel, pulling the others in after her. Water splashed up onto her face, but the tunnel held. They were moving fast, so fast. A flash of red made her tense. They were past the Blood Spell boundary. Up ahead were tall trees and streaming sunlight.

Her feet hit the ground, real ground. Water filled her sneakers, and Alex gasped at the cold. Nicki's hand was still in hers. She heard gasps behind her and took a few steps away from the tunnel, not releasing Nicki's hand.

"We're through," Aiden said. Then he coughed. "And wet."

Something moved in the trees. Alex let go of Nicki's hand and climbed up onto the muddy shore of the creek. Beneath her, Alex's feet sank into the mud. There were two figures. One was taller than the other with broad shoulders and blond hair in a loose ponytail. The second person's arm was around his shoulders. Alex recognized their clothing at once. It was Arthur and Scáthbás. Relief, excitement, and fear that they'd managed to catch them before they left again filled her chest.

She didn't wait. Shoving her hand forward, Alex released a blast of magic. It spun together, forming a lightning bolt. Scáthbás made an alarmed sound and Arthur waved his hand. A shield of shimmering black sparks formed in front of them. It was enough to hold back the lightning, even if Alex did hear Arthur grunting at the impact. Icicles shot past her, colliding with the shield, which shimmered and lightened in color. Two fireballs impacted seconds later.

"Really?!" Arthur shouted. "You want to do this now?!"

The shield shifted. Bran called a warning just before the magic swept forth, turning from a wall into a spear. Yellow magic swirled in front of them, solidifying into a wall at the moment of impact. Alex reached out and gripped the hilt of Cathanáil, pulling the sword free. It hummed in her hand, sending magic all through her arm and chest.

Bran's shield fell. More blasts of black magic filled the air, raining down on them. Retreating away from the stream, the mages all launched counterattacks. The water swept up around Arthur's legs, turning into ice and trapping him. Bran sent a yellow bolt towards Arthur's face.

Alex's eyes widened. She held her breath. A golden shield blocked the attack, and her eyes jumped to Scáthbás. The Queen's eyes were sharp and instantly went to Cathanáil. Alex's fingers tightened on the hilt as she raised it. Sparks shimmered across the metal and Alex braced herself.

More fireballs and icicles were flying through the air. Arthur had pulled himself free from Nicki's ice trap. Scáthbás' shield was holding. Alex saw the Queen's mouth moving, but couldn't hear her. Swinging Cathanáil, Alex remembered Chernobog's death and pushed her magic forward. A beam of magic exploded towards Arthur and Scáthbás. Ozone filled the air. The shield shattered into small fragments of gold flakes flickering in the sun.

Nicki screamed, sending blue magic rippling out around her. The stream between them and Arthur rose up and swept forward across the land. It exploded into sharp ice spears. One caught Arthur in the leg, another in the chest. Scáthbás raised her hands. Another shield formed over them, this one smaller and already flickering. Marching forward, Alex watched Arthur's hands, but he was busy covering a wound.

Scáthbás waved her hands. The water in the stream churned. Nicki released a beam of blue sparks, but Arthur sent a black bolt at Nicki. Aiden grabbed her and pulled her out of the way. A fireball exploded against the shield. It flickered. Alex swung Cathanáil again. This time bolts of light sailed off the blade, striking the shield all over. Two slipped through small holes. Arthur roared as one grazed his neck and the other hit his chest.

A water tunnel formed out of the stream next to Scáthbás. It was compact, barely large enough to jump into, but Scáthbás threw herself forward. The shield flickered out the rest of the way. Aiden's fireball just missed, hitting the swirling water and extinguishing in a sudden spurt of steam. Yellow sparks spun around Arthur's ankle, forming a rope and pulling him from the water tunnel. A snarl ripped from Arthur's mouth, and he twisted his body. A black bolt sailed through the air. Bran shifted to the right, avoiding the attack by inches. The yellow binding vanished.

Arthur jumped into the tunnel. Alex screamed, rage pounding and teeth gnashing. He twisted and looked back at her. His features were tight, desperation and frustration written on every new line in his face. Then, before Alex could move, the water tunnel collapsed, the water splashing back into the creek. Closing her eyes, Alex lowered her head in defeat, a sinking feeling in her stomach taking hold.

30

God of the Dark

Podlasie Province, Poland 983 C.E.

It was a small lake, locked between the hills and ridges of the valley. Water streamed into it from the nearby hills. In one place on the far bank it even formed a small waterfall. There had never been much in the way of fish here, so Dobiemir and others rarely bothered with the trek. The last time he'd been here the trees along the water had been thick with green and birds had been busily harvesting water insects.

Now it was still, and darkness hung over the valley. Swallowing, Dobiemir planted his feet on the ground. He couldn't run. This had to be finished. He and his village couldn't just live in fear forever. The stillness was wrong. The world wasn't meant to be so still, so silent. Even on a quiet day, there was always something: a breeze, the chirping of a bird, or a distant rustle in the grass.

"He's here," Cyrridven whispered. "Close by."

The Old One looked around with her odd blue-green eyes. Her right hand moved to the sword she carried, and she turned her face towards the water. "He's in the lake."

"Isn't that a good thing?" Baldr asked, sharing a look with his sister.

"Not necessarily," Odin said. He leaned on his walking stick and glared at the surface of the water. "Why now? What changed?"

Then the surface of the small lake began to ripple. Dobiemir's eyes jumped to a tree, but it wasn't moving. There was still no breeze. The temperature dropped, the air turning cold around them. His right hand went into the pouch on his belt and wrapped around the seal. Beneath his skin, the metal began to warm. He could feel the softly curving shape of the metal form. He'd used the symbol that Merlin and Morgana wore. The symbol was fixed to a round base of iron. It was solid and real.

"I do not know," Cyrridven said. "Let us hope that he is seeking the waters to rest and cleanse himself." Her tone wasn't very hopeful, and she turned to look at him. "Stay on your guard."

Dobiemir stayed back. He was content to let the Old Ones and the proper mages take the lead. Still, he inhaled slowly and felt the spark in his chest flutter. It was there, but it remained out of reach. Morgana caught his eye and then shifted closer to him, putting herself between him and the lake.

"Belobog!" Odin called. The Old One walked to the shore of the lake and pulled back his gray hood. Sif and Baldr flanked their father protectively. "Old friend, can you hear me? I wish to speak with you."

The water rippled, but there was no answer. Around them, the air grew colder, and Dobiemir's breath hitched. Looking towards the trees, he watched as the long shadows started to twist and grow. Backing up, he pointed to them, and Morgana growled.

"I don't think he's reverting to peace," Morgana said. "Brace yourself. Shadows are coming."

"Chernobog!" Cyrridven called. "Belobog. Whichever name you chose to embrace, speak with those who share your origin!"

Shadows emerged from the trees, slinking towards them with slow, deliberate movements. Morgana stayed close and her hands began to glow. Pressure filled Dobiemir's chest. It was like the spark was being smothered. Still, he tugged on it, willing it and pleading with it to emerge. To help him survive this.

Chernobog was rising out of the water. Something thick and black bubbled over the surface. Dobiemir stepped back, his feet sinking into the mud. The Shadows were circling them and the lake. If they tried to leave now, they'd be hunted down. Maybe seeking to end this wasn't such a good idea. Maybe they would have done better to leave Chernobog alone. The water sloshed, and a figure stood, stretching up and out of the lake.

The tall humanoid figure lurched towards the shore, long skeletal limbs stretching out. Chernobog was thin with stretched black skin that shined unnaturally in the dying light of the day. Turning towards them, Dobiemir gasped as he saw the face. It was sunken-in like a corpse's, with bones that were too defined and wide. Horns grew from its skull in a sick facsimile of a crown. It wasn't what he had imagined dwelt in the cave. But the eyes were the same. Those glowing, unnaturally green eyes swept over them all.

"Oh no," Odin groaned. "Belobog...."

"Chernobog," Cyrridven called up. "Hold." Bringing up her right hand, she gestured for the figure to stop. "Hold. Do not attack. This does not have to come to violence. But your Shadows are causing harm to the Iron Realm. The cold you release is killing the plants and threatening the humans with starvation. This cannot stand."

Dobiemir looked up into the face. There was a mouth, but it did not move. Chernobog said nothing. Dobiemir wondered if it even understood anymore. Staring up into the green eyes, he waited for it to do something. Yet it did not speak. It looked down at them from its position towering above them. Morgana and Merlin said it was an Old One like Odin and Cyrridven, but it was so much larger.

Then the thing lifted its arm and reached for Odin. Baldr pushed his father back and raised his right hand threateningly. Chernobog did not stop, smacking his hand down towards the ground. Odin and his children scattered. A beam of light from Baldr struck Chernobog, but the being showed no reaction.

The Shadows rushed them, suddenly violent and closing rapidly. They were rushing down the slopes of the valley, leaving the cover of the trees far behind. With trembling hands, Dobiemir pulled his knife from his belt and shifted toward Morgana. The female mage waved her hands and a wall of ice formed between them and the first Shadows.

"Let's see how these abominations like the ice," she snarled.

The wall shattered when the Shadows reached it, and exploded towards them in dozens of shards of ice. Several Shadows were hit and fell to the ground with resounding thuds. More came, and a whip of magic flashed through the air, striking the first Shadow and forcing it back. Green sparks appeared around the feet of the creatures, and they were pulled down into the soil as it turned to mud.

Turning around, Dobiemir looked back at Chernobog. The being was swinging its hands down, trying to catch Odin. The Old One was still trying to talk and shouting something about a place called Avalye. None of it made sense. Odin raised his hand, sending orbs of light towards Chernobog. They did nothing except illuminate the creature's face in the darkening day. Dobiemir looked up into the sky. There were no clouds, and he could see the sun, and yet all the light was vanishing.

"Stop using light!" Merlin yelled. "It doesn't affect the Shadows; it probably won't affect him."

An explosion made Dobiemir drop to his knees and cover his neck. Ringing filled his ears. The shouting increased. He knew he needed to get up. He was too vulnerable. His knees quivered, and he reached for the seal once again. It warmed in his hand, and he pulled it free from the pouch. Looking down at it, he allowed his thumb to trace the triskelion symbol. It was simple, but inside of it was bound his wish for this to be over. That was what he wanted, what he needed. Traces of magic flickered across the surface of the metal.

The ground shuddered, and Dobiemir looked up nervously. Odin fell to the ground, gasping for air and gripping the side of his head. There was no blood, but Sif's expression was panicked as she raced across the ground to her father. Baldr had pulled his sword and was slicing down any Shadows that came too close. Sif pulled Odin to his feet, putting his arm over her shoulder and started walking him further from the shore. Chernobog roared, lashing out towards Odin again. A wave of green sparks pushed the hand back.

There was too much. People were shouting. Both the mages and Old Ones were using their magic, filling the sky with flashes of light. The Shadows were snarling and swarming from different sides only to vanish in magical attacks. Chernobog was moving slowly out of the lake with heavy thunderous steps. Dobiemir spun around, barely dodging an attack by a Shadow that Morgana then killed with a large ice spear. His eyes couldn't focus on anything. Terror. Confusion. He was lost, and there was no way out.

Merlin hit the ground with a thud that echoed through the valley. Eyes wide, Dobiemir waited for the older mage to rise, but he was still on the ground. Shadows leapt forth and ran towards the man. Morgana waved her hands. Icicles shot through the air, impaling two of the Shadows. She rushed forward, placing herself between them and Merlin, hands at the ready. That left Dobiemir on his own, frozen in place.

The Shadows didn't care about him. Chernobog was just watching them now, no longer moving. His eyes glowed, making Dobiemir brace himself. Three Shadows rushed Morgana. An ice wall formed between Morgana and the Shadows. Silver sparks sprang into the air as she shifted her hands and readied herself. The Shadows leapt to go around the wall and Morgana flicked her fingers. Large spikes of ice burst forth and impaled the three Shadows.

Dobiemir caught sight of a small nasty smile on Morgana's face.

In the lake, the water churned and began to swirl. Cyrridven was standing on the shore, her arms thrown up into the sky. Her long dark hair fluttered in the wind. His eyes dropped to the sword on her hip, and his fingers itched. Water spun into the air, forming long vine-like structures that reached for Chernobog.

The black Old One roared as the water vines wrapped around his chest and dragged him back into the lake. Water splashed around his feet, and his hands flailed, trying to swipe at Cyrridven. A roar shook the valley. Dobiemir's grip tightened around the metal, making his joints ache. Chernobog's fist hit the ground. Everything shook, sending Dobiemir stumbling to his knees. It was hard to breathe. The cold bit into his skin, sinking into his bones. Pain radiated through his chest and limbs. Raising his eyes, he watched ice begin spreading out over the lake. A faint cracking filled the air.

Merlin was moving again, slowly rising to his knees, his face a portrait of pain. Green sparks surrounded Merlin, the old mage spreading his hands at his side. The color flared, growing brighter and brighter. A wind picked up, ruffling his hair and pushing on his back. Merlin's magic spun together, forming a spear above his head. It burst forth, striking

Chernobog in the chest. The being roared, clawing at the magic trying to burrow into its chest.

Dobiemir looked up into Chernobog's face. This wasn't working. His legs quivered. He could run, get back to Slavko. But then what? Why had they brought him here? Did Merlin and Morgana still hope that he could reach his magic? The spark jumped in his chest. He inhaled slowly, trying to imagine it like he was feeding a fire. The spark grew, and Dobiemir focused on the struggling Merlin. He was still on his knees. Sif had moved Odin away and was fighting Shadows with Baldr. Shadows were snarling at Morgana, and she was waving her hands wildly, throwing spears of ice at the advancing line encircling her and Merlin.

Chernobog truly was the dark god now. It was a winter's night in the middle of summer. This would spread. The Shadows would kill all the harvest that was left. People would starve, and his son... his son, who had been so weak, would surely suffer. The spark burned. Heat raced down his quivering limbs. Around him, the world slowed. He heard himself exhale. A purple glow appeared at the edge of his vision. Looking down, Dobiemir wasn't even surprised when he found the seal in his hand glowing. His fingers were stretched around the round object, holding it tightly in place.

The metal was hot in his hands. A strange thrum traveled from the iron into his body. His bones quivered, and his muscles twitched. It was comforting. There was power here, real power. Looking up at the dark form, Dobiemir's stomach tightened. Chernobog loomed above them. His tall form was blocking out the sun that was still valiantly trying to light up the area. Day meant nothing here. Darkness was spreading as all the light seemed to sweep towards Chernobog and vanish into his dark form.

Every moment the temperature dropped, but the metal in his hands kept Dobiemir warm. There were shouts from Merlin and Morgana as they threw everything they had at the Old One. Sif and Baldr were all throwing magical orbs at the Old One, but they had no effect. Nothing did. He watched long arms sweep over the landscape. Trees cracked at the impact, and the others were forced to scatter to avoid being crushed.

Then those bright green eyes found him. Dobiemir didn't flinch back. The fear was gone. Somehow, he felt no urge to run. It wouldn't help. His fingers tightened around the metal, and he breathed in slowly. They couldn't kill Chernobog. His power was too great. Maybe someday. He remembered what the Old Ones had said about sleeping. This being didn't want to be helped, it didn't want to be saved. But maybe he could be stopped.

Raising the metal circle in front of him, Dobiemir began to march forward. A bright glow spilled forth from the metal. A rich purple color. His color. There were no sparks of magic. Everything remained tightly bound in the metal. The thrum beneath his fingers intensified. Chernobog growled, the sound rolling across the area. Dobiemir kept his eyes on the Old One, trusting his other senses to keep him safe.

Chernobog roared. The seal in his hand was burning. Dobiemir screamed. The metal dug into his flesh, the heat charring his skin. More magic was spilling out now, circling Chernobog. The Old One reached for him, but streams of bright silver and green magic struck his chest. Merlin and Morgana. He didn't look for them. He didn't dare. Holding back his screams and tears, Dobiemir kept the seal aloft. The burning was worse now. His bones ached. Instinct screamed to let go, but the magic kept it tight in his hand.

Beneath his feet, the ground thrummed in time with his heartbeat. Every moment that passed was agony, and even the rush of cool magic up through his body from the earth didn't soothe it. His knees were locked. The edges of his vision were going dark, but those bright green eyes remained fixed on him.

He heard the lake water churning. The wind howled. Dobiemir was aware of the others but didn't look away from Chernobog. It was watching him. Waiting to see what he would do. Dobiemir didn't know. His heart raced, and the spark in his chest was a raging fire that was releasing magic he didn't know what to do with. The water around Chernobog was lashing against the Old One's legs, and an idea came to Dobiemir.

The Old Ones had talked about it, about sleeping in the waters. He didn't understand it, but perhaps it could work. The purple glow intensified. In the lake the sound of crashing waves increased. The waves rose up, twisting about the black form. It roared once again, fighting back. The seal grew hotter and hotter. It burned against his hand, the heat sinking into his flesh. But he did not let go.

"Lock him away," Dobiemir whispered. "Please, lock him away. Stop this. Put him to sleep." The words were lost to the wind but echoed in his mind. His chest burned, the strange illusive flare suddenly bursting with power and life. "Seal him away from my son and me."

Chernobog roared. Water spun around him, rushing over the black skin. The Old One made a frantic lunge for the shore, but vines of water pulled him back. His legs vanished into the water. Dobiemir didn't believe the lake was that deep. The surface of the lake began to glow purple. Dobiemir took another step forward, hope filling his chest.

His knees gave out, but he held on. Magic kept spinning around him, from him and filled the world. Chernobog's roars were distant. More water was twisting around his arms now. It was dragging him under. Dobiemir saw beams of light in different shades colliding with Chernobog's chest. He blinked his eyes frantically, trying to clear the sweat and tears from them. The others were gathered in a line. Streams of magic of different colors hit Chernobog's chest, knocking him back.

The seal burned his hands. His throat was aching. He was screaming. The hot pulse of magic in his veins was painful. Rushing up through him to the seal, still raised above his head. One last wave of water glowing bright purple sloshed over Chernobog, pulling him under. The last glimpse of the skeletal black hand vanished in moments.

Everything went quiet. Dobiemir looked around with wide eyes, his heart still pounding. The sky was brightening rapidly. There were no Shadows. Merlin was leaning on Morgana. The Old Ones were staring at him. Lowering his hand, Dobiemir studied the seal. It was dark. There was no more light coming out of the metal. Then, it began to crack in his hand, reddish lines of rust appearing on the surface of the metal. Crying out, he let go of the metal and frantically scooted back.

It hit the ground with a soft clatter, shattering into small pieces that quickly crumbled into dust. Morgana made a sound of alarm, but a gust of wind blasted past him, carrying away the pieces. Dobiemir glanced over at the mages, who were staring at him. Then he started laughing, collapsing back on the grass, looking up into the clear blue sky and letting the sun warm his skin.

31

Retaliation

I t was easy to worry about Alex. Very easy. Alarmingly easy. Even when he should have been worried about all of them since Merlin and Morgana were on their way, and they were not happy. At least they hadn't needed to call them for a pick up. Jenny and Lance had been happy to come out and shuttle them back to Ravenslake once they made it to the road and found a mile marker sign. But there was no getting around the very real possibility of Morgana lecturing them while Merlin gave them his best 'disappointed' face.

Still, as they unloaded from Lance's truck, Bran found himself watching Alex. Her posture was tense. No one had addressed the elephant in the back of the truck. They'd almost had Arthur, but the snake had slithered away again. ...that wasn't fair to snakes. Arthur was lower. Bran slammed the door of Lance's truck a little too hard and got a look from the other man.

"Sorry," he said.

"I get it," Lance said. He sighed and shook his head. "Arthur got this close to town. I hate even thinking about it."

Nodding, Bran inwardly grimaced. As bad as this was for them, it had to be worse for Lance and Jenny. The extent of Arthur's manipulations of them was still unclear. Bran suspected that cockroach had used magic on them, but they couldn't be sure. Instead, it remained a great big question mark.

And he was poking at the Iron Gates. Alex's vision had been dead on. The Queen's defenses were down enough that they could peek in. That probably meant something important. It was probably a hint, but Bran's head hurt too much to ponder it properly right now. Dragging himself into the house, he collapsed onto the sofa and sighed. The others followed suit, filling up all the soft surfaces in the living room and toeing off their wet shoes.

Avani came out of the kitchen, carrying a tray with a pitcher of ice water and sandwiches on it. Nicki all but whimpered with relief and adoration. Aiden snorted slightly at the display but didn't try to hide his fond smile. Avani smiled coyly and then winked at Nicki, who almost sputtered. At least the day had some redeeming moments.

Bran grabbed a glass and filled it with water from the pitcher. He gulped down nearly the whole glass on the first go, only now noticing the burn in his muscles. Apparently, he'd given more magic to Alex than he'd realized. But at least everyone was here, safe and sound. He poured a glass for Alex, who was staring off into space next to him. She jumped a little, blinking at him in surprise, but then took the glass and drank half of it.

No one said anything. Bran glanced towards Aiden, who was frowning and staying close to Nicki. Lance was holding Jenny's hand, and Avani had poured everyone else some water before she returned to the kitchen for more. Exhaustion and frustration filled the air and Bran didn't expect anyone to start a conversation. They'd been so close to Arthur and yet had failed to get him. Bran's hand twitched. They'd tried to kill him. Alex was wrong: it wasn't the same as killing the Fae. Maybe it was stupid to think this way, but it wasn't. There was a distinction that now made him light-headed.

Arthur was a problem. Bran controlled his breathing and tried to think it through rationally. Their enemy had proven himself highly capable of magic and had been using it much longer than any of them save Merlin and Morgana. He was manipulative, a good actor, and driven. Any one of those traits was dangerous, but combined they were frightening. Then there was everything they didn't know. If everything had been a mask, then there were depths to Arthur that they had no idea about, and that could be dangerous.

"I'm sorry we didn't get him," Nicki said to Jenny. "I'm not sure which of us wants him out of the picture the most, you, me or Alex."

"My desire for revenge is selfish," Jenny whispered. "And I know that I shouldn't wish him dead, but I do." Jenny shivered, and Bran's heart tightened with sympathy. "So, if you can kill him soon, I'll only be grateful." With a wobbly smile, Jenny added, "I might even give you a kiss."

Lance snorted, lowering his eyes when Jenny gave him a sideways look. Even bringing his hand up to rub his chin didn't hide his smile. Shaking her head fondly, Jenny leaned against his shoulder, releasing an exhausted sigh.

"Not sure you're my type anyway," Nicki said. "Plus, I like Lance."

"Not your type? I'm gorgeous," Jenny protested, even as she snuggled against her boyfriend.

Avani chuckled, setting a new pitcher of ice water down on the table. "As fascinating as this is, I believe Merlin and Morgana are pulling up."

They all tensed again. Jenny and Nicki's banter had brightened the mood, but now all that worry and frustration was right back in place. Bran wondered as he heard a car door slam if this was more a bad report card feeling or a dressing down by a superior officer feeling. Another car door slammed, and he looked at Alex. She was holding her glass of water against her knee and staring off into space again.

Morgana swept into the living room, her green eyes all but blazing. Her gaze landed on Alex first and then went through the room, checking on each of them in turn. Shoulders relaxing, Morgana exhaled and crossed her arms over her chest. Merlin came in a moment later and repeated Morgana's check of them all.

"Well?" Morgana demanded. "What happened?"

"I scryed for the Queen," Alex replied. She leaned back against the cushions and closed her eyes. Her expression was neutral. "She and Arthur were at a nearby Iron Gate, trying to break it down. With them so close I decided to try and attack them. We managed to intercept them at a stream where they were preparing to leave. Arthur was injured in the fight, but managed to avoid most of our attacks."

Nicki growled. Aiden reached over and squeezed her shoulder. Jenny's lips rolled tightly together and her fingers clenched into fists. Morgana frowned at all of them but was silent for a moment.

"That was reckless."

"No," Alex said. "It wasn't. We had a shot, so we tried to take it. Arthur's attacks and new magical items are a real problem. Sooner or later he's going to kill someone else's family."

Bile rushed up Bran's throat and he stilled, not trusting himself to speak or even move. Everyone in the room seemed to be in a similar position. Slowly, Bran looked sideways at Alex. Her eyes were open again, but they were vacant, as if she wasn't really seeing any of them. He hoped she wasn't seeing the death of her parents again. He didn't ask.

"Alex," Merlin sighed. "We would have gone with you."

"You would have been too late," Nicki said softly. "We barely made it before they left. I'm sorry that we didn't manage to kill either of them. It wasn't for lack of trying, but they are a fairly well-oiled machine."

"Not as much as you think," Alex said. She sat up, her brow furrowed in concentration. "Actually... things seem off between Arthur and Scáthbás. In my first vision they were fighting about Arthur sending the Fae after us." Setting her glass back on the table with a soft clink, Alex leaned forward and folded her hands. "I'm not sure how much longer Arthur is going to be working with the Queen," Alex said. Everyone turned to look at her. She had a pensive expression on her face; almost worried. "Their... dynamic, has changed," she said. "The Queen used to be the dominant personality, but now it seems to be shifting to Arthur. I saw him expressing a lot more displeasure with her. Outright impatience and frustration."

"That could be good for us," Aiden said. "If the Fae splinter."

"Yeah, but we know what the Queen wants," Alex said. "And while it's bad, Arthur is more of a wildcard. He's always done what Scáthbás wanted."

"Indeed," Morgana agreed. Her voice was cautious, and she crossed her arms over her chest, pacing a little. "Scáthbás is... controlling, and can make someone believe that a course of action is the best, but it is all mental. A person can shake that off." The 'I did' went unspoken. "And we just don't know what Arthur's motivation is outside of what Scáthbás wanted."

"To be a king," Alex huffed. She sank back into the sofa, staring up at the ceiling. "That's what he's always wanted."

"That's true," Morgana agreed softly. "But in the modern world... surely he knows that isn't possible?"

"I don't know," Aiden said. He was tapping his fingers nervously against the arm of the sofa. "The Fae have been living in hiding for years. They live on the edges of human society. There's a lot of resentment there he can tap into."

"But there aren't that many Fae," Morgana countered. "Their population has always remained low. They have difficulty reproducing in our world."

"Still, Aiden has a point," Merlin said. "You and I both know how easy it can be to stir up a mob. The Fae aren't human, but they are very much capable of anger and violence."

"I'm going to try again tomorrow," Alex said. Standing up, she stretched her arms and outright ignored Morgana's glare.

"You will not," Morgana said. She stood up and reached toward Alex, but the blonde shifted away.

"Yes, I will, because we can't keep playing defense, Morgana. You and Merlin used to seek out the threats! I don't remember everything, but I remember enough."

"Alex, looking for a fight isn't always the best way. And in the modern age of technology that could simply be playing into Arthur's hands."

"Something is wrong," Alex said. "Trust me. Arthur and the Queen; something is changing there, and we can't just be on the defensive when it happens."

Whatever Morgana was going to say was interrupted when the alarm bell began to chime softly. Looking up at the metal triskelion on the wall, Bran found it glowing and pulsing in time with the chime. Someday he was going to have to figure out just how that sound was produced, but not right now. Magic was enough of an explanation for now. Everyone jumped out of their seats. Lance and Jenny moved away from the windows with Avani, pulling their iron daggers out.

"Seriously?" Alex growled. Pulling Cathanáil out of the scabbard with one smooth movement, Alex headed for the stairs. "I'm getting Mjǫllnir too."

There was no arguing with her. Bran moved to the front window and pulled back the curtains. The sun was still out and would be for at least another hour. His eyes scanned the road and nearby trees. He didn't see any Fae, Sídhe or other threats, but the triskelion on the wall kept flashing.

"Outside or inside?" Nicki asked.

"Split up," Merlin said. "Aiden, Nicki, and I will guard the front. Morgana, you take Bran and Alex to the back."

"Alright," Morgana agreed. "Be careful. Keep an eye out for Arthur. This can't be a coincidence."

"He's probably hoping we're tired," Nicki said.

Probably, Bran thought. He was. There was a faint humming in his chest, but he'd still be able to help. Alex came rushing down the stairs, a weapon in each hand and a scowl on her face. She glanced at them, and Nicki gave her a small wave before following Merlin to the front door.

"You're with me out back," Morgana said. "No sign yet, but I have faith in your spell."

Bran followed the pair of women out back. Morgana was almost vibrating with tension, and Alex kept glaring at everything that moved, even the blades of grass fluttering in the wind. Then Bran caught movement in the trees. Pulling on his magic, he let the warm sparks swirl around his fingertips and waited. There was a distant rumble of thunder. He almost laughed. Arthur was making a mistake attacking now. Alex and Nicki were both worked up. If the evil mage knew what was good for him, he wouldn't be anywhere near here.

Something slammed into the wooden fence and Bran flinched. The wood cracked and fell to the ground, revealing dull violet eyes staring at them. A Fae stepped through the opening with several more behind them. They tugged at the next wooden boards, pulling the fence apart. Silver magic surrounded Morgana like an aura, and she stepped forward.

"Leave now or die," she said. "Our spells tell us that you mean harm. I warn you that none of the mages in this house have much patience left."

It was surprising that Morgana was even giving them a chance to run. None of them did. Morgana chuckled softly and snapped her fingers. Silver sparks shot forward, joining together and forming a wall of magical bolts. The first five Fae went down in moments. More came rushing out of the trees. Bran couldn't count them all, but there was at least a dozen.

The Fae came forward. They didn't care that the sun was still in the sky. Wearing sunglasses with their hoods pulled up, they rushed the house. Bran's throat tightened as three swung firearms out of their bags. Morgana shouted something, and a dome of silver appeared in front of them.

Gunshots erupted, but they were soft and muted. Just enough that the neighbors would assume a television was on too loud. Bullets hit the dome, crumbling upon impact. Raising his hand, he pictured the weapons being pulled away from the Fae. A moment later, all three were struggling against swirls of yellow magic to hold onto their weapons. Morgana's shield rippled for a split second before exploding towards the Fae as a shower of silver bolts. The Fae didn't have a chance to run before the bolts ripped them all apart.

"Check on the others," Morgana ordered.

Bran exhaled, his legs quivering. There was shouting. His legs were unsteady, but he forced himself to move around the side of the house in case it was more Fae. Instead, it was Merlin with the others, charging around the side and flanking the second wave of Fae. Stumbling forward, Bran looked around to check on his friends.

Blue magic filled the air just before a line of ice spike burst up from the grass and caught several Fae. A fireball exploded in the midst of another group, melting the ice which extinguished the fire before it could spread. More Fae were coming, and Bran's mind spun with confusion. Why were they here? Why did they keep throwing themselves at mages for Arthur? More were coming. It wasn't just Fae now. Red Caps were slinking in the shadows and a few other strange creatures were mixed in. At least the Brownies seemed to be staying peaceful and not joining the fight.

They were closing in — dozens of creatures pressing into the yard. Green magic formed spikes of earth that stabbed some alongside Nicki's ice walls. Lines of fire flicked through the air, igniting and blocking off some. But more kept coming. He didn't dare look at the others. He couldn't handle their fear along with his own. A flash of light off of a weapon made Bran lash out with his magic. The gun was pulled from the Fae's hands. There were more firearms scattered in the crowd. Using his magic, he snatched all of them that he saw and tossed them towards the back door.

Alex was spinning through the horde, swinging Cathanáil with her right hand and awkwardly flailing Mjǫllnir with her left. Fae were falling to the ground, either with broken bones from the hammer or long slices across their torsos from the sword. A pair of Fae grabbed Alex from behind, trying to wrestle Cathanáil out of her hand. Overhead the sky rumbled, and Bran looked up. Lightning flashed, and the Fae stopped for a moment out of surprise. It was all Alex needed. She lifted Mjǫllnir, and a bolt of lightning crashed down into the hammer.

Bright light filled the area. Bran slammed his eyes shut. When he opened them, the Fae around Alex were on the ground with wisps of smoke rising off their bodies. He shot off three magical bolts of his own, striking down a Fae, a Red Cap, and a strange feminine looking creature with goat's legs. His chest was burning, but he kept pushing on his magic. The sparks came more slowly. One Fae got too close, and a green bolt shot it down before he could react.

His knees gave out. Falling to the ground, Bran grunted as his legs hit the grass. In his chest his magic tried to spark to life again, but could only sputter. It was all too much for one day. Not even for one day; for a single afternoon. Chasing Arthur down had left them exhausted. A shout from Alex made him look up. The magical glow around her weapons was fading. Thankfully they were still lethal enough to keep her safe as she whirled them around.

Someone stepped up next to him. Bran hissed and reached for his dagger, but it was Morgana. She didn't look down at him but shifted protectively in front of him. Silver magic formed a shield in front of them just before another round of shots rang out. Bran flinched. So many weapons. Arthur was giving up on magic doing the trick. Bile filled his throat and mouth, leaving a harsh burn behind. Somehow though he managed not to throw up.

He forced himself to focus on the threat. Another fireball flew past what remained of the fence and collided with a Fae holding a gun. The firearm dropped to the ground. Another Fae tried to grab it only to be killed by a lightning bolt to the chest. Bran lifted his hand and pushed, pleading with his magic. Three guns on the ground were picked up in a pale swirl of yellow magic and dragged across the ground away from what little remained of the Fae forces.

A few Red Caps turned and fled into the shadows. Green bolts killed one last Fae that was trying to escape. The hole in the fence was half the length of the yard. Bran hoped that they wouldn't bother fixing it. There wasn't any point. It didn't slow anything down. The yard was finally quiet, and there was no movement in the trees beyond the yard.

Panting, Bran straightened up and turned to check on the others. His eyes moved over their small rank. Morgana and Merlin were in the best shape, their faces calm. Without exchanging a word, they both marched forward and began to check the trees. Aiden and Nicki were leaning against each other. Alex was near the destroyed fence, still standing up, but looking shaky.

"That was childish of Arthur," Alex grumbled.

She sheathed Cathanáil with a huff and headed for the house. Alex paused only long enough to look at the pile of firearms that they'd taken and curl her nose. Sighing, Bran followed her towards the back door. He had to agree. This was a childish retaliation, but hopefully, it would be enough for Arthur.

32

Dying Dreams

Alex was exhausted, and they now had a small armory of firearms that they had no idea what to do with hidden in their basement. Arthur had escaped with Scáthbás, and Merlin and Morgana were angry with her. This had been a wonderful day. Alex really wanted to throw something but settled for brushing her hair and glaring at her reflection.

"Now what?" she asked herself. "You missed your shot at Arthur and made him mad. How are you going to fix this?"

She didn't have an answer. Settling for braiding her hair, Alex listened for any noise from the others. The house was quiet. That wasn't a surprise. Even Merlin and Morgana had been pretty tired by the time they'd finally left the house. It had been a while to convince them that they didn't need to stand guard. Glancing at the clock, Alex grimaced. It was late, almost early, and as exhausted as she was, there was a strange urgency at the back of her mind. An itch she couldn't scratch.

Turning off the lights, Alex climbed into bed by the light of her cell phone and stared up at the ceiling. Her eyes slowly adjusted after the blue light from her phone vanished as the screen went dark. Sleep came gradually, giving Alex time to worry and wonder. There was a limited population of Sídhe creatures in the Iron Realm, and not all of them were going to help Arthur. Alex couldn't see the strategy here.

Either Arthur had already had the Red Caps in Ravenslake waiting for a signal or he'd sent them here with a water tunnel while he was injured from their fight. Neither option made much sense to Alex. Was he really just hoping for the guns to take out a few of them? They were a bit more durable than regular humans thanks to their magic, but bullets were serious business.

Slowly, her head began to feel heavy. She was drifting off, but in her chest her magic began to churn. Alex lost time. Opening her eyes, she didn't find her room and instead was standing in a familiar gray fog. Sighing, she resigned herself to another night of vivid dreams of long gone faces. But no one stepped forward — no one called any names out of the darkness. Instead, the gray fog began to shift and close in.

Looking around, Alex watched the colors shift and darken. She was dreaming. In her chest, her magic was fluttering and expanding, making it hard to breathe. Taking a step forward, she held out her hands. They passed through the fog. It curled around her fingers. Alex shivered. Magic tingled up her arms, tickling her and pulling the breath from her lungs. Then the world around her finished solidifying, and Alex was able to look at it all properly.

It was the dead Sídhe world. Swallowing, Alex pulled her feet out of the ash, but they sank right back in. A few feet away the remains of a building were half buried. There was a statue so worn down now that the facial features were almost completely gone. Overhead, the dark violet sky churned. There was nothing around her, and the smell of ash filled her nose. Closing her eyes, Alex pinched her arm, urging herself to wake up. She didn't.

"Hello."

The sound of a living voice made Alex spin around. She almost tripped as her feet failed to move as quickly as her torso. Then her eyes found the person who had spoken, and Alex tensed. Scáthbás wore the form of a beautiful human woman that hid her alien nature. Elaine Pendred was fairly tall with long blonde hair styled into an elegant, complicated looking bun. Arthur had her sharp blue eyes and long lashes. Despite having an adult son, there were few wrinkles on her face. Like Merlin and Morgana she was a hybrid, and nothing about her appearance betrayed her real history. Dressed in a dark pinstriped pants suit, she looked to Alex more like a lawyer or politician about to deliver damning closing arguments. With her human appearance, she didn't belong here anymore than Alex did.

"Hello, Alexandra," Scáthbás said. Her voice was calm, almost wistful. She almost smiled and took a few steps towards Alex.

"Stay where you are!" Alex snapped.

"I'm not here to hurt you." Scáthbás held up her hands, raising an eyebrow in annoyance. Alex shivered. It reminded her a lot of Morgana. The thought made her stomach tighten. "I'm dying."

The words took a moment to sink in. Tilting her head, Alex considered the figure and blinked. Scáthbás' impatience filled her face, and a rough growl escaped her. "I'm dying, you idiot girl! I'm lying in a puddle of my blood! No one is there to help me!" Her voice quivered.

Alex stared at her. She heard the words but didn't understand them. They didn't seem possible. Scáthbás' expression faltered, and she looked away from Alex to examine the landscape around them.

"Then why are you here?"

"I don't know," Scáthbás replied. Her eyes flicked back to Alex. "Perhaps your precious Iron Realm wants us to speak once. Or maybe because you've been trying to reach out to me and this is a lingering connection in your magic," Scáthbás smiled, a nasty and bitter smile. "Oh yes, I noticed you. Felt you poking and prodding, but you weren't the priority." Then Scáthbás chuckled, examining her fingernails. "We've never met, but I do feel like I know you, Alexandra. Arthur told me about you in great detail."

Holding back a shudder, Alex glared and fought to keep her face neutral. Scáthbás sighed and shook her head. "Enough of that. I doubt there's time for it. Arthur has killed me."

"Arthur?"

"Yes... the monster I raised finally turned to bite me." Scáthbás shrugged. "I saw it coming, of course. I'm not a fool. I just thought I had more time before he did."

Scáthbás looked around them at the ash covered landscape. Her eyes narrowed and she swallowed. Then she calmly walked over to the nearby statue that was half buried. With almost tender movements, she brushed away the ash from the face and studied it. Alex stayed where she was, ignoring the sting of the wind on her cheeks.

"Don't you ever wonder why we conquered those worlds?" There was a challenge in Scáthbás' voice. The tall blonde woman raised a delicate eyebrow and her dark painted red lips twisted into a slight frown. Meeting her eyes, Alex just stared at Scáthbás and waited for whatever was coming next. "You don't, do you?"

Scáthbás laughed darkly and shook her head. Pulling her shawl around her, Scáthbás looked away from Alex and stared out into the twisting fog. "Mages. I respect your power and your dedication to your realm, but honestly, you need to consider motivations more."

"Are you going to tell me or just hint dramatically?" Alex asked.

"Sídhean is dead." The words rang with a finality that echoed in the thick fog. Holding her tongue, Alex studied Scáthbás' face, but it was calm and resigned. It was a fact, but not a painful one. Seeing her confusion, Scáthbás explained, "It has been for centuries, long before I was born. The world was dying, so my ancestors began to move into another one, but they met with resistance. Desperation spurred refugees into forming an army and conquering the world. Many were left behind on a dying planet as it became harder and harder to cross over. The new world was declared New Sídhean, but death was there too. My ancestors kept marching deeper into our branch of the Tree of Reality to outrun the decay."

Strange images filled Alex's head. There was a withering branch made half of wood and half of stardust that was crumbling away. Thin and pale figures with long horns growing from their foreheads that branched out like antlers were moving across a dark, dusty landscape. There were small crying figures and a shimmer of golden magic on the horizon.

"I won't claim that everything we've done has been kind, but our culture is built on fleeing. We took worlds and unified them into an orderly society of multiple peoples that can live and work together. What was once many worlds is now Sídhean, and we were keeping the decay at bay. I took over and improved the lives of the slaves, using recent rebellions as proof that we needed some change." Scáthbás narrowed her eyes. "I treated Morgana as well as I knew how. I protected her from the more dangerous elements of the court and kept her healthy. The cunning that has served your realm so well she learned from me. And I am only trying to save my people. Three thousand years... the decay will be right on their heels."

"And I'm supposed to believe that you're some sort of good guy deep down?" Alex almost laughed at the ridiculous notion. Nonetheless, there was ice in her gut, and her magic was fluttering weakly. "You're saying those words from a stolen mouth. Elaine Pendred was a real person. You took over her life and destroyed it."

"I had to survive," Scáthbás replied. Her voice was too calm and even. She was just watching Alex. "I don't expect you to trust me Alexandra Adams, the Iron Soul of the Iron Realm. You've spent lifetimes either fighting or living in a tense peace with outsiders." Scáthbás looked past Alex at the strange churning landscape as the fog tried to solidify into something. "But it is complicated."

Alex debated with herself for a moment. But then the world flickered around them, and Scáthbás released a small sound of pain. Her fingers gripped the statue tightly as she swayed. Alex's mouth went dry. She didn't know what to feel. There was a spark of pity, but it was extinguished quickly by the reminder of what this woman was and the things she'd done. Still, not all of this was a lie.

"I'm aware that something is happening outside the Iron Realm," Alex said. She hoped she sounded calm and controlled. "The mages and I have discussed it. The Demons reported that they were fleeing a Darkness of some kind."

"Yes," Scáthbás said. She gestured around with her hand. "Yes; this is what comes. Life can't survive. Not sapient beings, or even the plants. It all dies, withers on the vine" Scáthbás studied Alex, her eyes glistening. Desperation, Alex thought. "I hadn't been queen long when I found Morgana," Scáthbás said. "Not long to my people, but to yours I suppose it was a long time. We live longer than you... maybe that was part of the problem." Scáthbás' eyes shifted to look out at the dead landscape once more. "Morgana... my dear girl. Strange, I'm a little proud of her now. I was angry with her for so long. But my son, my Arthur betrayed me for power: at least Morgana's betrayal was far nobler."

"I'm having a hard time believing this," Alex said dryly. "I- I've seen some of Arthur's past. You molded him into being vicious. You hurt him, lectured him and trained him. What did you think would happen? You're trying to play for sympathy now."

"I'm not perfect," Scáthbás agreed. "This body... this human brain with its chemicals and reactions... it feels so much. So much more than my kind do. More than I did as a Síd." Scáthbás breathing quivered. "I fought to survive, but it didn't help."

"Are you expecting me to feel sorry for you?! That's a stolen body."

"That's true." Scáthbás nodded calmly.

"Don't you care?"

"About that? No, not anymore. Never did, to be frank." Scáthbás straightened up and took a shaky step away from the statue. Her foot sank into the layer of ash. "That doesn't matter. One life is nothing. I enslaved humans because it kept the Sídhe busy. They poked and prodded, took slaves which justified my invasion to the nobility. Kept the short-sighted and vulgar power grubbers busy."

"Yeah, because that makes sexual slavery of children so much better."

"I protected Morgana from that."

"Oh, bravo," Alex sneered. Crossing her arms over her chest, she glared at Scáthbás. "Congratulations, you protected the child who was useful to you from being abused. Then fused her and the Changeling, which I'm pretty sure was painful, and made her a spy!"

"I was trying to protect my people!"

"Then why didn't you just move in?" Alex pressed. "Why did you do things the way you did? It was hardly the best course of action."

"Your world... it fights back. I kept hoping for a better way. Morgana might have... never mind. It doesn't matter."

"And Arthur?"

"Arthur..." Scáthbás lowered her head, and Alex thought there might be shame in her eyes. "Arthur was perhaps a mistake."

"You slept with your son," Alex growled. Her stomach turned at the words, and she barely held back a shudder. "That's not exactly sweet and innocent."

"Do you think that your mentors have never taken comfort in each other?" Scáthbás snapped. She whirled to face Alex with sharp, dangerous eyes. "I was lonely!"

"I don't believe that!" Alex raised an eyebrow now and crossed her arms over her chest. "I've seen parts of Arthur's childhood."

Scáthbás was silent for a moment, but there was no sense of victory. Instead, Alex felt ill and uncertain as she watched the woman's face. It was so human and seemed pained. She was grateful that she'd never had a reason to meet Elaine Pendred when she and Arthur had been dating.

"This...I am a Síd. I was born in one of our colonies. My father was a general, and my mother was a noble. I rose to power and unified disorderly, warring principalities into a true Queendom." Scáthbás looked back at her. "You find it difficult to change bodies and lives, Iron Soul? Imagine switching not only the body but your very species. I cast my spirit and my power, what remained of it, into this form. I only managed to grab on thanks to the mage blood that was already growing in the woman. Arthur was my link, my grip on existence."

Alex shifted uneasily. Feeling like she should say something, she licked her lips and tried to speak, but nothing came out. The look in Scáthbás' eyes was haunted, and the Queen was far away from where they were now.

"Medraut and I had a bargain. I kept that bargain to the fullest of my abilities. He was to be my consort. I keep my bargains."

"You were his mother."

"No, this human body was his mother," Scáthbás said. She looked disdainfully down at her own hands. "Using the Iron Chain, I restored myself a little."

Alex couldn't look away from Scáthbás. Her brain whirled as she tried to process what the former Queen was saying, but none of it made sense. There were hints of something like regret in Scáthbás' voice and flickers of more human emotions on her features, but nothing stuck around long enough for Alex to take it in.

Suddenly Scáthbás flinched, gasping for air. Bending over, she clutched at her gut. Alex froze. Scáthbás' statement about dying returning with brutal force. Then the Queen laughed weakly and straightened up.

"That bastard is just lingering and watching me die," Scáthbás huffed. "Doesn't even have the decency to make it fast."

Alex didn't say anything. Nothing clever came to mind, and there was another twitch of sympathy. It was all too easy to imagine it. Arthur sitting in a chair in that brick-walled room she'd seen them in, with Scáthbás on the ground in a pool of blood. Had she used magic to defend herself, or had he knocked her out first and then injured her? Worse, was she being tortured and this was just a desperate magical projection?

"What are you hoping to achieve with this?" Alex asked.

"Just... please..." Scáthbás paused and dropped her eyes. "Please, don't let them all die. We're different from you at our core. We're more selfish, far less naturally social. Your views of good and evil aren't the same as ours. You hate me, and that's fair. I'm not pleading for myself." Her tone had gone very soft. "I'm asking you not to abandon dozens of species to death. I don't have control over Arthur any longer," Scáthbás admitted. There was regret and even some sadness in her voice again. "I'm afraid that you're correct about my poor parenting skills. My destined consort has decided that he's better suited to take over himself. The faction gathering under him has no interest in the plight of the Sídhe. He'll allow the Iron Gates to stand forever now." Good, Alex thought, but guilt quickly pushed to the surface. "Don't celebrate that, Iron Soul," Scáthbás scolded, her expression fierce. "The death that creeps through the branches will come to the root soon enough."

Around them, the world flickered. Scáthbás swayed on her feet. Looking down at her hands, the former queen started to laugh hysterically as her limbs turned to mist. The fog returned, shredding their surroundings, pulling everything back into the haze. Alex watched the last spot she'd seen Scáthbás for a long time. There was nothing there anymore. Scáthbás was gone. Not in a great battle against mages, but with a desperate plea for Alex to stand against the Darkness.

She didn't know how to feel about that.

33

Departing in Peace

Podlasie Province, Poland 983 C.E.

For the first time in months, Dobiemir slept well. Baldr had all but carried him back to his home, the Old One unfazed by the miles-long hike. Slavko had worried over him, a strange reversal of how things had once been. He'd slept deeply, satisfied that Chernobog was gone. There had been no dreams; no nightmares crafted of his fears to haunt him.

The sun came up as normal, casting warm light on the world. It had been days since the battle at the lake and Dobiemir was finally beginning to believe that it was over. The air was cool as he stepped out into the morning light and stretched. His muscles burned slightly, but it was pleasant and reassuring rather than the pain he'd been fighting since the battle. It really was over now.

Flexing his fingers, Dobiemir breathed in the fresh air. He looked down at his hands in amazement. Somehow all that power running through the Seal had left only a slight scar in the shape of the triskelion on his hand, but there was no injury.

The spark in his chest flared. He could feel it now, see it, even if it didn't feel strong. It was there. All that talk about him being a mage had been true. A hysterical laugh bubbled up in his chest. None of this had hit him last night. The exhaustion had distracted him, but now it was a new day. Biting his lip, he contained the laugh, though his body still shook a little.

There was so much to do. He needed to speak with Merlin and Morgana. What happened now? Morgana had spoken of him returning to his normal life, but could it truly be that simple? Scanning the area, he saw no sign of the mages or the Old Ones. Had they already gone once he was safely home? Beneath his feet the ground thrummed softly, traveling up his bones and feeding the spark in his chest.

Sitting on the ground, Dobiemir closed his eyes. Morgana's words about connecting with his magic echoed through his mind. Now, they made sense. The spark in his chest fluttered happily at his attention. He pulled on it gently, almost cautiously. Unlike yesterday, his instincts didn't spur him to action. There was no frantic hum in his bones urging him on. His fingers tightened, searching for the Seal he had made, but it was gone. He remembered now, the way it had collapsed in his hands: he'd pulled out all the magic that he had put into it. Used it up, but Chernobog was gone.

Despite his unease, the magic responded easily, trickling down his arms. Opening his eyes, Dobiemir lifted his hands. Purple sparks orbited his fingertips, vibrating in the air. He could feel them. Dobiemir gaped at them, astounded by the sight of them. They were real. Looking around, he tried to find something to try the magic on. His eyes landed on a small plant growing nearby. Waving his hand, Dobiemir willed the magic at the plant with the command to make it grow. A stream of sparks rushed through the air and circled the plant. Focusing on his knowledge of the plant and recalling what it looked like at different stages, he tried to create the image of it growing quickly. The green leaves trembled as the purple sparks settled into them.

The plant glowed softly but grew taller right before his eyes. New leaves appeared and expanded, reaching towards the sun. A small flower bloomed. The hysterical laugh did escape him now. Birds went flying at the sudden loud noise, but that didn't stop him. It felt good. Cathartic. Finally, all the worries were gone. It almost didn't seem real. Didn't seem possible, but here it was.

"Father?"

He turned. Slavko was watching him with wide, worried eyes. Stopping the laughter, Dobiemir opened his arms and beckoned his son into a hug. The boy hesitated but quickly gave him what he wanted. After a few moments of hugging, the boy was shifting impatiently, and Dobiemir let him go.

"I'm fine," Dobiemir said. "Chernobog has been dealt with."

"That's what Merlin said last night," Slavko replied. "You were so tired. You barely even noticed me."

"I'm sorry. I used magic... it was... it's hard to explain. But everything is alright now. Chernobog is gone, and the Shadows are gone. We don't have to worry about that now." The urge to sweep his son into another hug built in his chest. "Life can return to normal."

Slavko almost made a face. "Not completely," he said. Nodding to the plant, he grinned. "You've got magic now."

"Yes, but that's a secret." Dobiemir gave his son a stern look. "You're smart enough to understand that you need to keep it a secret. Things have been tense enough around the village without more trouble."

"Of course, Father," Slavko agreed. His eyes were earnest. "I'd never put you in danger."

Dobiemir gave into the urge and hugged his son again. Slavko sighed but didn't fight back. When Dobiemir released him, Slavko grinned and headed off into the fields. Peace meant that it was time to focus on work again. There was a harvest to tend to, animals to care for, and now even some metalwork to do.

But it was safe again. Dobiemir couldn't help but feel lighter as he flexed his fingers. In his chest the magic hummed in response to his happiness. He'd be careful with it, he promised himself. He'd never reveal it to anyone but Slavko and would only use it to keep the crops healthy and his son safe. With luck, by the time he died, they'd have a bit more wealth to ensure his son's future. That was a worthy goal.

Nervous, almost frantic energy filled Dobiemir's body. He wasn't sure what to do with himself. Slavko was hard at work, but the ache in his muscles warned him off doing anything too vigorous. He settled on cleaning up the house a little. It had been neglected in the last few months. Opening the door and the window, Dobiemir allowed the breeze to air out the house a bit. He straightened the pots, pans, and baskets that filled the shelves. Using a small broom he swept the dirt out of the house and then restacked some of the firewood on the side of the house that had tumbled down.

Sometime later, after he got a drink of water and prepared some food for his son, Dobiemir caught sight of figures coming towards the house. Merlin and Morgana had their cloaks on despite the summer sun, and each of them carried a bag on their back. Something in their stride and expression told him exactly what was happening. Relief, eagerness, and a surprising sense of loss warred in his chest for a moment, but it passed quickly. The pair of older mages walked towards him.

"You're leaving?" Dobiemir hoped he didn't sound too excited or nervous. "Is it really over?"

"Over, no," Merlin said. "But Chernobog is asleep. He will be for some time. We can even hope that he may regain his mind." Morgana made a face. Her opinion on that possibility was clear, but Merlin either didn't notice or didn't care. "This area should be safe. We just returned from checking the lake, and Chernobog remains under your spell."

"So, you're leaving?"

"Yes," Morgana said. "I think that we have frightened the locals enough as it is. We don't wish to make things more difficult for you."

"I... thank you," Dobiemir said. "I hate to say it, but you're not wrong. Everyone has been on edge lately."

"That is fair," Merlin said. "But I think... I think it is time for you to focus on your own life now." Merlin smiled at him now. "You did well, Dobiemir: beyond what I thought you would achieve. But then again, mages do seem to find what they need when it truly matters."

"Ignore him," Morgana scolded. "You did very well. Don't worry about anything beyond that."

"Mind your magic," Merlin said. His hand came up to rest on Dobiemir's shoulder, and Merlin squeezed it. "People... sometimes they don't understand. If they realize that you have the power that they lack, then they may turn violent. And believe me, even when you have magic, a mob is a terrifying thing."

Dobiemir's stomach tightened with fear, and he nodded firmly. "I'll keep that in mind. I don't imagine that I'll need to use it for much."

"You may be surprised," Morgana teased. A more easy-going smile appeared on her face. "I hope that you have a peaceful life, Dobiemir. You deserve it."

"Where will you two go?" Dobiemir asked.

"We're heading east for a bit," Merlin said. "Sif informed us that there are some more... militant clans of Fae establishing themselves out that direction. We're just going to take a look and sort it out if needed."

Dobiemir almost offered to come with them. Something pulled at him, urged him to help and do his duty, but it vanished quickly. The two mages were looking at him, studying him, and Dobiemir had no doubt that they knew what he'd felt. They said nothing.

"We will meet again," Merlin promised.

"In my next life?" Dobiemir asked.

Merlin laughed, tossing his head back and letting the sunlight illuminate his features. "Then too, I'm sure. But I meant that we'll be passing through from time to time. Just to be sure that Chernobog stays asleep."

"If he does wake, we'll be back to help," Morgana promised. "Though... that seal you made did its job well."

"Thank you... I-I didn't want to fight," Dobiemir said. "I didn't want to destroy him."

"No," Morgana said. Her eyes were soft, and she almost looked amused. "I know you didn't. You are a good man, Dobiemir, and most certainly not a warrior." There was a hint of judgment in her voice, but it was more like fondness than true irritation. "I fear that despite your natural gifts, you make a poor battle mage."

"I just hope that your spell holds," Merlin said. His mirth faded away. "I hope that we don't regret how this ended."

"What has happened has happened," Morgana said.

The pair looked at each other, and Merlin nodded. Dobiemir wasn't sure how to take the words. Chernobog had once been good but now wasn't. He hadn't known what else to do. They might have spoken of Lokpal who saved Shiva, but he wasn't Lokpal. Not really. Instead of saying anything, he forced a smile and nodded.

"I wish you both a safe journey," he said. "And... if you need me..." the words trailed off. He knew what he meant to offer, but did not really mean the offer. "I want things to stay peaceful."

"We'll keep you in mind," Morgana said. She sounded calm and nodded to him. "You take care of yourself and your son. Slavko is a fine young man."

Morgana's smile was gentle, almost wistful, and Dobiemir once more found himself wondering about everything he didn't know about this pair. His mouth dried out as he tried to think of how to thank them. He had nothing of value to offer. In fact, the most valuable thing at his farm now was the forge they had made him and the supply of iron waiting for him to work. Giving up that line of thought, he swallowed thickly and forced himself to speak.

"I will, and thank you again for helping him," he said softly. The words were difficult. "I don't know what I would have done if I lost him."

Merlin nodded slowly, his eyes growing distant for a moment. Dobiemir wondered if Merlin was seeing him or someone else at that moment. A sad and all too understanding smile appeared on the man's face. Nodding in understanding, Merlin stepped back and adjusted his pack. Morgana was watching him with soft eyes. More history that he didn't understand. That was alright. He had what he needed: his son and his home were safe. The mages then started to walk down the road, away from his farm and the village.

Dobiemir stayed next to the animal yard, watching as Merlin and Morgana departed. Relief welled up inside him. It was over. This strange year was finally done. His eyes jumped to the distant trees. He couldn't see the lake, but he knew it was there. Chernobog was there and yet, Merlin and Morgana had explained that if he were to dive into the waters, he would never find him.

It was one more thing that didn't make sense — one more thing he didn't understand. Yet somehow, it was the truth. His seal had put the mad Old One to sleep, and with luck, Chernobog would rest for a long time. Nodding to himself, Dobiemir gave the road one last look just to be sure that Merlin and Morgana were gone. They were, and his life could finally return to normal.

Slavko came running up with a wide smile on his face. Dobiemir's shoulders relaxed, and he reached out to put his hand on his son's head. At least he had a healthy child to prove that the darkness that had taken over this valley had been lifted. There wasn't anything more that he could ask for. Looking towards the trees, Dobiemir knew that he'd be going to that lake from time to time to check on Chernobog. But for now, he followed his son into the house for some lunch, at peace with the world and his life.

34

Battleground

The commons food court was packed. Almost all of the tables were filled past capacity, leaving next to no room for Alex to navigate to the corner table that Jenny had somehow found. If it had been one of her mage friends she might have suspected the use of magic. As it was, she didn't think that Jenny was that far along yet. Setting her tray down, Alex plopped down into her seat and tore open the small ketchup packages.

"Burger again?" Jenny teased.

"I like burgers," Alex said. She shrugged and then took a sip of her soda. "They make good ones here. Surprisingly. And the fries are top of the line."

It was a bit difficult to get comfortable in the wood and metal chair. Cathanáil was secure on her back, and while the sword wasn't that long, the tip of it still hung off the edge of the chair. Alex shifted a bit until she found a reasonable position. She sort of missed being able to lean back in chairs, but the sword was very much in the way of that. At least the spell hiding it was holding strong.

Lance came over a moment later with his burger and handed Jenny a small basket of onion rings. She kissed his cheek and alternated between eating her salad and the onion rings. Bran and Aiden joined them a bit later with their Asian rice bowls, and Nicki bounced over with a sandwich. Avani arrived last with her salad and a stack of books that filled one corner of the table.

"So, what's up with the Professors?" Nicki asked.

"Professor Yates had a sub today," Alex said. "He's out sick." She stressed the word sick and made quotes with her hands. Lowering her voice, she added, "He and Morgana are probably scrying for the Queen."

"You said she's dead."

"Yes, and I'm sure she is, but those two will be trying to verify it."

"Which does make sense," Aiden said carefully. "No offense."

"None taken." Alex took another sip of her soda. "I get it. But that wasn't a dream. I felt my magic working. She reached out to me. Besides, the look on Arthur's face when they fled... I could tell that he was angry with her. Something had changed."

"Too bad this doesn't mean he'll leave us alone," Nicki grumbled.

"No, he won't," Alex agreed. That much she was certain of. "He's too obsessed at this point. He's not crazy; that would be too easy. I think there's something else at work."

"You said he wants to be king," Jenny said. Her voice was soft, and she shifted towards Lance. "And lately he's been outfitting the Fae with modern weapons. That may indicate that he really is setting his sights on Earth. On conquest."

"If he could get rid of us that would make it easier," Bran said. He tapped the end of a pen against his lower lip. "No one else with magic would be around."

"I'm not sure if that would be the end of it," Alex said. "Merlin and Morgana could..." she trailed off.

"Could what?" Jenny asked.

"Uh... I'm not sure," Alex said. "I had this stray thought that they could... never mind. Not sure where it came from."

"Maybe a memory," Bran suggested gently.

"Maybe."

Alex sipped her soda and slumped in her chair as much as Cathanáil would allow. It scraped against the wood and a student at a nearby table turned to see what the noise was. There was nothing for them to see of course, but Alex straightened up, reminded that even Nicki's brilliant scabbard had limits.

"I need to figure out a way to hide the hammer," Nicki said. Her eyes were tracing the scabbard. "I know that Arthur wants the Sword... well, actually, does he still want it?" Frowning, Nicki looked at the others. "I mean, the Queen wanted to open the gates, but if Arthur isn't interested then do we think he still wants the Sword?"

"Probably," Jenny said carefully. She paused and considered her words. "It's not just a magical item, remember that. It's also a symbol. In terms of mythology, that is Excalibur, the Sword of the king."

"And he wants to be king," Alex finished. "That makes sense, and he did have experience with this sword in his previous life, unlike the hammer." A vague memory tugged at Alex, pushing its way to the front of her mind. Medraut had never seemed obsessed with the sword, but he had resented the respect that Arto had. "And Jenny's right; add to that the modern ideas about the sword, and he probably does see it as something more. Plus, he saw me use it to kill Chernobog." Alex dropped her voice for that last part lest they freak someone out.

Everyone turned their attention to their food, and Alex held back a sigh. They didn't know. She hated not knowing. Even scrying, if successful, could only tell them so much. Drenching some of her fries in ketchup, Alex glanced around lazily. People were chatting all around them. It was safe and public. In his seat, Bran suddenly shuddered and had to grip the edge of the table. Lance reached over and put a hand on his shoulder to steady him.

"Bran?" Aiden called. Then he lowered his voice. "Did you see something?"

"I...I'm not sure." Bran looked up with wide eyes, searching the area. "There was smoke or dust. I'm not sure where."

That wasn't much to go on. Frowning, Alex checked their surroundings again. Bran was still shaking his head and trying to figure out what he'd seen. Suspicion crawled up Alex's chest and settled in her throat. Exhaling slowly, she pulled on her magic. The spark in her chest burst to life. Alex cast it out, pushing the magic out around them.

Closing her eyes, she focused on what was around them. There were so many people that for the first few moments it was all just a haze of outlines. The walls of the building took shape as the magic flowed over them like water. Still nothing strange. Then a black tangle drew Alex's attention. Her eyes swept through the room. It wasn't here. It was moving above them. Looking up, Alex frowned at the upper floors around them, surrounding the food court. Her magic stretched out further, trying to find the tangle that was eluding her.

"Alex?" Bran called.

"Something is here," Alex said. "It's one of those medallions."

"Shit," Aiden hissed.

They all stood up, and Alex froze, suddenly debating what to do. It was the middle of the day. The Student Union building was full of people. If something happened... if there was another firearm involved, then this would get ugly very fast.

"Jenny, Lance, I need you to get out," Alex said softly. "Pull the fire alarms to clear the building and call Merlin and Morgana."

"You sure?" Lance asked. "I mean... pulling the alarms?"

It was Bran who answered, "If there's another gun here then people have got to clear out."

"You think the dust-" Lance began to ask.

"I have no idea what I saw," Bran snapped. "Just go."

Heading for the staircase, Alex was aware of the black tangle of magic moving. Not quickly. It was almost pacing. They reached the second floor, but it was still above them. Heart pounding, Alex led the others upstairs. Around her, the world kept shifting in color. Bright lines of magic outlined the staircase, and vague blobs of color were the people. Behind her, the other mages were distinct.

Alarms went off just as they hit the third floor. Downstairs in the food court, students looked up and around in confusion. There was grumbling, but most people grabbed their things and started filing out the front doors. Around them the side rooms and offices opened as people headed for the exits. Alex didn't. The black tangle wasn't far now.

A strong chemical scent hit her nose, filling her nostrils and making them burn. Magic hummed over her arms. Curling her nose, Alex shook her head. Her magic was flaring up. A sound of alarm behind her made her turn. Bran swayed, nearly stumbling into the wall. Aiden caught him, holding him up and swinging Bran's arm around his shoulders. Alex turned, her vision clearing enough that Bran's wide green eyes were distinct. They were filled with horror.

"Bomb," Bran gasped. "It's Arthur. There's a bomb."

That's what it was, Alex realized with a jolt. At least Bran's magic had made the warning clear. Swinging around, Alex narrowed her eyes and looked for the tangle. It was moving, but at least it was on the same floor. Dashing forward, Alex ran for it. The others were right behind her.

"Alex, wait!" Nicki shouted. "We pulled the alarm! Everyone is getting out! We should too!"

She stopped and blinked. Her magic was humming, but the black knot was moving downstairs now, probably using a back staircase. Nicki was right. Exhaling, Alex eased her hold on the magic. Her vision shifted back towards normal, and she turned back to the others. As soon as she nodded, they all raced for the stairs. Rushing down them, Alex glanced around. People had taken the alarm seriously by the looks of it. A few people were moving slowly towards the door, apparently not thinking anything of it.

Then she felt it. A sudden change in the air that made her turn back around. Out of the corner of her eye, something was flaring and sparking. Her magic shuddered. Turning and throwing her hands forward, Alex screamed. Magic flashed around her. Pushing everything she had forward, she thought of only one thing: stop the explosion. Air shimmered. Her hands were suddenly touching something warm and solid. A dome glowed in her vision before her magic started to fade. She couldn't see the dome now, but she could feel it. An ache in her chest added to her pain.

There was a push, a hard shove against the dome, but it held. Opening her eyes, Alex saw the air darken in the dome. It swirled and shuddered. Behind her, Alex heard screaming and shouting. It wasn't too close. She hoped it wasn't too close. Her hands trembled. Then someone was behind her and put a hand on her shoulder.

More magic flowed into her chest. Inside the dome, there was dust and ash, curling in the air. The pressure kept hitting the dome, struggling to break free, but Alex held it. Another hand touched her right shoulder. Another jolt of magic reinforced the dome. It shuddered. Waves of pressure were bouncing inside the dome, slowly weakening, but every hit shook her. More magic pumped into her body and Alex released a shaky breath. Her friends were here. But the horror of what was happening didn't escape her.

Arthur had planted a bomb. Right in the middle of the Student Union building. At the busiest time of the day. He'd probably even made sure that they were on campus for classes and lunch. Her hands quivered. The dome shimmered. Alex bit her lower lip. Tears gathered in her eyes. She wanted to tell the others to run, to leave, but she couldn't

Then the shaking stopped. The pressure eased, and Alex's hands fell. Dust hit her face as the shield collapsed and she coughed weakly. The Student Union building was destroyed. Half-collapsed in a pile of rubble. Gaping at the destruction, Alex almost fell to her knees. Her magic was gone. Exhausted. She hadn't stopped it; just contained it. Swallowing, she stared. How many students had been in there? Not everyone paid attention to fire alarms unless they smelled smoke. More shouting echoed up behind her. Bran grabbed her hand and pulled her towards the doors.

"Alex, come on, we have to go," he said. "The whole interior is ripped apart. People are watching."

"But-" She coughed again and followed meekly.

People were screaming outside. There were shouts and phones and cameras everywhere. A few other people were running away from the building. A crowd was gathering, and some were pushing towards the doors. Bran never let go of Alex as they maneuvered through the people now trying to investigate.

They reached the grass. Alex's stomach gave up, and she bent over as she started throwing up. Nicki pulled her hair back, and the others circled close to her. She didn't release Bran's hand. Distantly, Alex heard sirens. A bomb. Her mind was stuck on repeat. Arthur had used a bomb.

He'd made a bomb and planted it in the school. How had things gone this far? Why was she surprised?

"Easy," Nicki said. She slowly straightened up, certain there was nothing left in her stomach. Grimacing at the taste in her mouth, Alex spit frantically on the ground. Nicki pulled her away from the mess. "Just keep breathing," Nicki instructed.

There were shouts now near the building for everyone to get back. Alex didn't bother turning to see who it was. It didn't matter. Everything would be chaos right now. Glancing around at the other buildings, she saw people flooding out of them. The crowd was thickening, but Nicki and Bran kept tight hold of her and kept moving them away.

"Nicki!" Jenny's voice called out. "Over here!"

She blinked and looked up, still in a daze, but trying to fight free of it. Jenny was standing on top of a small retaining wall at the edge of the sidewalk. Lance was next to her on his phone. Expressions of relief flooded both their faces. Jenny jumped off the retaining wall and dashed towards them.

"Oh god," Jenny gasped. Throwing herself forward, she hugged Alex. "Oh, thank God, you're all okay!" Pulling back, Jenny reached to touch the sides of Alex's face. "If you hadn't sensed him...he...it..."

"They're okay, Jenny," Lance assured her. He gently touched Jenny's shoulders as she trembled. "It's okay. You pulled the alarm: people got out." Jenny spun around and hugged him tightly. "I got ahold of Morgana," Lance said. "She was nearby in class. She'll be here soon."

"Good," Nicki said. She finally eased her grip on Alex's arm. "Good."

Lance studied all of them. Then he turned slightly, still keeping one arm around Jenny, and picked up his messenger bag. "There's a bottle of water in here."

Bran nodded and dug it out, handing it to Alex. "Here, maybe it will help."

Saying nothing, Alex took the bottle and walked over to the retaining wall. Everyone was silent as she poured some water into her hand and rinsed out her mouth. There was dust on her skin. She stared at it as the water droplets on her hand turned it into a fine layer of mud. Her jeans were covered too. Jenny appeared at her side and extended a package of tissues. Taking them with a nod, Alex cleaned off her hand and then rinsed her mouth again.

It helped — a little. Fire trucks were driving up onto the lawn alongside police cars. Officers were urging the crowd back and setting up a barrier. Alex wasn't sure if it was smoke or dust rising off the building, but another section collapsed, twisting inward and falling across the tables and chairs that had remained intact.

"You did great," Aiden said. He reached over and squeezed her hand. "It's impossible to say right now how strong that bomb was, but you must have stopped at least half the explosion."

"If not more," Nicki softly added. "We're alive, and it took out only one building."

"You stopped it?" Lance asked. His eyes were wide. "Wow... I mean, that makes sense, but wow."

"A shield," Alex said softly. Her voice sounded rough even to her. "I didn't even think about it. Contained the explosion in a dome."

"That trapped the pressure waves," Bran explained. He touched her shoulder again softly. "That's why it was hard to keep it up. The pressure waves were trapped and kept bouncing. Probably shredded everything inside the dome, but kept it from going out."

"Maybe that would have been better," Alex said softly.

"No," Aiden said. His voice was firm. "The area of effect of an explosion is huge. A lot bigger than movies make it seem. It would have probably killed everyone inside the building and blown the rest of the building apart."

Alex didn't know if that was true. She didn't know anything about bombs. But her fingers twinged as she remembered how hard the dome had fought back. Her whole body ached, and she vaguely remembered getting a couple of magical boosts.

"Thank you for helping me."

"You're welcome," Nicki said. "But we were also saving our own lives with that too."

Grabbing onto that thought, Alex nodded and closed her eyes. The sick feeling was still there, but the haze was shifting. Horror was still dominating, but at least she was grateful. If they hadn't been there, it would have been worse. If Bran hadn't had a vision of the explosion, then she wouldn't have used her magic to find Arthur. Her legs tried to collapse.

"I got you!" Lance caught her and lowered her to sit on the retaining wall.

The shouting and screams around the ruins of the building were louder. Alex hoped that any recording equipment was all destroyed. She didn't look over at the building. Alex didn't know if she could handle it. Folding her hands in her lap, Alex watched them shake.

"Alex!" Morgana's voice cut through her thoughts and Alex looked up to find the older mage rushing towards them. Dropping to her knees in front of Alex, Morgana took her hands in her left hand and brought up her right hand to gently touch Alex's face. "Are you alright? You're filthy."

"We were next to the blast," Bran explained quietly. "Alex contained it with a dome, but a lot of dust got thrown out when it dropped."

"The blast... so it was a bomb?"

"Yeah," Alex managed. "Bran had a vision, so I used my magic to sense the area. I felt one of those medallions of Arthur's. I think it was him. Jenny pulled the alarm, and we went upstairs after him, but then we realized what it was and tried to run. We didn't manage to get out of the building. I just reacted."

Nodding, Morgana leaned up and kissed her forehead. "That's what matters most. Merlin and I need to contain this," Morgana said. She released Alex's hands and stood up. "All of you, go home and stay together."

"I don't think anyone saw me," Alex said. "There was nothing to see." There hadn't been. The dome had been only a shimmer in the air. There hadn't been any distinct lines or colors like in the movies. "Nothing to record."

"Be that as it may," Morgana said. "Police are going to be all over the school. Your dome also means that the bomb exploded oddly so they'll be a lot of questions. We have to be sure that this doesn't get any worse." She rushed off towards the crowd and Alex could only wonder what her plan was.

Any worse. It could have been worse. Alex knew it. If she hadn't sensed that something was wrong then the bomb then... Her stomach turned at the very idea. It had been lunchtime, the building had been full of students before Jenny pulled the fire alarm. He'd already proven before that he was willing to kill. Happy to kill.

"I can't believe he did this," Jenny whispered. "I mean... maybe it's stupid. I know he's evil and maybe crazy, but... this seems pointless."

"It's proving a point," Bran said. "Arthur wants us focused on him, wants us to see him as a threat." Nodding towards the collapsing building, Bran swallowed thickly. "He can hit us where we live without needing magic."

35

All Over the News

It was all over the news. A bombing at a college campus that most of the United States had never heard of. Suddenly the University of Ravenslake had notoriety. Alex wanted to turn off the television and go upstairs to her bed, but she had made the mistake of sitting down when they got home. Reporters had descended and were talking with frightened. and in one horrible case, excited students.

In the background of the interviews, people were crying and huddling together. The police were trying to keep everyone back. The President of the University and the suddenly far too small campus security team were urging students to go home and wait for news. Classes were canceled for at least the rest of the week.

But there was no news. The police hadn't made statements beyond that experts were coming in. People kept bringing up the fire alarm going off and the media was speculating. One station said that the bomb was a prank gone sour or a plea for attention without the intention of harming anyone. Another suggested that there were multiple people and someone had gotten cold feet. Alex knew the truth. Gratitude that she'd thought to have Jenny pull the alarm overwhelmed her senses.

She wasn't sure how long she sat there on the sofa watching the news feed. Time slipped past, and her only movement was to change the channel occasionally. Avani was in one of the armchairs, watching silently. Alex was sure that the woman was keeping an eye on her. Maybe that was wise. There was an itch to go and hurt someone, preferably Arthur.

Now one channel was talking about if the attack was done by religious fundamentalists. It made her flinch — one more thing for others to be blamed for. She knew who was behind it. The temptation to call the FBI almost choked her, but Alex knew that she needed to talk to Merlin and Morgana first. It was tempting to set law enforcement on Arthur, but that might make everything worse.

Alex turned her head a little as Aiden collapsed on the sofa. His shoulders slumped, and for a split second Alex feared the worst. Aiden looked up and must have guessed her train of thought because he rushed to reassure her.

"My dad is fine," Aiden said. "Freaking out, but he was on the other side of campus."

"Good." Alex sighed in relief. "That's good."

"Bran's still talking with his mom. Judging from what I heard, she's panicking a little. Not sure about Jenny's dad or Nicki's Gran."

"I'm sure they'll all be grateful that they're safe," Alex said.

"This is..." Aiden gestured at the television. "I can't wrap my head around it. Part of me keeps thinking that Arthur is crazy to draw human warfare into this. It's so dangerous, and if he draws attention to himself, he'll lose. Magic or not, they outnumber him."

Nodding in agreement, Alex just stared at the television. It had cut back to an image of the collapsing Student Union building. Only one section of the wall remained upright. Everything else had started falling inward. People were beginning to notice that something wasn't right.

Alex clenched her fingers into fists. The explosion was all wrong. What would they make of it then? Had that been Arthur's goal? To expose them?

"I don't know," Alex said. "I don't know what his game is. He proved he can hurt us, but we already knew that."

"This was more than hurting us," Aiden said. His voice was almost a whisper. "A lot more."

"I was expecting to find the house on fire," Alex admitted. "For him to try and take the Sword."

"He might know that you're carrying it now."

"I suppose."

Footfalls on the stairs saved Alex from having to turn that thought over in her head. She turned as Jenny walked into the room. Her long hair was up in a messy bun, and her face was full of defeat.

"Daddy wants me to come home," Jenny said. She leaned against the wall, staring down at her phone. "He's really shaken. Wants me back in California."

"That's understandable." Alex ignored the flare of worry in her chest. If Jenny separated from them, then she wouldn't be able to keep her safe. "What do you think?"

"I don't know," Jenny admitted. "This is bigger now. Maybe it's stupid, but when it was just swords and magic, there was this... detachment, maybe, to the danger. Then the guns started showing up, and that was scary, but this was a whole other level. Sorry, I'm not explaining myself well."

"No," Alex said. "It's fine, I understand. What do you want to do?"

"We need to all talk first," Jenny said. "But... but if you need me to go somewhere else, somewhere safer, then I won't take it personally."

The idea had merit, but Arthur knew Jenny. Without some serious magic, he'd find her. Alex kept that to herself, not liking the way her mind jumped to her brothers. She missed them, but suddenly that dull ache didn't hurt as much. Matt.... Matt would have been terrified for her over this. As it was he could be another shocked college student seeing it on the news, and just be grateful that no one he knew was affected.

Bran came up the stairs from the basement, all but dragging himself up using the railing. He nodded to them and went straight into the kitchen. Aiden sighed loudly and grabbed the remote to change the channel again. Another student was being interviewed and talking about the fire alarm. Hopefully they wouldn't be able to get fingerprints off of it. The last thing they needed was Jenny and Lance pulled in for questioning.

Standing up, Alex started to pace. She couldn't help it. The news kept going. The faces just kept talking and showing pictures being taken off of the internet. Alex hated cell phones. This hadn't been an issue in any other life. The voices in her head agreed. Aiden watched her with soft, worried eyes, and Alex sighed. It helped, but only for a moment.

"I have no idea what to do," Alex admitted.

"No one is expecting you to," Bran assured her. He glanced towards the television. "Any deaths?"

"Unknown," Aiden answered. "They're still searching the rubble, but so far it seems like people were mostly outside or close to the outer doors."

"Thank God for that," Jenny said. "But it might make Arthur even angrier."

"That's a lovely thought," Alex muttered. "I wish I knew where he was."

"No scrying," Bran said firmly. "You're still shaking, Alex."

Looking down at her hand, Alex scowled when she found that Bran wasn't wrong. Her hands were trembling. She shoved her hands into her pockets. Everyone was looking at her with worry, maybe pity. Alex wasn't sure; it was hard to tell, and the voices were almost panicked. Sitting down, she exhaled slowly.

"I guess you're right," Alex said. "I just..."

"You did great, Alex," Nicki said. "Just breathe and try to relax."

Alex nearly glared at Nicki. Relaxing wasn't going to help. She couldn't just turn off the adrenaline still pounding in her veins or the desire to go and rip Arthur apart. Nicki gripped her shoulder and all but pushed Alex back down onto the sofa.

"Exhausting yourself isn't going to help."

"How are you not freaking out?" Alex demanded.

"Oh, I'm close!" Nicki snapped. "It keeps going through my head that if Bran hadn't had that vision and spurred you to check the area, then we and a lot of other students would probably be dead!" Nicki was shouting at the end. But then she inhaled slowly and rolled her shoulders. "But magic was looking out for us. We're safe. But Arthur might have something else up his sleeve, so we need to focus on recovering and not doing anything stupid."

Pressing her lips together, Alex huffed and crossed her arms over her chest. The sword sat awkwardly on her back against the cushions, but she didn't dare take it off. She was pouting, but she didn't care. Nicki watched her with warning eyes until she nodded. Then Nicki sat down and looked at the television.

"This isn't going to go away easily," she said.

"How is your Gran taking it?" Aiden asked.

"Not great, but she's trying not to panic at least."

"They closed the public schools," Aiden added. "Mom picked Aisling up; she's at home. I think I'll stay there for a few days after we talk with Merlin and Morgana."

"Do we know when they'll be here?" Avani asked. "They are professors. I'm sure that things at the school are chaos."

"Makes me glad we don't live on campus anymore," Bran said.

"Any news?" Lance asked, coming down the stairs. He went straight to Jenny and sat down next to her.

"No," Alex said. She uncrossed her arms and picked at a stray thread on the sofa arm. "Nothing for sure. How did your parents take it?"

"Not bad actually," Lance said. "Dad thanked me for calling right away. Told me if I want to come home for a bit that they'll have my room ready. I think they'd like that."

"My mom almost demanded it," Bran admitted. Alex looked at him, and he grimaced slightly. "She's... horrified by the idea of this. Doesn't know it has anything to do with us but is scared that it happened."

"What did you tell her?"

"I'm going to stay here while things calm down, just in case there are announcements I need to hear. She wasn't impressed with that."

Alex nodded, grateful that at least for the time being the others would be staying. She had no idea of what to expect from the school. Would a lot of students leave? The semester had barely started. What happened to your tuition if you left due to something like this? There were probably policies in place about all this, but she had no idea how it actually worked. She glanced towards the door. At least no cops had shown up at their place yet.

"I'm sure Merlin and Morgana will take care of things," Bran assured her. "And we were still inside when you stopped the explosion. People outside wouldn't have been able to see or record us. All they might have is us stumbling out of the building afterwards."

"That could still be important," Lance warned. "But you weren't the only ones. A few people came out of some of the side doors. You could always say that you were in one of the small classrooms during the explosion."

"Maybe," Alex said. "We'll just have to see."

"We should figure out a story," Bran said. "Just in case. Like we found an empty classroom to eat in and didn't think it was a real alarm, so we were packing up our stuff until we heard the explosion."

"That could work," Jenny agreed. "Of course, you don't have your things. Other than your wallets and phones, you left everything at the table."

"Shit," Alex groaned. "You're right... I think that table was inside the bubble, so our books are destroyed."

"So, they're shredded," Nicki said. "As expensive as books are, that isn't the key issue. The classroom idea works, and we can plead stupid kids who didn't believe the alarm. Jenny and Lance had already left, but hopefully Morgana and Merlin will clear any footage of her pulling the alarm."

"My head hurts," Jenny muttered. "We need to talk to Merlin and Morgana. We just don't-"

There was a sharp knock on the door. Everyone tensed and straightened up. The knock came again, and Alex thought that she recognized it. Standing up, she gestured for the others to stay put. Opening the door, Alex wasn't surprised to find Morgana on their doorstep. There were furrows between her eyes and an air of exhaustion hung over her.

"It's Morgana," Alex called to the others. "Come in."

Stepping to the side, Alex gestured for Morgana to come in. The professor gave her a grateful nod and moved past Alex and straight into the living room. All but collapsing into an armchair, Morgana sighed and dropped her face into her right hand.

"What's the news on campus?" Aiden asked.

"It is chaos," Morgana admitted. "There were policies for an emergency like this, of course, but it was like everyone forgot them. Classes are canceled for at least the week, and students are being restricted to dorms and the cafeteria only. Everything between Hartung and Campus Avenue is being blocked off while they investigate." Morgana chuckled darkly. "They've got barriers up between Greek Row and the area just to make sure they don't do anything stupid."

"What about the explosion?" Alex asked. "Is anyone noticing that it was... weird?"

Green eyes met hers, and Morgana nodded. "Yes, it's been noted that something is off. There's damn near a crater in the center of the building while the outer area doesn't show much damage. The FBI is coming in to investigate, in fact they may already be here. Rumors are all over, of course. Thankfully so far no fundamentalist groups have tried to claim the bombing."

"So, what have you been up to?" Bran asked. He suddenly appeared from out of the kitchen with a tray of tea. "You look exhausted."

"Thank you," Morgana said drily. But she took a cup and poured herself some tea. "Damage control. We heard about the alarm fast enough to remove fingerprints from the ones by the main doors."

"East door," Jenny said quickly. Her whole body was tense.

"That was the first one I did," Morgana said. "It's the main one into the food court." Sighing in relief, Jenny slumped against Lance. Morgana watched them and took a sip of her tea. "After that, we cast a spell to confuse anyone who saw you come out and disrupt any cell phone footage. That one was a little concerning... I'm not sure how well it worked, and it is sure to cause questions." Morgana shook her head. "We kept ourselves hidden, which is utterly exhausting."

"Where is Merlin?"

"He's at the admin building. As I said, it is chaotic. I'll have to report soon, but everyone is so badly shaken that my absence won't be an issue for a little longer."

"Thank you for helping contain everything," Alex said. "I don't want to be questioned."

"You still might be," Morgana cautioned her. "You came out after the bomb went off. There might be questions about your survival."

Bran cursed softly. "Yeah, anyone inside should be dead just from the shockwave."

"Maybe: the seemingly small explosion but the shredded interior will confuse them for a while," Morgana said. Her lips curved into a strange almost sarcastic smile. "There is a clear line, I'm afraid, where your dome was. Merlin and I were able to muddy it a little, but the police were right behind us. Everything inside had been torn up into small pieces while things outside were mostly intact."

"The pressure waves kept bouncing," Bran explained. "The shield, well, shielded us, but it didn't cancel out the pressure."

"Still, it was well done," Morgana said quickly. Her eyes softened, and she looked at all of them, including Jenny. "We will deal with the aftermath as best we can, but far worse would have been losing you to Arthur's attack."

"At least people were able to get out," Jenny said.

"Yes," Morgana agreed. "Setting off a bomb at the Student Union during lunch was clearly an attempt to kill as many students as possible and make a statement. With all of you having different majors and very different classes at this point, you're rarely together on campus."

"What happens now?" Jenny asked.

"The university is starting to make calls to students to make sure that everyone is accounted for," Morgana said. "Be sure to keep your-"

"I don't mean that," Jenny said softly. "I mean, what are you mages going to do? Are you going to leave Ravenslake? Arthur knows where you and Merlin live. Nothing is stopping him from bombing your houses. We at least have Timothy here to keep an eye on the alarms and he has a cell phone; as weird as that is. Are you going to go on the road to hunt him down?"

"You just started your junior year," Morgana said carefully. "If you decide that you need to leave now then there is time for you to finish your educations at a later date."

"Do you think we should?" Aiden asked.

Morgana opened her mouth but hesitated. She looked down into her tea. "I don't know," she said softly. "This is... Merlin and I have never dealt with anything like this. In the past, the wars were public because everyone knew about the Sídhe. But the world changed, and we started hiding the conflicts, but even then, it was always about magic. I- I'm honestly not sure what the best course of action is now. Arthur escalated to using guns and now this... I'm very worried about how far he will go." She looked up and met Alex's gaze. "I dare say that you were right about the Queen's death. With her dead, Arthur is doing things his own way."

"So, what do we do now?" Nicki asked. "Wait it out?"

"We need to see what happens on campus first," Morgana said. "I don't want you to draw attention to yourselves by taking off. If other students leave, then it becomes an option. I hate the idea of retreating, but destroying Arthur is now our greatest priority."

"So, we wait," Bran said. He didn't sound impressed.

"We need to plan," Morgana corrected. "Arthur has changed the battlefield on which we fight. Tomorrow, once people have rested, we can start trying to scry for him and see what we can learn."

Despite her desire to go upstairs and crawl into bed, Alex turned her attention back to the television. Arthur was pushing things into real warfare. Modern warfare. She should have taken the guns as a warning, but she hadn't. Whatever Arthur was after, he was going to fight for it using whatever tools he had. Regret that she'd ever trusted him welled up in Alex' chest and she looked down at her hands. He had to die.

But what did he really want? Was this all about becoming King of the Iron Realm, or was there something more? Had he truly dismissed his mother's concerns about the Darkness or did he have something planned? She didn't know. But Alex knew that Arthur had to die. That would be the starting point of anything that came next.

9 780999 117194